Sausage!

Thanks for reading
my book & I'm glad
you liked it.
When I write the sequel
I want you to be
the first to read it.

Tim xx

3

Prologue
January 12th, 2022
400km south of the Cocos Islands, 3500km northwest of Perth
(Indian Ocean)

Lieutenant Glen Robertson squinted through the sparkling sea-spray and adjusted the strap on his Austeyr semi-automatic rifle. Whistled a jaunty ditty through his teeth, and flexed his foot in the floor strap as Fitzsimmons, laughter-lined eyes narrowed against the breeze, launched their rigid-hull inflatable over the soft swells. Bumping legs next to him was the heavily freckled Andrews, the latest addition to their party.

'I'm telling you boys, she's the one,' said Ahearne.

Robertson stopped whistling so he could reply. 'How long have you been seeing her?'

'Two weeks,' said Ahearne without irony.

'Gillette,' shouted Robertson over the roar of the motor. 'How long is this cruise?'

'Eighty glorious days!' the heavily muscled Gillette shouted back.

'What?' said Ahearne, trying to suppress a grin. 'She's not stupid, she knows she's hit the jackpot.'

Robertson smiled, shook his head and started whistling again. Everybody had their own way to keep their minds from pre-mission jitters. Ahearne's was to gossip about women.

Of course, nobody believed it, least of all Ahearne, but lying to each other about their women was something sailors had been doing since the first bark canoes.

They were en-route to a leaking, wooden fishing trawler overloaded with asylum seekers out of Jakarta called the *Bau Anjing*. Robertson's CO had tasked his team with taking control of the little boat and guiding it back to the HMAS *Melbourne*. There, they would load the *Anjing's* passengers into life rafts, and the frigate would tow them back out of Australian waters.

4

Every detail of the mission was cut like crystal into Robertson's memory, as though a high-speed camera was playing it super slow-motion in his head. Things had been quiet on the Atlantic approach to West Australia, and the *Bau Anjing* was the first illegal boat they'd seen for a while. The closer they got, the less he thought the term 'boat' applied to the *Bau Anjing.*

'Look at that piece of shit,' laughed Fitzsimmons. 'Junk by name, junk by nature.'

Harsh but fair, thought Robertson. The vessel was indeed a decrepit piece of garbage. Glen Robertson pondered a moment as his squad began to settle and prepare for their mission, the levels of bravery, stupidity, and desperation a person would have to feel to get into a barely seaworthy vessel like this and sail across an ocean! It had the traditional low stern, sweeping hull, and high pointed bow typical of most Indonesian refugee boats he'd seen. Bloody tragic thought Robertson.

There was a boxy wheelhouse at the rear of the vessel. Part of his brain registered it as a good place for belligerents to fire from cover, then scanned the splintered gun whale for logical places to board. As he examined it from a tactical perspective, the part of his brain concerned with aesthetics decided it was pleasing from neither an aesthetic nor a functional point of view.

The junk was only about twenty-five metres long. Robertson could see the rotting hull barely covered by flaked blue paint near the waterline, and salt-washed red covered the majority of the ship's rotting hull timbers. The wheelhouse was yellow, the deck had once been green but was now a chipped shade of vegetable compost grey. To Robertson it looked like a child had painted it with a rainbow colour scheme in mind, the truth of it was a jarring combination of colours everywhere, like a renovator removing layers of wallpaper from an old house.

Mouldy bilge water stained the side fore and aft, and the slime glistened in the hot sun. Desperate, skinny people crammed the deck; men, women and children, who'd strung up makeshift shelters over the deck with sheets on poles. The cloth hung limp and listless in the dense atmosphere, like a flag of surrender. Whoever was piloting this poor gypsy's trawler cut the puttering diesel motor as the RHIB drew close.

Overly large eyes in burnt, gaunt brown faces stared out from under shade-cloth. The whole scenario made Robertson uneasy.

He matched vectors with the junk, and they closed to board. The illegals seemed skittish somehow, sharing furtive glances with each, mothers clutching children close. A wizened old man in tattered robes stood on the gun whale and subtly held up his hands in a placating gesture that Glen couldn't figure out. Usually, they just displayed a mix of sullen defiance and fear; this time, it was like they were trying to tell them something, without telling them...

The old man stared at them meaningfully and shook his head. *Stay away...*

'This all feels a bit weird,' said Fitzsimmons.

'Just a routine pacify and tow, sailor,' he said, more to himself than Fitzsimmons. *Quit being so jittery and focus.* Every detail, every second - the faster things got out of control, the slower it plays back in your brain...one second everything is routine, a microsecond later -

Able seaman Andrews was crossing between the two vessels, about halfway down the junk and five metres from the wheelhouse. Suddenly, a rustle of gasps from the illegals and then someone stifled an abrupt scream as three dark, sinewy men emerged from the wheelhouse with AK-47 rifles, hollow ends pointed. Andrews lined up the taller smuggler with his Austeyr and Robertson activated the megaphone on the RHIB, turned it to full volume, 'Put down your weapons! I say again, put down your weapons!'

6

Completely ignoring him, the men shouted at Andrews, spittle flying through the air, gesticulating with their barrels for him to get off their boat. They looked as panicked as Robertson felt.

Andrews was completely open; he had no cover.

'Andrews, you're coming back across, slowly,' called Robertson. Andrews nodded, his Austeyr still trained on the three smugglers.

At that moment a side-swell slapped into the junk, staggering Andrews who stumbled towards the gunmen. One of them fired, three rounds from an AK jolting Andrews' body as the bullets smacked into him, two into his bulletproof vest, one through his neck. The bullet deflected into the RHIB next to Robertson, puncturing the skin. Red blossomed into the air as Andrews staggered, dropping to a knee. Blood spat out of Andrews' body onto the deck, splashing off the gun-whale and into the ocean, mingling with the chipped paint. A micro-second of stunned silence that lasted forever...*Jesus fuck*...thought Robertson as he fingered off the safety on his rifle and the world held its breath...then Andrews brought his weapon up, selected full automatic with a distinctive 'click' that echoed impossibly loudly, and hosed the smuggler with bullets, blowing him right over the side.

Hell broke loose. Bursts of fire spattered from the wheelhouse as more gunmen weighed in with their lead, firing on the crew in the RHIB. Robertson watched in horror as Andrews collapsed, clutching his neck, gurgling wetly, eyes screaming for help. The two smugglers left on deck had retreated behind some civilians, hosing the Australians with 7.62mm rounds, safe from return fire under their unwilling human shields. Muzzle flash was coming from the wheelhouse-

'There's minimum three more inside!' Robertson shouted, trying to get a bead on the shooters through the human shield. Point blank range with multiple automatic weapons, Robertson ducked behind the wheel console in the RHIB, trying to shrink down to a pinprick, keep low and find an armed target

7

amongst the mass of people on the junk. The RHIB crew started dropping, roars of pain and anger, muzzle-flash from their Austeyrs, screams from the illegals and the salty tang of blood and seawater...Keeping low, Glen peeked around the wheelhouse console, targeted a gunman, steadied his breath and squeezed the trigger as a woman dashed across his line of sight. Going against all of his training, Robertson jerked his rifle upwards at the last second; she disappeared and he didn't know if his bullet was the reason.

With the smugglers shooting from behind the asylum seekers, the boarding crew could do nothing to defend themselves without harming civilians. Bullets slammed into them and their craft; they were being cut down. The 50.cal was next to Fitzsimmons, mounted in front of the wheel.

'Fitzsimmons,' Robertson yelled. 'Get on that fucking gun!'

Fitzsimmons crouched behind the weapon, cocked it and swung it around, like a wrathful god.

'I can't get a clear shot!'

Robertson took a second to take stock. Andrews was dead. Ahearne was dead. Gillette was down, screaming and clutching at a gaping wound in his stomach. Unlucky, thought Robertson, that it missed the body armour. *Us or them,* he thought fatalistically.

'Light it up!' he bellowed.

Fitzsimmons lit it up. It was like trying to gouge a splinter with a jackhammer. He'd aimed primarily at the shooters, but there were so many civilians in the way.

One .50 caliber round will punch through five human beings without any trouble, and Fitzsimmons was pouring fire at point-blank range. Blood spurted into the air. Body parts exploded across the deck like liquid fireworks as people burst apart; as though someone had rigged them with internal detonators which were all going off at once. Bullets were shredding the *Bau Anjjing* itself, splinters of timber and flecks of paint flitting into the air, suspended momentarily in the soft

8

ocean breeze. Fitzsimmons bellowed incoherently, like a gorilla beating its chest. Women and children shrieked in panic, pain and terror.

The shooters dove further behind the asylum seekers for cover but Fitzsimmons started shooting *through* their protection and hitting them anyway. Robertson glimpsed a woman clutching a child to her chest, cowering next to the wheelhouse, when the kid's head just exploded, splattering blood and brains all over his mother's face. Her shaking hands held the air where his head had been. She stared at her empty hands. The thumping concussion, the licks of flame and the brutal efficiency of the machine gun was like a hellish combine harvester, processing human beings; people one minute, clouds of blood and meat the next.

A smuggler dropped, a round hitting him in the shoulder, blowing his entire arm off in a spray of viscera, and catapulting him back into the wheelhouse. His AK went flying, bounced off the gun-whale and into the ocean. Fitzsimmons had taken out most of the gunmen but in doing so had slaughtered most of the people on deck. He now turned his fire onto the wheelhouse where the last two shooters were. Within seconds the wheelhouse was reduced to a cloud of sawdust and slivers of paint. The incoming hail of bullets ceased, and Fitzsimmons realised there was nothing left for him to target. The big gun finally silenced, smoking lazily. The moans and whimpers broke through the ringing that still filled the air; cries of pain and shock, the ticking of the cooling gun and Fitzsimmons gasping hoarsely. Robertson huddled behind the wheel in disbelief, absently slapping another clip into his Austeyr. Flakes of green paint drifted serenely in the breeze, and sunlight seemed to cruelly peek through the clouds, as though God had decided to start paying attention again.

He stared, stupefied, at the little flecks as they slowly sank to the deck in front of him. So graceful, almost elegant in their descent. He was only broken out of his reverie by Fitzsimmons calling hoarsely.

'Glen...what have we done?'

He swallowed ashes. His whole crew was dead, except for himself and Fitzsimmons. Not to mention the butcher's yard on the refugee ship. 'Get on the radio to *Melbourne*. Tell them to get a medical team out here right now.'

Chapter 1
February 22nd, 2035
Washington, DC, 2100 hours

Deep in the corridors of the West Wing, Jacqueline Lafitte, Prime Minister of Australia thanks to a landslide majority vote in the 2033 election, waited patiently in the White House Situation Room. Her day had been full of the usual media-driven symbolic ceremonialism accompanying a state visit to Australia's most important ally, so she was glad to finally be meeting the President away from the flock of nagging journalists that followed her every step.

If he ever arrived.

Jacqueline's back was straight but not stiff; she was superficially a picture of patience. She had neatly crossed her legs and delicately folded her arms on her lap. However, those who knew Jacqui well, like Louise Abbott, Foreign Minister, could tell instantly that she was annoyed at the delay; a minute thinning of the lips, the hint of a raised eyebrow. However, to the American president, Jacqui was sure she'd appear entirely unruffled. Calm and well poised. South-east Asian stock from her mother's side had gifted her high cheekbones, delicate bone structure and caramel skin. Her father, with his heavy Gaelic roots dating back to the convicts that had settled Australia, had bestowed upon her soft green eyes, a full mouth and honey-coloured hair that had naturally maintained its thickness and colour despite the stress of office. She wore a white blouse under a tailored navy suit with two buttons undone; more casual than usual for a head of state. Her choice of attire reflected her youth at thirty-seven, yet was still well within the parameters of sterile, political fashion. Jacqui was tall for a woman and could have graced the covers of fashion magazines the world over (if she'd had any interest in such frippery). As a result, she looked the US President straight in the eye during their staged handshakes.

11

Louise Abbott eyed her ruefully. Jacqueline was the standard by which other women measured themselves and invariably came up short. She was composure personified, exuding an infectiously calm confidence that had captivated an entire nation. The most rattled anybody ever saw Jacqui Laffite look was when she was moved to a display of wry amusement, usually when journalists tried to implicate her in one of her colleagues' scandals.

With an obnoxious slamming of doors, Marion M. Cain, President of the United States, emerged from the corridors of the West Wing and marched into the White House Situation Room; cleft chin up, broad shoulders back, and a swarm of men and women in drab suits behind him. Jacqueline half expected the sound of trumpets to follow soon after. None did.

With an economy of motion, he flanked the long mahogany table and strode towards the patrician woman waiting for him at the end. President Cain's salt and pepper hair was cropped close in military fashion, his buttons shone as pristinely as his shoes, and if Jacqui hadn't had her fair share of military men, she'd have been quite impressed.

Beneath a navy-blue jacket, his broad shoulders and barrel chest were a testament to his past in the USMC, special forces. Cain lacked height, but behind frameless glasses, his tanned face and clear blue eyes conveyed a strength of character that more than compensated for his relatively modest stature. A man who could act with incredible compassion or cold ruthlessness, President Marion M. Cain hadn't charmed or inspired his way to the Oval Office; he'd bludgeoned his way there through sheer force of will. President Cain was a man who spoke less and did more, a quality sadly lacking in most people, she thought, glancing at Louise Abbott.

Jacqui knew that as far as POTUS was concerned, this meeting, like most with the Australians, was more about rubber stamping and relationship maintenance than a real discussion of the issues. The yanks allowed that the Aussies had some good ideas, but at the end of the day knew which side their bread was buttered on. Jacqui knew Cain didn't expect much negotiating.

That said, she knew he was always happy to meet with the Australian Prime Minister. He showed some paternalistic respect for her, very young as she was for the job, while fully aware she was nonetheless a very shrewd operator and shared his pragmatic perspective.

'Ladies,' he said as he firmly shook Jacqui's hand. 'My apologies for being late. I wanted to quickly cover something of concern to us before the formality of tonight's supper. I'd like to introduce you to Dr. Gemma Beale. She's the Undersecretary of Commerce for the National Oceanic and Atmospheric Administration,' he said, making way for the bookish woman to introduce herself. 'As you're aware the NOAA puts together seasonal weather forecasts for all the major regions around the world.' President Cain proceeded, 'The outlook for South-East Asia is cause for particular concern. We expect continued deterioration in conditions on the ground around the Bay of Bengal, and we're hoping that Australia will take a leading role in any response required.'

'What's the specific area of concern?' asked Lafitte.

Cain gestured to Dr Beale who activated a screen displaying a map of the globe.

'Thank you, Mr. President.' Jacqui honed her attention onto Beale, who appeared to be, and spoke with the brusque matter of factness of a very competent bureaucrat.

'We're observing a combination of factors that point to an extremely severe storm season centred on the Bay. Storms that were a 'once in a century event' in 1980 are now occurring every two or three years.'

On the screen, black dots represented mega-storms. In 1980, there were a few in disparate parts of the globe, however, as Beale cycled through years until the present day, the speckling of dots slowly coalesced into thick black bands, like a spreading infection.

'Storms are one thing, but it's the secondary consequences that cause most of the damage,' she continued, changing the graphic overlay of the globe to represent agricultural output. 'We've seen food output drop in fertile regions right around the world, no matter what we do to fight it. This is attributable to two factors; changing rainfall patterns, moving away from traditional food bowls, and massive storms wiping out crops which are unusually vulnerable due to heatwaves and water shortages. Farming infrastructure, built for specific places and conditions and built up over centuries, can't keep up.'

Abbott and Lafitte shared a look. Australian wheat and beef exports were setting records. There was so much space in Australia that it was easy to move production to where the rain was. Output was way up, which, coupled with massive food shortages to the north meant that Australian farmers were enjoying boom times.

Beale continued. 'Southeast Asia was able to support such huge populations because it *had* a thriving and productive ecosystem; now, they simply can't grow enough food anymore, due largely to pollution, overpopulation, land clearing and, most importantly, climate change.'

Lafitte nodded.

'In India, the interior is dying of thirst because Himalayan glaciers that fed major rivers like the Indus and Brahmaputra have melted off over the last twenty years. The Ganges gets most of its flow from monsoonal rains and now regularly flood with disastrous results because the monsoon is that much more intense. Border wars with China and Pakistan are a direct result of competition to control the remaining source-waters. Mumbai is built on reclaimed land and large parts of it are unlivable due to the storms; same goes for Kolkata.'

'Ladies,' said the President, 'the point is we expect the worst for the region this year. Gemma's team is predicting weather will be extreme, even by current standards; typhoons, floods and so on, that will wreck entire districts and leave millions homeless and starving.'

'We've led plenty of humanitarian missions in the region in the past,' said Lafitte. 'We're not about to start holding back now.'

'I'm glad to hear that, Jacqui,' said Cain. 'We cannot allow India to descend into chaos; it is a crucial part of our China-containment strategy. Borders are already falling apart, and we need to be prepared to help them stabilise things if the situation gets worse.'

Lafitte wasn't sure where this was going. In the grand scheme of the Australian-US alliance, Australia was a 'price taker'. She knew the US would never labour the point, certainly not publicly, but Cain had to know she'd support any mission which helped maintain the status quo in Southeast Asia.

'We used to send our aircraft carriers to the region. Ostensibly for humanitarian purposes but really to let any would-be separatists not to get any funny ideas; but my predecessor thought it rubbed the Chinese up the wrong way, so we stopped.' The disdain on his face made it clear what he thought of that decision. However, from now on if required, we're going to resume military-backed humanitarian missions to the Bay of Bengal.'

'I can't see an issue, Marion,' said Lafitte. 'We share the same priorities regarding regional stability as you. As you know, we can configure our two helicopter landing ships for humanitarian deployment at short notice, and we're set up to integrate into US-led taskforces.'

Cain nodded. 'Thank you, Jacqui. Our two nations have worked together for over a hundred years; we don't have a closer ally.' He held out his hand. 'We'll always be at your side.'

Chapter 2
May 6th, 1035 hours
Kolkata

Thousands of cinder-block and corrugation shelters crammed together and meandered like old rail cars across the low hills of downtown Kolkata. A massive tropical storm was dumping gigalitres onto the city, and the thin tin roofs vibrated like timpani's under the water pressure, adding a percussive backing track to the wild cracks of thunder and gusting wind.

Fadi Manoj brushed strands of thick wet hair out of his eyes and peered under the awning of his slum-home. Average height and slender, he blinked through long, sodden eyelashes. His eyes were a window into a thoughtful, intelligent soul, but right now they were scrunched up against the weather; while the winds weren't hurricane powerful, the rain was *heavy*. The street was empty, and rain drummed into the roof, trickled down the inside of the shack, pooling on the floor. The entire alley outside was floating away, garbage buoyed by rising water. A packet of noodles sailed through his door and an eddie swiftly sucked it into a vortex with a plastic bottle. He watched them circle each other until the bottle swept forward and pinned the noodle packet against the wall.

Still, Fadi had seen much worse, and while awful, today's weather was just a low-grade flooding event. Something you just paused to accommodate, rather than prepared and hunkered down for, like with the hurricanes.

The most recent flood had destroyed the slum on the lower edge of their hill. Mother Nature had been sadistic that day, three hundred kilometre an hour winds turned corrugated rooves, like the one over Fadi's head now, into flying blades that shredded people like confetti as they ran, seeking shelter that didn't exist. The last monsoon had flayed Kolkata; today was just a garden variety tropical storm.

16

I mean, thought Fadi, *the rain is pretty much falling vertically, no chance of getting killed by flying metal.*

'Shouldn't we go, Fadi?' piped the skinny kid by his side, shaking his head dramatically to get the hair out of his face. He looked up at Fadi, open and questioning. Fadi ruffled his little brother's hair and the kid scrunched his bulbous nose and ducked out of the way with practiced alacrity.

'I told you, Jay, we're waiting for Auntie Varsha. Didn't I already tell you that a thousand times?'

'Yea, but how long? She should be here by now.'

Fadi sighed. The kid was right. Where were their cousins and Auntie Varsha? He bent to pick up an apple as it drifted past at ankle height. It was going to flood around here, third time in as many months. It was already overflowing, technically; apples don't move around under their own steam. He lobbed it into the street where it bobbed along serenely with the rest of the rubbish. He was nervous about what they were about to do, and he envied the apple's ignorance.

Mother had given them rigorous instructions to wait for Auntie Varsha, who was admittedly, seldom on time. Still, Fadi hadn't heard from her; and despite her reputation, he couldn't believe she'd be late today of all days. Maybe something happened and they couldn't get through on the phone. He rechecked his phone: Nothing from Auntie Varsha, but as he stared, a video call popped up. It was mother.

'Fadi! Do you have your things? Come to the docks right now!' A seething mass of people behind her were forcing their way across a small gangway, which connected the shore with an enormous and worryingly decayed coal bulker. The ship was a wall of flaking black paint and rust, like sunburnt skin peeling on an industrial scale.

'Yea, it's all here.' He shifted the bundle on his back. Everything worth taking was wrapped up in a bedsheet slung over his shoulder. 'Auntie Varsha hasn't come yet, did you speak to her?'

17

Mother shook her head, making her wet hair swing angrily across her eyes. 'I can't reach her, I don't know what's going on, but it doesn't matter, you need to come now. They've started loading people, the ship's leaving as soon as the last person is on board. Is Jay with you?' she asked, panic creeping into her voice. He'd known things were desperate, but he'd never seen such concern in his mother's eyes.

'I'm here, mum!' called Jay, snatching Fadi's wrist to pull the camera onto him.

Fadi pushed Jay out of the way, refocusing the camera onto himself. 'I'll go find them, what if they're waiting for you to call? Maybe her phone isn't working because of the storm.'

'No!' she snapped. 'There's no time. The ship is leaving. Get here now! You have to come now, Fadi.' She cut the link.

'Shit,' he swore softly.

'You shouldn't swear!' said Jay sternly. Fadi grunted. He couldn't believe his mum would abandon his auntie and cousins like that. His mother was unflappable, like a cliff before a raging sea. Even when father died her sorrow had been measured, dignified.

But now...

Apprehension settled over him as he looked around their tiny home. The dirt floor had turned to mud, and a collection of rubbish swarmed around the leg of the plastic table in the corner. On the sill, an electronic photo album flickered as water seeped into the circuits. Mother and father stood arm in arm with a much younger Fadi grinning in front of them. Father was beaming as he held an infant Jay. Proud. Fadi was determined to look after his mother and brother with the same steadfastness his father had before he'd died.

His mother's sari was orange and yellow like the blazing sky stretching behind them. Cousin Adrita had married that afternoon. Fadi tendered a smile as he reminisced about the last time the whole family was together. Auntie Varsha had been incandescent with happiness and the late afternoon sun

18

had infused the sky with deep fractal reds and oranges, bathing them with warmth as they danced, and laughed through the slum.

It felt like a long time ago.

Jay fidgeted in the doorway impatiently as Fadi lingered, recounting that day just a moment longer; the sun had receded slowly behind the hill, perfectly warm on their backs. That monsoon season, storms had destroyed all the crops, so his father and the other men in their district had joined the Kolkata coastal militia. The militia set off inland to fight for a share of the produce still growing in central India, but his father had never come home.

A gust of wind blew the picture off the sill and it fell in a puddle. The little image-generator short-circuited and his family disappeared.

'Come on kid, time to go,' he said, grabbing Jay's hand. He took one last look around his home and then swung out under the awning into the torrential rain.

They descended the hills near Dhapa Road and moved west down Haldane Avenue. The road was blocked here, some trucks crossing a flooded intersection had become stranded.

Fadi flew down the side streets heading west towards the river, Fadi's long legs eating up distance, while Jay struggled not to trip.

'Stop dragging me, it hurts!' Jay whined.

'Shut up and move,' snapped Fadi. 'If we miss that ship, we'll never see mother again.' Jay pulled a face and struggled on in silence.

In these low-lying suburbs, the roads were submerged, forcing them to lift their knees high with each step to clear the water. They sprinted down Queen's Way and cut across the sodden racecourse. It looked, and felt, more like a swamp now, thought Fadi, as they veered onto Khiddirpore Road.

The streets before the racecourse were eerily quiet. They saw a gnarled old man leaning against his shopfront, chewing paan under a plastic awning. Water poured out of a gap between the canopy and the shopfront, splashing a skeletal shoulder. He ignored it. Most of his teeth were missing from the drug, and creased lips curled in over his gums as his jaw moved. Like a camel, thought Fadi, the shop owner staring at them through hooded eyes as they rode by. He seemed to know where they were going, what they were doing. *Take your desperate measures young men. It won't make any difference...What's coming is coming for us all.*

'What are you looking at,' muttered Jay. '*Stupid* old man.'

When they rounded the edge of the racecourse onto Khirddipore Road, Fadi glanced up and saw for the first time, the bulky silhouette of the coal carrier through the rain haze. The hull was black but tinged all over by a revolting bruised red where the rust had taken hold. The ship's superstructure was white, spattered with rust, and heavily pockmarked. Oily black smoke pushed up through the rain out of the triangular stack, culminating in a sight and smell that made Fadi think of a crematorium chimney. He finally felt, in his guts, the immensity of what they were about to do.

Fadi's family had daydreamed about moving to Australia since he was a young boy; his mother insisting that 'India is no place to raise a child anymore,' and his Father wishing that weren't the truth as he found excuses to stay. Fadi had distant relatives in Melbourne who had everything; a nice apartment, a car, food on the table every night, even the doctors in Australia were free.

But, he'd always daydreamed about the end result; not how to make it happen. He was glad it was raining so Jay couldn't tell how clammy his hands were. When he'd been a child, the first genuinely massive storm had smashed into Kolkata, flooding the Hoolie River and wiping out crops and property. Hundreds of thousands had died, so the United States had sent aircraft carriers, teeming with choppers, to the Bay of Bengal to fly in emergency supplies and medical care. While the flying machines were exciting, they felt hardly as impressive as the floating fortresses that carried them. Fadi would come down to the bay area to stare at these great vessels in wonder and fantasize about sailing away from Kolkata with his family in one.

The ship at the dock reminded him of those moments, but this ship didn't inspire quite the same confidence the US carriers had.

His phone vibrated. It was mother, looking even more frantic than before. 'Where are you? Get here now! Nearly everyone is on board, and they're leaving any minute!'

Dammit. Fadi squashed his doubts and gave Jay a brotherly clip over the ear. 'Let's get a move on, Jay,' he said as they continued their sodden dash down the road.

Only a few minutes later, they arrived at the docks with Jay dragging his little feet and Fadi, whose own lungs were burning, pulling him along; half holding him up. Almost everyone had disappeared into the hold, and the last few people were filing into the ship via an overhead gangway. He picked Jay up and raced over the concrete, across the ramp, and onto the deck.

'Welcome aboard,' spat a stale smelling man in greasy blue overalls as he swung the gangway away from the bridge. He grabbed them by the wrist and pulled them to a line of people jostling through a hatchway. Fadi searched for his mother. He eventually spied her, waiting pensively to the side of the line.

Fadi put Jay down and slumped to the deck, panting. Jay rushed to his mother who took him up in her arms. 'Brave little man,' she said. 'You made it!'

Fadi looked down the deck. Thousands of people were being manhandled down hatchways by hard-faced men with batons in their hands and rifles slung on their backs.

'Move your desperate asses, it's down the guts or over the side!' one of them shouted. There were still hundreds of people milling about when a low-frequency vibration shuddered dramatically through the deck.

People disappeared down the hatch, Fadi's family edging closer until he was staring into the black pit of the hold. He peered in. The ship seemed to swallow light and spew sound; the murmur of thousands of voices jostling in the dark wafted up like a breeze sweeping through a forest. Odours too boiled out of the hatch; already the musky smell of sweat wafted up. Fadi's mother kissed Jay on the forehead and climbed down, Jay following after without a moment's hesitation. To him, it was still a game.

Fadi waited long enough for his brother to disappear in the gloom and took a final look at his home city. He bit his lip to tamp down on his apprehension. Thousands of people crammed into a barely seaworthy ship during hurricane season made him...jittery. Not scared, he told himself. Just...jittery. He grabbed the rung of the ladder and stepped into the hold.

The big bronze alloy propeller eased into motion, and the old bulker inched away from the shore.

Chapter 3
June 25th, 2035
Briefing Room 2, Parliament House, Canberra

Commodore Glen Robertson picked up his pen, put it down and again, and tried not to fidget. The meeting hadn't even started, and he'd already covered his notepad in mindless doodling. He peered at the mess of squiggles and tried to figure out how to make it resemble an actual real-life object. *An impressionist masterpiece, open to the interpretation of the beholder,* he thought. He marvelled at his lack of artistic ability; out of sheer boredom, he'd been filling notepads with scribbles since school and had never once created anything worth keeping. *Fortunately for me,* he thought, *if you need art, you can go to the shops and buy it.*

He flipped to a fresh page and looked around to see if anyone had noticed.

Prime Minister Jacqueline Lafitte was looking across at him, a small smile playing on her lips. He tsked to himself. She was still a lovely looking woman, despite her androgynous suit and political haircut. Cunning as a used-car salesman and compelling as a...well, a beautiful woman. Reading the set of her shoulders and the tilt of her jaw, he could tell she was as willfully stubborn today as she'd ever been. He grinned to himself; he was genuinely proud of what she'd accomplished since they'd known each other.

Suddenly he frowned, remembering why she'd dumped him; not because she didn't love him, or he'd broken the trust. No, she'd broken things off because she'd one day wanted to be PM, and as she'd told him with tears in her eyes and hands shaking with emotion, 'I can't become PM if my partner is the guy who slaughtered all those refugees on the *Bau Anjing.'* She'd broken her own heart that day, but that was the key thing to remember about Jacqui; beautiful, smart and personable as she was, the one word that described her better than any other was *pragmatic.* No matter the price, she did what she thought she must.

Well, things turned out pretty bloody well in the meantime, he thought, glancing at the epaulette of rank on his shoulder and his long-term girlfriend who happened to be across the table. *So no hard feelings.* But he didn't forget he was dealing with a very uncompromising woman.

He resisted the urge to pick up the pen again, opting instead for a subtle swing on his swivel chair.

Defense Minister Nicholas Whittey (thick wavy hair, tall, telegenic, boorish moron), head of Navy Vice Admiral Jason Futcher (ageing poorly but intelligence shining brighter than ever) and the head of ASIS, Director-General Cam Holloway (Glen felt the same way about the old spymaster as he did a venomous spider trapped under an upturned jar) were there, as well as a bevy of military and civilian advisors/hangers-on that reminded Robertson of some tragic reality TV show, with everyone scrambling and back-stabbing their way up the bureaucratic hierarchy. Not everyone could be an action-man, he supposed.

He let out a slightly too audible sigh, earning him a playfully exasperated stare from his girlfriend, Alice, who in some bizarre twist of fate, was also at this meeting. He tried to mouth something back, but her attention turned as Lafitte opened.

'Thank you, everybody, for being here. As you all know, we've got a disaster on our north-west shelf, compromising our border sovereignty. Today I want to figure out how and why this is happening and then assess our options. Director-General Holloway, can you give us an update please?'

Holloway nodded.

'For those of you who didn't already know, we collaborate closely with US surveillance and intelligence organisations. Specifically, we have access to their satellite feeds in areas of mutual interest, like, southeast Asia. There is a pattern to what we've seen in the last few months, but we only figured it out after the third ship came through. Alice Robertson will be taking us through it. Alice is our southeast Asia expert and ASIS liaison with the Navy on intelligence matters.' He nodded to the tanned, petite woman to his left. 'Alice, you can take it from here.'

Alice was wearing a white blouse tucked into a shin-length black skirt. Tanned skin contrasted sharply with the white shirt, and delicate, toned arms attested to her addiction to surfing. Her nearly waist-length hair was dark brown, almost black, thick and combed to one side. She had a pixie-like, impish beauty that made her look younger than she was and today Alice was wearing glasses - not because she needed them, Glen knew, but because they made her look a little older, given the company.

The analyst took control of the meeting. Robertson was impressed, but not surprised by his girlfriends composure in such company. No nerves at all. He let a small satisfied smile creep onto his face.

Lafitte's lips compressed when Alice stood up. The two women couldn't stand the sight of each other but (thankfully) were too professional to let it show.

'Thank you, Cam,' said Alice. 'I think it's worth providing some background to events, so we're all on the same page. Then we can discuss our options and the consequences of each.' She changed the view to close-up satellite footage. Ships of all shapes and sizes, from lighters to supertankers, were beached on a giant mudflat on the edge of a giant, rundown warehouse complex. The scene stretched for kilometers in both directions, like a post-apocalyptic industrial nightmare. Pollutants leached into the water, green and black mixing on top of the mud of the rotten sea. The ships had much in common, they were all old, rusted and decaying, beyond use, and in various states of dismemberment. The scene had an air of majestic sadness about it.

25

Alice began.

'This is an aerial view of Chittagong, second largest city in Bangladesh. Specifically, we're looking at the Chittagong dock area, where the famous ship-breakers of Chittagong work. It's on the Karnaphuli River, which is one of the world's biggest producers of scrap metal; obviously from old cargo ships and bulk freighters waiting to be broken up. As we know, the Chinese and Indians imported vast quantities of coal and ore in the first part of the twenty-first century, chiefly from Australia and Brazil, but since the market for these raw materials has dried up, millions of tonnes of old freighters are lying at anchor waiting for the oxy-acetylene torch. As the Director-General mentioned before, we use US satellite assets, which are equipped with low-level AI and programmed to send alerts to our counterparts at the US National Reconnaissance Office if they observe unusual activity in their area of observations.

'We're aware of Australia's mineral export history, Alice. What's your point?' said Defence Minister Whittey. Robertson gave him a flat glance. It wasn't smart to interrupt Alice.

'The point is, those boats shouldn't be going anywhere,' continued Alice as though he hadn't spoken. 'Chittagong is a ship graveyard. The first hint we had of anything unusual was when a satellite spotted a large ship leaving the Chittagong port district, one that had been laid up for a substantial length of time. Usually, it's a one-way journey to the scrappers in the Karnaphuli River. Its atypical movement caught a spy-sats' eye, and it got alerted up to the National Reconnaissance Office, where analysts tracked its progress to Kolkata. But since it wasn't doing anything hostile or dangerous, they closed the file.'

Defense Minister Whittey spoke again 'Isn't it...unusual that the Indians let this unregistered ship sail into their territorial waters unmolested?'

'We thought so. However, as it wasn't identified as a threat, we didn't follow it too closely. Also, we'll deal with the Indian response later in the briefing.'

'Ok, go ahead,' said the minister.

'The ship steamed up the Hoolie River to the Kolkata docks where it moored for about three days. Cursory surveillance revealed large crowds of people around the ship which dissipated after a day or two.' She spread her hands. 'It wasn't investigated further because there's always large crowds everywhere in India. But then something interesting happened. The ship left the port and sailed down the Hoolie river to the open ocean and kept going south. The satellites sent another alert to the analysts, who had no idea what was going on. They cross-checked shipping registries for information on the vessel and found it was an old Indonesian primary goods freighter called, *Akita*. It had been sold for scrap three years ago and has been sitting on the beach ever since. Our people checked with the Indian Navy, who'd been tracking the ship too. Turns out an opaque shell company purchased it, and it was scheduled to be refit at the Kolkata docks, but nobody knew by whom or for what purpose.'

'So, you're telling us that even at this point, the Indians didn't investigate this rogue ship?' interrupted Whittey.

'That's correct,' said Alice.

'And you didn't think to press the issue with them!' Whittey exclaimed.

'It's not my job to press the issue,' said Alice wryly. 'You'll have to address that question to the Navy.'

'It's not our business to tell them how to patrol their territorial waters.' Admiral Futcher shrugged. 'Besides, they've got bigger problems, like their embryonic civil war.'

Whittey drew an angry breath but before he could speak Robertson cut in.

'With all due respect, Minister, there are thousands of vessels of all sizes sailing around the islands between Jakarta and Kolkata; tracking them all would be futile. Furthermore, the vast majority of older freighters, especially ones bought off the scrap heap, are owned through shell companies-it's just not that unusual.' Glen caught the look from his girlfriend telling him, 'Thanks for your help, but I had this anyway.' Her masterfulness at refusing to ask for help was just one of the things Glen Robertson loved about her.

Admiral Futcher spoke up. 'Thank you, Commodore. Shall we carry on?' he said to Alice.

'The Indian navy was nowhere to be seen when it steamed south,' she went on, the tiniest smile beginning to play at the edge of her mouth. *I love you too*. A quick look from Jacqui did wonders to wipe the smile off Robertson's face. 'Apparently they made a few half-hearted attempts to hail it, which were ignored. We've spoken to the Indonesians; they didn't know where it was going, but they didn't send their navy in to investigate either. It sailed across the Indian Ocean to Oakajee Beach in Geraldtown, WA, where it ran aground, and 24,517 refugees climbed off it.'

'The consequences of which we are well acquainted,' said Lafitte. 'Alice, what is the intelligence community's take on why they are coming?'

'Well, this will take us off track a little...' Lafitte waved her on. 'As always, people seek refugee status for several reasons, but lately, the number claiming climate refugee status has gone through the roof. Each rich nation has a UN-mandated minimum intake due to our retroactive culpability regarding climate changes.'

Whittey snorted. 'Imagine if we tried to 'retroactively' blame India and China for having three billion babies and ruining the world's environment? Ridiculous concept.'

Alice grinned. 'Well, we *have* seen increasingly severe weather patterns, especially around the tropics, over the last decade. Low lying countries, like Bangladesh and parts of India, keep getting hammered by storms. They can't feed themselves because crops get flooded, and it's caused massive population dislocation in these places because people are starving and can't live in the storms zones.'

'Most have moved inland,' added Holloway, 'That's why they're on the verge of civil war. There's just too many people with different religions and backgrounds competing for less food.'

'This creates a market for people who want to leave,' said Alice. 'Especially since inland food bowls are starting to fail because of drought. So, the logical choice for many is to migrate overseas.'

'And they'll pay,' said Holloway. 'People we've interviewed from the *Akita* tell us they paid up to five thousand US dollars for a place on that ship.'

'People smugglers,' said Abbott with disgust. 'We solved that problem once. We can solve it again.'

Lafitte arched an eyebrow. Abbott was always looking for something to bash with her fist.

'At present, after three ships have landed,' continued Alice, 'there are eighty-three thousand, six hundred and ninety asylum seekers interned in temporary shelters a few kilometers outside Geraldtown. When they arrived, we found most were severely dehydrated and had symptoms of malnutrition, ranging from mild to severe. A large proportion were infected with various strains of bacteria and sepsis of the blood, mainly stemming from atrocious hygiene on the voyage. People were transported in the cargo holds of the ships, which were awash with human faeces, urine, and vomit.'

'The good stuff,' muttered Whittey. Robertson nearly burst out laughing; the Defense Minister was often unintentionally funny like this.

'Why were conditions so appalling?' asked Abbott.

'There's no plumbing or sanitary facilities of any kind installed, so all the...waste, pooled in the bottom. Rough seas on the way over didn't help, especially for people who'd never been on a boat in their lives. The refugees report they weren't allowed on deck at all either. For security reasons, apparently.'

'Now they're interned in a camp. Because it's so remote, it's been a real struggle to get supplies and medical care out there.' Alice looked at Lafitte. 'After twenty-three escaped into the desert, we had to put a twelve-foot fence around the compound.'

'It's for their own protection,' defended Whittey. 'Twelve died from exposure before local authorities could find them.'

'This whole situation is making us look like fools,' said Lafitte. She looked coolly at Admiral Futcher. 'The people smugglers have made a mockery of our border sovereignty, not to mention our navy. The Indians are telling the world we're abusing their citizens, detaining them illegally and then letting them die in the desert. Indian communities in Sydney and Melbourne are on the verge of rioting, demanding we let them in. Not to mention shock jocks on their soapboxes unearthing every latent racist in Australia, who want us to send the damned 'queue-jumpers' back where they came from. Then there's the bleeding hearts brigade who want us to help the refugees *and* go after the smugglers.'

'We should certainly pursue the smugglers,' said Whittey. 'Make an example of them.'

'The tabloid media is being helpful, as always,' said Lafitte. She dropped a newspaper on the table. 'NAVY IMPOTENT AS BROWN TSUNAMI BREAKS ON GERALDTOWN shouted the headline.

I wonder if she's more upset about the strategic situation, or the poll numbers showing her support tanking, Robertson scribbled on his watch and sent to Alice.

'It's imperative another shipload of illegals does not land here,' said Lafitte. 'Anyone identified as a people smuggler is to have the book thrown at them. I want them paraded in front of the media and locked up permanently. Send a message. We'll need to work with our regional partners to make it happen.'

Easier said than done, thought Robertson. This was classic Jacqui, he thought. Speaking with total certainty about things that were more complicated than she wanted to admit. That had always been her problem; pitch black or snow white, and always prepared to ignore facts if they didn't fit her world view. It made her an inspirational leader if you didn't follow the issues closely, like most voters, and unfortunately for most people in this room, it also made her a pain in the ass to work with. 'Work with our regional partners' was a nice soundbite but Robertson strongly suspected the Indian Navy was on the take. How else would these tankers get through? If Robertson was right, they weren't going to extend themselves by helping the Royal Australian Navy.

Alice continued. 'Two more ships have landed since the first. We tracked them the whole way in but didn't have the capability to turn them around. Perhaps Vice-Admiral Futcher is best placed to outline Navy procedure going forward?'

'Thank you, Alice,' said Futcher. 'Operation Sovereign Borders, implemented by the Abbott government in 2013, set the benchmark for denying illegal entry into Australia by sea. Illegals had been using old fishing boats or similar vessels to bring people in, so it was relatively easy to board them, pacify the crew and either tow them back to Indonesian waters, or transfer them to life-boats and do the same.' Futcher looked at Robertson as he spoke. When Robertson met his gaze, the Vice-Admiral looked away.

Yes, thought Robertson, it was easy. Most times, things went to plan...He drifted away from the meeting for a moment, and suddenly he was a twenty-year-old midshipman again, piloting *Melbourne's* RHIB. Pulling alongside that Indo fishing trawler, five young men completely oblivious they were seconds away from disaster.

He took a deep breath, brought himself back to the present. Maybe he needed to revisit the shrink; that mission kept popping into his head at the most inconvenient times. He always remembered the flaking paint so well; the way it chipped and flew everywhere, floating, spinning serenely, like a dandelion seed in a whisper of wind, on a day when youthful serenity was blasted out of existence forever.

Meanwhile, Futcher was still droning on. '...However, the new tactic precludes the use of RHIBs because of the ships' size. The freighters they've used so far have been well over forty thousand tonnes each, and they timed their run in such a way that we had no frigates in the area, which can affect fast-rope insertion by helicopter. Patrol boats have attempted to intercept the bulkers, but they don't have the capability to board, and these ships didn't comply with requests to identify themselves. These actions add weight to the Director-General's conclusion that elements of the Indian navy are in some way complicit with the smuggler operations, namely by reporting on Australian frigate locations.'

'So, from now on we'll be using helicopter insertion teams to board, pacify and tow. Same strategy, slightly different tactic to previously. The teams will commandeer the ships, pacify the crews and passengers-'

'Pacify?' interrupted the PM. 'That's not a very nice word, is it?' It was more a statement than a question.

'The boarding parties will be briefed to act with as much restraint as the situation permits. However, your policy dictates that we turn these ships around, which has the potential to cause upset amongst the passengers.' He rolled a shrug. 'How you sell it to the public is up to you, but operational realities dictate our tactics.'

'Ok, Futcher. But keep it clean. I *do* have to sell this to the public.'

'Excuse me, sir,' interjected Robertson, 'but what about the possibility the smugglers resist our attempts to board?' The *almost certainty* they'll resist our attempts to board, he thought.

Futcher nodded; he knew it was a fair question, especially from Robertson. 'Boarding parties will be accompanied by a squad of clearance divers for security.' He addressed the broader group. 'We plan for contingencies of course, but the other ships haven't had any weapons aboard, and the crews have shown no aggression. Our assessment is we're unlikely to encounter resistance.'

He resumed the briefing. 'Once we have compliance, we'll bring aboard pilots, medics and engineers as necessary to keep the ships running. We'll turn them around and sail them back to Indian territorial waters. The *Melbourne,* under Commodore Robertson here, will use this tactic on the *Tamil Nadu.* It left Kolkata only yesterday and has been observed following the same pattern as the previous three ships to arrive...'

Robertson, bored, reopened a private link to Alice.

'You're so damned sexy when you act smart,' he tapped across. Nodding along to the Admirals briefing, she arched an eyebrow.

'No wonder you're so damned horny all the time,' she shot back.

Jacqui Laffitte glanced at Glen, seemed to read his mind, then shifted her gaze to Alice, whose face confirmed her suspicions. She sighed inwardly. This crisis was developing into the biggest test of her political life, and she didn't need feelings for Glen Robertson resurfacing. She resisted the urge to admonish him with a look and returned her attention to Admiral Futcher.

Chapter 4
July 1st, 1700 hours
HMAS *Melbourne*

On the bridge of the HMAS *Melbourne,* Robertson leaned on the forward console and peered over the wall of water his frigate was about to plow into. Cords of water flowed over the bow and lashed the superstruture as the ship pitched in a sea state six ocean, and the old *Hobart* class destroyer creaked in protest.

Nobody noticed; rough seas were par for the course these days. Attention was split between the towering waves and the sensor suite display in the middle of the bridge, which was showing a stylised three-dimensional representation of all naval, aerial and submarine assets within the designated range.

Robertson was commanding the task force assigned to intercept the *Tamil Nadu*, so the *Melbourne* was at the centre of a faintly luminous, transparent blue sphere within the display. Sonar tracked a few whales, displayed in the bottom half of the sphere and marked 'O' for organic. Cutting the sphere like a sliced onion was a ring of concentric circles, representing the ocean surface. The patrol boat *Broome* was close by on that plane, and further out was the destroyer, *Brisbane.* They were both tagged in yellow. A flashing red dot three hundred clicks out was the transport ship, *Tamil Nadu.*

Robertson's lips thinned as lukewarm coffee spilled from the mug in his hand. He tossed the tepid dregs down his throat and grimaced. Foul.

'Who made this coffee?' he called. 'Sterling,' he said to the weapons officer. 'It was you, wasn't it?'

'What makes you say that, sir?' replied Sterling.

'Because it's weak, bitter, and finished,' he said, tipping his empty mug upside down. The bridge crew tittered, including Sterling. 'Can't get enough, can you sir.' Sterling taunted.

Robertson's red-rimmed eyes creased as he searched for the bulker over the six-metre swell. Heavy grey clouds blanketed the ocean, and in the dreary light, the waves were like black glass.

Robertson chuckled softly as he peered through the teeming spray. 'Look at this shit.' Sterling said, pointing out to the wicked seas. 'Hey Max,' he said to the navigator. 'Where the hell are we? We're clearly off the coast of Norway.'

'You should be glad,' Max deadpanned back. 'The North Sea matches your personality.'

The bridge laughed again, and Sterling managed a rueful grin.

'Norway wouldn't be so bad,' Max yawned. 'The weather's ordinary but the women are very...*liberal.*' He smacked his lips.

Janice Conlan, Tactical Action Officer, roller her eyes. 'They'd have to be to let you anywhere near them,' she muttered.

'Stop flirting you two. Target will be visual in moments,' Robertson weighed in with the natural voice of command. He'd modelled it on his grandfather, a stern man whose mantra was that it was far preferable to be respected than liked.

Their target (was that even the right word?) was close now. A tell-tale pall of black smoke was visible against the clouds, even though the ship was beyond the curvature of the earth.

The *Tamil Nadu* had left Kolkata twelve days earlier, giving Robertson plenty of time to transfer back to his ship and get on station.

Battling giant swells and a category two tropical cyclone, the ancient forty-five thousand tonne bulk-carrier had steamed a slow, erratic course south-west into the Bay of Bengal. Battered by storm cells, it had meandered in looping circles, like a lazy dog chasing its tail. Once in the open ocean, the hundred-mile-an-hour winds had abated somewhat, and the ship turned directly south. A few days later it passed Smith Island, then the first islands of the vast Indonesian archipelago. When the giant landmass of Sumatra came into view, the ship changed course again to a more south-westerly heading, tracking a parallel route to the Indonesian coastline as it curved to the west.

Eventually, the ship left Sumatra behind. Changing direction for the final time, it now pointed straight towards Geraldton, a remote port town on the edge of the Australian continent.

As a matter of routine, the Royal Australian Navy tracked everything that came within three-thousand clicks of the northern Australian coastline. Lacking any commercial transponders the *Tamil Nadu* had come to the attention of the low-level AI-equipped surveillance satellites soon after it left Kolkata. The silent birds in the sky had photographed the ship leaving port, and once it had passed Sumatra, transmitted its location to the 'Laverton Over the Horizon Radar', which had followed its progress. Laverton had updated the position and heading of the *Tamil Nadu* to the *Melbourne*, guiding Robertson to intercept.

Australia was rich, free and democratic and had therefore been a favourite destination for people smugglers for years, and until 2015, no government had known how to deal with the issue. Often, crews deliberately sabotaged boats when the Navy came into view, blowing holes in the hull or wrecking the engines, so they had to be rescued and transferred to the mainland. Then, policy was changed: The Navy allowed any ship that was sabotaged to sink, and the passengers were packed into cheap lifeboats, towed back to Indonesian waters and set adrift.

This approach adjusted attitudes and promptly stopped the flow. Its architects clapped each other on the back and toasted a job well done because soon the flow of refugees had slowed to a trickle of irregular, isolated events. Potential customers didn't want to pay five, ten or twenty thousand dollars for a return trip to the middle of the Indian Ocean. They'd tried a few other tactics, like landing in New Guinea,but the Aussies just intercepted anything coming from there too. Besides, nobody wanted to go there because it was a basket case itself and the chances of getting stuck were damned high. Then in 2022, the *Bau Anjing* incident happened and deterred trips even more.

As a last ditch effort, the smugglers set their sights on New Zealand, but that was a bridge too far; most of the boats sank on the way, and after a few actually landed, the Kiwis dropped their international nice guy act and adopted the Australian approach anyway. New Zealand had turned into a life raft for sinking Pacific Island nations; they were full. Demand was there, no doubt about it, but smugglers couldn't get them to the antipodes.

The way was closed.

Robertson thought back to those missions with something akin to nostalgia, primarily because in the last six months, everything had changed. Someone had the bright idea of loading giant bulk carriers with tens of thousands of passengers, and two of them had washed up on the beach at Geraldton. He couldn't help but admire the gumption, it was a ridiculous idea, which, impressively enough, they'd somehow pulled off. He figured they must have paid off elements of the government *and* the navy to swing it, which meant some powerful financial and political backing. He wondered how far up Indian society their support went.

Anyway, the bureaucrats upstairs decided twice was enough, so now the *Tamil Nadu* was Robertson's mess to clean up. *Third time's the charm.* The only issue being that you couldn't factor in luck in military operations, unless it was bad. And Robertson's mind kept circling back to the fact that this was the same mission as the *Bau Anjing,* but on a much larger scale.

The Australian taskforce was holding position by tracing lazy circles on the edge of the EEZ while they waited for the Indian vessel. When the *Tamil Nadu* had closed the gap, Robertson made his way to the helicopter hangar aft. He pulled the aircrew in close, hiding from the whipping spray inside the hangar bay door. He addressed Osborne, the pilot. Straight out of the naval aviator mould, Osborne was stocky, cocky and utterly sure of himself which was exactly why he needed to hear what Robertson had to say.

'Our intel people have told us there shouldn't be any resistance,' he said, 'but you need to forget the official party line. Stay sharp. These are desperate people we're dealing with here, and they do desperate things.'

Osborne nodded, slightly confused. 'Sir, no specific threats have been identified in any of the briefings we've too…'

'That's exactly my point,' snapped Robertson. 'The intel people don't know everything. So you're going to keep an eye out for any funny business,' he continued, 'Watch your threat boards and monitor activity on that ship…I want your Hellfire's pre-targeted on that bridge. Understood?'

'Yes sir,' Osborne said. He exchanged looks with his co-pilot.

Robertson caught it. 'Gentlemen,' he said sharply. 'I can tell you from personal experience these are the missions where shit will spray at high pressure if you take your eyes off the ball.'

A few minutes later he'd ordered a bemused Osborne to take the big Seahawk into the air, spinning up and lifting off the flight deck. Robertson magnified the zoom on the bridge camera, stabilising the image and focusing on the bridge of the incoming ship. If there was trouble, he figured it would come from there, because that's where the smugglers were likely living. That's where he would have been. He turned to his communications officer.

'Try them again on all radio frequencies. Same message; acknowledge, ID and compliance with previously stated requests to reverse their heading and leave Australian territorial waters.'

'Sir.'

'And call the *Broome* onto station for any contingencies.'

'Yes, sir.'

Robertson wasn't particularly enamoured with this mission. There were thousands of refugees on that ship who would be most displeased when he told them they were not welcome and were going right back from where they came. He couldn't blame them if they felt that way, but it meant there was a real security threat to his specialists who were going to be on board the *Tamil Nadu*. It'd take nearly two weeks to plod its way back to Kolkata. Apart from the engineers and the civilian naval pilots being flown over with the boarding party, a medical team and security force would embark as well. All in all, plenty of time and plenty of scope for something to go wrong. He ambled back to the bridge and tried to figure out how this mission would go south.

Tamil Nadu

Fadi sat, propped against a corroded ladder that led up to a cargo hatch on the ship's deck. The rusty metal scratched his back, but he ignored it and peered into the cavernous dimness through eyes tight with discomfort. He was breathing through his mouth as much as possible to filter out the dense fog of human waste and vomit in the air. Nobody was allowed on deck - rough seas meant the risk of being washed overboard was too high, according to the smugglers. *Stupid*, thought Fadi. If he wanted to risk it, what did they care? Assholes.

Practically everyone had been seasick as soon as they hit the open ocean. Thousands of people had vomited until their stomachs knotted and bile came out. The smugglers hadn't bothered installing toilets, so people went where they sat in the gloom.

His mother held his hand, weak and clammy. She'd been horrendously ill, first seasickness and now some sort of gut infection. He'd been cleaning her up as she voided her bowels. At first, he'd tried vainly to hide his disgust. If nothing else, his violent wretching, while he washed her, gave things away. She'd reminded him that she'd done the same for him, not so long ago. It had made him laugh but hadn't stopped the retching. After a few days, however, he'd become desensitised, and now it wasn't much worse than dragging muck out of a drain. She turned to face him, eyes dull.

'I'm sorry, Fadi,' she croaked. 'This is not what I expected. They said the trip would take six days and we could wash on the deck once we were at sea.'

'It's ok; you weren't to know. It'll be worth it once we get there.' He squeezed her hand. 'Do you feel any better?'

Cleaning up her mess was bad enough, but the real hurt came from her humiliation. She pretended the situation didn't bother her, but once as he'd washed her, he'd seen her biting her lip, tears streaming down her face. After that, he made sure not to look into her eyes until well after he was finished. And now, he could see she was starting to succumb from dehydration.

The thousands of travellers surrounding them had been nervously optimistic when they'd bunkered in and moved down the Hoolie. The main hatches had to stay closed, because of the typhoon outside, or the space would have slowly flooded. So they'd sailed to sea with just a few access hatches and strung fluorescent lamps for light. Many had winked out, and now the few left were more like stars in a night sky - visible but not much use for seeing.

The ocean never seemed to calm down enough to allow them on deck, and the vague optimism quickly evaporated. There were no toilets, so people relieved themselves in bedsheets, then where they sat. There were two levels, and the people below had a real risk of human waste raining down on them. Vicious fights started when bottom dwellers tried to force their way up to the top level, and space ran out. Food became contaminated unless it was in tins or plastic bags, theft and outright robbery became commonplace.

Before long, the unholy stench of decomposing bodies added to the reek. There was no escape from the pungent, almost sweet odour. It was so thick that breathing through his mouth, Fadi could taste it. Hell, he could almost roll it around his mouth with his tongue. Every breath was a conscious choice to ingest the smell. Fadi was sure that anyone introduced suddenly to the hold of the ship from the outside would immediately collapse unconscious in shock.

He glanced at his mother, who hadn't answered; she'd fallen asleep. Jay was curled up next to her, twitching. He wondered what the little man was dreaming about?

Fadi had to get out of here. Checking his family one more time, he stood up and started climbing the ladder he'd been using as a backrest. A young girl sitting nearby stared at him. Her big eyes were white in the murky light. 'What are you doing?' they seemed to say. He brought his finger to his lips. *Shoosh.*

At the top, he poked his head through the small hatchway and felt daylight on his face, breathed fresh air again for the first time in twelve days. Spray from the ocean swept across the deck and caught in his hair, prickling his face, rejuvenating his skin. He closed his eyes and inhaled; it was the purest, most exalted, cleansing sensation he'd ever felt in his life. The underlying sea-sickness was still there, and he was weak and giddy from dehydration, but compared to being in the depths of the hold, he felt reborn. He opened his eyes and took in the scene. Five gantry towers, painted a faded cream and flecked with oxidised iron, punctuated the deck. Someone had used frayed hessian rope to lash thick metal cables to the gantries. Some lonely seagulls wheeled forlornly around the superstructure to the rear.

A distant thudding sound caught his ear, and he peered at the sky, the spray and glare of an overcast day stinging his eyes which had adapted to darkness. Against the grey clouds a speck hovered, no, it was moving closer. It closed and resolved into a helicopter. Maybe a military chopper? Resting his elbows on the deck, half in and half out of the hatchway, he settled in to watch the chopper approach, a little mesmerised. Maybe they were close to the Australian shoreline, and the aircraft was coming out to meet them - give them medical supplies? Then something darker occurred to him. He knew that twenty years ago, the Aussies had stopped the refugee flow by turning the little ships around. What if that chopper

41

had people on board who were going to turn the *Tamil Nadu* around?

'To hell with that. I'm not spending another two weeks in this floating sewer,' he muttered. *Not that there's anything you can do about it,* he thought angrily. The helicopter was close now. For the first time, he noticed movement high up on a wing jutting out the side of the bridge. A group of agitated agents seemed to be arguing with each other, Fadi could read the tension in the group as they gesticulated and pointed angrily, casting worried glances at the rapidly closing chopper. The group turned to one man who dashed inside and came back carrying a rectangular box over his shoulder. He disappeared behind the railing for a moment. When he came into view, there was a long tube slung over his shoulder. At right angles to the tube was attached a grip, and the man held it like an unwieldy rifle. Fadi didn't know much about guns, but if that's what this was it was a strange one; most of the barrel seemed to extend behind the man's shoulder, with only a short length in front. Weird. The thudding grew louder, and Fadi swivelled to watch the chopper approach over the bow.

Suddenly over the beat of the aircraft came a violent whooshing sound, like a high-pressure tap on full blast. A flame streaked from the bridge with a savage rip as the rocket motor ignited and the missile flashed across his vision before he could get a lock on it, straight towards the helicopter. The aircraft had been slowing as it descended; it now abruptly veered up and to the left, like a human recoiling from a striking viper. The engines whined as the pilot dodged, and he almost succeeded, but the rocket slammed into the side of the aircraft as it frantically peeled away. Fadi stared, shocked, at the retreating aircraft; it had survived the initial strike and reversed trajectories, flying back the way it had come, trailing black smoke from a gaping hole in the fuselage.

The body, contorted and bent, glowed orange as flames licked at the jagged edges where sheet metal had been moments before, and the engine note had changed. The chopper was losing altitude even as it clung to the air, trying to get as far away as possible. Fadi stared in disbelief. What the hell was going on?

'What are you doing up here, you reeking puddle of horsepiss?' said a rough voice behind him. Fadi turned just in time for two agents to grab him under the arms, wrench him out of the hatchway, and drag him across the deck. 'What are you doing? Let go of me!' he shouted, struggling in vain to break free. 'Shutup,' one of them grunted and clipped him over the head with a metal bar. Fire flashed through his skull. Too weak, and now stunned, they hauled him quickly to a door in the superstructure and threw him inside. The door clanged shut and darkness enveloped him.

HMAS *Melbourne*

Robertson peeled his fingers off the console and tried to think about how to resolve this diabolical mess. What a complete, unmitigated disaster. He had flashbacks of that ill-fated mission fifteen years ago which he had tried so hard to banish from his thoughts...

He composed himself. 'Comms - get onto Captain Moriarty on the *Broome* and have them get in there and check the helicopter wreckage for survivors. Then hail the *Tamil Nadu* again. Broadcast: Stop immediately and submit to boarding or prepare to be fired upon. Weapons, bring the three-inch gun online, illuminate the superstructure. Arm torpedo tubes one through four and draw a bead on stern of the ship.'

He looked out the bridge windows, his gaze alternating between the superstructure of the big ship where the SAM had come from and the small islands of debris in the ocean that had been the Seahawk.

He'd *known* this mission was going to be a disaster, a repeat of the *Bau Anjing.* He'd been slightly nervous - more standard mission jitters really, as the Seahawk flew over the waves but he'd only expected any opposition to emerge, if at all, once they'd boarded and explained to the crew what was going to happen. He berated himself; the *Bau Anjing* should have taught him that. *No. That's bullshit talk. You can't predict everything in combat, but you can react to the best of your ability.*

'Come *on*, Moriarty,' he breathed to himself, willing the *Broome's* captain to get in there and fish survivors out of the water. He was fuming at Osborne who had been taken by surprise. He'd reacted instantly, maxing out the turbines and savagely pulling the machine sideways and up, but Robertson had identified another problem; he'd guided the sinking Seahawk a few clicks back towards the *Melbourne*, but he'd eventually ditched *right in the path of the Tamil Nadu,* which was still bearing down on the half-submerged Seahawk.

The patrol boat captain's voice crackled over the bridge radio. 'This is Moriarty. We've disengaged the overspeed governor and are heading to the crash site at thirty knots.'

'We're running out of time, sir,' Conlan said. 'We have to stop that ship somehow, or at least get it to change course or it'll steam right over the boarding party.'

'Sterling, fire a warning shot with the Melara across the bow,' he said. The three-inch gun barked and a splash plumed scant metres from their quarry.

'No reply to any attempts to hail them, they're either ignoring us or just can't hear us,' said Conlan.

'Conlan, how long till it arrives at the crash site?' said Robertson.

Conlan grimaced. 'Less than five minutes, sir.'

'Sterling, if we launch a Mk 48 now when does it hit the back of that ship?'

'Sixty-four seconds, sir,' called the Sterling.

Worst case scenario that gave Robertson just over three minutes for the *Broome* to arrive, pick up survivors and get out of there. Not long enough. Specifically, for this worst-case scenario the *Melbourne* was carrying some heavyweight torpedoes, which were more than adequate for blowing the propeller off the back of the *Tamil Nadu*...but it would still take minutes to stop, and the real issue was he didn't know how much damage an MK 48 would do. They were seriously heavy hitters designed to cut warships in half. On one hand, the *Tamil Nadu* was ten times bigger than most warships, on the other, it was old, barely seaworthy, and unarmoured.

He blinked, ridding his mind of unbidden memories of Fitzsimmons pouring fire into the *Bau Anjing*. He peered at the console to check on the patrol boat's progress.

The *Broome* had arrived at the crash site, prowling amongst the wreckage for survivors. The fuselage of the Seahawk bobbed on the swell, half-submerged and listing, the two visible rotor blades ending where shrapnel had smashed them off halfway down their lengths.

'Sir, target is maintaining speed and vector,' called Conlan.

Robertson could see for himself - the *Tamil Nadu* hadn't changed course, hadn't slowed down. 'How long till collision?'

'Two minutes, thirty-seven seconds,' said Conlan, who'd set up a timer on her screen. If he launched a torpedo now, it would take sixty-four seconds to hit the back of the ship. He doubted if it would stop before hitting the debris pile, but the loss of steering would almost certainly change its course.

'Sir, *Broome* says it has found survivors. They're trapped in the cabin and it's going to take some time to free them.'

'They have sixty seconds to pull anyone else out. They must clear in sixty seconds.' Robertson commanded.

Comms relayed the order and Robertson clasped his hands behind his back. Mainly to prevent him from fidgeting nervously. Maybe kill thirty thousand Indians or definitely kill five Australians.

Sterling glanced at his captain, willing him to order the torpedo free. 'Sir, we have to launch now to prevent the collision!'

45

'Do not fire!' he snapped.

He'd give the *Broome* an extra thirty seconds to get any survivors out. That still gave them thirty seconds to get the hell out of the way before the *Tamil Nadu* drove over the top of them. Should be plenty of time.

He picked up the comms unit and spoke directly to Moriarty, captain of the *Broome.*

'Moriarty, this is Robertson. You now have ninety seconds to rescue any survivors and then you will *clear the area.* No heroics! You will be clear at thirty seconds to impact.'

There was silence on the bridge. Now, it was too late to fire the torpedo. Unless the *Broome* could get those men out of the water, or the *Tamil Nadu* suddenly changed course, he'd just signed their warrants.

The timer on Conlan's screen ticked down.

One minute, forty-three seconds...

'*Melbourne,* this is the *Broome,* we're having trouble getting to them all, the metal has warped, and we have to torch through to free them,' came Moriarty's voice over the speakers. 'We have a diver in the water...'

'What the *fuck,* Moriarty!' shouted Robertson. 'Recall your diver *immediately!*'

The ship was close now, barely a few hundred metres away.

Fifty seconds...

'Negative sir, we've freed one, but there's four more alive still trapped,' replied Moriarty.

The bulker still hadn't changed course or speed. The immense shape was threateningly close now.

'Sterling, as soon as the *Broome* has cleared the area fire on the bridge. Take out the entire superstructure and ready the second Seahawk for launch, combat boarding operations.'

Thirty-two seconds...

The Broome was still on station. The bulker loomed larger.

'Moriarty, break away! Get out of there!'

'We're close, only need a few more seconds!' crackled the radio in response.

'You have a direct order to clear the area. Your entire crew is at risk. Breakaway now!'

'There's time for one more then we're leaving!'

Seventeen seconds, the bulker was barely half it's own length from the patrol boat.

'Get clear! Clear the area now!' spat Robertson.

Seven seconds...

The *Tamil Nadu* reared up next to the *Broome,* dwarfing the little patrol boat, a colossal mechanical tsunami cresting.

'We've got them, we're leaving,' shouted Moriarty, his words echoing around the *Melbourne's* bridge, and the little boat's engines roared into life...

Two seconds...

The *Broome* squatted down under full acceleration. Too late. The *Tamil Nadu* crunched into her side, picking her up and bulldozing her through the water. An awful rending, tearing sound reached across the waves as the *Broome* skipped sideways, pincered between the oncoming waves and the freighter's bow. The entire bridge of the *Melbourne* watched in horror as the patrol boat caught a swell and flipped over, forced under the big ship, torn to pieces in a shrieking, grinding lacerating of metal as it disintegrated like a scrap shredder was consuming it.

Robertson struggled to swallow, his mouth dry like hot ash. Apart from the radar, beeping course updates, the bridge was utterly silent. Robertson's heart pounded painfully in his chest. Bits of the *Broome* drifted to the surface. As it materialised Robertson saw it was upside down. Conlan covered her mouth with her hands in disbelief.

Robertson turned to Sterling who was watching him expectantly. Robertson couldn't believe it had come to this, but he knew what he had to do. He delayed a second more, then spoke to the bridge.

'You know our orders. No more ships are to reach Australian waters. Furthermore, ramming a ship in the process of rescuing crash survivors is a hostile act. We don't know who's on that ship, but they *are* hostile. Sterling, arm torpedo tubes one and two. Fire one torpedo on my mark.

Sterling nodded. 'Yes, sir. Tubes one and two armed and operational, sir.'

'Fire one.' Saying the words, Robertson suddenly felt wholly disconnected from the situation; like an alternate consciousness was drifting over his shoulder, telling him it was the right thing to do. It wouldn't bring the crew of the Seahawk back, or the *Broome,* but the ever defiant *Tamil Nadu* had hostiles on board, and it was his job to stop it reaching Australia.

Just following orders, echoed a voice in his skull. *Where have I heard that before?* He squashed it.

Sterling punctuated the silence on the bridge by calling the torpedo home. 'Fifteen hundred metres to impact. One thousand metres to impact. Five hundred metres to impact.'

The *Tamil Nadu* steamed on, a small gash in its bow from where it had collided with the *Broome*. It looked like a giant scratch, something you could cover with a band-aid. Hitting the patrol boat was an insignificant event in the life of the old freighter. Activity on the superstructure had ceased; obviously, the smugglers had retreated inside. Maybe they were as shocked at what was happening as the Australians. For a moment, it could have been just another ordinary freighter on the high seas.

Too late to think like that.

'Imminent impact.' said Sterling.

A bright flash under the surface, like a silver sun rising from the depths to illuminate the stern of the ship-then the ocean exploded. Scalding streams of sea-water spat into the sky, and simultaneously but much more slowly, the entire rear end of the ship lifted totally out of the water. Robertson had never seen anything like it. A split second later the detonation blasted pulverised metal into the air, a steel-grey cloud of debris shooting up and out from behind the bridge superstructure. The tearing thunder of the explosion reached them moments later.

'Impact on target,' said Sterling redundantly.

Nobody spoke. Robertson had sent an emergency signal for ships in the area to help pick up survivors in case the freighter sank, and had ordered the *Melbourne's* remaining Seahawk out to search for any survivors from the *Broome*. As they watched, the big ship slowed and then stopped making headway, the stern sinking lower into the water. To Robertson's knowledge, nobody had ever fired a Mark 48 into a cargo ship like the *Tamil Nadu*. He didn't know what to expect; no one did. The Mark 48 was a heavy-duty weapon with some serious stopping power. It had, in fact, been designed for use in submarines in an anti-shipping role but was filling a capability gap on the Australian destroyers because of long-term delays procuring a lightweight torpedo for the Navy. A lightweight would have been much better suited to take out the propulsion unit and little else, but he knew that wasn't going to 'cut it' in Canberra if this mission went south. He could already sense that perhaps the 48 had been overkill, but what was his other option?
Just following orders.

Tamil Nadu

Fadi sat on the floor, back against the wall, brooding. Twenty minutes ago he would have done anything to get the hell out of the hold, but now he wasn't so sure. A few minutes after he was locked up a metallic tearing sound had echoed down the length of the hull, filling him with trepidation. Was the hull breached? But the engine note didn't change, and neither did the movement of the ship on the water, and his thoughts returned to his immediate situation. What had happened to

49

the others who'd come topside? Maybe he should've stayed down with mother and Jay.

All speculation ceased when a massive explosion rocked the ship, as though a petulant giant had picked it up and slapped it aside in disgust. The concussion flung him across the room and he felt the entire deck shift up, and then gradually drop away, lurching crazily as it settled back into the water. He gathered his senses...light was filtering into his little world - a thick cloud of dust motes riding a shaft of daylight; the door had burst off its hinges.

He staggered through and peered around, not believing his eyes. The superstructure had been largely ripped apart, with the rear half sagging into the ocean. The back of the ship just wasn't there anymore. A mess of wreckage was strewn all over the water, bobbing on a boiling, frothing sea. The ship kept shuddering, great creaking sounds emanating from deep in its bowels, an ailing giant. It sounded like the ship was coming apart on the inside, the mechanical equivalent of what so many passengers had endured on this voyage. He looked around, dazed. He could hear muffled shouts and screams from the hold.

HMAS *Melbourne*

'Ok Sterling, what you got?' Robertson's mind raced. If the *Tamil Nadu* sank, a lot of people were going to die, whatever the *Melbourne*, and the *Sydney*, did about it.

Sterling brought up some data on his screen. 'Doesn't look good, captain. She's already two metres lower in the water, mostly at the stern. Now she's come to a complete stop and with the ass blown out of her, water's just gushing in. I've brought up a schematic of those old bulkers; it's not the *Tamil Nadu,* couldn't find her blueprints, but a ship made by the same manufacturer, similair vintage and displacement.' His screen displayed a two-dimensional cross-section of a cargo ship nearly identical to the *Nadu.*

'These ships were compartmentalised, with four or five holds; if one or two breached and filled with water, the ship should stay afloat. However, we've almost certainly blown through the bulkhead between the engine compartment and the first hold. That probably won't be enough to sink the ship, but it would explain why she's already noticeably stern-down.'

'Sterling, the explosion lifted the stern clear out of the water. I've never seen anything like it. I need to know your assessment of its ability to withstand that sort of stress,' said Robertson.

'Well sir, I suspect we've broken her back. If we have, I'm guessing at least one other compartment, but probably more, are compromised. If you break their backs, the middle holds will fill up and they're useless as ships, but they won't sink. However, as I said, we've probably blown through the engine compartment into hold one, and broken her back too, so I would expect her to go under....'

'How long?' Robertson cut him off suddenly.

'She's gonna sink fast, sir,' Sterling replied with grim hesitance.

Tamil Nadu

People scrambled through the hatches, sprouting onto the deck like weeds, turning and dragging others out frantically.

Fadi pushed forward, searching for Jay and his mother. 'What 's going on? What's happening down there?' he demanded from a group of girls who were clutching each other, huddled crying near the railing.

'There was an explosion. The bottom of the ship cracked open,' sniffed one into her fist. 'Water's pouring in. People are fighting to get out.'

'The scaffolding, is the scaffolding still intact?' Panic crept into his voice. 'My mother was on the top level!'

One of the girls looked at him, eyes brimming with tears. She bit her knuckles. 'It fell, everyone on the top-level got dumped onto the people below. Lots of people are trapped. People were already drowning when we climbed out.'

Fadi dashed away from the girls towards the hatchway, tried to force his way through the crowd. He had to get down there, find them and get them out. No way, *no way* was he going to let them die in that hold!

'Get out of the way!' bellowed a burly man who was manhandling people through the hatch. Another man pulled Fadi to the side and held him there. 'You're not going back down there, kid.'

'But my mother is in there, I have to get her out!' He pushed against his captor but the man just held him tighter.

'Let her take her chances same as everyone else! Everyone has someone down there. Help us clear the hatches or get lost.'

Fadi went berserk. Striking manically, he jammed his hands in the man's face, dug his filthy nails into his eyes and raked them down his cheeks. The man roared in pain and surprise, and Fadi tried to skirt around him. But the man was too quick. Fadi felt his brain slam against his skull as the big man tackled him into the deck, grabbed him by the hair, and pounded his head into the metal. Fadi thrashed wildly, his limbs clipping bystanders, then he felt the weight of another man pinning him to the deck, and the first man let go of his hair and regarded him with angry, bloodshot eyes.

'Please,' ground out Fadi through gritted teeth 'My mother is down there. Please let me go and get her.' The man contemplated him for a moment, licking a trickle of blood off his lip. Then his fist came down, crunching into Fadi's nose. Hot pain shot across his face, and suddenly, he was drifting...

...The damp velvet hands of a thousand angels were gently holding him aloft, caressing him, enveloping him. They rippled up and down his body, across his chest, up to his neck, teasing his mouth, then down again, he was the strings on a harp, being touched by the fingers of virtuoso musicians. It felt wonderful. He could see his mother - she was drifting near him on her own cloud of euphoria, contented bliss radiating from her sleeping features.

'Hey, mother,' he began, but it was all too much effort...he sank back...she'll be fine...She looked beautific, even as she started to float away, born on the hands of the invisible angels. He wanted to reach out and touch her, pull her back towards him, but he just felt too lethargic, and she drifted into the distance, slowly disappearing. The hands felt more fluid now, less like velvet and more wet, like thick honey, and they were pulling him deeper into their embrace as they enfolded him even more. 'Breath Fadi...' whispered a voice... 'you have to breathe...'

He jerked awake, gasped in shock as he inhaled a lungful of seawater. He doubled over and coughed violently, vomiting up salty water even as the panic welled up in him. A shot of adrenalin broke his lethargy and he scrambled to stay afloat, thrashed towards a chunk of metal floating nearby. He'd never been a good swimmer and he was terrified. He managed to flail his way to a piece of debris and clung on gasping for air, raspy coughs heaving the water out of his lungs. He gathered himself. Where was the ship? He couldn't see it. He spun frantically, looking through three hundred and sixty degrees, there was no sign of the *Tamil Nadu*. Had he been washed overboard? There were clumps of people, like him, clutching flotsam, scattered around. Not very many. Definitely not everyone who'd been on board. He couldn't see his mother, or Jay anywhere, no matter how desperately he searched or how hard he peered at the little clumps of people surrounding him, as far as he could see.

'Mother!' he screamed. 'Jay!'

His voice echoed across the glassy black ocean.

He cried out again, his voice sounding tiny and the water swallowing his shout.

Grief welled up inside him, along with the anger that had grown in his chest during the voyage, until the emotion of the loss of his mother and Jay and his impending death overcame him, and he drifted numbly, like so much debris, as shock settled in and mercifully leeched him of all feeling.

HMAS *Melbourne*

On the bridge of the *Melbourne*, they watched the *Tamil Nadu* sink with alarming speed, even as they steamed towards it and deployed all the RHIB's to pick up survivors. The back of the ship disappeared first, captured air blew out of the hull as water rushed in, the remains of the superstructure protruding above the surface like a giant mangled periscope. The deck finally followed. The water crept up the length of the deck, slowly reeling in the bow, herding stranded passengers to the front.

When they ran out of room on the deck, one by one, and in groups, two here, three there, families holding hands, they waded or jumped into the water and paddled away from the receding ship. A dispassionate part of Robertson's brain saw penguins leaping off an ice flow. He'd wondered if he was broken emotionally the first time he'd experienced this sensation. Over time, he'd come to accept it, sometimes welcoming it - it helped him work through a crisis. By the time the *Melbourne* arrived, only the bow of the big ship was poking through the dark ocean surface, and soon it fell away, swallowed by a wave. A few hundred people littered the water. He had no idea how many had been on board, but knew, in all probability, the ship would have dragged most of the passengers down with it. Wreckage strewn about the area from the *Broome*, the Seahawk and junk from the deck of the freighter made the little clumps of people hard to distinguish.

The rescue operation continued well into the night, with RHIB's picking up survivors and bringing them back to the frigates. Robertson stared at the spot where the *Tamil Nadu* had disappeared, issuing orders woodenly. Finally, memories of the *Bau Anjing* broke through, and there was nothing he could do to stop them. His face became a stony mask, denying the outside world any knowledge of the raging battles tormenting his conscience.

Chapter 5
July 7th, 1600 hours
Lok Sabha

Sonal Malhotra, leader of the National Democratic Alliance and Prime Minister of India, approached the speaker's podium in the Lok Sabha - the lower house of the Indian parliament. An unprecedented silence in the chamber. Opposition MPs watched him intently, even his own MPs were boring holes in his back with expectant eyes. Hushed murmurs came from the gallery above. The usual lampooning cat-calls, shouted questions, and groans of mockery that ordinarily filled the chamber were, Malhotra realised, a blanket you could hide behind; even when you were thundering into the microphone. The Lok Sabha was the closest it had ever been to silent, and as Sonal made his way to the microphone, he felt exposed like a beacon in a storm.

He buttoned up his jacket and roundly stared at each section of the chamber, the gallery, opposition MPs. Let them see his resolve.

'Madame speaker, in light of the tragic and utterly unjustifiable death of some twenty-four thousand Indian nationals at the hands of the Australian Navy, we convene a special parliamentary session. Today, both sides of parliament affirm our solidarity with the families of those who lost their lives in the sinking of the 'Tamil-Nadu'.

He felt a sudden surge of pride in his country, and rage at the injury the Australians had so brazenly caused. His back straightened, and his tone became harsh.

'We affirm our universal condemnation of these actions, and that our resolve in gaining reparations from Australia will not waver. Today we send our condolences and our hearts to the families of the victims, so needlessly taken before their time.

'To the families of the deceased, we say: Nothing can bring your loved ones back, but take strength from the knowledge that in their deaths, we will vigorously pursue redress.

'Today we will also clarify the will of the Indian people on the issue of climate change refugees, and the responsibilities that developed countries have in supporting us in addressing the compelling problems we face as a result of their wanton abuse of the environment over centuries.

Hereafter we make it firm Indian policy to not only support, in principle, the concept of retroactive culpability on climate change, as pertaining to those developed nations that we deem fit to nominate.'

He stole a moment to look around the gallery. The opposition leader, jaw jutting, and eyes hard, caught his eye. Gave the slightest nod of support.

'Furthermore, it is now the policy of the Indian government to protect the rights of those citizens seeking to exercise their rights under retroactive culpability status.

'I ask you this. Why should the Indian citizen, in seeking a better life for himself, and his family, by way of removing himself from his traditional home, now made unlivable by the affliction of extreme weather events, for which he has no responsibility, face the risk of death at the hands of the very governments who are responsible for his hardship, for his dilemma?

'Our strident belief is that he should not! Our strident belief is that when Indian nationals exercise these rights, destination countries should do all they can to accept and integrate these refugees into their societies. We believe retroactively culpable countries owe climate refugees this basic human right.'

He put down his script and spoke from the heart.

'From this point forward, it is our policy that the Indian government will spare protection to any citizen exercising his rights in this fashion. In this, both sides of the chamber are in

unanimous agreement. For this, I acknowledge and thank the opposition parties.

'Our policy is not to organise the relocation of Indian nationals to other states without the consent of the receiving nations. However, any Indian citizen with the wherewithal, the desire, the inclination and strength of character to exercise their rights in this respect will gain the protection of the Indian government.

'We will never allow the tragedy, the catastrophe, of the Tamil-Nadu, to ever be repeated...'

He swept from the lectern and strode to the exit riding a wave of thunderous applause.

July 9th, 1630 hours
Sydney

The afternoon sun beat down relentlessly on Sydney harbour. Ultramarine water joined the burnt blue sky through the curved sails of the Opera House. The harbour sparkled like a diamond, the brightness crisscrossed by the tracks of countless faded yellow and green ferries joining the various ports along the Parramatta River. The arc of the Sydney Opera House cut blazing white streaks through the backdrops of the office towers behind it.

Jacqueline Lafitte gazed at the harbour briefly, enjoying the spectacle. Just like a beautiful summer's day, she thought, trying not to reflect on the fact that it was the middle of winter. She'd take her silver linings where she could.

Despite the aberrant weather, she never got sick of the view from Kirribilli House, situated as it was on the easternmost point of Sydney's north shore. Built in the 1850s, the House was a twin-gabled cottage; more modest and far smaller than the Opera House, but as home to the Prime Minister when in Sydney, arguably much more important.

She snapped the venetians shut and sat at the head of the conference table. She slid a plate with neatly folded chopsticks to the side, flicking a piece of chicken onto the desk. Popping it into her mouth, she picked up a chopstick and stabbed it at the screen on the far wall.

'Watch this, ladies and gentlemen. Watch it very closely.' Admiral Futcher, General Hammersmith, Cam Holloway from ASIS, Abbott and Whittey were all there. Thankfully they'd left their staffs behind. She let them twitch for a moment before continuing. 'I am open to suggestions as to how we should solve this unmitigated catastrophe.'

Glen fucking *Robertson.* She hadn't thought those words in a long time. She'd made many sacrifices to get where she was, and giving him up had hit the hardest. But you can't become PM whilst married to a refugee killer, so she'd done what she had to, and cast him aside, and subsequently thought about him every day for years, her heart making cruel comparisons between Glen and her husband that her head tried to stop. After all these years she thought she'd finally forgotten all about Glen, thrust him right out of her head. Well, he'd come crashing back into her mind like an uppercut to the jaw. He was all she could think about. All she was *supposed* to think about. Perversely, she was glad because it was going to happen anyway - now she could embrace, *indulge* it (if she was honest with herself), and not feel guilty. If she didn't know it was ridiculous, she would've almost thought he'd done it deliberately. The cocky bastard.

Louise Abbott studied the PM with interest. Abbott had recently been in Kuala Lumpur for the East Asia Summit involved in trade talks with ASEAN nations. The official line was that she'd come back to Canberra to be part of the crisis talks she was now attending. In reality, the Indian delegation had threatened to completely derail the entire process if Australia didn't immediately withdraw, so, diplomatically isolated, and politically marginalised, she'd been on the first flight back to Sydney.

Abbot continued to stare at Jacqui. The PM was renowned as a skilled negotiator, and law-maker; she'd had a mostly excellent term so far and seemed to be able to weasel her way out of most issues by merely exuding warmth and likability. Jacqui was undeniably beautiful, and Abbott felt she got an easy ride from artless men and a sympathetic public who gave her an easy ride due to her looks. Abbott felt that the ever-lovable PM was a façade and that behind it all was a paucity of substance like a wedding cake hollowed out from within.

She blinked and dragged her attention to the big screen at the end of the room which had been showing grainy military images from a hovering drone that had been rapidly launched from the *Melbourne* straight after the SeaHawk went down. It caught the end of the Seahawks frantic struggle back to the *Melbourne,* trailing smoke, a small splash as it ditched in the ocean. Fast-forward to the *Broome* entering the area, searching for survivors. The little craft just seemed to be sitting in the water, the small figures, from the height of the drone, seemed non-plussed. There was no sense of urgency in the footage.

From on high, without sound, it all looked very undramatic.

'Stop it there,' said Jacqui. 'Do we have any footage of them firing on us?'

Futcher answered. 'We don't. There was a recorder in the chopper, but it sank with the wreckage. This drone footage is all we have.'

Jacqui frowned. 'Are you quite sure? It seems all we have is evidence incriminating us and exonerating them.'

'Quite sure, Jacqui,' said Futcher.

She grimaced and took a deep breath. '*Shit,'* she whispered, then spoke for the room. 'It's nobody's fault, but we're going to pay dearly in the international community for that little fact,' she said looking at her colleagues. 'Ok. Carry on.' She shook her head in resignation.

The coal carrier moved into shot and slowly closed the gap to the little patrol boat. The *Broome* looked like a toy, with no business in the open ocean. The *Tamil Nadu* overran the patrol boat, which disappeared entirely from view for some seconds, only to resurface in the wake of the ship, upside down and in many pieces.

Fast forward again; the sudden flash of the torpedo, the writhing ocean and the ship arching into the air. An inset showed the perspective from *Melbourne's* camera, which revealed the ship visibly bowing in the middle as the rear lifted out of the water. The footage ended soon after with grainy images of people emerging onto the deck and desperately swimming away from the ship as it sank.

Abbott spoke into the silence. 'This is not what we had in mind when we said "stop the boats"', she said to Admiral Futcher.

He closed a notepad in which he'd been writing. 'You did not?' he asked sarcastically. 'Perhaps we misinterpreted the directive that no more ships are to reach the Australia coast.'

'Holloway, how many people were on that ship when it went down?' asked Lafitte.

Holloway couldn't believe what he was about to say, 'Our best estimates come from satellite images of the crowd on the dock prior to leaving Kolkata. We counted about twenty-five thousand. We rescued six hundred and seventeen. In all probability, over twenty-four thousand people went down with that ship... It's the largest single loss of life in maritime history.' The silence stretched, as those present digested the news.

'An ironic touch, sending them in coal ships,' said Lafitte, almost to herself. Burning coal was what had caused the climate mess in the first place, and Australia had been the world's biggest coal exporter for years. 'Right, what are the Indians telling us?'

'Their figures match ours.'

'Those clever bastards engineered this crisis from the bottom up,' mused Futcher.

'Malhotra wanted a war to keep his coalition together, and this Robertson cowboy handed it to him on a platter,' Whittey muttered.

'Well, the footage doesn't help us deny the fact that Robertson acted without cause,' said Abbott. 'And it's not as though we can admit to the world it was official policy to sink that ship.'

'So you want to make him a scapegoat?' asked Futcher flatly.

'I don't see an alternative. Unless you want to take the blame for twenty-four thousand dead Indians,' Abbot shrugged.

Jacqui opened her mouth to refute Abbott, and caught herself at the last minute. Abbott's point was well made; under no circumstances could the world think that torpedoing refugee ships was official Australian policy. Anyway; it wasn't, and what Glen had done was the result of a series of incredibly unlikely events. Unfortunately, judging from the videos, there was no evidence to justify his actions either. It made her sick, but they would have to hang Glen out to dry for this.

'Whatever the case, we've played right into their hands,' said Lafitte. 'Malhotra effectively admitted that those refugee ships were *de facto* official policy in his speech, and Holloway had floated the idea the Indian Navy was on the take. We have to acknowledge the likelihood that large parts of the Indian government are being paid off too.'

Whittey spoke up. 'Now we've given them an excuse to invoke this retroactive culpability garbage that's been circulating the UN for years. The Philippines, Malaysia and Indonesia all back Malhotra. They have climate problems themselves and need someone to blame. We'll be flooded if they start sending ships too!'

'It doesn't matter what the Malaysians and Indonesians say,' said Lafitte. 'Only what they do. Obviously, they'll play up the populist aspect of this, Australia-bashing is a regional sport because we're rich and they're poor, and it plays well to the voters. But I don't see the leadership doing anything about it, because they all own property in Sydney and send their kids to our universities. Besides, this isn't their problem.'

'We should take the Israeli approach,' said Whittey. 'Instead of placating the Indians, we should hit them so hard nobody else tries it on.'

'No.' said Lafitte. 'We're not butchers, and we're not becoming international pariahs on my watch. Since Malhotra's speech, three more coal ships from Chittagong have put to sea. It's almost certain they're heading to Kolkata to pick up refugees. Question is, will Malhotra deliver on his promise to escort them?'

'This might be a stupid question,' started General Hammersmith, 'but has anyone tried picking up the phone and talking to them?'

Jacqui grinned ruefully. 'We've tried, but they're more intent on righteous indignation than discussing a solution. Malhotra won't entertain us. Frankly, he's been handed a gift in terms of stabilising his coalition around him, and he won't throw it away to rapproach with us.'

Futcher looked up from his notepad, 'There's been a build-up of frigates and destroyers in the Bay of Bengal, and we think at least three are in the area for reasons other than normal transit, refit or other standard operational circumstance.'

'What's your point?' demanded Whittey.

Futcher peered at the Defense Minister. He had to conclude the man was an imbecile. 'Our assessment is that they're forming an escort force to protect ships leaving from Kolkata,' he explained slowly.'

'Ok, here's the deal.' Lafitte leaned forward slightly and let her gaze settle on each of them. Some met her gaze; some didn't bother. Abbott stared back at first, then found something on her notepad to study.

'Malhotra is giving the go-ahead for these people smugglers to do their thing, with government protection. They aren't even people smugglers really, more travel agents since they're sanctioned. They're going to send hundreds of thousands, maybe millions of refugees over to us, and if we try to stop them, we'll end up in a shooting war with the Indian navy. If we don't stop them, we'll have millions of the poorest, least educated slum dwellers from south-east Asia sucking up our resources and undermining our society. My position, the government's position, is to reject the notion of retroactive culpability. No more tankers with refugees are getting through. I need a full assessment of our warfighting capability. Game this out. Can we do enough to deter Indian aggression without actually sinking any more of their ships? What if other south-east Asian states become involved? Other developed countries are going to watch this very closely because it has consequences for them too. If we let the Indians in by the millions, they'll expect that they can follow suit. Any questions?' She looked at each of them in turn. 'Good. They're not refugees anymore. They're illegal arrivals. I'm going to call the Americans. Let's find out if all the blood and treasure we spent on this alliance the last hundred years is actually worth anything.'

July 11th, 1600 hours
Parliament House, Canberra

Lafitte sat in parliament, flanked by her senior ministers. She absently fingered the silver pendant around her neck. It was a simple piece that Glen had given to her after his first command, and she'd worn it ever since. She liked its simple elegance.

The legislative chamber was full; no MPs had anything better to be doing today. The public gallery was over-flowing, as were the press stands. Journalists too far down the pecking order to get gallery access were crowding the halls of Parliament House, waiting for their colleagues to relay information.

Abbott leaned over. 'You sure you've got this?' she murmured.

'I'm sure. We all agree. They tried to force our hand.' She spared Abbott a wry look. 'It's too late to back down now, anyway.'

She tamped down her anxiety. This was decision-making orders of magnitude more important than any call she'd made before. Her resolve had always inspired people from all walks of life, from the halls of corporate power to the dregs of welfare row. People trusted her.

Now, she had to trust herself.

The Indians had delivered her a choice. The world was breaking apart, and hundreds of millions of people were being swept from their homes like boats on a storm surge. Most were poor, and most blamed rich countries like Australia. If Australia folded, it would open the floodgates around the world. She stood, buttoned her jacket, and strode to the podium.

'Madame Speaker, the honourable leader of the opposition, and members of parliament: I stand before you today, in my capacity as the elected leader of the Australian people, to put forward the sentiment and will of the Australian people in regards to the tragic sinking of the *Tamil Nadu*, the tragic sinking of the HMAS *Broome* and the shooting down of an Australian Navy helicopter, with such terrible, unprecedented loss of life.

'I thank the leadership of the opposition, with whom we have consulted extensively regarding this crisis, and from whom we have full and unwavering support for today's response.' She inclined her head to the opposition leader as she spoke.

'The people of Australia are united as one in expressing our deepest and most sincere condolences to the families of those Indian nationals so tragically lost at sea. These events will be forever etched into our national consciousness, and for Australia to have a part in such a horrific event is a matter of genuine and profound regret. To the people of India, we can only offer our most heartfelt sympathy for your loss. Were we able to make things right, we would stop at no lengths to do so.' She paused for a moment, and the sound of camera shutters clicking echoed down from the press gallery.

'The Australian people understand the grief, the frustration and the anger expressed in India at present. We see and hear the calls for retaliation from various quarters, and we take this moment to commend Prime Minister Malhotra for his wisdom and his restraint. We hope that cool heads can prevail.

'We also use this opportunity to outline the events leading up to the sinking of the *Tamil Nadu*. Such events, deplorable as they are, must be placed in context. In the months leading up to this tragedy, three ships carrying over eighty thousand illegal immigrants came to our shores. Conveyed by retired bulk freighters, these ships, by virtue of their size, were able to circumvent Australian border protection officials, including our navy.

'These ships all originated their journeys from Kolkata. They were all conveying Indian nationals. Of deep concern to the Australian government was a clear and complete disregard for Australian border sovereignty. Also of concern, was a notable lack of response from the Indian authorities, who were notified of, and aware of, the passage of all three ships.

'The loss of untold thousands of Indian nationals is an appalling event. However, such events do not happen in a vacuum. An Australian navy helicopter en-route to land a party of engineers, medics and a pilot to guide the ship back to Indian territorial waters, was shot down by crew or passengers of the *Tamil Nadu*. The Australian patrol boat HMAS *Broome*, in attempting nothing more than to rescue the crew of the helicopter, was rammed by the *Tamil Nadu*. There were no survivors. In total, 38 Australian sailors lost their lives.' She paused, let the facts linger in the air.

'The events leading to the sinking of the *Tamil Nadu* are still under investigation. However, the Australian government contends that if the crew of the *Tamil Nadu* had not acted with such aggression, if indeed the ship had been headed off by Indian authorities before reaching Australian territory, this situation could easily have been avoided.

She paused for a moment. She'd never seen the chamber so utterly silent. 'Without apportioning blame, it is essential that both sides are heard, such that the most appropriate response can be developed.

'Today, we also outline the Australian response to the notion of retroactive culpability. This concept originated at the turn of the century during climate negotiations, where developing nations contended that, as the responsible parties for greenhouse gases in the atmosphere, developed countries had to shoulder the majority of the cost and effort in mitigating climate change.

'We reject this notion in its entirety. It is impossible to historically and quantitatively apportion blame for today's weather patterns, by nation, in any reasonable, or fair manner.' Her expression never wavered at all, and her lack of emotion conveyed the fact that the Australian government had decided.

'It was the great American leader Benjamin Franklin who said, and I quote; 'Without continual growth and progress, such words as improvement, achievement and success have no meaning.'

'Civilisational growth and progress are as intrinsic to human nature as nurturing a family. Since humans diverged from primates, we have sought better, more productive ways to feed ourselves, enhance our security and further our species, creating the intricate web of civilisation in the process.

'One stage in this eons-long evolution is the industrial era. Unfortunately, this period of development created large amounts of pollution; but progress is the natural state of humanity.' She spread her hands; surely, any reasonable person could see the logic here.

'Progress, change, and a constant pushing of the boundaries are what it is to be human. It is part of the human condition. This curiosity led us from agrarian, to industrial, to information societies. To apportion blame upon those nations that led the way for all others, a path which they follow gladly, is to accuse those societies of the crime of being curious, of extending ourselves, of being human beings.

'Another basic tenet of human nature is the desire to have and to rear a family. The people of some nations have done this to a much larger extent than others. Australia has twenty-five million people; India has one point two billion people. The environmental stress created by all those mouths to feed, all the resources consumed to live, in comparison makes Australia's historical contribution to climate change a trivial thing indeed.'

Her voice became iron. 'It would be opportunistic indeed to stand here and suggest that Indians, by vastly overpopulating their land, by stripping their forests and fouling their waterways, by pushing their environment to the limit, and by not taking full advantage of contraceptive technology have, over the course of their history, been the architects of their own demise. Imagine if there were only thirty million Indians? There would be room, and resources for them all to live comfortably.

She spread her arms wide. 'Retroactive culpability for having too many children? Such a suggestion, made in seriousness, would be rejected widely and completely. Who are we to question the right of Indians to a family?' Silence was her answer.

'So, we don't. Yet here we are, being judged. We, in Australia, ask the question; what right does any nation have to question the historical imperative of Australia to pursue that very human activity; progress and economic security?

'We fully reject the notion of retroactive culpability. We strongly assert our right to border sovereignty, and will take all necessary measures to defend this right. We will choose who comes to Australia, and the manner in which they arrive...'

Chapter 6
July 6th, 1350 hours
Geraldton, Western Australia

'Shut up and listen up!' shouted the navy guardsman. Fadi dragged hooded eyes off the burning concrete of Diamantina Peer and peered at the man through the rustling throng of Indians clumped on the dock. Two hundred and twelve in all, the sum total who'd been picked up by the *Melbourne,* which loomed next to them. They'd all been ushered off the ship and told to wait, and they did so, ringed by men with rifles.

Two hundred, more or less, plus a few hundred more in the other ships. A few hundred, out of twenty-five thousand. His family, not included. He ground his teeth and swore under his breath at the guardsmen.

He glared at the destroyer as if he could sink it with the heat of his gaze as the crowd rustled around to face the speaker.

'He's the same as the agents on our ship,' whispered the girl next to him. 'I hate him'. He scowled and turned to tell her *of course you hate him, he's the enemy*, but the words died in his throat. She glanced at him quickly, then turned away, a sad cast to her eyes. The words became stuck and he stared stupidly. He worked his jaw so he could speak. 'I wish there was some way to sink that ship,' he muttered.

'Do you now?' she said, softness in her tone.

'Yea. Tie those loudmouths to the anchor and send it to the bottom,' he said, nodding to the guardsmen surrounding them.

'It's not going to sink from you glaring at it,' the girl, said, putting her hand on his shoulder and gently turning him towards the guardsman who had spoken.

He tried to summon up a retort, but nothing came. Just a deflated 'yea' echoing up from the depths of his mind.

'What do you think this asshole wants?' he eventually muttered, pointing to the sailor.

'Welcome to Australia,' shouted the asshole. 'We will now transport you to temporary accommodation where we'll provide you with food, shelter, and any medical treatment you require. We will be conducting you by coach.'

'Apparently we're going on a holiday,' whispered the girl.

Fadi grunted. He was getting sick of being told what to do and where to go by armed men he knew nothing about, and said so, receiving a grunt in agreement.

'Each coach will have a team of guards to prevent any disturbances,' continued the asshole, pointing at the soldiers. 'We will treat you with all humanity,' he called out. 'But make no mistake; you are in this country illegally and you have no rights beyond those we choose to grant you. Do not test our hospitality.'

The trip to the internment camp took half an hour. They'd quickly passed through Geraldton and headed east into the desert. The girl from the dock, Khandi, had tilted her head back on the headrest and fallen asleep straight away, snoring softly. He'd stared out the window, trying to drink in this new, alien land. He soon concluded there was nothing to see apart from spindly plants clinging to sandy dirt and the endless blue sky, stretching away forever. The drone of tire-noise and the pleasant coolness of the air-con gave him nothing to focus on besides than the loop in his head playing of the last interactions he'd had with his family. Old memories of his father, and more jarringly, his mother and Jay. Over and over it played against the sensation of numbness that had engulfed him until they'd pulled off the highway and jostled towards what looked to Fadi like a giant shearing shed. A massive silver biscuit tin, ringed with a razor-wire topped fence, discarded in the desert. It must have been three hundred metres long on each side.

They'd been led inside, issued blankets and taken to communal showers where the men and women had been separated and washed under supervision. Then they were given wrist bands with numbers, and assigned to sleeping quarters; eight-foot-high plaster walls dividing the giant space into dormitories of fifty army surplus bunks for the refugees to sleep in. Next, they were assessed by medical staff, prodded, inspected and probed. It had felt the same as boarding the *Tamil Nadu;* there they were cattle getting onto a truck, here they were horses at an auction. A few times Fadi witnessed a refugee lash out at the medics; on both occasions, guards with batons had materialized out of nowhere and belted them until they were on the ground. Their hands were zip-tied behind their backs, and they were dragged away.

A few days passed in a stupefied haze of adjusting to camp life. Fadi was permently tired and grainy; at night all he could see was the ship sinking with his family, and during the day he was numb from exhaustion and grief. To get away from the unwanted stimulation of the social areas, he'd found a spot on the outer perimeter of the camp, and he sat there now with his back against the corrugated wall of the structure, staring into the desert. The background buzz of eighty-thousand refugees echoed softly behind, discernable words sometimes rising out of the anonymous hum. Some men were kicking a sad-looking soccer ball in the dirt in front of him. Dust chased their footsteps, carried on a cool breeze, which flicked his hair across his face.

Khandi jogged up and plopped down beside him. 'How was your medical?' she asked. 'Did they find what's wrong with you?'

'There's nothing wrong...' he grinned sheepishly. 'No, they didn't. But whatever it is they think I caught it from someone on the bus over here.'

She snorted and punched him on the shoulder. 'What's that?' he asked, nodding at the package on her lap.

'Something the doctors gave me after my examination.'

'That's not fair, they didn't give anything to me.'

She lobbed it into his lap. 'What are you gonna do with a box of tampons?' she giggled.

'Put them in your mouth to shut you up,' he laughed.

July 11th, 1830 hours
Kolkata docks

Izhar Khan pushed into the corrugated metal wall and worked a tight muscle in his back. That was it...right there. A bit more pressure, it felt...good. A nerve jangled in his neck, and he drew deeply on his cigarette. Good grief his office was hot and humid. A man shouldn't have to work in such conditions, it really was intolerable. Sweat dribbled down his chest, and his unbuttoned shirt gave him excellent access to a hairy, flabby stomach that he scratched vigorously.

The office, a rather grand name for the tiny space, which was just a small shipping container with holes torched out for windows holding a metal desk, a metal chair and a TV. Sitting on top of three other shipping containers, it's one redeeming feature was that it afforded him a clear view of the beautiful scenes on the docks below.

Three bulkers, line-astern, were roped up to the docks - he'd found them over at Chittagong and paid bottom dollar for them. Lines of people queued to get on board. He'd never go to sea in one, he wasn't that brave, or stupid, but his genius engineers had somehow gotten those old pieces of shit running again and sailed, or steamed (whatever, he was an entrepreneur, not a sailor) them to Kolkata. The ships were bought and paid for, and ready to go with tickets selling fast. When that insane Australian had blown the *Tamil Nadu* to hell, it had put a big fucking dent in demand for 'one-way pleasure cruises to Australia'.

He remembered the shock of learning about the *Tamil Nadu.* He'd been nursing a persistent hangover when his phone had lit up with friends telling him to turn on the TV. He'd watched, utterly stupefied, as all the news channels had interrupted normal viewing to report on the sinking of that ship. News anchors, talk show hosts, everyone with a pulse on TV was recoiling in shock at the disaster, most calling for swift retaliation against the bastard Australians. On and on it had gone, and no matter how many times he changed channels, the news was always the same. He'd gone into a panic; he'd never anticipated such shocking press! Frankly, the Australians were incredibly out of line; while certain governments rather unfairly labelled him a 'people-smuggler', he preferred to think of himself as an unsanctioned travel operator. Still, it was risky business; he'd had to pay a lot of hush money to a lot of politicians and naval officers to get those boats through without being stopped, and with the *Tamil Nadu,* he'd finally broken even. It'd been an anxious period; he'd had debts to pay and everyone (particularly his father who had sanctioned the entire operation) was watching him like a hawk to see if he could make the operation stick. These next three ships were supposed to be gravy, but demand had plummeted as quick as that sinking coal carrier when news got out about Australia's hard-line. Twenty-four thousand drowned, he mused, will give even the bravest soul pause for thought.

Pirates west of Sumatra had become a real problem in the last few years, which is why he'd armed his pilots and engineers with RPG's and some shoulder-mounted surface-to-air missiles. In reality, they were just refugees who had the skills he needed to get the ships across the ocean, so he'd given them and their families free passage, armed them and told them he'd arrange large cash bonuses to be paid by his Australian contacts if and when the ships reached the Australian west coast. Khan had no way to know for sure but had an exceedingly strong hunch that the Australians were telling the truth; that his men, desperate to get to Geraldton, had done the unthinkably stupid and attacked an Australia warship. Maybe they were worried about being arrested and imprisoned as smugglers; who knew? He'd never admit it, but he just didn't see the Australians sinking a ship full of refugees without good cause. Luckily, there was nothing to prove his hunch, and now the Indian government were playing up their victim status to the hilt.

When Khan learned the ship had sunk, he'd gone on a four-day drug and alcohol-fuelled bender, taking out his rage on his endocrine system and the unfortunate whores of Kolkata.

But then, as though Brahma himself had been listening to Izhar's most earnest prayers or his drunken tirades, that puppet Malhotra had pledged to protect any ships full of climate refugees with the might of the Indian Navy. Sales for the voyages he was organising picked up slowly at first, then with increasing velocity when it became clear the Indian President was firm on that retroactive culpability policy. Khan had barely even heard of it, but it was a gift from above because before long his agents quietly working the slums, the refugee camps, and aid agencies (basically anywhere desperate people needed somewhere new to live) had sold another seventy-five thousand spots, and his ships were full.

That presidential announcement...incredible! Khan's bribes had never reached that high up and whilst he most certainly wasn't afraid of giving himself credit where due, he was aware this was an astounding piece of good luck. On reflection though, it only balanced out the bad luck brought on by that devilish Australian destroyer captain, so really, things were only as they should be.

Seventy-five thousand people, every single one representing two thousand United States dollars, filing onto his boats in an orderly fashion...it was a wonderful sight. His only expense, now he'd paid off all the politicians, were the ships, meaning his margins were beyond his wildest dreams. A few grubby lawmakers had tried to wheedle more cash out of him, but he'd put them off; a damned good thing too, because Malhotra's speech meant he didn't have to hide what he was doing anymore. In a way, he wasn't even unsanctioned, perhaps even respectable! -helping, as he was, to emancipate his countrymen and women from the clutches of violent weather, starvation, and conflict. Khan didn't give a bent copper about humanitarian missions, but the fact was, India was going to hell, despite Malhotra pretending to be the head of a big happy family. Why else would he be selling so many tickets? Actions spoke louder than words.

His sources told him that way out in the Bay of Bengal, two Talwar class frigates and a Kolkata class destroyer were waiting to escort his refugee carriers to Australia's west coast. Those Australians better know what was good for them. No way would they start a shooting war with the Indian Navy. The Aussies had some nice boats and decent submarines, but nothing like a *Kolkata* class destroyer. They'd get blown to pieces if they engaged in a pissing contest with him this time. Khan was confident that his ships would get through, and that was good for business. He was so confident that he'd already reached out to his contacts in Chittagong to source more ships.

Khan put the cigarette to his lips and sucked back deep, a sweaty smile splayed across his face. Life was good. If fortune truly favoured the brave, he reflected, then he had courage in spades, because he was making an absolute fortune on those people down there.

July 12th, 2300
Canberra Hyatt Hotel

Jacquie waved the waiter over and ordered a soda water on ice. She was sitting in a padded chair in the lobby of the Canberra Hyatt Hotel. Thick rugs covered mahogany parquetry, various sumptuous sofas and armchairs arranged in little squares across the space. Chandeliers provided a soft orange glow, supplemented by stand lamps distributed around the floor. It was, reflected Jacqui, reassuringly bland luxury, just like every other five-star business hotel lobby she'd ever been in. More important than the décor was the time; it was late and mostly empty.

Slumped on the sofa opposite Jacqui was Keiran Knight, a short, slender man in a crumpled suit. Keiran headed up the Fairfax Media Canberra bureau. He had a notepad nestled on his lap, and a cheap pen cocked and ready for use in his fist.

They waited in silence as the waiter brought Jacqui's soda. After it arrived, Jacqui ignored it, peering instead at the dull light reflecting off the chandelier. She hated what she was about to do, but she couldn't see any other way.

Keiran waited patiently - he knew she had something to say, or she wouldn't have called him out here.

'Alright Keiran,' she said eventually, resisting the urge to slump in her seat like the slovenly journalist. 'This is an off the record conversation.' The rumpled man *mm-hmm'd* his assent. Most of his conversations with Jacqui were off the record.

Just get it over with, she scolded herself, sighed, then prepared to rip off the sticking plaster.

'As you know, we have a growing refugee crisis, and we're working on solutions to stop those tankers getting through. The Australian government is working closely with the Navy to resolve this. That said, notwithstanding my speech in Parliament yesterday, our strategy is *not* to sink these ships on the way in. What happened last week was a combination of unfortunate circumstances and a rogue Navy commander operating well outside his rules of engagement.' She mentally shrugged. She'd said what she needed to; the hardest part was over.

'So the government or the Navy never sanctioned the sinking of a refugee ship?' murmured the little man in a disconcertingly deep voice.

'No, of course we didn't,' she snapped. '*Obviously* we're trying to figure out a humane solution to this mess, massacring civilians isn't something we chat idly about during cabinet meetings.'

'So…what you're telling me is that the government wants to distance itself from Commander Glen Robertson's actions.' He glanced up from his notepad and into her eyes.

'Something like that. It makes sense; he does…have a history of violence against refugees.' There. She'd said it. *What an utterly appalling thing you're doing, Jacqui,* she mused.

'Mmm,' intoned the journalist. 'He also has a history with you.' Jacqui arched an eyebrow and waited for what was next. 'I assume that's not particularly relevant to this story?'

'Not relevant in the slightest,' she said, the words dripping like acid off her tongue.

Keiran suddenly sat up and looked directly at Jacqui. 'Ok, Jacqui. Sounds to me like you want us to do a hatchet job on Commander Robertson for you, hang him out to dry like jerky on a rack.'

Jacqui usually found dealing with Keiran mildly unpleasant, like cleaning a dirty toilet bowl. Tonight's conversation was an altogether revolting experience, like unplugging a blocked toilet by hand. *But it's you, not him that's doing the revolting things,* she told herself and carried on. 'We need to distance ourselves from what he did, or our diplomatic options disappear.'

'I think I understand what you need,' he said nodding to himself. 'Anything else I need to know?' said the little man abruptly, meeting her eyes again.

'Nothing you can't research on your own.'

'Then we're done!' He stood up and pocketed his notepad. 'Always a pleasure to do my bit for the country, Jacqui,' he said, inclining his head at her and strolling away.

'Glad you can help,' she muttered bitterly under her breath.

Chapter 7
July 13th, 1730
Balgowlah, Sydney

Glen put the sander down, took a deep breath and blew the sawdust off the lump of timber straddling the sawhorses in front of him. He brushed the remaining fluff off with his hand, then half-heartedly blew on his chest to dislodge the sawdust stuck in his chest hair and sweat. None shifted. He hefted the wood over his bare shoulder with a grunt and dumped it onto the pile of identical lengths of timber that were going to form the back deck in the home he and Alice shared. He could see Alice through the kitchen window, earbuds in, chatting to someone on the phone while she chopped up some vegetables for dinner. He paused for a moment to enjoy the view; he loved how utterly unselfconscious she was. It was her trademark. No matter what she did, or who was watching, she was just herself, take it or leave it. She looked up and took in the pile of freshly sanded lumber, which earned him a wink. Facing out as she was, she was looked out onto a sprawling plot of newly mown lawn that meandered down to the harbour. White flagstones curved from the kitchen to the water; a small boat was tethered to a timber jetty and water lapped gently on the pebbled shore. He'd completed the little dock over the last few weeks, and the deck was his next project.

Alice had finished her call and wandered outside. She stood on a short staircase, three steps to ground, and leaned against the vertical pillars he'd already installed and crossed her arms. 'Looking good babe. Need a hand?'

He jammed his hand into the icebox next to the sawhorse and pulled out a tin of beer. Cracked it open and took a long swig. 'All good babe, I'm done for now.' He stared at the naked wood, wondering what he should do next.

'Glen, is everything ok?'

He blinked and shook his head. 'Yea babe. I'm good. It's strange how productive a man can be when he's trying to forget a whole bunch of things,' he mused, surveying the jetty and the budding deck.

Smiling sympathetically, she hopped off the small staircase and slipped under his arm, putting an arm around his waist. 'You always forget things, Glen. I don't think that's the problem.'

He laughed ruefully, a faint-hearted sound that died a quick death in his throat.

With her free hand, Alice picked the larger pieces of wood out of his thick chest hair. With the hand around his waist, she guided him toward the stairs and into the house. 'That's enough forgetting for today, sweetheart. Sit yourself on the couch and I'll bring you dinner.' She eyed him reproachfully. 'But have a shower first!'

'Yes ma'am,' he saluted, grinning, and to Alice, it was like the sun bursting from behind dark clouds. She gave him a playful slap on the backside as he sauntered away.

A few minutes later, they were sitting together watching the evening news. He'd showered and was shovelling the Caesar salad she'd put together into his mouth.

The reporter onscreen was warbling on about some mundane local council issue. Alice picked up the remote to change the channel when it cut back to the anchor, who announced the latest development in the Indian refugee crisis. Glen put his hand on Alice's. 'Leave it here for a second babe.' Alice looked at him with concern, then let go of the remote.

'Senior sources from within the Australian Government claim that Commodore Glen Robertson was acting outside mission parameters when he torpedoed the *Tamil Nadu*. When asked by journalists to comment, Prime Minister Jacqui Lafitte was unequivocal in her condemnation of Commodore Robertson's actions...' the scene cut to Jacqui, flanked by journalists in the halls of Parliament House somewhere.

Jacqui kept walking, the throng of reporters moving awkwardly in time with her. 'It's not Australian government policy to target civilian vessels. It never has been and it never will be,' she said as if the questioner was a moron.

A journo shoved a microphone under Jacqui's nose. 'Prime Minister, surely Commodore Robertson was acting with a degree of freedom such that he felt his actions were justified, a freedom which must have been authorised higher up the chain of command?'

Jacqui stopped suddenly and squared up to the cameras. 'Let me be very clear. The Australian government condemns the actions of Commodore Robertson, and never sanctioned such action.' She paused and looked directly into the camera. It was like she was in Glen's living room, standing on their carpet, about to cast judgment on him in his own home. In front of Alice. His eyes became hooded, and his expression flat.

'*I* condemn the actions of Glen-' she hesitated minutely then continued, '...Commodore Robertson. Let me assure you all that we're working closely with the Indians to resolve this, and the broader refugee question, as soon as possible. Thank you, that will be all,' she finished and swept through the throng and down the green-carpeted hall.

Alice turned the TV off. 'Glen...' she started tentatively.

He stood, waved her off. Never in his life had he felt so betrayed. And by Jacqui of all people!'

He started talking but it was hard to articulate his feelings, the words came in clumps. 'I know she's bloody-minded. But this. I mean, I get *why* she's done it...I just can't fathom *how* she could be so ruthless.' He clenched his jaw. He wanted to put a sledgehammer through the TV. He wanted to find her and tell her what an absolute piece of shit she'd turned into...

Alice stared at him in a mix of sympathy and anger, eyes wide, concern etched on her face like a beacon. 'I mean, you were in the same briefing as me. Am I a fucking moron or did she not say that *no more boats were to get through* in front of every senior defence officer in Australia!' His fists opened and closed, like jaws groping for a neck to clamp down on.

'That fucking *bitch,*' he finally managed. Alice stood up and went to him.

'Glen, it's not your fault,' she said, taking his head in her hands and forcing him to look in her eyes. 'It's just politics, she's just doing what she has to do. No different from what you did...' He shook his head and broke her gaze. He didn't want her to see him this way; his rage at Jacqui fanned even hotter. He tried to focus on his girlfriend.

'You're right, of course, you're right...it's just...' He trailed off, struggling to say what he meant. It was just that the only thing damming his guilt for sinking the *Tamil Nadu* was he'd been able to convince himself he'd done it to protect his country from an avalanche of illegal arrivals, sanctioned from the highest levels of government and command. Yet now Jacqui had hung him out to dry and the dam had burst, releasing a tidal wave of emotions to sweep through him. 'Its fine babe, I'm ok. I just need...some time.' He turned away and his back was an impenetrable wall blocking Alice's attempts to reach him. He wandered outside, picking up the box of beer as he went. Went down to the jetty and drank, pacing up and down, as the light faded.

August 21st, 1900 hours
Indian Navy Ship *Mumbai*

Captain Chakradev Khurana sipped tea and broke bread in the mess of the INS *Mumbai*, a *Kolkata* class destroyer and the lead ship of a seven-ship flotilla, that slowly, ever so bloody slowly, approached the West Australian coastline. The INS *Tabar* and INS *Trikand*, both *Talwar* class frigates, shadowed the Mumbai, one a speck on the horizon astern and starboard, the other thirty kilometres ahead. An attack sub, the *Kalvari*, slunk under the waves, tracking the fleet.

Khurana didn't know where *Kalvari* was right now, but it knew where he was and would be on station somewhere close by. The *Kalvari* was a *Scorpene*-class sub, which meant that it was both silent and deadly; however, it wasn't really designed for missions that ranged so far from home. Fortunately, the rate of progress was so incredibly torpid that fuel economy was much higher than normal.

Khurana couldn't see the last three ships in the convoy because they were over the horizon to his port side. He could, however, see the palls of thick black smoke belching from their stacks. The smoke was moving faster than the ships, getting blown ahead of them by a south-easterly breeze. Those old boats were real slugs, the captain mused to himself. He didn't mind so much the slow pace though; he felt blessed with good weather and calm waters since they had left Kolkata. All things considered, they were making easy money.

Praveen, the *Kolkata's* weapons officer, was spooning curry and rice into his mouth across the table from him. 'The intel people keep telling us the Aussies are bluffing and won't put up a fight,' he said between mouthfuls. 'What do you think?'

He shook his head, dismissing the assertion. 'I don't believe that. They've invaded every country the US has in the last hundred and thirty years. And that's a lot. I don't believe they'll suddenly become reticent now they perceive their territory is under threat. The Aussies may be on their own this time, but I do wonder at the wisdom of sailing right into Australian territory with a relatively small force.'

'They *have* let us get far closer than the *Tamil Nadu* ever got.'

'I don't like it,' said Khurana. 'We'll soon be in range of their shore-based fighter planes. That will tip things heavily in their favour.'

Like people right around the world, most especially back home, he'd been disgusted by the sinking of the *Tamil Nadu*. Those lumbering giants over the horizon were *his* charges to protect.

He turned to his weapons officer. 'Praveen, tell the team repairing the vertical launch hydraulics we'll be running combat testing on the system in thirty minutes.'

Praveen's fork paused halfway to his mouth, reversed course and settled back on the plate. He stood up ran out the door, shouting orders as he went.

Chakradev also finished his meal and made his way back to the bridge. Regardless of what his intel people said, he anticipated a fight, and since the mission had been announced, his crew had been running combat drills to prepare for one.

Canberra
Old Parliament House
August 21st, 1900 hours

Jacqui Lafitte picked her way through the gardens at Old Parliament House. The building was a flat, broad neoclassical slab, its whitewashed façade shining like a solar reflector in the Australian sun. It was at the base of Capitol Hill and had been the seat of Australia democracy until 1988 when Parliament had relocated to the new building which had been cut into the top of the same hill. The old building had been relegated to museum duties, and the surrounding gardens were a favourite place for her to escape her colleagues and be in her head for a while.

'John,' she said to the head of her security detail. 'I just need a little time to think if you don't mind.' He nodded, and his team had formed a perimeter around the gabled garden plots she now wandered through. Her chief of staff had been messaging her incessantly about mundane items so she'd told him she was busy and put him on silent. She wanted to at least pretend to be alone. She wended through the shrubs and blossoms, drinking in the scents and absorbing the colours. Sunlight sparkled off the plants, and while the air was crisp, the sun prickled her neck with warmth. She loved these gardens for their mild chaos. Roses grew in tangled thickets, leaning over thick hedges to encroach onto the grey paving which was half-submerged under the carpet of grass. Eucalypts leaned haphazardly, jutting up through the roses, bark dangling like a homeless man's beard from their trunks. They reminded Jacqui of her father on family occasions; tie undone, clothes rumpled, wine spilling from his glass, drunkenly charming, compelling despite, or perhaps because of, the chaos. Fundamentally unreliable.

The rose bushes were like her mother, beautiful, wild, and raw, trying and failing to corral her father into respectability.

The plants had been allowed, encouraged even, to flourish and grow unkempt by the groundkeepers, (or neglected, depending on your view of the aesthetics), with fewer constraints than the plants in the galleries and other museums around the city. She breathed in the gardens thoroughly; on one hand, they represented a quiet misrule that she felt contrasted the straight-jacket of political rules constraining her, while, on the other hand, they were an echo of the constant and systematic chaos of parliament.

Bees buzzed loudly in the perfumed air. For Lafitte, it was a serene oasis, a bubble within the turbulent maelstrom that was her life. The tranquillity slowed down the spinning gears in her mind until they matched speeds, then meshed, and usually, without actually thinking about anything specific, she left the gardens with clarity and renewed direction on any issue that had been bothering her.

Today was different. She usually wore quiet, resolute confidence like a suit, as naturally and easily as breathing, but suddenly the right the way forward had never seemed so elusive. It should have been simple; her job was to keep her country safe, yet little seeds of doubt had been sewn in the garden of her mind, causing her to question the path she was taking. Easily quashed, like weeds, but like weeds, they kept coming back. The only way to keep her country safe was to shut these people smugglers down, but in the meantime, the refugees kept coming. How could she turn them around, send them home, and keep her humanity?

She stepped carefully off the stone paving and onto the lawn, which like the shrubs, needed cutting. The grass itself was a memory, and as always, it came unbidden. Annoyed, she pushed it away. She toyed with the pendant around her neck, unaware of what she was doing, and recollection swept through her.

In the final year of her post-graduate studies in international law, Indonesia held presidential elections and voted in a hardline Islamic coalition government for the first time, led by the United Development Party. Then, three days before Christmas, Typhoon Newman smashed into the southeastern islands of the Indonesian archipelago. A category six storm that ruined crops on the verge of being harvested, causing tens of millions of people to run out of food. From Bali in the west to East Nusa Tengarra in the east, a mix of Hindu, moderate Muslim and Christian peoples inhabited the islands. They were at the centre of the political spectrum and the natural political enemies of the new President, whose government dragged its feet in responding to the crisis.

The international response was also blunted: Not only were local resources tied up with other disasters (the Philippines had their hands full with Chinese encroachment on their territorial waters and Malaysia was dealing with fallout from the same storm), but the President made it clear this was an Indonesian problem, to be dealt with by Indonesians. They didn't want foreign militaries on their soil, and he politely but firmly declined offers of assistance.

The situation on the ground quickly deteriorated. Food, water, and shelter were eventually distributed, but Muslims were prioritized, and relief was scarce. Christians to the east and Hindus to the west heard there was help in the central Muslim islands and flooded in. Before long, violence flared up along religious lines and the government, so slow to respond to the crisis, was quick to send in the troops. The situation became desperate. Peaceful neighbours had become deadly enemies. Words like 'massacre' and 'brutality' began leaking out to the wider world and the Australian government formulated a response.

Australia's top universities recognized that this was a learning opportunity to take advantage of, so they assembled a group of the most promising post-graduate students to game out a political response to the crisis. Jacqui Lafitte had joined, somewhat reluctantly. As a junior diplomatic advisor to the Prime Minister on South East Asia, she felt she could have been contributing far more usefully in her day job. Unfortunately, the response group was the final requirement to complete her thesis. The ambassador to Indonesia had told her with a tired twinkle in his eye, 'Go. Enjoy yourself, and don't worry Jacqui; there'll be plenty more crises for you to deal with.'

Also present in the response group was a deep-chested young naval officer called Glen Robertson. He'd stood up, tracking his gaze around each of them like a surveillance radar as he announced to the group he was completing a masters of strategic studies. He'd made eye-contact with Jacqui, and it seemed to her a twinkle of amusement had momentarily crept into his hard gaze, then he'd swept onto the next person, and she'd known instantly that there was something intriguing about him. Not like that - at just under six foot tall he was too short for Jacqui's taste...but still. Maybe it was the old eyes in his young face?

At the end of the first week Glen said his goodbyes and quickly left the group like he did every other day. Greg, the human rights advocate from Melbourne who had been fawning over her all week, suggested the rest of them all meet at a local bar to unwind; who was interested? The idea didn't particularly appeal to Jacqui, and she tried to exit stage left without being noticed.

'We'll see you there, Jacqui?' called Greg plaintively.

Jacqui turned - they were all looking at her, and for some inexplicable reason, she didn't have a plausible excuse ready to go.

'Ah...yea, sounds good,' she heard herself saying, mentally berating herself for being caught by surprise. *Oh well, a few drinks, then home, won't hurt.*

'Great!' said Greg with relieved excitement. 'We'll be at the Caucus; it's a cool little bar not far from here. From eight.'

Jacqui arrived early; the sooner she started, the sooner she could leave. The Caucus was a dark, moody place with isolated booths and a curved bar topped with a massive slab of dark mahogany. Behind the bar, shelves lined with a vast selection of whiskey, rum, and gin were backlit dimly, an alcohol coloured pall filling the space. The place was virtually empty, and she went to the bar to order a drink. A solitary broad-shouldered man was leaning on the bar, left leg crossed behind his right. His right elbow supported his weight, and his left arm dangled by his side, two fingers loosely holding a tumbler of some dark liquid. It was Glen. He smiled as she approached as though he'd been waiting for her.

A spike of excitement arose in her chest; she squashed it. He'd practically ignored her all week, unlike the other men in the group who'd eagerly courted her opinion. He'd only interacted with her when necessary and always in an entirely professional way. His perspectives were impressive, and his contributions showed insight, but predictably, he'd consistently overstated the importance of the military's role in any response.

He pointed to the spot next to him, and she sat down on a high stool beside him. 'I'm surprised to see you here. Didn't realise you'd got the memo,' she said.

'I don't need a memo to have a drink,' he said, bemused. 'In fact, I'm surprised to see *you* here.' On the high stool, she was nearly eye-level with him. His eyes, which had appeared so cold during the seminar, now shone with amusement, like he was listening to a joke nobody else could hear.

'Why? Don't you think I'd enjoy a drink?'

He arched an eyebrow, a twinkle in his eye. 'Not so much. You seem kinda buttoned up.' The twinkle turned into a grin. He nearly laughed when she gave a small *harrumph* and looked away. She picked up a drinks menu and pretended to study it.

'What? I've been here every day this week, and this is the first time you've showed up.'

'Is drinking a hobby of yours?' she asked airily, flipping through the menu.

'Not at all. It's part of my training, which I take very seriously. Same as you,' Glen said, eyeing Jacqui's toned thighs appreciatively. 'If you want to get good at something, you have to do it every day. Mastery through practice,' he finished with a satisfied look.

'Is that what you've been doing every day after the seminar?' she asked incredulously, pointing a delicate finger at his drink.

'Most days, yea. After being surrounded by such clever people all day it's nice to take the edge off.'

She fixed him with a condescending smile. 'Glen, are you self-medicating with alcohol?' she asked in a talking-to-a-child voice. 'Are you an alcoholic?'

He snorted a laugh at her audacity. 'Depends who you ask, Jacqui,' he smiled. 'I don't consider myself to be one, but someone with a more judgmental, puritanical mindset,' he inclined his head in her direction very slightly, 'might consider that I am.'

She ignored his jibe and his smug grin. 'That's pathetic.' She snorted. 'Alcoholics tend to be useless, self-absorbed, emotional wrecks of men.

He eyed her with renewed interest, then pointed to the drinks menu page on which she'd settled. 'I didn't pick you as a whiskey drinker,' he said, and she looked down, confused. Was he smirking at her? Idiot. She shook her head and snapped the menu shut. 'Arak, please,' she said crisply to the bar girl. That wiped the smug look off his face.

'Arak,' he mused, eyeing her with renewed interest.

While her drink was poured they sat in silence. The pungent odour of aniseed wafted across the bar.

'Ice?' asked the bartender. 'Yes, please. And water,' she said a little too quickly. 'So...' she asked curiously, 'how do you get away with your habit when you're supposed to be setting an example?' He laughed gently, nodding. 'Jacqui, the navy trains people to be proactive, to respond as the situation demands.' He thumbed his chest. 'Which is exactly what I'm doing. I was sober; I wanted to be drunk; therefore I'm drinking. Trust me. My CO would heartily approve.'

'I didn't realise being drunk is an operational requirement in the navy.'

'It isn't. Not everything I do is for the benefit of my career. Not all of us have your laser focus.'

'I don't understand you, Glen. This week, in that seminar, we were all in there trying to find humane solutions to real problems, and you kept pushing the military line.' She didn't know where she was going with this but ploughed on. 'You kept pushing an option you're smart enough to see beyond. It felt like you were compensating for something, acting dumber and tougher than you are.'

He peered at her. 'What are you driving at, Jacqui?'

'Well,' she said breezily, 'It seems to me that men like you, you join up to pander to your fragile male egos.'

He burst out laughing, 'You're bang-on the money. I'm just compensating for my insecurities with big guns and expensive equipment. Once I get sick of that, I'll cultivate a smug sense of intellectual superiority and jump to negative conclusions about everybody who disagrees with me.' The merriment welled up in his eyes. 'And then, you and I will have one more thing in common,' he finished, He looked at her with sparkling green

90

eyes and she struggled to pull her gaze away for just a moment too long. How he could he insult her like that yet make her want to burst out laughing at the same time? Her hand itched to slap him, then the bartender finally interrupted their staring contest with an order request, 'Would you like another drink, lady?' Grateful for the excuse to look away, she swung her head to the serving girl.

'Yes. Same again...thanks,' she said briskly.

The bartender looked to Robertson, who wiggled his nearly empty drink in such a way that the bartender clearly understood meant, 'One more.'

'Look, Jacqui. I'm really not trying to impress anyone. I find it hard enough to impress myself. I was just trying to get drunk. Alone.'

'Trust me, I'm sorry I interrupted.'

'You could always leave.'

She began to move away, then hesitated. 'I'm meeting the rest of the class here, so...'

They sat in relative silence, engaging in dead-ended conversation about nothing important when finally he turned to her and said, 'I've pretended not to, but I've been watching you in action over the last few days, Jacqui. Somehow, against all probability, you're even more intelligent and more brilliant, than you are beautiful. It's...amazing... to watch you in full flight.' He shook his head in appreciation. 'The other guys on this committee...well, I think you're going to break a few hearts over the next few weeks.

Slightly mollified, entirely suspicious, she shrugged. 'None of the men on this committee are my type.'

'Well, well, look at you two sneaking in here early!' said a voice behind them. It was Greg, the tall, slender Melbourne academic. His foppish fringe obscured horn-rimmed glasses. He took in the tension between Jacqui and Glen and flicked his hair off his face.

'You know Glen, you look incredibly familiar,' he said, squeezing a stool between Jacqui and Glen and planting himself on it. 'I'm quite sure we've met before this week.'

Jacqui glanced at Glen, who seemed to roll his eyes inwardly.

'Sorry, Greg. You don't look familiar at all. Your memory must be much better than mine.'

'It's certainly possible. I do have an excellent memory.' He repositioned his glasses. 'Are you sure you haven't been in Perth recently?'

'I spend most of my time on the east coast these days, so I highly doubt that's it. But, hey, you could be right.'

'I usually am,' said Greg. 'But, there's a large naval base out in Perth, isn't there? Have you ever been posted out there?'

'There you are. We must've met on a night out a few years ago, and it slipped my mind. Sorry.' He frowned in consternation as Greg casually crossed his legs. He couldn't bring himself to like a man who could - and did - cross his legs while sitting down.

The academic spared a surreptitious glance at Jacqui who was chatting to the others, pretending not to eavesdrop. 'No, that's not it. I tend not to socialise with people in the military anyway,' he said with an apologetic smile. 'A vodka orange,' he said to the bargirl who slid his drink over to him. 'To new friends, and a peaceful resolution to the Typhoon Newman crisis!' He toasted the group.

He turned back to Glen. 'It's bugging me; I really must figure out where I know you from. Wait! I've got it!'

'Tell us, Greg. We're dying to know.'

'They *should* know. The fact is, I recognise you from the Royal Commission into the massacre of seventeen refuges en-route to Australia from Indonesia five years ago.'

Robertson fixed Greg with a clear-eyed stare. 'So what, Greg?'

Greg glanced around the group. 'I wanted to see if you had the courage to admit to the group what you did. Instead, you pretended not to remember who I am. I wonder what else you haven't cared to remember about that awful episode?'

'I'm not proud of what happened that day. I think about those people every day of my life. But it's done, Greg. What we did is over. And so is your part in that awful episode,' he echoed the words of the academic. 'The best thing we can do is learn from it, so it never happens again.'

'What are you two idiots talking about?' demanded Jacqui.

Greg looked slightly wounded at her insult. 'This man,' Greg pointed at the naval officer, 'was on the boarding party that murdered those innocent people from the *Bau Anjing*. It was all over the news and caused a massive diplomatic incident.'

'How do you know all this, Greg?' asked Jacqui.

'Because *I* was on the refugee advocacy board representing refugee rights, assisting the prosecution of the sailors responsible,' he pronounced.

'But Greg,' said Robertson quizzically, 'the three of us who survived that incident were acquitted.' He half-heartedly suppressed a wry smile. 'If you'd been any good, I'd be in gaol, and yet here we are enjoying a pleasant conversation about old times.' He finished with a shrug.

'Our conversation was hardly pleasant' started Jacqui wryly.

He turned to her, freezing a sputtering Greg out of the conversation, and fixed her with an intense gaze. 'However you care to describe it,' he said softly, 'I was enjoying myself until this fool interrupted us.' The smugness, the merriment had disappeared, replaced by a feverish intensity that made it impossible to look away.

'Don't call Greg a fool,' she finally muttered at him softly. 'It's not nice.'

'No, it's not.' Glen suddenly broke his gaze and cast his eyes around the group, suddenly back in surveillance radar mode. 'I better leave you all to it.' Nodding to Jacqui, he threw the rest of his drink down and placed the glass carefully on the bar. He turned and strode away.

Greg shook his head. 'Men like him are the cause of all the misery in our world,' he said ruefully.

Jacqui tapped her ringed fingers on her glass, *pinging* softly. 'Shut up, Greg,' she said absently.

Back in the present, Jacqui left the gardens of Old Parliament House and made her way to a conference room. It was Glen who had taught her to do what needed to be done, regardless of the personal toll. He'd carried the guilt of the *Bau Anjing* refugees with him all those years-it was why he drank. But he'd never let it influence his thinking or decision making in a way that compromised his mission. She'd always aspired to leadership, and saw that mode of thinking as critical; the greater good was the only consideration, regardless of personal cost. This crisis was testing that approach to her limits.

Chapter 8
Parliament House, Canberra
August 21st, 1930 hours

In the new parliament building, Nick Whittey, Cam Holloway and Jason Futcher from the Navy gathered around a conference table near Jacqui's office.

Jacqui studied her team. She was adept with most matters of state and was usually able to formulate positions on her own, then take guidance from her experts to tweak the details. With this crisis, the process was reversed. Her advisors were shaping her policy, and she had to know she could trust them. She had a ridiculous urge to get in touch with Glen, see what he thought she should do. *Idiotic. This was all his damned fault.* Guilt flared in her stomach at the sudden recollection she'd thrown him under the bus to the media.

'We have to make a decision,' she said, trying to focus. 'We can interdict the ships, land a crew on each and turn them around, like last time. Or just let them land and deal with them ashore, which is a lower risk option.'

'Landing crews is risky, and the INS sending escorts will make it harder to do without something going wrong. We'd have to neutralise them if interdiction is the preferred method,' said Whittey.

'Taking out those INS vessels is tantamount to declaring war on India,' said Abbott.

'Louise is right,' cautioned Holloway. 'We have to be careful here.'

'Are there any alternatives to engaging the Indian ships?' asked Lafitte sharply.

'No.' said Futcher. 'Apart from letting them through unmolested, there's only the diplomatic option.'

'One way to avoid a fight with the INS is to let them land and bring everyone ashore. We can treat them, bring them back to health, and refloat the ships they came on; add a few creature comforts, like toilets, load them with supplies and send them on their way,' said Nick Whittey, Minister of Defense.

'The people getting off those ships are very sick, Nick. They need a lot of care, and many of them wouldn't survive a return journey without being here for weeks first.'

'That's their problem,' shrugged Whittey. 'In some ways, if some don't make it back across, it'll stop others from trying in the first place.'

'We shouldn't use these people as pawns,' said Abbott reproachfully.

'They're not pawns!' scoffed Whittey. 'They dealt themselves into this situation when they tried to come here illegally! This amounts to emotional blackmail. Are you saying we should capitulate?'

'You're not listening,' said Abbott more forcefully. '*If* we let them in at all, we have a duty of care to bring them back to health before we put them back on those ships. If not, they'll die on the way home, and we might as well sink them on the way in.' She spread her hands. 'It'd be more merciful.'

'If those ships land, we need to build another massive camp, so they've got somewhere to live; and strip more doctors and nurses out of the hospital system to care for them.' Whittey looked at Futcher, who nodded.

'I don't like it,' Laffitte said. 'It sends the wrong message.'

'And let's be realistic. Once they're here, it'll be bloody impossible to get rid of them. We need to stop them at sea.' Whittey added.

Lafitte considered her options in silence for a moment. It felt like they were using a military solution to solve a humanitarian problem...But...

'Whittey is right. We cannot let those ships through. We're not barbarians, and we won't be packing thousands of people into ancient ships and forcing them to sea. So, we have to stop them getting here in the first place.' She turned to Futcher. 'Can we stop them without sinking them?'

Futcher nodded. 'Yes, it won't be a problem. We already have a task force assembling to meet them. Two subs, two frigates, and a destroyer are converging on a point two hundred nautical miles northwest of Geraldton.

'That's rather close, isn't it?' asked Abbott.

'It's the limit of our exclusive economic zone. We'll tell the Indian warships not to proceed further and we'll escort the freighters in. Once they reach our territorial waters, twelve miles out, we'll board them, turn them around and sail them back where they came from. There'll be a hundred and eighty miles between us and the Indian ships; they won't be able to do anything.'

'And if the INS escort the bulkers past our EEZ?' asked Lafitte.

'Then we'll sink them,' replied Futcher, 'and board the bulkers anyway.'

'Is that going to be as easy as you make it sound?' asked Abbott.

'Nothing is easy. But we won't lose a confrontation with the Indian Navy that close to our shoreline. They have comparable naval capabilities to us, but we've have deployed a squadron of F-35's to RAAF Pearce, and we'll have full sensory control of the battlespace. We think they believe we'll blink; there's no real military logic to it that we can discern. Anyway, our top cover will be well within strike range of the flotilla at the EEZ. In essence, we're pursuing the same boarding tactics as last time, but with air cover for the helicopter boarding crews provided by the *Hobart*. Besides, we'll be monitoring the bulkers for any sign of shoulder-launched missiles, or any SAM's, with guns trained. If the Indian ships become aggressive, we'll have F-35's out of Pearce providing a stand-off strike capability, and the two Barracuda attack subs as contingency.'

'This doesn't add up,' said Abbott. 'The Indians must know that they'll get shot to pieces in a confrontation if they're sailing into our backyard.'

'It's a game of brinkmanship,' said Lafitte. 'Like Futcher said, they need us to blink first. They have world opinion in their favour, they have a larger navy, and they have nuclear weapons. If we back down, they win. If we sink their ships and turn the refugees around, well, they win, because the world will condemn us, and they can come back harder, stronger.'

'But we might deter them from trying again,' said Whittey.

'That's the problem with making unilateral statements when stating critical policy,' said Abbott. 'No wriggle-room.'

'Sure,' agreed Lafitte. 'But sometimes ambiguity isn't an option. We agreed that our borders are our borders. You agreed on that too, Louise. States control their borders and that means they decide who comes in, and when. Until that changes, my position is that it's not acceptable to disregard international norms because you have internal issues.'

'It's possible,' said Cam Holloway, 'that those rules aren't as hard and fast as they used to be. There are so many people flooding across borders everywhere; the Middle East, Asia, from Africa into Europe because of warming and civil war; attitudes are shifting. If the perception is that new realities trump established tradition, we might be well and truly on our own.'

Lafitte nodded. 'I don't say this lightly, but it's a risk we have to take. We have our allies, the US and Japan who will weigh in.' Abbott didn't look convinced. 'Does anybody here seriously believe the US and Japan will reinterpret their immigration rules because of some people smugglers?' Lafitte said addressing Abbott specifically. 'I don't think so. This is our country, and we need to defend it.'

Futcher spoke. 'I'll issue instructions to the task force deployed to interdict the Indians. Those ships won't get through.'

Chapter 9
September 5th, 1700 hours
Indian Navy Ship *Mumbai*

Chakradev Khurana's convoy had made it to within two hundred and fifty miles of the Australian coast when his comms officer signalled to him. 'Captain, the Australians are reaching out to us. They wish to communicate directly via secure line.'

Khurana thought the implications through; it wasn't entirely unexpected they were making an overture - both sides hoped there was still a chance there might be resolution somehow, without anyone seen to be backing down; or, maybe it was an ultimatum. There was only one way to find out.

'Patch them through.'

On the destroyers' screen, an Australian sailor appeared. The woman was tall and thin, almost gaunt, and the distortions of the signal made her cheeks look cadaverous. She held her captain's hat crooked under her left armpit.

'Good afternoon,' said the Australian. 'I am Madeleine Malm, commander of the HMAS *Hobart*. Am I speaking with Captain Chakradev Khurana?'

'You are,' Khurana said. 'How may we help you?'

'Captain Khurana, my instructions are to let your warships no closer than the outermost point of our EEZ, two hundred miles from the Australian coast. We will escort the freighters in and deal with them in our territorial waters. I am also to convey to you that we intend no harm to the passengers and that we will treat them with all humanity.'

Khurana paused. His job was to escort those ships to where they needed to go. That said, he could monitor the situation just fine from two-hundred miles out.

And tactically, he was just as effective at distance, perhaps more so. He had hypersonic cruise missiles, and the Australians did not. If this woman was telling the truth, then Khurana could go home having fulfilled his mission, with no shots fired. That was a win. If she was lying, he had sixteen two tonne anti-ship missiles that would be slamming into Australian hulls at Mach 7 three minutes after he gave the order to fire.

'Commander Malm,' he said, 'we will keep station at the limits of the EEZ. Be aware that we will be monitoring the situation. My role is to ensure those refugees make it to Australia safely. If I think you are acting to prevent this, or I doubt their safety, we will act to secure it.'

Malm gazed at Khurana. 'We understand your mission, Captain, as I'm sure you understand ours. Rest assured we mean your countrymen no harm.'

Khurana frowned even as he nodded. He felt he was missing something. 'Is that all, Commander Malm?' he asked.

'That is all, but Captain Khurana,' she said, warmth softening her features slightly. 'I hope that we'll meet again soon, in happier circumstances.'

Khurana raised his eyebrows. 'Thank you, Captain. As do we all.'

That was a strange conversation, he thought as the image disappeared. Despite Malm's entreaty at the end, he was sure there was a hidden message in her words. If the Australian navy wasn't here to engage Khurana's force, why was it there?

'Captain,' said Ramakrishnan, the XO, when the line cut. 'There's no reason for the Australians to be here unless they're going to interdict those ships. They don't need escorting in.'

He grunted. 'That Australian bitch is playing word games and I don't like it.' He turned to his sensors team. 'I want to know everything that happens on those Australian ships, down to the tiniest detail. Get a drone in the air for over the horizon monitoring. If a seagull shits on the *Hobarts* anchor chain, we log it, understood?' Then he turned to Praveen on weapons. 'Get me a firing solution for all three surface targets, incorporating the sixteen Brahmos on *Tabar* and *Trikand*. If they do anything, anything at all, besides escort those freighters to the beach, we take them out.'

Commander Malm cut the link and turned to the XO, lieutenant commander Gary Schmidt. 'What's the status of that Seahawk?' she asked.

'Fueled, armed and ready to rock,' said Schmidt. 'The boarding party is in the hanger, waiting for the green light.'

Malm nodded. She had orders from the highest levels, so there was no ambiguity about her freedom of action. 'Once those freighters cross into our territorial waters, launch the Seahawks. There's no way the Indians will just let them land and do their thing. Any resistance that stems from the freighters themselves, we deal with using the guns. We'll continue to monitor those surface ships.' She turned to the team manning the radar and the fire control system. 'All countermeasure systems are on active alert. Weapons, you are cleared for weapons release if you detect any incoming threats. Those Brahmos IIs will be inbound at Mach 7, so it's critical we paint them and shoot them down as quickly as possible.'

The situation screen had expanded its represented volume to include a flight of four F-35 Lightning II fighters which had launched from RAAF Pearce, an airbase two hundred kilometres down the coast from Geraldton. The stealthy planes were loitering over the ocean north of Geraldton, loaded with anti-ship cruise missiles. Two black lozenges, the two Shortfin Barracuda attack subs, lurked under the water. They were slinking closer to the Indian taskforce, one from the north, the other from the south. The *Hobart* and the two frigates were positioned ten miles from the three freighters, shepherding them in slowly.

Malm was an icy and calculating commander, a leader who never let pressure or unexpected turns of events shake her resolve or compromise her decision-making ability. Perhaps her crews didn't love her; she was too distant for that, but they did hold her in very high regard, and they trusted her implicitly. She looked at her screens.

'They face an overwhelming array of firepower and it would be suicide for them to start a fight. Von Harten,' she said to her weapons officer. 'Can you think of any scenario where they'd initiate hostilities?'

'I'm not sure, Captain. I don't like this whole situation. The way I see it, we can't execute our mission without preventing the Indians from fulfilling theirs.'

Malm nodded. 'Yea. That seems to be the crux of it.' It seemed somehow inevitable that missiles would be streaking across the sky very soon, no matter what.

This irresistible sense of impending violence was growing a crater of unease in the pit of her stomach. She'd never had it before, not in training, drills or exercises, and she didn't like it. She spared a thought for Glen Robertson. That man was widely considered the best naval mind in the Australian surface fleet, and he'd felt compelled by circumstances to make what seemed like a senseless decision. Malm's situation was far less ambiguous; in the event of a weapons release, at least enemy warships were threatening them. Not for the first time she felt a conflicted sense of admiration for Robertson's uncompromising approach.

She found her current situation unnerving. Her ship's primary mission was air-defence. Malm and her crew had drilled ceaselessly to shoot down airborne threats like aircraft and hypersonic cruise missiles; they had the best sensors and missiles on earth - it was the reason the ship existed. She looked at her crew, diligently running final calculations and preparing for the worst, and tamped down on her anxiety, hard. It was their time, and they would feed off whatever emotion they sensed from her.

The freighters and her surface ships were inching towards the territorial line, twelve miles from shore. There was nothing to do but wait, plan for the worst, and hope like hell for the best.

INS *Mumbai*
1750 hours

A drone, flying high above the ocean and midway between the Australian and Indian ships, sent a video feed back to the *Mumbai's* bridge. Chakradev studied it intently. 'There's a helicopter dialling up on the flight deck over the stern of the Australian destroyer,' he mused to himself.

'Captain, choppers are spooling up on the flight decks of all three Australian warships,' ventured Praveen.

He shook his head. 'Inconclusive' he muttered. Then louder, to the group. 'Commander Malm's words were ambiguous, vague, which means she's hiding something. Those freighters are only fifty miles from the beach at Geraldton. Very shortly they'll be in Australia territorial waters, which is when Captain Malm implied something would happen.' He pursed his lips, thinking, then spoke slowly, clarifying the situation. 'Our mission here is to prevent the Australians from interdicting those refugee ships. If those ships don't make landfall in Australia, for having been sunk or otherwise intercepted, we've failed. I think those helicopters are going to land on the freighters and turn them around. There's no other reason to put Australian personnel on them this close to shore.'

'Could be medical teams?' said Praveen half-heartedly. He didn't really believe what he was saying.

'No.' Khurana shook his head. 'Those helicopters are there to deliver boarding parties to take control of the ships and turn them around. Question is, how do we stop them?'

'Sir, if you're right, our surface to air missiles only have a range of seventy kilometres. So they won't be any use,' said Rama the XO.

'Yes. You're right. Any ideas?' *Come on,* he gestured at his senior officers, demanding their input.

'Sir, we do have two Rudra helicopters in our hangar, plus another one on each of the frigates,' said Praveen. 'They can be fitted with air-to-air missiles. With those, we might be able to deter the Australians from trying to land boarding parties on those bulkers.'

Khurana pointed at his weapons office like he'd just scored a goal; that was what he was looking for.

He turned to his XO. 'Get our Rudra's loaded up with Mistrals and get them in the air,' he said. 'The *Trikand's* as well. I want them shepherding those freighters in. If the Australians launch helicopters they will be intending to interdict those freighters. As such any Australian helicopters that closes within a kilometre of those ships is to be regarded as hostile and shot down.'

HMAS *Hobart*
2045 hours

The water turned a steely grey as dusk settled over a placid Indian Ocean. A keen eye from Oakajee Beach might have been able to spot the three Australian surface ships, which were strung a few kilometres apart about ten miles from the coast. On the bridge of the *Hobart,* Commander Malm looked east at a cloudless sky, glowing orange from the sunset. The freighters, now Malm's charges, were boxy black dots, silhouetted against the horizon. Malm was about to give the order to launch the Seahawks when her Tactical Action Officer office spoke up.

'Captain, we're tracking three helicopters which have just taken off from the *Mumbai* and the *Trikand*.' They look like Rudras, and they're heading this way.'

Malm acknowledged the information and pondered what this meant. Three Seahawks were spooling up on the Australian ships, about to take off and drop the boarding parties. She knew the light helicopters on the Indian ships that could be configured for air-to-air operations, specifically against other rotary-winged craft. It was exceedingly rare though, and if it occurred, it was over land, in support of ground troops. Malm had never even heard of a chopper shooting down another chopper in a maritime environment - did those Indian boats even have the right weapons on board?

There's no need to send them out to observe, she thought. Especially not three. If Khurana actually believed she was going to let those ships land, he didn't need those helicopters to view the situation up close and personal, because all modern warships had drones for observation and scouting. The incoming choppers could mean only one thing, Khurana was expecting the Australians to board the freighter, like with the *Tamil Nadu,* and he wanted to stop it.

The sensors officer spoke again; 'Captain, a visual feed from the drone shows those Rudras are carrying some sort of externals weapons on their hard-points. It's inconclusive exactly what, but the hard-points do appear occupied.'

Malm thought furiously. That cagey Indian bastard. She had to take out those helicopters otherwise her flight crews were in danger. But by doing so, she'd be guilty of firing the first shot, essentially declaring war on India. She wasn't prepared to do that. Australia was already seriously on the nose internationally, and throwing first, no matter how provocative the Indians were being, wasn't an option.

This must have been how Robertson had felt, torn between saving his own, and causing a catastrophe.

'Launch the Seahawks. Target the Rudras with SM-6s. If they become hostile, take them out. But we cannot fire first.'

Moments later, the Sea Hawk on the flight deck lifted off, whumping past the bridge and off into the sunset. Choppers from the two frigates joined it, and the three helicopters set off over the ocean in formation.

The opposing rotorcraft quickly vectored towards the refugee ships. One wrong move here would end in catastrophe. She'd make another overture to the Indians, see if she'd misread the situation. 'Open a line to the *Mumbai,'* she ordered. Maybe she could convince Khurana to let them land.

INS *Mumbai*

Ramakrishnan glanced at the comms screen; a new channel was asking to be opened, blinking red at him. 'Captain,' he said. 'The Australians are calling.'

'What the hell could she possibly want?' demanded Khurana of nobody in particular. The Australian helicopters were minutes away from landing on the freighters; Did Malm want to do some last-minute horse-trading?

'Sir, she may be calling to clarify what those choppers are for,' said Rama.

'No shit that's what she's calling for,' Khurana snapped. 'But what could she tell us that we don't already know?'

'Sir, if those choppers are full of medical teams or something other than a boarding party to turn the ships around, shooting them down would be a giant mistake,' said his XO.

Khurana nodded. But how could they know, until after they landed? 'You're right. But if Malm lies about them being medics, or whatever, and we let them land, we're fucked, we'll never get them off. We'll have failed our mission.' He pointed at the radio receiver that Malm was waiting on, red light blinking enticingly. 'I want to know what she's got to say,' he said eventually, 'but this is her chance to feed us disinformation that could lead to the wrong decision.'

'Sir, the Australians will be within a kilometer of the freighters in thirty seconds. The Rudras are in range of the Australian aircraft now and awaiting orders,' said the communications officer.

'Sir, the Australians...' queried Rama.

Khurana decided. 'Cut the line to Malm,' he commanded. He wouldn't give her a chance to bullshit them into letting those choppers land. He watched the Australian choppers on the radar. They continued to vector in on the tankers and he watched them cross the one-kilometre line in silence. He then picked up the receiver and spoke to the commander of the flight of Rudra's. 'This is your captain. You're ordered to fire. Take out the Australian helicopters.'

HMAS *Hobart*

'No joy, Captain, *Mumbai* left us hanging,' reported Malm's communications officer. *Shit,* breathed Malm silently, and was about to issue the order to fire on the Rudras when frantic shouting came over the radio from the SeaHawk pilot. 'Missiles inbound, we're under attack!'

'Engage hostiles, weapons release,' she ordered tersely. Von Harten acknowledged her order, pressed a button and six small trapdoors swung open on foredeck of the destroyer, just in front of the bridge. In rapid succession, a volley of SM-6 missiles whooshed out of the launcher and rocketed over the horizon. Long claws raked towards the Rudras. A stream of encrypted chatter between the ships targeting computer and the missiles' electronic brains identifie, then locked them onto the fleeing aircraft.

Madeleine Malm was not nervous anymore. Her endocrinal system had dumped every available millilitre of adrenalin into her blood and events had, from her perspective, slowed down to the extent that she could pick and choose what she reacted to on her terms.

She felt calm, calibrated; on a hair-trigger but in complete control. Clarity of purpose. All the safeties in her brain had been disengaged and bypassed. Her mind, her crew, and her ship were a tightrope walker on a razor's edge over a chasm, locked in the sweet spot between perfection and oblivion. This was why the *Hobart* existed. Sad it had come to this, she thought, and inhaled deeply, breathing in the reality of the situation. The *Hobart* was a naval-engineering masterpiece with an exquisite integration of high technology and raw destructive power; but at the end of the day, it was just a tool, and tools weren't much good unless they were being utilised.

The *Hobart* finally had a purpose.

'Time to kill - thirty seconds,' said weapons.

'All ahead to the crash site. Assemble rescue crews and prepare the RHIBs for launch,' commanded Malm.

The *Hobart* emerged from the rocket exhaust smokescreen, and Malm calculated her next move.

The attacking Rudras were now speeding back to their ships.

But, a three-hundred kilometre an hour helicopter can't outrun a four thousand kilometre an hour missile. The Rudras had fired on the Seahawks at the limit of their missile range, six kilometres, then turned and sprinted to safety.

On the sensor display, the helicopters were represented as letters; HAR (hostile aircraft; rotary) and numbered *one, two* and *three.* The SM-6s rapidly closed the gap to the choppers. The *Hobart* had been specifically designed to shoot down airborne threats, which meant she was packed with fast missiles designed for attacking fighter jets; taking out those Rudras was shooting fish in a barrel.

Malm watched the first missile merge with HAR1. *'Like harpooning a beached whale*,' she thought.

'Impact on target, hostile one rendered neutral,' announced weapons, trying to keep the tension from his voice. On the screen, HAR1 was blinking, indicating that the system had acknowledged the kill. Shortly after, the other two helicopters began blinking on the screen, and the weapons officer announced their destruction. The Rudras were now rapidly expanding shards of metal sinking towards the water, but Malm felt no satisfaction. She was concerned about a new threat.

Confirming her suspicions, Lieutenant Holmes on the radar cried out;

'Captain, launch detected, missiles inbound, low trajectory...' Radar struggled to keep his voice measured as he processed the information. 'They're going supersonic. We're tracking ten, no wait, twelve, ah shit, they're still launching, all platforms are launching, this is a saturation attack!'

Events were exploding out of control. Malm did the maths in her head even as the screen displayed time-to-kill information. The *Hobart's* sensors were tracking the inbound missiles, thirty in the air from all three Indian ships. Travel speed; seven times the speed of sound; arriving in four minutes. Impact was something Malm was very keen to avoid; the *Hobart* would be nothing but an incandescent debris field if even one of those BrahMos II missiles got through.

'Engage inbound hostiles with SM-6s, first wave. Ready Sea Sparrows for second intercept wave, sixty-second stagger. Call up those F-35s, get them in the fight. I want those Indian ships on the bottom.'

She hadn't even finished issuing orders when the forty-eight-cell launcher on the front of the destroyer started spewing fire. Trapdoors swung open, launching SM-6 surface-to-air missiles. The rocket engines made a giant, rasping sound as they accelerated towards the incoming BrahMos II at Mach four. The missile launch embroiled *Hobart* in a roiling cauldron of flame and rocket smoke, and when the ship finally emerged into clear air, Malm caught a glimpse of the two frigates in the distance; silhouettes under their own towering columns of rocket exhaust that stretched away into the stratosphere.

Malm quickly scanned the consoles for critical information; sixteen out of thirty missiles were heading towards the *Hobart*. The less dangerous frigates were targeted by seven each, but even one missile would obliterate anything it hit. It was incredibly difficult to shoot down something travelling seven times the speed of sound, but the Indian ramjets had to penetrate a sophisticated, layered missile umbrella, which is why they'd fired thirty of those venomous projectiles at once. The Aegis combat system on the *Hobart* was tracking each BrahMos II, integrating information from the sensors on the distant frigates and guiding the SM-6s home. The Indian missiles were lethally fast, and after launch all but one had swooped in low over the ocean, rocketing along scant metres above the surface. The final missile had stayed at altitude, its active radar illuminating the Australian ships and relaying course corrections to the rest of the salvo, which had split into three groups and flew low to hide among the background clutter of the choppy ocean swell.

Malm took stock of the rapidly evolving situation. She'd started the battle with thirty-two state-of-the-art SM-6 missiles, and sixty-four of the smaller, shorter ranged, Evolved Sea Sparrow surface-to-air missiles, which could be quad-packed into each cell of the forty-eight-cell launcher. Now, she was down to twenty-two SM-6s and a full load of Sea Sparrows; make that a half load. The second defensive wave, thirty Sea Sparrows, shrieked out of the launcher even as she did her mental gymnastics, embroiling the bridge again in blazing exhaust. Never before had a warship launched so many missiles in such a short amount of time; less than three minutes after the first shot and already half of her missiles were airborne. What happened next would decide if they lived to see the next sunrise or not.

'Ten seconds to initial merge,' said the weapons officer. The SM-6s had flown a looping flight path, flying high, the better to search for the ocean-hugging Brahmos. Scanning downward with their active radars, they locked onto the speeding ship-killers red-hot exhaust signatures.

The two opposing missiles were going to catapult into each other at incredible speed, barely one-hundred kilometres from Malm's taskforce. The weapons officer reported that two SM-6's had locked onto the high-altitude Brahmos II, the missile acting as the eyes of the inbound salvo, and the target they needed to take out first.

'Merge initiated,' cried Weapons as the seeker Brahmos II started evasive action, jinking up and down. The first SM-6 changed direction too late and exploded harmlessly in the sky. The second SM-6 had approached from a slightly different vector-and with a closing speed of Mach ten the Indian missile had flown directly into the second SAM's path. Within a fraction of a second, the SM-6s proximity fuse triggered, and the missile exploded. Warhead fragments tore into the big ASM, shredding it and causing it to flail out of control. It was instantly torn apart, the hyper-velocity air ripping the suddenly un-aerodynamic shape to pieces.

Just above the surface, the remaining Brahmos II registered the loss of their eyes, and the designated secondary began to rise in its place, just as the rest of the SM-6s shrieked out of the sky in a screaming kamikaze attack, straight into the barrage. The ship-killers sensed the threat and began slewing, turning S bends and increasing altitude to evade. From the *Hobart*, Malm looked west, eyes drawn to the hot engines of the flock of Sea Sparrows, then to the explosions under the horizon flashing orange against the now charcoal sky. Malm and Khurana were projecting incredible destructive power far away from their ships; an invisible and distant arm wrestle.

But not invisible for long, and not distant enough for comfort.

'Recording six, make that...eight hostiles shot down by the first wave!' cried the radar officer, who was tracking the remaining missiles. 'Twenty-two still inbound, time to impact, forty seconds!' In the top of the BRU, a timer was counting down the seconds before the first of the remaining projectiles would collide with the *Hobart* and the two frigates.

Malm said nothing. In ten more seconds, the Sea Sparrows would start to explode amongst the remaining inbounds.

'Impact in ten...' said radar.

'Fire the decoys!' snapped Malm, and the Nulka decoy launcher spat the little rockets into the air, it's small thruster cartoonish after the battery of light and sound from the missile launchers. The Nulka would emit the same electronic signatures as the *Hobart* and try to fool any remaining missiles into targeting it instead.

The noise from the little rocket motor had barely dissipated when Weapons spoke rapidly.

'Sea sparrow merge initiated,' he said, and the SAMs began exploding above the sea. This time the explosions were above the horizon; the BrahMos' were barely twenty-five seconds away.

Missiles flashed on the sensor display as they were taken out.

Radar spoke: 'Confirming, oh shit, that's thirteen kills, seven still tracking; three heading for us, two each at the frigates!'

Thirteen wasn't enough. A second salvo of Sea Sparrows erupted out of the launch tubes, tearing off into the twilight, rapidly swinging down from vertical, to clipping the ocean waves. Over the water, their own missiles launching illuminated the other Australian ships. The frigates, with much smaller missile payloads, had just expended their last defensive weapons.

The screen showed the F-35 fighters vectoring in at Mach 1.5 to launch their own cruise missiles, but they were still hundreds of kilometres out. The *Hobart's* fate would be decided well before they dealt themselves into the game.

'Ten seconds!' called Radar. The bridge crew faced the setting sun. Malm could see the hot exhaust reflecting off the waves now like a giant fuse strung out to sea, lit and streaking towards the ship at breathtaking speed. Radar announced the final volley of Sea Sparrows shrieking home; after the explosions Radar spoke up once more; 'Four kills, three remaining inbound.'

'Fuck that's fast...' breathed Malm as she watched a BrahMos II slice a glancing blow into the *Newcastle* at eight thousand kilometres an hour, the kinetic energy alone visibly rocking the ship over, tearing through the hull and pulverising the guts of the frigate like a giant hollow-point bullet. A fraction of a second later the warhead exploded, lighting the ship with orange fire from within like a giant Halloween lantern. Overpressure exploded out of the funnel, the bridge windows, and other weak points, ripping the frigate open. The *Newcastle* buckled in the middle and sagged in the water.

Malm and her crew were just passengers now; there was nothing left but to trust their defensive systems. The flashing sensor display showed the Nulka had successfully drawn the second-to-last hypersonic away from the ship-it exploded harmlessly a few hundred metres off the starboard bow. Malm heard the industrial shredding sound of the auto-targeting Phalanx chain gun spin up, vomiting flames and seventy-five, twenty-millimetre shells per second into the sky; the *Hobarts* last-ditch, Hail Mary attempt to avoid sharing the fate of the *Newcastle*.

The missile was barely five-hundred metres from the *Hobart* when the shells struck home. The warhead exploded and fragmented. Flaming streaks propelled in all directions, a dark firework detonating, and...they'd survived! Malm had the tiniest fraction of a second to hear Weapons begin a whoop of triumph and feel relief sagging through her body when the remains of the big missile, reduced to hot shards of hypersonic shrapnel, blew through the bridge like a shotgun blast through a human skull, ricocheting off the walls like a bullet in a pillbox, reducing every human there to red mist.

INS *Mumbai*

Captain Khurana took stock. He'd just taken a frigate and a destroyer out of the fight. From what he could gather the *Hobart* had been critically damaged somehow, but it was still floating, and the IR feed from the drone showed only superficial pockmarks from missile debris. One frigate remained, with nothing more than eight, ancient Harpoon anti-ship missiles left. Khurana was confident his missile screen could deal with that threat.

His radar operator spoke. 'Captain, I'm getting some strange returns here. Sporadic signal on an aerial threat, it appears to flash into view at intervals, then disappears.'

'What vector is it on?' he asked.

'Well, we've been tracking it for the last half-hour. From the few plots we've had, it appeared to be holding station approximately four hundred kilometres away. Then, the locations of the last three times it's popped up on our sensors indicate that it's closing on us, at about one and a half thousand kilometres an hour.'

A stab of anxiety pulsed through Khurana's stomach. 'Where are they now?' he demanded.

'We're correlating data with the *Talwars* to triangulate them. The last time we pinged them, they were one hundred and fifty kilometres out. We think each time we paint them, they change course. That was… twenty-four seconds ago.'

Khurana's mind worked furiously. There was only one reason the Mumbai's sophisticated radar wouldn't be able to get a lock on an aircraft; it was using stealth.

'F-35s,' he breathed. Not good. 'Where did they come from?' He barked with panic rich in his tone. His crew could barely shrug a response. Not only were the fighters hard to detect, but the Long-Range ASM missile they fired, was just as stealthy and could well be in the air already.

'Our best chance to get a lock is when they launch missiles,' he said. 'Opening the bomb-bay doors magnifies their radar return. The second they come within the envelope of the Baraks, get them in the air.'

Minutes later the radar operator spoke again, voice ringing with tension; 'Painting four aircraft. Returns indicate they're firing missiles, I think, it's hard to say but possibly eight missiles inbound. The aircraft now appear to be maneuvering away from us, heading back to the Australian mainland...'

Khurana swore softly. The jets had launched the missiles well out of the range of his Barak-8 surface-to-air missiles. His only hope now was to try to pick them up on his sensors and shoot them down. Those LRASMs would split up and approach his ship from totally different vectors. For all it did the same job as his BrahMos IIs, it went about its work in a completely different way. A silent assassin versus a steroidal berserker. The BrahMos II could maneuver to a certain extent but mainly relied on pure, unadulterated speed to evade countermeasures and make the kill. However, a giant missile, streamlined for speed and burning enough fuel to hit Mach seven had a prominent heat signature and made plenty of electro-magnetic noise that screamed 'look at me' to every sensor on the ocean. The LRASM took another approach; it dawdled into its target at barely one-thousand kilometres an hour, an eighth the speed of the BrahMos. An invisible fucking slug thought Khurana. His weapons officer looked up and shook his head, nothing.

'Keep looking,' he snapped. 'There's only eight of them, and we know approximately where they were fired from.

Minutes passed, and still the Mumbai's sensors couldn't get a lock on the missiles. At least with the BrahMos II, you were either dead, or you weren't; there simply wasn't time to be truly terrified. Khurana could see the tension building in his crew as they searched in vain for the elusive, flying bombs. Wide eyes and sweaty brows crowded the bridge, tremors caught in voices conspicuously casual or forced-confident when reporting in. His radar operator grimaced silently at his instruments, peering at the data feed, trying to triangulate the missiles using an information feed from the Talwar's as well. Periodically he raised his hands in anguish as his equipment turned up nothing. Khurana could feel the panic in himself too and had to check himself from issuing orders for the sake of it.

Would breaking the silence give his crew a much-needed injection of confidence? Not good, here he was second-guessing himself. He affected calm and waited.

Sudden chatter from the *Trikand*, they had a visual on a sea-skimming missile that they still couldn't raise on their sensors!

'Captain!' cried one of his deck officers, 'I can see missiles, look!' Khurana followed the sailor's out-flung hand, out the window on the bridge. Coming in low over the port bow, Khurana glimpsed a black shape; like a bat, visible only by the moonbeams reflecting off the water that it obscured. 'A billion-dollar ship and we're relying on lookouts!' seethed Khurana The 'bat' was hurtling across the top of the waves towards the *Mumbai*. The two Vympel close-in weapons systems on the front of the ship waved around spastically, giants pawing in the dark, as their radar caught traces of the incoming missile and spat thirty-millimetre shells into the ocean almost at random. 'Get a fix on that missile!' he screamed at a terrified Praveen.

In the distance, far away under the horizon, a dirty fireball lit up the night sky.

'Sir, the *Trikand* has been hit, the *Trikand* has been hit!' cried his communications officer.

'Forget the fucking *Trikand*!' he roared, 'get a solution on that missile, or we're next!' jabbing his finger at Praveen. Secondary explosions erupted on the horizon as the *Trikand's* missile magazines blew the ship apart.

'Manual fire!' screamed Khurana, veins bulging on his forehead as the shadow flashed closer.

The weapons operator took remote control of the guns, and through an optical targeting site on his screen, designated where he wanted them to spew fire. The two mounts, each with twin six-barrel thirty-millimetre rotary cannons, swung around to the path of the missile. Praveen pulled the electronic trigger desperately.

'Hit it!' bellowed Khurana as the Vympel's thundered into life, blasting gouts of flame and twin, lancing tracers of shells shooting into the night, like supersonic, red hot needles pushing through dark flesh. The rounds converged on the point targeted by the weapons officer, who kept fucking missing, so onwards the missile rushed, a vampire silently stalking its victim. One thousand metres...five hundred metres...

'Hit it, *Hit it!*' spat Khurana.

'Shut. Up,' whispered Weapons, a split second before the missile exploded in an orange fireball...barely two hundred metres from the Mumbai. Pieces of shrapnel splashed white in the ocean, some pitter-pattering off the superstructure and tinkling into the water.

The big cannons fell quiet; smoke wafted from their turrets. Stunned silence on the bridge, then an elated Weapons banged his fists into his console. 'I got it! I bloody got it!' he roared in triumph, glaring around the bridge; a final moment of emotional release before the second missile, approaching from the stern, crashed through the helicopter hangar at the back of the ship. The four-hundred-and-fifty-kilogram warhead detonated, heavy metal rods tore through the hull at three thousand metres a second, just as the third stealth missile, also unseen, tore through the side of the Mumbai's bow, demolished the bulkheads around the vertical launcher, and penetrated her forward missile magazine. The fireball set off sixty-four Barak-8s, annihilating everything forward of the funnel. Ripped in half like an axe through a tin can, the blazing remnants of the INS *Mumbai* slipped under the waves scant minutes later, thick plumes of oily smoke the only testament she'd ever existed at all.

Chapter 10
Sydney
September 1st, 2300 hours

Ex-Commodore Glen Robertson slumped on his barstool, shoulders stooped, elbows on the bar top. He faced the screen above the bar, but the noise drifted over his head. A half-drunk bottle of beer dangled from his left hand. It was getting warm. Why was he drinking beer? He hated beer. He swirled it, regarding the spinning amber liquid as it started to froth. Filth. *You're drinking beer because you're a recovering alcoholic trying to only relapse a* little *bit*. 'Do it right or not at all,' he muttered to himself; he shoved it away and ordered a whiskey instead. The bar stank of stale beer and commercial quantities of industrial disinfectant. The pokies room towards the back of the bar, inconveniently located right next to the toilets, permeated what little atmosphere there was with every obnoxious arcade sound. He swivelled his gaze away from his glass and towards one of the men who'd been sitting at the same pokies machine since Glen arrived. The man looked like a poster child from a meth clinic, but instead of rat gauntness, slabs of loose fat hung off him. He looked like several blocks of butter mashed together then left in the sun. Youngish, but with thinning hair and grey speckled stubble, black gaps in tobacco-stained teeth. A vintage Metallica t-shirt retreated up a hairy apron of fat that dangled over the front of his board shorts.

The recovered meth junkie sidled up next to Glen and ordered a drink. At the same time, the screen above the bar cut to an update on the repairs the Navy was doing on the HMAS *Hobart.* Glen had known Captain Malm. Had a high professional regard for her. He'd spent the last few weeks wondering if she was dead because of him.

Junkie snorted and leaned on the bar. 'Useless fucking navy losers. Can't even beat the Indians. What do we even pay their wages for, eh?'

Glen's face curled into a sneer, then his eyebrows shot up, then finally he almost laughed. What else could you do? He raised his eyes to the roof, as if an answer was hiding amongst the exposed ventilation piping and dangling electrical tape. 'Jesus Christ,' he muttered audibly, shaking his head.

Junkie gave him a dirty look then wandered back to his machine, smacking the buttons with practised authority. Four or five other specimens just like him tapped away at the colourful money pits around him. Sounded like a mindless child's game to Glen. *But for mindless adults. Should show the Indians footage of this pub,* he thought bitterly. *That would stop them in their tracks.* To think he'd torpedoed that ship for that conniving devil-woman Prime Minister and these drop-kicks. To think Malm had died for them.

He took a breath as if he was about to confide in the drink, then sighed and took a swig instead. He grimaced. If it wasn't the coffee on the *Melbourne*, it was warm, shitty whiskey. What did he have to do to get a decent drink?

Well, he didn't have to worry about the *Melbourne's* rancid coffee anymore. He'd been suspended indefinitely, pending a full military investigation into his conduct up to and including his sinking of the *Tamil Nadu*. He was getting hung out to dry and his career was effectively over. Lafitte needed a scapegoat, and there was no way in hell she was going to pass up a chance to make him pay. He knew why she'd done it, but this was twice she'd ripped his heart out. He got it, intellectually, but emotionally, he wanted to strangle her.

He cycled through events in his mind. Poorly defined mission parameters, the wrong weapon system, an unprovoked attack. Not to mention some seriously bad luck. None of those details mattered. Besides, maybe he wasn't really a scapegoat; he'd blown that freighter sky high and killed more people in one go than nearly anybody else in history. He'd almost certainly plunged Australia into war.

119

He focused on the big screen above the barmaid, who was more interested in her phone than the customers. The news ran through the international reaction to the sinking of the *Tamil Nadu*. Universal condemnation, expressions of shock and dismay. Initially, Jacqui had run with the line that the Indians had fired first, but there was no real evidence, and it was easier just to offer Glen up on a plate and distance herself. The outrage was relentless. No politician ever missed the chance to be horrified. The General-Secretary of the United Nations was telling the world that such contempt for human life was, 'Incomprehensible in this day and age. Australia, once a model international citizen, an open country with a vibrant multicultural society, had slowly become an international pariah as it ignored climate change and turned its back on the world,' the General-Secretary said. 'At first, it was more a diplomatic point - Australia didn't want to help. But then people started starving and losing their homes, and it became a human issue, not just an abstract scientific and diplomatic one.' he continued, 'The *Tamil-Nadu,* was an atrocity, the culmination of years of obfuscation about the realities of climate change. This time there was a real, human consequence.'

Leaders in Africa said they had taken refugees from across borders for years, in times of famine, disease and war, in their hundreds of thousands, their millions. *You had no choice. Doesn't count,* Glen thought.

Who did Australia think it was, refusing to help in such a barbaric fashion? Middle Eastern leaders blamed the United States for emboldening their allies to be so ruthless. Only countries, like Israel, under the protection of the Great Satan, would dare to behave like this. Syria's president wanted to know what kind of regime murdered helpless people waiting at the gates of salvation? Robertson almost cracked a smile.

ASEAN nations issued a joint statement, closing ranks around India. Australia was quickly becoming a dirty word, spoken in the same breath as Soviet Russia or Pol Pot's Cambodia. Lafitte, being compared to the most ruthless leaders in history. Some commentators were saying that Australia's racist stance put it on the same level as Nazi Germany. Ironic, that he and Lafitte were cast as partners in crime, part of the same heartless machine. She had been a pain in the ass when they dated, and she was being a pain in the ass now..

At least the British and Americans were casting it as an appalling accident, instead of premeditated murder. President Marion Cain announced, 'nations have a right to choose who crosses their borders. Although the right to protect your sovereignty does not confer the right to murder civilians.' Another almost-smile twitched at his lips. Robertson got what Cain was trying to achieve but really, how did these people sleep at night?

He ordered a whiskey.

He knew he was in some sort of catatonic state, so emotionally, he'd shut down. His mind constantly replayed the ship going down, and the night and day they'd spent fishing as many of the survivors out as they could, but it was just a feeble attempt to right a catastrophic wrong. They'd recovered some of the drowned Australians too.

Some.

He'd forgotten how much he liked to drink. The slow descent back into apathy was perfect. Sober, his mind was like an echo chamber, amplifying the negativity. The booze subdued his gloomy thoughts one drink at a time. The thoughts still banged around up there, but his head was now a padded room. Besides, what else could he do that would help? Nothing; they'd hung him out to dry until the formal investigation started. So, he found the dingiest, quietest pub he could, parked himself at the bar, and washed away his feelings. He even felt a twinge of nostalgia for the years after the *Bau Anjing*, further heightened by his inability to recall any specific details about that period of his life.

121

He was starting to feel nicely detached. He could watch the bad press, or think about the sinking ship, without his stomach screwing up into a knot, or going through a list of 'what if's', and things he could have done differently.

He missed his crew. A selfish, small thing compared to everything else, but persistent, like a pebble in his shoe. He loved commanding those sailors, and his crew loved him. They would have followed him anywhere.

Out of the corner of his eye, he noticed a slender brunette approach the bar. She headed straight towards him, and he had a moment to enjoy the sight of her tanned, toned arms and figure-hugging skirt before he realised it was his girlfriend. He muttered a curse to himself. Maybe she would go away.

The TV now showed footage of Indian and South-East Asian youths rampaging through the streets in Australian cities, trashing cars and torching local government buildings. Two police officers had died. White vigilantes had caught up with the rioters soon after, and there'd been some running street battles in western Sydney since. Twelve rioters and ten vigilantes were dead, as well as several bystanders. Footage played of Lafitte telling reporters, 'There is no place for such actions in Australia and anybody identified as takieng part incivil unrest and ethnic violence will be tracked down and charged. Australia is an inclusive country, proud of its multicultural heritage, and in testing times, we have to pull together, not fly apart.'

That cat is well out of the bag, he thought.

'Taking a trip down memory lane, are we?' said Alice, leaning into his field of vision.

'You know how I get nostalgic sometimes,' he replied wryly. He took in her delicate, almost mousy features, with clear, piercing brown eyes and a tiny flutter of excitement filled his chest momentarily. After all these years...

'Are you coming home tonight? The dog misses your conversation.'

He shifted on the stool. 'I, um...actually no. It doesn't look like it.'

She sighed and settled on a stool next to him. She ordered a whiskey, the same as his. 'Things are really escalating,' she said pointing to the TV. 'Quite a situation we found ourselves in.'

'Quite a situation I caused; you mean.' He finished his drink. The barmaid was ready with another one.

Her whiskey arrived too. She evaluated it briefly then set it aside. 'No, Glen. I mean what I said. We're all in this together. Nobody who understands the issues blames you. It's been brewing for years. It's been coming since the first drought turned their crops to dust and the first typhoon wiped out their coastal cities.'

'Yea...but you can't blame the weather, can you.' He pulled a face. 'And I sure as hell kick-started things, didn't I.'

'Well,' she said delicately. 'You just poured fuel on the fire.' She paused. 'A lot of fuel.'

'Fuel on the fire,' he echoed. 'Sounds better than a Mark 48 up the ass of an unarmed refugee ship.'

'We've all reviewed the data, Glen. Nobody blames you for the decision you made. Besides, you were following orders.'

He made himself ignore the concern in her eyes. 'Just following orders, eh.' He grunted. He knew he was being petulant and resented himself for it. Wished she'd leave him alone, and not see him acting like such a baby.

'I know what I was doing. Doesn't seem to matter to those assholes,' he waved his drink towards the TV. 'And I'll never be able to forget the sight of that ship going down...' he said emptily. She said nothing. She'd heard it a hundred times already. He changed the subject. 'What were you doing reviewing the data?'

'We were trying to get a visual on the smugglers, trace them back to their associates in India.'

'How'd that go?'

'Not so well. There's no footage of the SAM launch and nothing near high resolution enough to get a positive ID on anyone. We did debrief the survivors,' she said, trying to draw him out. This sparked some interest in Glen. 'Oh yeah? Any of them know anything?'

 'No. We think all the smugglers were in the superstructure when the torpedo hit.' The spark died. 'They were directly above the point of impact. Half the explosive force went straight up through the superstructure. They're nothing but vapour.'

'Hmm.' Of course they were.

'I killed all those people, Alice' he mumbled into his drink.

'Sure, Glen. But that's on *them*. Not *you*. Done is done. You command a warship. Your job is to safeguard our naval approaches, and that is what you did. It's time you realised that and stopped drinking yourself stupid.'

'It helps me forget,' he shrugged.

Her eyes grew spikes. 'While you're wallowing in self-pity, the world is going to pieces around you.' Her jaw hardened. 'Not to mention your relationship.'

A tiny spark of anger lit inside him. 'Give it a rest Alice. I didn't ask for your help. I'm trying to get drunk and forget about all this entire clusterfuck.'

'While better men, like those police officers, die for your stupidity?'

'What? You said it yourself; it was going to happen anyway. I just lit it up.'

'Doesn't mean you can sit on the sidelines.'

He turned to face her. 'Do you have any idea what you're talking about?' he asked sharply. 'I've been stood down. My career is over, I'm done. They wouldn't put me in command of a bathtub, and nothing will change that.' She stared back. Was she stupid?

'Are you stupid, Glen?' she asked irritably. He blinked. How the hell did she do that? Against his better judgment, he bit.

Chapter 11
Alexandria, Sydney
September 4th, 2115 hours

Glen Robertson wiped the sweat off his brown and swore under his breath as he walked into the dingy pub in Alexandria, Horseshoe. Alexandria itself was an abandoned industrial wasteland, which had recently developed into trendy warehouse conversions.

A cesspit within a dump, he thought to himself. Precisely what he was after, but tonight, for some reason, the pub was packed. He frowned. A lone surviving relic from the industrial days, the pub was an anachronism, somewhere he could usually count on to be virtually empty; he came here for the solitude, not the atmosphere.

His shirt clung to his chest in the sticky evening air; he needed something cold in his hand ASAP.

Jayden Jones, youthful-looking with his slender, fit frame and sandy hair, shot Robertson a quizzical look. He wasn't suffering in the heat like Robertson.

'You said this place would be empty,' said Jones.

Robertson shrugged. 'It usually is. I mean, look at it.'

The Horseshoe had stubbornly clung to its dowdiness even as the rest of the area blossomed. No self-respecting city girl would be caught dead in the place, but it had perversely become a popular kick-off point for local guys looking to get in a few cheap drinks before they moved onto bars with better prospects. It was a throwback to the nineteen-sixties; the chipped, fading cream and pale green wall tiles were only slightly more appealing to look at than the brown, threadbare carpet. Robertson's shoes stuck to the floor as he walked to the bar.

Jones wrinkled his nose. 'The reek of stale alcohol gives it a bohemian air. I thought you came here to be miserable?'

'I do. Usually, everyone's buggered off by now, and it's just a few sad old men and problem gamblers.'

'A sad middle-aged man in their midst.'

Robertson barked a humourless laugh. 'Exactly.'

'I wonder what the occasion is.' Jones asked obviously trying to steer clear of the depressive hole Robertson seemed so keen on pursuing, 'At least there's some atmosphere. I was afraid we'd only have each other's company all night.'

'Heaven forbid,' said Glen, with what Jayden could have sworn was a genuine smile touching the edge of his lips. He pointed at the bar, 'Let's get a drink.'

Jones had been Glen's CO from the *Bau Anjing* days. They'd gone on trial together, and Jones had insisted on taking full responsibility for what had happened, despite being back on the frigate when the shooting started. After their acquittal, Jones had been granted an honourable discharge from the Navy. Their friendship had stayed rock solid, and they'd lived together, drunk together, and helped clean up each other's messes. Robertson had been best man at Jones' wedding, and a perilous choice to make a speech on such an important day which had paid off; A standing ovation had met Robertson's speech. Jones had breathed a sigh of relief, but in hindsight, it hadn't mattered: Jones' wife left him for her yoga instructor a few years later and he'd lived in Robertson's spare room during the breakup.

'Good crowd in here tonight,' Jones said as they worked their way past some tired, old men dribbling into their beers. They were scowling at a large group of loud Asian men who were drinking fast near the bar.

At the bar, Robertson ordered the house whiskey. Cheap and nasty, Robertson downed it in one gulp. It prickled on the way down, and heat spread through his stomach as pungent fumes wafted out his nose.

Jones grimaced. 'I'll choose the next one.'

'You do that,' said Robertson. Christ, he hated whiskey. It was all just liquid road base as far as he was concerned. But he drank for the final result, not the journey.

New drinks arrived and Jones raised his to Robertson. 'I can't tell you how glad I am you dragged me out tonight. The perfect way to start my weekend.' He made a show of looking around.

'You dragged me. Yet another error of judgment on my part to let you.' Robertson said as he took a swig of the top-shelf whiskey Jones had ordered for them both. It still tasted like whiskey.

'Don't be like that! Surely there's nowhere else you'd rather spend Friday night.'

Robertson grinned. 'Somehow I'd forgotten how relentlessly positive you are.'

'I'll take that as a compliment.'

Robertson smiled despite himself.

'Now Glen,' said Jones, becoming serious. 'We need to have a chat.'

Robertson felt himself deflating. 'Really? You gonna tell me what I need to hear, dish out some tough love?'

Jones raised an eyebrow. 'You're an idiot, Glen.'

Robertson pretended to be offended.

'No, seriously, I think you're a fool and you're acting like a real dickhead,' Jones pressed.

Robertson dropped the fake smile and abruptly conceded the point.

'I know!' he said vehemently. 'But Jayden, I can't stop thinking about that ship going down. Then Lafitte...I did what they wanted, and they're crucifying me for it. You know the International Criminal Court is talking to the government about trying me for crimes against humanity, and the government hasn't shut them down yet' He shook his head. 'I don't know what to think.'

'I know it can be unfair, Glen. After the *Bau Anjing,* they let me quit on my own terms, but it wasn't voluntary. You know that. The Navy was all I knew, and I was out on my ass and starting from zero. And I wasn't even on the boat with you and Fitzsimmons, was I.'

Robertson shrugged, drink halfway to his mouth. He couldn't argue. Jayden had done as much as he could to take the responsibility off Glen and Fitzsimmons.

Robertson pointed over his drink. 'OK. So what's your point?'

'Look, I know that last thing you need is another lecture. So, this isn't one of them. I just want to tell you what I see, as a third party.'

Robertson raised a dubious eyebrow.

'Firstly, everyone has turned on you. The government, the Navy, the media are all eating you alive. But you never cared what anybody else thought before. Suddenly what they think upsets you and you're pushing away the only people interested in sticking by you.'

'I'm here with you, aren't I?'

'Ha. That's only because I said we could get pissed together, not because of my delightful company. I could be anyone.' Jones got serious. 'End of the day, you've got an ego problem.' He had a drink. 'I've seen you do this before, Glen. When you're up, you're king of the world. When you're down, you're worse than useless. The thing is when you have a command, or a woman, you don't get the luxury of being down. You've got to manage your emotions better.'

Robertson ground his teeth. Jones was right. But...'You can't just decide not to be rock bottom, Jonesy. It doesn't work like that. You need a circuit breaker.' He studied the lines on his palms. 'I know I'm screwing everything up with Alice. My career is dead, my relationship is going down the toilet, and I can't sleep at night for seeing that ship sink with all those people on it. But I don't know what to do.' He looked at his friend. He could feel hotness behind his eyes. 'I'm just really ashamed.'

'You're not a victim, Glen,' said Jones harshly. 'You're a commander in the Australian Navy and the boyfriend of a woman who definitely doesn't need you, and is only with you because of who you are when you haven't forgotten yourself. Start acting like it.'

'Alright..! You're right. So what should I do?'

Jonesy studied his friend for a moment, who seemed to be at least considering his words.

'I won't labour the point, but it's time to stop turning your back on the people who are there for you. It's like you want to be alone. You're self-sabotaging. It's senseless.'

Robertson nodded. 'Yea. Ok. I'll think about it.'

'And Glen?'

'What?' he said, exasperated.

'Tonight is your last night on this,' said Jones, waggling his glass. 'Alice won't have it, neither will the Navy, and neither will I. And most importantly, if you have any self-respect left, you'll cut it out for your own benefit.'

'Bloody hell! I wish you'd stayed home tonight' Glen chuckled, his usual cockiness returning to his voice.

Jones pointed at the screen above the bar showing reruns of the race riots which had caused so much damage in Sydney and Melbourne the past week.

'Things are really unravelling. If they can't get things under control soon, they're going to have to send in the army.'

'Yea...' Glen cracked some ice in his teeth and grimaced. It was an awful situation.

'At some point, they're going to drag you back into this, you know.' Jones said. Glen gave him a sideways glance.

'That's what Alice said,' he muttered.

'She's right. Yep. They're not going to paint you as a hero though, so play your cards carefully when they call you, you understand?' Glen nodded. Two people he respected most in the world were coming to the same conclusions, so he had to consider the possibility, however ridiculous it seemed. He was suddenly keenly aware of the group of Indian men on the other side of the bar who'd been staring his way for the better part of the last hour.

'Check it out,' Jones said, pointing to the screen above the bar.

'...riots in Australian capital cities. At peak hour on Wednesday, over two-hundred thousand Indian and other south-east Asian immigrants gathered in George St, Sydney's busiest thoroughfare, to protest the government and the Navy. The protestors pelted rocks and bottles at riot-police who tried to disperse the crowd.' The camera zoomed in on a group burning an effigy of an Australian sailor.

'Burning effigies in the streets. I didn't think we did that, here,' said Robertson quietly.

Jones patted his friend on the back. 'You're much more handsome than he is, don't worry, son.'

The footage continued: Police had moved in with shields and batons to arrest protestors, who fought back. They were capsicum sprayed, hog-tied and hauled into police wagons. The crowd rushed the police line, swamping it in moments, then rampaging down George Street, smashing cars and shopfronts; trampling everyone in their way.' The anchor continued breathlessly; '...eight police and twelve protestors dead, with hundreds arrested. Earlier today, Premier McGibbon declared a state of emergency and requested military aid from Canberra to bring order to the streets...'

It was the same in Melbourne, Brisbane, and Perth. More rioting, more damage, more deaths. Australia had never seen anything like it.

'Jesus, Jonesy. What have I done?'

His friend clapped him on the back. 'Look, Glen. I know you're feeling a bit down about all those refugees, losing your command, starting a war and probably losing your girl. But in your self-centred, world-revolves-around-me way, you're forgetting two very important things.'

'But fortunately, you're going to remind me of them.'

'I am!' He hefted another whiskey. A smoother one. 'Firstly, this was all gonna go down anyway. You're not quite as important as you think you are. Indians and Pakis, Arabs, Muslims and Jews, Christians, Russians, Chinese and Japs, they all hate each other's guts and the world has run out of space. What do you think is going to happen?'

'I know all that. It's...difficult being the guy that brought it to Australia.'

'Rubbish. We brought it upon ourselves. We should've got on the green bandwagon. Then we'd at least have moral high ground for turning those ships back. I mean, we had to do it, either way, can't let them all in, but the way we went about it makes us look like gold plated assholes, doesn't it.'

'Yea. You could say that. What's the other thing I'm forgetting?'

'Well, obviously, you make me feel morally superior. When we go out from now on, no matter how obnoxious I behave, I'll never be the most hated man in the room. It's carte blanche to behave like a pig,' he said, smacking his lips.

Robertson laughed. 'You're such a dickhead, thank you,' he began, but Jones was distracted by the TV. The news was running a profile story on Robertson, tracing his career through the navy. His face floated in a cutaway on the top corner of the screen while the anchor described the botched refugee mission he'd been part of fifteen years ago. Talk in the pub slowly ceased as people nudged each other, pointing at him. Suddenly the only sound was the TV voiceover; '...not for the first time, Captain Robertson has been involved in the slaughter of innocent boat people...his commanding officer at the time, Jayden Jones, was discharged from the navy...' and the clunk of glass on wood as the old men in the corner put their drinks down and looked around in confusion at the menacing silence.

The big group of Indian men stared at them.

'Looks like you're equal most hated man in the room, Jayden,' said Glen out of the corner of his mouth.

'I think we're in deep shit,' muttered Jones.

'You reckon?'

'I do.'

'Think we should leave?'

'I'm still thinking about it,' said Jones sardonically.

A big man, with a thick black beard and low buttoned shirt, approached them. 'Well, well. Look what we have here. Captain Glen fucking Robertson, out for a drink with his boyfriend.' Thick chest hair plumed out of his shirt, and he'd wrapped an Indian flag bandana around his head. He spread his arms wide and turned to his friends. 'Looks like it's our lucky day. What do you think of that, Captain fucking Robertson?' he grinned.

Robertson was estimating the numbers with the big man. Five, ten, maybe twenty drunk, angry men ready to do violence. They could've been in any of the mobs that had been trashing the city. Probably were.

'What've you got to say for yourself, mate? Not so tough now, are you? No playing God now, with none of your Navy buddies to back you up.'

'I won't hold it against you if you want to slide on out of here…' Robertson said out of the corner of his mouth to his friend.

'Fuck you, Glen,' Jones said dismissively. 'You ready for this? We probably should've noticed them before now,' he finished under his breath.

'I was captivated by your conversation,' he muttered back. 'It's Commodore Robertson,' he said more loudly to the Indians. 'Not Captain. You will address me with the correct rank.'

Hairy-chest took a step forward, and some of his friends moved to cover the door. Robertson's eyes darted around, searching for a weapon. There were the whiskey glasses, but he didn't want to go there just yet. Nothing else was near to hand.

'You're a murdering bastard and a child-killing, racist piece of shit.' He stepped up to Robertson's face, hot beer breath in his nostrils, spittle landing on his skin. 'The bastards running this country, bastards just like you, think they're better than the rest of the world.'

Jones cleared his throat. 'You have to admit, we do have a superior kill ratio,' he said.

'*Jesus Jonesy,*' Robertson had time to mutter partly in wry amusement, part shock at the audacity of the comment...then the bar exploded. A stool went through a window, and glasses smashed above the bar. Hairy-chest shoved Robertson in the chest and he slammed into the counter. Jones wrapped his arm around the man's throat and squeezed, hard. Robertson elbowed him in the face. Twice. Good connections, resulting in bone-shattering each time. Another man sprung forward. He grabbed Robertson's shirt and threw his fist straight at his head. At the last second Robertson ducked and took it on the top of his skull.

Crrrunch, light exploded behind his eyes.

He sagged, struggling to stay conscious, and forced his muscles to work. His attacker threw another punch and closed, leading with his head. Robertson had no room to swing his arm. Instead, he crouched and sprang, arcing his elbow onto the point of the new guy's chin. Felt bone crush bone and watched in fascination as the guy's head snapped back sickeningly, teeth splintering. Blood spurted from his mouth, and a piece of tooth hit Robertson as he went down.

Must've bitten his tongue.

He dodged a flying fist, stiffened his arm and caught the man's jaw with his forearm. The big guy dropped like a book off a shelf, but the next giant Indian was already diving towards him. He turned at the last minute, absorbing some of the impact but was still slammed back against the bar. A fist connected with his eye socket, cutting him. One guy was around his legs, pinning him. With nowhere to move, he wrapped his arms around that guys' throat and pulled him in tight. Rolling to the ground he positioned the guy on top of him and...squeezed. He felt the trachea cracking and his face turning purple as he clutched at the forearm crushing his windpipe. Robertson shuddered but held on. If he could use the use this guy as a shield, it might save him from the worst of what was coming.

From the ground he glimpsed Jones knock over a stool as he backed away, then pivot and punch someone clean in the face. The guy pitched forward in slow motion, not even on the ground when two more assailants rushed his old CO, dragging him to the ground.

'Hang on, Jonesy!' Glen roared into the mayhem, as three men moved towards him.

The first man sized up the gap between the floor and the man Robertson was choking, planted his hind leg, and sent his other booted foot hurtling towards Glen. Robertson tried to shift, but the kick found its mark, cracking one of his ribs. Pain streaked through his side, like someone twisting a knife, then a second man grabbed his friend and started dragging him, and Robertson still clinging to the man's neck, across the floor. Robertson gave the neck another squeeze - the man scrabbled weakly now, virtually unconscious.

Struggling with his continued consciousness, Robertson let his hostage go and staggered to his feet just as the kicker teed off on him again. His boot smashed into Robertson's arms, which he'd covered his head with, just in time. He absorbed some of the kick and clamped down on the man's leg with a tight ball and socket grip. Fresh adrenaline surged through his system, giving him enough strength to rise to his feet, levering the captured leg and twisting it violently as he rose and driving his attacker into the floor with a sickening crunch. He thought he felt a knee ligament snap and then the third man's fist crashed

136

into Robertson's broken rib. Pain and light flashed through his skull and he staggered sideways into a stool, picked it up and broke it over the man's chest.

This bought him a few seconds to search frantically for Jones…There! He was balled up on the floor, surrounded by men who were taking turns kicking and stomping him. Robertson roared and flew into the group, cracking skulls together and pushing men to the floor. He offered a hand to Jones who staggered up, bloodied and beaten. A burly security guard pushed his way in, trying to shepherd the two swollen sailors to the exit.

'Stay together and we can force our way out!' the security guard, called out.

They began pushing through the crowd as a trio, riding the punches. The guard dropped, hit from behind. Robertson grabbed his shirt as a second guard stepped in, smearing someone's nose across his face with a brutal right hand, blood spraying. For a moment the mob pulled back, realising that in bar fights, unlike riots, people fought back.

On some unknown cue, they swarmed forward, and quickly both guards were on the ground under a hail of boots. Robertson glimpsed one holding his head with his arms; the other was lying unconscious on his side, and still, the kicks landed, to his head and body. Other men picked up furniture and hurled it over the bar. Another group climbed the counter and began to pummel the barman. A bargirl cowered against a fridge in terror as she watched her manager get beaten to a bloody pulp.

'Move!' He grabbed Jones's shirt, and they staggered outside.

'Jesus Christ! What just happened,' muttered Jones thickly as they limped down the street.

'You don't look so good,' said Robertson. Blood was streaming down his friend's face.

'Neither do you. Are your ribs broken? You're breathing shallow.' Robertson was hunched over, protecting his side.

137

'Yea, I think so. Let's get the fuck out of here.' He felt his face swelling up already. Jones was a mess, gashes above his eyes fanning blood down his cheeks, arms black and red from the kicks.

They heard the door crash open behind them and turned to see the mob streaming out of the pub, sprinting up the street towards them.

Sirens wailed in the distance - they were close and would arrive very soon. But too far to stop the mob from reaching them first.

There was nowhere to run. Nothing to use as a weapon. The two friends looked at each other, then charged towards the onrushing gang. Using their bodies as cannonballs they smashed into the crowd, Robertson felt rather than saw Jones go down beside him. Had time to connect his fist to one man's jaw then was knocked off his feet. He lay huddled in a tight ball, arms over his head while the blows rained down. The last thing he heard before darkness came was the screech of tyres as the riot squad arrived.

Chapter 12
September 5th, 2300 hours
Parliament House, Canberra

Lafitte slipped off her shoes and undid her jacket. She was back in her office, again, behind her desk. The lights were dim to reflect the late hour and the blinds were open. She glanced briefly out the windows at the distant twinkling lights of Canberra and sighed. Defense Minister Nick Whittey sat to her left and was not troubling to hide his displeasure at having to attend this meeting.

God, he was sick of this, he thought. His wife was cooking lamb chops and had promised him a massage tonight, but he'd had to cancel and come here to listen to some fusty, self-satisfied egghead. He leaned on the table, put his head in his hands and rubbed his eyes, blocked out the light and massaged his eyeballs. Nice and deep, really jammed his knuckles in there. Felt good. Images of lamb chops flitted across the back of his eyelids. He swore he could smell them and emitted an unwitting low groan of despair. On his left sat Louise Abbott. He heard her sighing. As if she was above it all.

'Aah...mm...' he grunted, feeling tension wash away. For a moment he even forgot about the giant, steaming canyon of shit his government, indeed, his country, seemed to be paddling up at full speed. Reluctantly he opened his eyes, seeing double for a few moments while his eyeballs realigned themselves. As he'd feared, Lafitte was still there, back ramrod straight, elegant face composed (if a little more haggard than usual), clearly expecting him to live up to the superhuman standards she set for herself (and presumably, being moderately and permanently disappointed). God, there was one gorgeous, but buttoned-up woman. He was glad she was such a pain in the ass, it was the only thing that made being around her bearable.

And there was Abbott, watching him like he'd just farted in bed. He got along with Abbott at least, as far as you could get along with such an ambitious snake. Except she kept throwing ridiculous objections to the Indian problem into the mix, on *humane* grounds. And somehow she'd caught Jacqui's ear, at least enough to stay her hand on the obvious military solutions while she explored other options.

Hopefully, the smug nerd in the ill-fitting green jacket sitting in front of them, Apostolos Giovanoglou, would change her mind. The opportunity cost this man represented, reflected Whittey, was four, possibly five succulent, well-crumbed lamb chops. Giovanoglou's jacket, Whittey noted with consternation, had elbow patches, which, in Whittey's experience, was a sure sign the meeting would go far longer than necessary.

Lafitte had come to the same conclusions as her defence minister. She rested her red-rimmed gaze on Giovanoglou, an internationally feted professor of applied mathematics at ANU, a fellow of the Lowy Institute and the International Institute for Strategic Studies in Washington. He was feted as one of the most brilliant strategic forecasters in Australia. Her husband ran a strategic risk consultancy, and when she'd asked who he recommended in this sphere, he'd recommended Apostolos without hesitation.

Whittey shook her head. It took a particular type of conceit to be at once so independently wealthy yet so poorly dressed.

'Jacqueline, I'm afraid I can't give you a specific answer about where things will head based on your current policy setting. Nobody can predict the future, and no machine can either.'

The politicians shared bemused looks.

'Well shit,' said Whittey. 'What the hell do all those investment banks pay you for?'

'On the other hand,' said Apostolos, ignoring Whittey completely, 'it is possible to look at the international system and discern what attributes it's displaying. From there we can make general, educated guesses about what might happen.'

Lafitte shared a look with Whittey. His face echoed what she was thinking.

'Apostolos, we have a choice. If we let the illegals in, they'll come in millions and Australia will cease to exist as we know it. If we block them, we'll go to war. I need to know if I'm making the right decisions, or if there's a third way I'm not seeing.'

'Of course, Jacqui; may I call you Jacqui?' She waved him on. 'I understand the predicament,' he said, pulling a faux-vintage e-pipe out of his jacket pocket. 'Do you mind if I smoke?'

Lafitte blinked. 'Go ahead,' she said, a little impatiently. Apostolos nodded in appreciation and drew deeply from the pipe, exhaling vapour with obvious relish.

'Thank you. I admit, it's a vulgar habit, but it's become a crutch for me over the years. It helps me order my thoughts.'

'...Jesus...' muttered Whittey under his breath.

'If it helps you get to the point, I'd consider it a small price to pay,' said Lafitte.

'Hmm,' said Apostolos, slipping his pipe away. 'Jacqui, the international system is extremely complex. In academia, we have a term for systems like it. They're called, rather conveniently, *complex systems*. The biosphere, the stock market, and so on are all such systems.'

'We're aware this is a complicated situation,' said Abbott. 'Do you have any insights we might have missed?'

'Not complicated,' said Apostolos sharply. 'Complex. They mean different things. A complex system has specific properties. It's resilient; resisting and absorbing change...until it breaks. Think; the world financial system before the Global Financial Crisis of 2008. Even though it defied all logic, prices went up to ridiculous levels, people kept investing, and the system absorbed incredible distortions and nobody, or at least irrelevantly few people, were the wiser...' he nodded gravely, staring distantly at the desk. 'Yes...such incredible resilience.' A pause, then more brightly; 'You can predict *what* will happen but not *when* it will happen.'

'If we could predict the future,' said Whittey, 'we'd all be on a desert island getting fed dates by mermaids.' He looked at the women. 'I would be anyway. You said you could predict what *can* happen? That would be better than nothing.'

'Bear with me, you'll get your answer,' said the professor. 'Analysts, strategy types, and so on usually look at trends and see normal distribution curves. The further from the mean, the less likely it is to occur. Now, that's fine if you want to reliably predict how likely it is that someone two metres tall will come through the door. Complex systems don't work like that. That analysis can't predict 'black swan' events.'

Lafitte rubbed her eyes. 'You're saying we didn't see this coming because we've been studying it wrong?'

'In a nutshell, yes. Although you can never tell when things are going to happen, you should be able to predict what will happen.'

Abbott jumped in; 'How do you even know if a system is complex in the first place?'

The professor absent-mindedly took the e-pipe out again. 'Such arrangements,' he said, pausing to inhale, 'are ones with moderate diversity, for example, relatively few types of actors or agents. An example you'll recognise is nation-states.' Cinnamon-strudel aroma wafted through the room. Whittey resisted the temptation to pick at crumbs on his plate leftover from lunch.

'It's simple to discern other characteristics of complex systems in global politics: Nations all interact to a reasonable degree with each other, for example through political forums or war, and are interconnected with each other as well, in this example, through trade and economics. Finally, each nation can adapt, to varying degrees. Now, this interaction and influence is not recognised in standard decision-making processes, where decisions are made as if in a vacuum.'

142

'Not so sure about that,' said Whittey, moving the plate further away. 'Obviously, we try to anticipate what impact our actions will have.'

Apostolos shook his head minutely. 'Of course, you're trying, Nick. But you're probably failing, not least because everybody else is doing the same thing. Feedback loops and so on. You can't predict this type of system; it takes too much computing power to be practical. That's one reason over eighty percent of brokers and fund managers consistently underperform the market, even though it's mostly algorithm-based. They try to predict the performance not only of the underlying asset but also the market - in which they participate - on the price of the stock. Since they interact with each other, they create feedback which induces adaptability.'

Lafitte frowned. 'By that logic, diplomatic activity is a waste of time; which is demonstrably not the case.'

'In truth, most diplomatic activity just cancels itself out. Our failure is not recognizing that the system itself is changing. It's why Australia has gone from a well-respected international citizen...' he shrugged, 'to where we are today. Take our hard line on boat people for example; so many people are refugees of some type these days, they have a critical mass, a political voice.'

'How can you be sure this isn't just another crisis, and that the system itself is changing?' asked Abbott.

The professor examined his pipe. 'Jacquie, Louise...Nick. A system works, and absorbs imbalances until the imbalances overpower its inbuilt stability; its self-reinforcing nature.' He shifted his gaze to the politicians. 'Think of a pyramid. Slice the top off, so that it's more of a parallelogram, then invert it, and we'll call it the economy. If you pile things on top of it, in a nice balanced way, it will grow upwards, getting ever larger. A nice growing economy, we all like those, without a hitch, small at the bottom, getting wider at the top. Now in the real world, vested interests, poor decisions, and unexpected events mean that more is added to one side than the other. Over time it creates an imbalance, but since it hasn't fallen over before, nobody is too worried. One day the pyramid starts to wobble. Two things happen. Firstly, the wobbling helps redistribute things more evenly, like a bucket of sand that flattens out when you shake it. This is called creative destruction. Secondly, people and politicians run around, shifting things around to restore balance. Sometimes, when they're showing unusual foresight, they shift things around before things start wobbling.' He smiled brightly. 'But let's be realistic here. Usually, they only do so much because the wobbling fixes itself…and usually, they're hobbled, or at least influenced by special interest groups who like things just the way they are,' he said.

'Recessions and financial crises,' said Lafitte, unimpressed. 'These aren't cutting edge concepts, Professor.'

The professor continued patiently, 'Recessions and financial crises, correct. If you're talking about the financial system. But we're talking about the international system, where a wobble is a war. We're talking about the world's biosphere, where instability in our pyramid means droughts and violent storms, permanently changed weather patterns. But you missed a step, Prime Minister. Eventually, the imbalance overpowers the inbuilt stabilisation mechanism, and the pyramid, which has been upright for so long, falls over. That is what's happening now; our system is breaking. Currently, our pyramid is in freefall. This hasn't happened for hundreds of years. Nobody knows what's going to happen when it hits the ground.'

'Look, Apostolos,' said Abbott, 'it's ok if you don't have any new insights. Nobody else does either.'

Apostolos sighed. He had given up on the foreign minister. At least the PM was looking at the professor with renewed intent. He went on, 'The insight I have for you is this: Firstly, the

144

biosphere, the environment, is undergoing a systemic change and nobody knows what the new normal will be.'

'This is not news,' said Whittey impatiently.

'But it is,' snapped Apostolos. 'It's news because billions of people don't know where to plant crops, or how to stop them from being destroyed by storms and drought. This massive dislocation, in turn, is stressing the international political system, to such a degree that I believe that system is in flux too, searching for a new equilibrium.'

Lafitte exhaled. 'There's no third way...' she said in a tired voice. 'The big revelation is that no matter what there's going to be conflict and things will change permanently.'

The professor leaned back in his chair, satisfied that at least the Prime Minister understood.

'Just great,' muttered Whittey, 'I get the privilege of watching the system collapse just as I hit the peak of my career.'

Abbott snorted, 'Stop whining Nick, it's probably your fault, somehow.'

The professor frowned, while the PM looked suspiciously like she was suppressing a smile. 'You asked what was likely to happen,' he said. 'Well, I'm telling you. The system is broken and searching for a new normal. In the meantime, you get to choose war or a massive influx of refugees.'
He shrugged, 'Personally, I think both options lead to each other, so it doesn't make any difference what you do...but, as I keep saying, who knows where the pyramid will land?'

A knock sounded on the door, and an aide poked her head into the room.

'Sorry to interrupt,' she said after Lafitte waved her in. 'We've received urgent word from Defence that the navy has engaged Indian forces off the West Coast. We're waiting for details, but the navy is in a full-scale naval engagement, and the refugee ships are still heading for the coast.'

Lafitte looked at Apostolos sharply, who gave the slightest shrug. 'It's starting already,' she breathed. She hadn't believed but had desperately hoped there was some course of action, a set of decisions she could take that would make this problem evaporate. Reality had suddenly, brutally snapped into focus.

All Lafitte could see was blood and flames.

Chapter 13
Sydney
September 6th, 1030 hours

He tried to open his eyes, but the lids seemed stuck together. He pulled harder, and his lashes made little cracking sounds as the sleep-induced gunk holding them together peeled open. Grainy crap dropped into his eyes, making them water. He lay very still. Light filtered past the curtains in the lounge room window. It was impossible to sleep. Every part of him aching, and his ribs...each breath felt like someone was grinding shards of glass into his side. He would have shaken his head ruefully, but his neck was locked stiff, and his brain was throbbing against his skull. Glancing at the table next to the fold-out couch, he searched for the little white box. *There you are.* All he had to do was reach across - but to reach across he had to roll over, and that meant using his side muscles...*This is ridiculous.* He wormed his way across the bed an inch at a time and got his hand on the industrial-strength painkillers the doctor had given him before she discharged him from hospital the night before. Hospital-grade drugs. The good stuff. There's even a silver lining to getting bashed, he thought. Maybe he was picking up some of Jonesy's optimism.

The doc had looked at him disapprovingly and told him he'd been very lucky; he'd presented with severe bruising on his face, arms and back. And of course his side, but apart from a few ribs, only his eye socket was fractured. Can't set either of those, so they'd dosed him up on morphine, and sent him home with a tersely delivered warning to take it easy until his face and ribs healed. No permanent damage, she'd said.

Moments after their heroic, but mostly symbolic, charge into the angry mob, who'd made the most of their chance to generally beat the sense out of them, the cops had arrived. After days of rioting and violence, they hadn't come in with a soft touch. Armed with tasers and rubber bullets, they'd approached the mob from both ends of the street, cutting off any escape, and opened fire from a distance. Robertson had briefly regained consciousness on the ground to the popping of gunfire. The cops hadn't waited for people to stop resisting or hit the ground - it seemed to Robertson like they'd only stopped shooting when their bullets had run out. The police had then walked in and severely bashed anything that moved until everyone was face down, hands zip-tied behind their back, most definitely not resisting or talking back.

Robertson and Jones were admitted to St Vincent's Hospital, where Jonesy was sent to intensive care. He had bleeding on the brain, and they needed to drill into his skull to release the pressure.

'He'll be fine if you get out of our way and let us do our job,' the surgeon had said to him. 'The best thing you can do is go home and come back in the morning. He'll be under the whole time anyway; you won't miss anything.'

Robertson forced himself into a sitting position, fighting for every inch and wondered where Alice was. She wasn't there when he came home, but he'd been too sore to notice and passed out on the couch. He checked his phone. *Five missed calls. Shit.* He dialled her number - no answer.
He popped four morphine pills out of the blister pack, washed them down with water. Was overcome by the sudden urge to piss.

He'd put his phone on the toilet tank, and as blood-streaked urine tinkled into the bowl, it vibrated. He peered through gummy eyes. It was a video message. From Alice. *Oh no...* He'd planned on going home last night. After what Jonesy had said - to make things right again. But then they'd been jumped, and spent hours in hospital. He'd been discharged well past midnight, and he didn't think his face in current condition would inspire the reaction he desired.

He glanced at himself in the mirror above the toilet. Lips swollen spastically, face a rainbow of blue, black and maroon

148

palettes, left eye looking like a split plum, swollen shut. His face was covered in antiseptic cream giving it a greasy sheen. *What a mess.*

'Play,' he croaked.

Her face appeared on the screen. Piercingly intelligent brown eyes stared at him. Her lips were paused slightly apart while the video buffered. It gave her a childlike appearance.

She was quite beautiful, he marvelled for the thousandth time. Not in-your-face beauty, but the type of woman who gets more attractive the more you stared at her, the more you understood who she was.

He wondered what she wanted.

'Glen, I heard about what happened last night. We've been monitoring the rioters - some online personality is directing them, and we track their movements. Your name was flagged. You and Jayden.' Her eyes flashed, caught somewhere between anger and concern. 'What the hell were you thinking, going to a place like that?' She shook her head. 'Anyway, it doesn't matter anymore. I'm just letting you know I've been seconded to Operational Command and I'm flying back to Perth tomorrow. .'

Robertson swore softly as a pit opened in his stomach.

'I don't know when we'll see each other again.' Her eyes seemed to bore into his head. 'But Glen, when we do, we need to talk.'

The image disappeared.

Robertson stood, cock in hand, and tried to process what had happened. He simultaneously marvelled and rued how women did that; tell you you're in deep shit, but not what why (although in this case, he could hazard a guess) or what they intended to do about it, so it stewed in your mind like a saucepan boiling over.

Half the punishment, he supposed.

Her words sank in. She was right! In what universe could it possibly have been a good idea to go drinking last night, anywhere at all? He was the most hated man in Australia! She'd only echoed what Jonesy had been saying.

He started suddenly, as something cracked inside him. He tried to process how he'd felt before the morphine kicked in.

People he respected kept telling him he wasn't responsible for the deaths, for the riots, and now for his friend who was recovering from having a hole drilled into his brain.

Maybe it was time to stop feeling guilty. Maybe it was time to stop blaming himself for events much more significant than him, than any one person. Alice had been right, he was pathetic, wallowing in self-absorbed misery, and Jones had been right too - who did he think he was, able to do so much damage single-handed? He wasn't God, or even that ice-hearted Jacqui Laffite, pulling strings on an entire nation.

Resolve washed through him. Or was it the morphine kicking in? Fucking hell, he never even knew what he was feeling anymore. Well, something washed through him, and it was telling him to get off the booze, to get off the painkillers, and to stand up and be counted. He was a Commodore in the Australian Navy, and somehow he was going to make it his business to help his country through this crisis.

He limped back into his bedroom. His back was a little straighter though, and his one visible eye was now glinting, where before there had been only dull lifelessness. Picked up the painkillers regarding them for a moment. Crunched them up and threw them back through the bathroom door, into the toilet. No more dulling of his senses. If the price was some pain, well so much the better to remind him of why he was fighting.

His phone vibrated again. Someone was calling. He ordered it to pick up, and Commodore Leighton Swan's craggy, bulldog head appeared. Robertson's commanding officer, his ruddy jowls merged with his neck, which was much shorter than it was wide. Robertson thought his CO's head looked like a well-used chopping block. Swan thought Robertson was a maverick, a new age touchy-feely sailor who cared too much about his crews and too little about his commanding officer's requirements. He'd been amazed when Robertson sent that torpedo into that bulker. Didn't think he had it in him.

As far as Robertson was concerned, his CO was a man for whom strict adherence to protocol substituted for any sort of imagination, lateral thinking, and intelligence in general. They had a delicate relationship.

'Robertson. How have you been keeping,' he barked. Swan didn't ask questions; he demanded answers. Even if he had no interest in the reply.

Robertson automatically stood up a little straighter. 'Morning Commander. Just fine, thank you,' he mumbled around his split, swollen lips.

'You look like shit.'

'Yes, sir.'

'I'd heard reports that you've been flagellating yourself with guilt about all those refugees you drowned. Like a Catholic in confession. Apparently, they weren't exaggerated.'

'Sir. This,' he gestured at his face, 'isn't entirely self-inflicted. And it looks worse than it is.'

'That's a shame. Because it doesn't look that bad to me,' snapped Swan. 'Nothing more than you deserve, the disgraceful way you've been conducting yourself the last few weeks.'

'Yes, sir. May I ask what this call is about?'

'You may,' his CO growled. 'This call is about the fact that the Navy is down one destroyer captain, a role for which you, theoretically a least, are qualified. Therefore, this call is about the urgent and unfortunate requirement the navy has for you remove your head from deep inside your ass because, despite strong and wide-ranging misgivings held by not only myself but the entire chain of command, you are being recalled to active duty, effective immediately.'

For a moment, he was too surprised to speak. He could barely keep the grin off his face, even though he knew it would cause his lips to crack.

'Do you understand, Captain Robertson?'

He nodded, careful to keep excessive enthusiasm from his voice; 'Yes sir, fully understood. Where am I reporting to?'

'A driver is already on the way. You're reporting to Garden Island, where you'll be briefed then shipped out to the *Hobart* which is undergoing repairs in Perth.'

'Yes sir, thank you, sir!'

'Is that a smile? Are you trying to smile at me, Robertson? Wipe it off your face. Consider this a wartime contingency, not vindication of your record or ability.'

'Yes, sir.'

'And Robertson. What is that greasy slop all over your face. It makes you look like a drug addict in remission. Wash it off. Your head is already testament to the fact you're useless in a bar fight, no need to advertise that you're an alcoholic as well.' The projection disappeared.

The words were supposed to sting, but Robertson didn't care.

He was back.

Chapter 14
September 8th, 1900 hours
Canberra

Jacqui Lafitte glanced at her watch and sighed. Twenty-seven minutes past the hour. She'd been hopeful, if not optimistic, that the meeting would start on the hour as scheduled. She was about to ask her aide to get another cup of tea when the screen on the wall blinked. President Cain was calling.

'Good to see you again, Marion,' said Jacqui when his face appeared on the screen.

'You too, Jacqui. Hope I didn't keep you waiting,' said Cain brusquely. He wasn't looking forward to this conversation. 'Louise, Nick, nice to see you both again,' he said to Lafitte's ministers who were sitting next to her.

Lafitte shared a sidelong look with Whittey, while Cain went on.

'I'm afraid I have to keep this brief. I've got a hundred boxes to tick today, and the list keeps growing.'

Abbott glanced at Jacqui. Cain was always business, but today he seemed even more arms-length than usual. If the Prime Minister was worried, it didn't show.

'Suits us,' said Lafitte. 'Things are moving very quickly. When we last spoke, I asked for a commitment from the United States that you would honour your ANZUS treaty obligations should tensions between Australia and India escalate into a shooting war. Regretfully, in the last twenty-four hours, the Indians came to our waters and sank two frigates, damaged a destroyer and grounded three more of those freighters on Oakajee Beach.

'Now, we've mobilised most of our fleet to the Indian Ocean and are tracking another *five* bulkers moving through the Andaman Sea, off Indonesia. Two hundred miles from them are five Indian warships, who appear to be escorting them. We will not cede our borders, and the Indians are intent on shipping their people here under armed escort. We're at war, Marion.'

He spread his hands. 'We're in a tough situation here guys. Have you exhausted all diplomatic options?'

'Discussions with the Indian leadership aren't going well,' said Jacqui.

There was a pregnant pause.

'As I'm sure you can appreciate, we can't just take up arms against India. They're too big, too powerful, but more important; they're the main part of our China containment strategy. Have been for the last twenty years. You know this, Jacqui.'

Jacqui clasped her hands on the desk. She wanted to reach down the line and wrap her fingers around Cain's neck; instead, she waited impassively.

Cain shrugged. 'As you also know, we have commitments to various other nations in the region which are designed to keep China in check.'

'We're aware of your commitments, Marion. That's why we're here,' said Abbott, a touch of venom lacing her words.

'The dilemma we have is this: If we openly back Australia, China may be more assertive in the South China Sea because they'll feel we're distracted. Besides, India is China's biggest rival in Asia. Nothing would make the Chinese happier than to see us at each other's throats.'

'Nothing would make the Chinese happier than seeing the US renege on its longest-standing alliance,' said Whittey. 'Your credibility will be shot to pieces, and it'll be every man for himself in southeast Asia.'

'That's not our assessment, Nick. Other weather-exposed nations we have security arrangements with - the Philippines, Indonesia, and so on, are very supportive of India's position. We can't have them thinking we'll turn on them over what is essentially a refugee problem. If we let that happen, it opens the whole region up to manipulation.' He shrugged again. 'The

154

fact they're climate refugees does you no favours. One pm my time I'm going to make a statement on the matter. I'll be reaffirming our commitment to the regional alliances we have and outlining our policy when it comes to refugee flows.

'Your selective policy regarding refugee flows,' said Whittey.

'Which in this specific case is to do nothing,' said Lafitte flatly.

'Jacqui,' Cain said squarely to the Prime Minister. 'At this stage, we feel there is scope for Australia and India to work out their differences, and as such, we're going to continue to monitor the situation.'

'What is there to monitor?' barked Whittey. 'We're at war; you're our ally. You honour the treaty. What am I missing here?'

'This *is* a test case, Marion,' said Lafitte pointedly. 'My response was in large part formulated on the premise that the US would back Australia in the event of an escalation. You gave me your personal assurances. If you've led us down the garden path, it will do irreparable damage to our alliance.'

'We thought that by backing you publicly, the Indians would back down. But they called our bluff. The fact is, their importance in containing China is more important to the US than Australia's problem with its refugees.'

'Great. Just great,' seethed Whittey. 'You're a real piece of work, Cain.'

Cain gritted his teeth. Lafitte's eyes sparkled; there was no friendship in them anymore.

'Marion, if you abandon us, the whole idea of sovereign borders goes down the drain. You'll have Africans streaming into Europe and even more Mexicans pushing north than you do now. If you leave us hanging being an ally of the United States will become meaningless.' Lafitte pointed at the man on the screen. 'We've been at your side in literally every war you've waged since 1900. All that blood was supposed to buy something, Cain.'

155

Cain gritted his teeth. 'I know, Jacqui. This is an incredibly unfortunate state of affairs. We'll throw our diplomatic weight behind you, don't worry about that. The issue is that the international community has already judged you. You can't wash your hands of warming. Nobody can.'

'But that's exactly what you're doing,' accused Lafitte.

'Look around, Jacqui. Warming is killing your neighbours. They're falling apart, they can't feed themselves, and they need scapegoats. You're rich, isolated, and to blame. You know how this works.'

Whittey snorted. 'So what if nobody likes us? Since when was being popular a prerequisite for a workable alliance with the US? Everybody hates the Israelis, or the Saudis but you're not pulling any punches in the Middle East.'

'We can't just pick a side this time, Nick. We can't go to war - we can't even support a nation at war - with India. The Chinese have enough of their own problems to possibly do something really stupid, like invade Taiwan - but only *if* containment fails. We're just not up to doing it alone anymore. We need the Indians.'

'What's the point of those damned marines in Darwin,' said Abbott angrily, 'if you're not going to deploy them when we need it?'

'They're for China, not India. Don't obtuse, Louise,' Cain snapped. 'You want me to unravel the entire regional power structure, and I won't.' He jabbed a finger into the desk. 'How did you let this happen? You let a tiny humanitarian crisis turn into open conflict.' He glared at the Australians. 'My view is there is scope for a diplomatic solution. Find one, and fast.'

Later that evening, Louise Abbott strode the halls of Parliament House, knocked once on Nick Whittey's office door, and let herself in.

The Defense Minister was leaning back on his chair, eyes closed, hands closed behind his back. Jaunty K-pop music wafted from speakers. His feet, clad in fluffy slippers appropriated from a cheap hotel, were crossed on his desk.

When Abbott let herself in his eyes flew open, and he nearly fell over backward in shock.

'Jesus woman, ever hear of knocking?' he grumbled.

'I did Nick; you didn't hear it,' she snapped. 'Switch on, it's time to stop playing the fool. And turn that ridiculous music off.'

'What do you think this is? You can't just barge in here, wake me up and call me an idiot,' he complained.

'I said you were a fool, not an idiot, but if the shoe fits. Now pay attention. We've just been hung right out to dry by the Americans. We signed that alliance in blood, literally, and that bastard Cain has completely stood us up.'

'He fucked us,' said Whittey angrily. 'We should consider kicking the marines out of Darwin for a start.'

'What are you talking about? The marines go nowhere. We still need them, useless though they may be. The point is that not only was the relationship supposed to be ironclad, but the PM staked our policy on her personal relationship with Cain. Follow?'

'Well, yea, she's blowing it. She should have made a hero out of Robertson when he sank the *Tamil Nadu,* not had the navy pull him off duty.'

'Exactly. She's too soft. Her judgment throughout this crisis has been...lacking. They're invaders, Nick, we should be treating them as such, not putting them up in package holiday standard accommodation when they storm our beaches.'

'Of course. We should be sending them straight back where they came from. Or stopping them coming in the first place.'

'Nick, somebody needs to push Laffite in the right direction on this. I'm going to take steps to make sure it happens. Can I count on your support?

Whittey leaned back and found his precarious balance point again. 'If it stops those boats, I'll back you all the way. Whatever it takes.'

Chapter 15
September 15th, 2330 hours
Sonagachi, North Kolkata

The black, saloon car picked its way through night time traffic towards Sonagachi in North Kolkata. Traffic created in equal parts by vehicles, animals, and humans, was unbearably heavy, forcing the saloon to crawl through the streets. Pushers skulked in alleys, and vendors sold what looked like dried fruit from wooden carts but was regular produce shrivelled from drought. Caged monkeys, dogs, and even a wilted peacock, stared mournfully, dodging pebbles lobbed by kids.

Religious and garden variety lunatics stood on crates shouting manifestos at the throng.

One of the many benefits of communism, thought Pham Dinh Vuong from the back seat, was that such people were assigned to an asylum. The Communist Party in his native Vietnam didn't tolerate religious fanatics.

The car drove past a group of snake-charmers sitting in a circle, antagonising cobras coiled in wicker baskets with droning flutes.

From the cocoon of the limousine, he noted the swathes of bored hookers crowding doorways and lining alleys, trying to catch the eyes of the businessmen, while simultaneously ignoring the small-time drug-pushers and black-market gangsters sauntering through the biggest red-light district on the continent; waiting for their turn to earn a few rupees. Women from all over, even some girls from his country, had slipped between the cracks and washed up here.

'Such a globalised world we live in, eh Cadeo?' he said to the tightly muscled man in a suit sitting impassively opposite him.

Many of the girls looked barely high-school age to Vuong. Their pre-pubescent attempts to be sexy would have been pathetically amusing if they weren't so sincere. Terribly sad, but who could escape the laws of supply and demand?

159

Cadeo grunted. 'People are pigs, no matter where they're from. Even more so here than home,' he said flatly.

'Far worse than pigs, Cadeo. They are people. And for that I am grateful, for how else would I have made my fortune?'

Cadeo affected a tiny, knowing smile. His boss liked to couch his self-congratulations in hokey philosophy. If you didn't know him, it would sound like sage wisdom.

Electronic billboards exhibited close-ups of impossibly perfect, naked bodies. It seemed ridiculous to Vuong, given the uninspiring reality of the flesh-and-blood examples thronging the street.

On the side of the road, the hookers eyes were lidded with boredom, occupied with more pragmatic tasks like sharing food, fixing each other's hair and gossiping.

Cadeo cast a critical eye over the scene. 'Perhaps I'm getting soft. These days I prefer the seamier aspects of the human condition at arms-length.'

'Or perhaps you've become used to the finer things in life. However, sometimes, we can't help but get our hands dirty.' Cadeo's willingness to get his hands dirty was precisely why he was Vuong's most trusted enforcer; the chances of him going soft were about as likely as Vuong sending his teenage daughter to Sonagachi on work experience.

The car had picked them up from Netaji Subhas Chandra Bose International Airport where they'd flown into from Ho Chi Minh City late that evening. Now, turning off Jatindra Mohan Road, onto Sovabazar, progress slowed to walking pace as the car filtered through swathes of pedestrians. A mangy dog cocked its leg and started to piss on a cart, yelping when the vendor sent it on its way with a well-aimed kick to the ribs. Passing schoolgirls cooed in sympathy for the dog.

Vuong noticed some older hookers intercept a group of young gangsters and attempt to seduce them into coming upstairs. They were receiving a lukewarm response.

160

Sonagachi was a giant brothel, drug den, black-market and party town, inhabited by people born into lives of prostitution, drug-dealing and crime; servicing the wealthy and elite of Kolkata city, and India as a whole. Extreme behaviour was unremarkable in Sonagachi, and ordinary people were driven away or crushed. With money, even the sickest, most depraved individuals could get whatever sexual or drug-induced high they craved; but with connections, you could go a step beyond and cash in on it all.

Which was exactly what he intended to do.

'Cadeo, we need to discuss our strategy. I want you to know why we're here, so you don't say the wrong thing out of ignorance. Izhar Khan has built a people-smuggling enterprise that would have made the 18th-century slave traders green with envy. Whilst it is incredibly profitable now, they are taking advantage of a soft Western nation that is still concerned about how other nations perceive it.'

'You don't think that will continue,' prompted Cadeo.

'It's a softness born out of security and prosperity. However, Australia is now no longer secure, so they will shed their softness in due course, and very shortly become closed to refugee shipments again. Meantime, as you know, in exchange for fake passports and passage to Western nations, we have secured from Afghan security forces thousands of small arms, automatic rifles and so on.'

'You already have some buyers for those,' said Cadeo, wondering where this was going.

'Yes but I want to sell *all* of them to Khan, in exchange for several boatloads of refugees. He can build the cost of the weapon into the cost of passage.'

Cadeo tried and failed to repress a laugh bubbling up from his throat, like a methane bubble in a peat bog. This idea was absurdly audacious, even for Vuong.

'We don't have several boatloads worth of guns, however,' Cadeo ventured.

'No, nor do we have several boatloads of refugees. But one ship should be ample to get rid of all our weapons, and we'll tell Khan we've got untold millions of people who want tickets to secure the relationship.'

The car stopped outside a pink-concrete façade, nestled between a hole-in-the-wall curry house, and one of the better-maintained brothels Vuong had seen. A giant security guard kept the red, wooden door clear of people queueing for a late-night snack. The door swung open as Vuong and Cadeo got out of the car, and a beautiful girl emerged to meet them. She looked about fifteen.

'Mr Vuong, sir, welcome to Kolkata. Mr. Khan hopes your trip from the airport was a pleasant one. Come this way, if you please,' she said coquettishly.

Vuong took one of her hands and guided it to his other, which had a roll of cash in it. The girl's eyes lit up momentarily, giving her a youthful aspect utterly out of character. 'After you, young lady,' he said with a smile. 'Thank you, Mr. Vuong, sir,' she said a little breathlessly and turned into the brothel. Vuong could feel Cadeo's look of wry surprise on his back. Vuong liked to be kind to the people in front of him so he could forget about the thousands of people who suffered unseen because of his business activities.

As he walked past, the bouncers nodded to him. He took a final look around and noticed the old hookers had changed tactics and were now goading the punks into coming inside. They were questioning their ability to please a real woman. The kids looked at each indecisively. He chuckled. Crafty old chooks. Those hookers weren't so different to him; in business, as in life, you had to do whatever it took to succeed.

Izhar Khan sat at a private booth in Rati's Emporium. Rati's was an exclusive underground bar, cabaret, and brothel, right in the guts of Sonagachi. Named after the Hindu goddess of carnal desire, Rati's was an understated, yet lavish, meeting place for Kolkata's wealthiest and most powerful men. Of all the venues in his portfolio, Khan had chosen this club because it was a considered combination of decadence and discretion. Nothing ostentatious tonight, only understated quality.

Not like him at all, according to his father, who espoused the view he was overstated mediocrity - on a good day.

Khan sucked back on a vaporiser loaded with cocaine. He remembered 'the old days' when you had to suck it right up your nose like a barbarian, but nowadays he could augment his already considerable charm and magnetism in a far more civilised manner. In truth, Khan didn't care how he got high - he'd stick the damned stuff up his ass if he had to! But he couldn't deny the vaporiser made it much more convenient, not to mention socially acceptable. He gulped down a beer and drummed a pattern on his legs. By God, the girls on tonight were truly excellent - he hoped his little chinki friends would be impressed. His most beguiling girls, gathered from all over Sonagachi; innocent-seeming yet seductive, an irresistible combination of coy shyness and magnetic beauty; willowy Africans, contrasting with gorgeously petite Thai girls, some bewitching, hard-edged Eastern Europeans - girls from every corner of the world; something for everyone! If his little chinki friends didn't appreciate the effort he'd gone to...well, he owned clubs catering to the homosexual crowd too, although he took more of a hands-off approach to managing those venues.

By God, he was thirsty.

'Izhar, yuvā mitra, you must keep your wits about you. No more,' said the old man sitting to his left, putting a restraining hand on Khan's arm. The man could have passed for twenty years his junior, except for the brilliant white hair on his head, eyebrows, and beard. If only he bothered to invest in some hair dye...but not everyone could afford to be as fashionable as Khan, he supposed. Dark, inscrutable eyes recessed deeply in a heavy brow, and a proud, aquiline nose gave the man an air of powerful nobility. Even in such a classy brothel, he seemed strangely out of place, as if he was too dignified maybe. The old man was right. Khan was wired like a junkie. He needed to focus during this meeting, 'Best to come back to earth a bit, eh?' Khan slurred back at the older man.

'Lina!' he shouted to the shimmering maître-d standing near the bar. The blonde, Swedish beauty glided towards him, her flat, honey-coloured stomach glistening in the dim light. She leaned down and spoke, a genuine smile lighting her perfect Nordic features. 'What can I get you, Izhar, my dear?' She rested her hand on his knee as Khan leaned across and auspiciously found himself level with her small, yet firm breasts.

He addressed her cleavage with a hoarse whisper, 'Lina darling, you know that you're my favourite, don't you? Another whiskey, the Japanese one. Straight up, a triple measure.'

'Of course,' she said, caressing his hand and only breaking eye contact to turn back to the bar.

By God these girls are good, thought Khan, idly wondering just how many bad decisions Lina had made to go from a private school in Stockholm to Rati's Emporium by the tender of age of twenty-two. Not that he cared of course - the girls staffing his clubs represented the summed total of thousands of bad decisions, which he was primed to take advantage of. Anyway, that whiskey would straighten him out a little, ease the old fossil's concerns. Drugs, Khan knew, were like gravity; what goes up must come down and frankly, it was better to manage the process yourself than let nature take its course.

Khan didn't like being babysat, but without Dilip Sood, the smuggling operation would still be just another good idea. Sood was a lifelong friend of his father, who in public was a scrupulously legitimate man. He was old friends with many leading politicians from both sides of the spectrum, but was nonetheless like a bridge connecting two sides of a river - one side home to the (nominally) tax-paying, socially responsible corporations of the New India, the other where buyers and sellers traded everything from drugs, passports, sex, weapons and influence.

India was neighbours with perennial basket cases Pakistan and further out, Afghanistan. Of course, there was money in passports, drugs, and weapons! Those barbarians loved that stuff, couldn't live without them. For decades, the only currencies in the outlying villages of southwestern Afghanistan had been guns, heroin, women and mobile phones. They weren't interested in anything else. Well, he was here to help. He was the oil that kept the giant Kolkata money machine rolling on, lending his contacts to people with that requirement - for a fee of course.

Enter Dilip Sood, a man who didn't exist in a boardroom or corporate tower, who was nonetheless one of Khan senior's most trusted associates, representing a partnership of over forty years with Izhar's father.

As for Izhar himself; by a cruel twist of fate, Khan senior, upon succumbing to his wife's nagging desire for one last child, had been saddled with his youngest, least bright, least competent, most indolent son Izhar, a profligate purveyor of decadence and perennial abdicator of responsibility. Perhaps his seed had passed its use-by date when fertilising the ovum that turned into his son, a man whose only reliable trait was chronic non-achievement; who had nevertheless pulled off the incredible - not only had he made a business out of this ridiculous people smuggling idea he'd come up with - but had gained military support from the government. The sheer audaciousness of it had impressed him: Izhar had pre-sold all the places to fund the purchase of the first ship, relying on Dilip Sood's connections to bring it all together.

Khan senior wondered if his son had finally grown up, but was more inclined to suppose every dog has its day, and that massive internal problems meant the Indian government was looking to unify the country against an external enemy.

165

The old enemy China was too powerful and Pakistan still (in theory) had nukes, but Australia only had a small, distant army, so was not to be feared, and conveniently was full of rich, white people, who everybody hated. And the stupid Aussies had gifted New Delhi a humanitarian cause to support.

So, as far as Khan senior was concerned, the stars had finally aligned for the son he wished he'd never had, but that didn't mean he was going to give him any more rope than strictly required to hang himself.

And that was why Dilip Sood sat next to a completely inebriated Izhar Khan, waiting calmly for their guests to arrive.

Vuong's hostess led him and Cadeo down a dark hallway that opened into a lavish private club. Antique lamps provided pools of dim orange lighting, and on a stage in the far corner, a beautiful black girl, draped in an artfully slitted gown, crooned nineteen-thirties jazz classics to a small backing band. Vuong's shoes made no sound on thick, red wine coloured carpet, and water cascaded down one wall, lit by luminescent blue lights from within. Men drew deeply on cigars and vaporisers loaded with drugs, creating various scented clouds that swirled around Vuong as he passed, like a ship through thick fog.

Their hostess led them to a table where two Indians and two foreigners sat. As they approached one stood, dressed in expensive silk slacks, velvet slippers and a white canvas shirt, noticeably strained around the middle.

'Mr Vuong, welcome! And your friend, Mr. Trang, is that right? Please, sit down! I'm so glad you came. I,' said the man with a self-deprecating bow, 'am Izhar Khan,'

Vuong shook Izhar's hand, trying not to curl his lip from the fish-like clamminess of his hands. The strange scent of expensive cologne and deeply entrenched body odour battling for primacy wafted up his nostrils, and he tried to avoid staring at the cigarette burn on the man's shirt. 'Mr Khan, a pleasure. We are so glad to make your acquaintance.' Vuong shot a quick

166

look to Cadeo, whose carefully blank expression still conveyed wry amusement.

Khan appeared to have noticed the charcoal on his shirt. 'How did that get there,' he muttered to himself.

A serving girl glided to their table, and they all ordered drinks. Khan introduced the other men. 'This is my associate, Dilip Sood.' A dignified old man inclined his head. 'Here,' he said gesturing to a slight man seated to his left, 'we have Hugo Dioquino, from Manila, and our Indonesian friend is Adi Widjojo.'

Khan sat down. On the table was a thick Cuban cigar and a vaporiser. Puzzling over which to pick up, he settled on the cigar. Best not to overdo it in front of these vipers.

Cadeo and Vuong sat down in perfect unison. Cadeo poured his employer a glass of water from a crystal pitcher in the middle of the table as his employer began, 'Gentlemen, we're all present, so we should begin. I believe that business is about seizing opportunities as they present themselves. I also know that your countries, like India, are suffering greatly as famine and war continue to erupt all over the Asian continent.' He turned to Adi Widjojo. 'Only this week a category five hit North Sulawesi, killing thousands. The same storm had an impact on Davao as well, Mr. Dioquino; are not thousands more of your countrymen dead or homeless?'

Both men nodded. 'This is true. In the last few years, hundreds of thousands of my countrymen have died in these storms, millions more are homeless and starving,' said Dioquino. 'Typhoon Hamm is a timely reminder that there are opportunities we must be taking advantage of.'

'Indeed,' puffed Khan around his cigar. 'As much as this saddens us all, it also presented a chance for me to get into the travel business. Naturally, people don't like famines, or wars and would in fact rather be somewhere else, like Australia, for example, and are happy to pay handsomely to get there.'

The serious little Indonesian picked up a glass of ice water. 'Mr Khan, can you tell us how you managed to put together such a successful operation?'

Khan waved his empty glass at Lina who fetched another. 'I developed close ties with those gentlemen who own the ship-breaking yards in Chittagong, and they directed me to the least-unseaworthy ships on their beaches. At the same time, I used my connections within the Indian state to ensure the navy would not intervene if a few old cargo ships started steaming around again.'

'In what quantity can you purchase these ships?' asked Widjojo. The little man eyed Khan's pipe and whiskey with a mild look of disgust. Khan got the feeling he'd offended the man's Muslim sensibilities bringing him here.

'In whatever quantity I wish,' he said breezily. 'There are hundreds of ships in Chittagong, not to mention the Alang breaking yard in India. Then, there's the beaches in Karachi, Pakistan. I haven't sounded them out, but they're just as crooked as everywhere else, if not more so. As long as those Islamic madmen consuming that country don't get their hands on it, there'll be plenty of ships; trust me. I guarantee the best ships!' he laughed a little too excitedly. 'But at least they probably won't sink. Unless the Australians make them sink.' He stopped abruptly, the vague feeling of having said too much settling over him.

'How many do you need?' said Sood, steering away from his partner's lack of tact.

'I'm sure we could fill two or three boats quite quickly,' said Widjojo.

'Mr Khan, it is important to me that you do guarantee the best ships. A ticket I sell must deliver a person to their destination. I have a reputation to maintain,' Vuong added.

Khan grunted. 'Yes, of course, it's vital that all of our customers are safe; like I said, we get the best ships.'

'How many ships are you able to secure for us at short notice?' said Widjojo.

'There are nine ships suitable for such a crossing that are available right now. I'll split them between you on a first-come, first-served basis. Everything happens out of Kolkata docks, and it's up to you to get your passengers there. If you need a ship, you must pay me up-front, in full, for the cost of the ship, plus my commission. That works out to be…' he pretended to make some calculations in his head, 'ninety million US dollars.' That was fair, he thought, ten million dollars' worth of fat per ship. 'The shipyards wouldn't sell ships to anyone but me, certainly not any 'foreign devils'; after all nobody else has retroactive culpability backed up with the force of the Indian Navy on their side.' Khan spat the words in what amounted to a slurred, sales speech. 'My…our union contacts' he corrected glancing at Sood, 'have operations out of the Kolkata docks all sewn up.'

'And the Kolkata docks are the only place ships full of refugees will be leaving from,' Sood added trying to compensate for his partner's lack of charisma,

'Mr Khan, do you earnestly believe your government will send its Navy to protect ships full of Indonesians, or Filipinos?' asked Widjojo.

'They will if we mix the cargoes. If each ship is at least half Indian that should motivate our friends in the Navy. So, I'll pay your fees on a pro-rata basis.' He sucked on his cigar and exhaled smoke as he spoke. 'Let's face it, it'd be a good thing if the Aussies sank a ship full of Indonesians, it might bring your Navy into the fight; can't ride on our coattails forever you know.'

'I think the less conflict, the better,' replied Vuong. 'We should not provoke the Australians any more than necessary.'

'Well, unfortunately,' Khan said with a tinge of sarcasm, 'what we're doing here is considered pretty provocative by the

Australians. You may have noticed they're rather opposed to unscheduled arrivals.'

'They are,' said Vuong placidly. 'I am concerned that they may begin to enact harsher measures once they make landfall.'

'The Australians caused this mess. Retroactive culpability says so. They have plenty of space, plenty of money, plenty of everything. Screw them.'

'If the best thing passengers can hope for is for the Aussies to shove them into a concentration camp, it will quickly reduce demand for tickets.'

'That's not my problem,' said Khan. 'I only provide transport. And fuck the Australians. They've got problems? There's fifteen million Pakistanis fled into Punjab! Why? Because Pakistan is a viper pit of brainwashed, furiously masturbating jihadists raping and beheading their way across the country, fighting for the few regions that produce food in the name of Allahu Akbar. Good thing too, because it keeps their army off our back in Kashmir, where we're siphoning off what's left of the source waters there...' he trailed off, mildly embarrassed.

He signalled Lina again; he was starting to feel a bit paranoid and needed another drink. The economics of this deal were pretty clear cut; they were just here in person to avoid electronic surveillance. How had they worked him up so?

'Don't misunderstand me, Mr Vuong,' he said, drawing deeply on the cigar. 'That's all very nice because it's left us with a large pool of desperate people. Why do you think my country is using this retroactive culpability crap as an excuse?'

'Indulge me for a moment, Mr Khan; what is the best thing a passenger can hope for if they get on one of your ships at present?'

Khan shrugged. 'I don't know. To get shoved in that putrid concentration camp in Geraldton for fifteen years, probably.'

'And the worst thing?'

'The worst thing?' he echoed. The worst thing, as far as Khan was concerned, was running out of drugs, alcohol and women -

probably in that order. Although really they were like a tightly-knit Venn diagram - take away one and what are you left with? Two circles on a page. Nothing. A horrifying prospect. He dragged his mind back to the question.

'To get blown up en-route?'

'That's right!' Vuong clapped his hands, startling Khan. 'Neither are compelling options if we are to make this a sustainable business, for millions of passengers.'

'He raises a valid point,' said Dioquino. 'One boatload is a nice windfall. But it will bring us to the attention of the Australian military. They might not have a powerful army, but their special forces are world-class.' He looked thoughtful. 'To make it worth the risk we need to make many shipments, not just one.'

'Mr Khan, people will stop buying tickets once they realise it's a one-way ticket to a concentration camp,' said Vuong. 'We must allow them to control their own destiny. Don't you think?'

Khan was fed up. Nuance wasn't his strong suit at the best of times. This wasn't the best of times. He had no idea what Vuong was getting at and said so.

'When people realise they're trading one version of hell for another, nobody will want passage on Mr. Khan's freedom cruises,' said Vuong to the group. 'What we should be doing,' he slapped the table for emphasis, 'is selling the chance to make a new life for themselves. A new life in a new land where they'll have to fight, no doubt, but where, if they fight hard enough, they'll have a chance of succeeding, of winning.'

Khan looked at him, stupefied. 'What on earth are you talking about?'

'What I want us to do, Mr. Khan, is supply every man, every person who gets on those ships, with an assault rifle. Other weapons. Ammunition. So that when they get taken away to that concentration camp, they can fight back. Imagine what twenty thousand desperate Indian or Vietnamese with rifles

171

could do? And that's just one ship. If three, or four ships landed? That is something we can sell to desperate men with big dreams.'

Khan burst out laughing. Not food, or first aid packs, but assault rifles. Of course. What else could you possibly want on a hellish trip across oceans? *Pavitra ghoda kacara ...Holy horse shit*, he thought.

'Mr Vuong, that's the craziest fucking idea I've ever heard. You must be even further removed from reality than I am, which is most concerning. Let's pretend for a moment I agree. There's one little problem. Just where in hell are we going to get tens of thousands of assault rifles?' he asked triumphantly.

With a small smile, Vuong raised a finger and said, 'I am aware of several large caches of weapons and ammunition. I believe my colleagues from Manila and Jakarta also have friends in their respective militaries who could assist.'

'I'm not entirely sure about this...'

'Mr Khan, this is not a suggestion. It is a condition of doing business with us. We are happy to be your 'travel agents', but we also have other business concerns that must be taken care of. We have put to you that between us we could fill nine boats, rather quickly. This is ninety million dollars, purely for ship brokerage. A good deal, you must agree. Truly, the choice is yours.' A tiny smile playing at the edge of his mouth, but eyes were steel hard.

Khan's mouth was suddenly dry. He looked at Dilip Sood, who remained inscrutable. *You made this bed. Now you have to lie in it.*

Tonight was supposed to be some idle chit-chat, agreement on basic terms followed by some civilised debauchery, whoring and general back-slapping. What an ensemble of beautiful women he'd assembled, the best drugs, and it was all going to waste. Well, it wouldn't because he'd get around to them eventually, but...these men were made of ice.

He went through the motions as the meeting wound down, and his guests got up to leave. Dilip Sood was the last to go, placing a firm hand on Khan's shoulder.

'We will discuss the implications of this meeting in the morning. When you're sober,' said the old man, and he too left Rita's Emporium. Lina came over and sat down on the sofa with Khan, her knee touching his, one hand on the inside of his leg, the other resting on his wrist. 'Izhar…is everything alright? You seem upset.'

Khan pushed her away. Stupid whore. He wasn't upset, just…thinking. Ninety million was nothing to sneeze at, but still…

Chapter 16
The Lodge, Prime Minister's Residence, Canberra
September 10th, 2000 hours

'To be, or not to be, that is the question: Whether 'tis nobler to suffer, the slings and arrows of outrageous fortune, or take arms against a sea of troubles...' The monologue warbled on, punctuated by sweeping gestures and tortured facial expressions.

Craig Laffite leaned over to his wife's ear and whispered: 'Sea of troubles indeed...one might even say your life is imitating Shakespearian art.'

Jacqui cocked an eyebrow. 'You have no idea. Sometimes, when I'm cooking your dinner, I contemplate poisoning your food.'

Craig snorted. She'd never once cooked him dinner.

The Laffites sat on the back deck of the Prime Ministerial home in Canberra, screen set up on a wicker table, red pebble drive and beyond that, the spreading garden greenery. A bottle of white wine lay in a cooler and a glass dangled from her hand, condensation beading in the warm spring air.

She was staring at the screen blankly. Craig got up and went inside, mumbling something about grabbing pate and crackers. She heard the screen door closing behind him, and flicked the streaming service over to the news amalgamation channel.

More violence in the capital cities, red-faced news anchors demanding the government act more decisively on the boats *now,* general criticism of Laffite's handling of the crisis. More people wanted the Indians dealt with brutally and decisively. War frenzy was starting to take hold. The one positive; an increasing proportion of commentators were of the view the Indians needed to be taught a lesson. The ethnic rioters had only hardened public attitudes, and even refugee sympathisers were beginning to want vengeance. Other than that, though, more of the same. She sighed and changed the channel; this one was running a profile on Glen Robertson.

She sat up straighter. Footage of Glen after his last cruise, post the sinking of the *Tamil Nadu*. Fifteen years later, and she still felt that *pang* in her body every time she saw him. He still walked with a parade ground set to his shoulders. Even after the horror of his mission, there was an easy confidence to him; a defiance jaded only by a haunted look in his eyes.

'Foolish woman,' she muttered to herself. She was the Prime Minister, not some giddy teenage girl. The door behind her slid open, and she quickly changed the channel.

She didn't acknowledge her husband when he approached, his hand outstretched with a block of chocolate for Jacqui.

She closed her eyes. Dammit. She smiled at Craig apologetically, noticed how his shoulders stooped when he walked, how his eyes darted around. Once, it had been so endearing. Now she felt guilty for finding it insufferable. What was wrong with her? She'd always prided herself on her pragmatism; when she'd dumped Glen, it was certainly the pragmatic, if not emotionally satisfying, thing to do. She'd felt a sort of delicious irony that the man she'd learned that 'whatever it takes' attitude from would now be a victim of it. Craig had been a logical replacement; all the right connections, high-achieving, well-spoken, six-foot-three inches of gravitas in a blandly corporate, easily-managed package. Now she was beginning to wonder if her head's grip over her heart was as firm as it once was, or even desirable.

'No chocolate?' he said, waggling it once and putting it on the table. 'I'll leave it here, just in case,' he said and flopped down next to her.

Jacqui sighed. Craig was such a caring, gentle man. She was so lucky to have him.

She grimaced and brought the wine to her lips and switched back to Hamlet.

Stars now twinkled in a cloudless sky, blue ink brightening to soft yellow as the earth spun away from the sun. The languid shape of a jacaranda tree blotted out parts of the sky, the blossoms smattered pools of purple, nearly black, as the night finally blanketed them. The crisp scent of jacaranda blossoms perfumed the air. Crickets droned hypnotically, and distant aircraft roared mutely. A sense of splendid isolation, like their only contact with civilisation was miles high and utterly oblivious to their existence.

'It really does feel like we're a million miles from anywhere,' he said.

'Shush,' said his wife. 'I want to know what Ophelia's got to say next.'

He chuckled. Jacqui had seen this a hundred times. Taking a swig from his beer, he rested his hand on her arm. Jacqui sighed and moved over. She wanted her own space.

He turned the monitor off. Jacqui frowned at him.

He waved towards Parliament House. 'You're thinking about work.'

'I was trying to forget about work,' she snapped. Then felt a pang of guilt - he was trying to help. 'Yes,' she relented. It's all still bouncing around in there.'

He looked at her expectantly.

'Look, it's one thing ordering the Navy to war; I can deal with those consequences. But we just haven't figured out what to do with those bloody refugee boats. We took the last bunch that came through. Another sixty-thousand damned illegals. We're fighting a shooting war to stop the arrivals, and winning, but letting them in anyway, sending the wrong message. They can't continue to roll up on our beaches, and we can't just sink them without losing public support. We're damned either way. There's well over a million ethnic Indians in Australia, and it seems half of them have organised into violent groups and are causing systematic damage. And now neo-Nazis, white supremacists, every idiot redneck with a chip on his shoulder are using it as an excuse to go to war in the streets. We're at the point of ordering the army out to clamp down on things. It's a complete disaster.'

'You're doing your best. You're a good person, Jacqui and if you have to take a hard line, it's because of external circumstances.'

He stroked her arm again 'The only option is a hard line. There are a billion people up there so an open door policy won't work,' she said grimly, more to herself than Craig.

She sat up sharply. 'You know there's easily over two hundred and fifty thousand people in that Geraldton camp, mostly men, and the numbers keep growing. The women and girls in that camp are walking targets. They can't do anything alone, for fear of being gang-raped by sex starved so-called refugees that we're supposed to be showing compassion to.' She snorted in disgust and pulled her arm away from Craig again. His touch suddenly felt...inappropriate.

He picked up his beer with his now surplus hand.

'What options are there?' he asked. He already knew the answer, but he hoped by getting Jacqui talking she'd realise she was doing the right thing.

'Well, another ship just left Kolkata, so we need a stronger deterrent.'

'It's the navy's failure, Jacqui. They keep screwing up when they try to turn the ships around.'

She had a sudden urge to defend the navy, which she crushed. He was spot on.

'Well, in their limited defence, circumstances keep changing. The first time around caught everyone by surprise. Second time, we all know what that idiot Robertson did. A great deterrent that turned out to be, bringing the Indian Navy into the picture.' She considered that for a moment. 'Maybe we need more Glen Robertsons,' she eventually muttered.

Her husband was usually so tranquil, and Jacqui felt guilty satisfaction at the way Craig stiffened next to her. 'Time to put these issues with Glen to bed, Jacqui.'

'There are no issues, Craig,' she said scornfully. 'Apart from him taking us to war.'

'It was going to happen anyway. It's just an ironic twist that it took Glen Robertson to do it.'

'Hmm.' She gazed out through the jacaranda trees at the remnants of sunset, ribbons of orange hanging from the trees. There he went being all reasonable again. 'I know that Craig. I mean the Navy is just doing its job, but every time they do anything we get the worst possible outcomes and every time, Futcher shrugs his stooped over shoulders and mumbles something about operational realities or operational constraints. *Excuses*...Glen Robertson,' she muttered. 'He always has an excuse. He's a charming, charismatic incompetent. He's a lovable buffoon. His people skills are the worst thing that could've possibly happened to him because they paper over the giant cracks in his judgment. He's never had to deal with his issues because he hoodwinks people into liking him, so they make allowances for his idiocy.'

'He's not that calculating Jacqui. And besides, this isn't going to help.'

She grunted in agreement. 'You're right - he's not that calculating. He doesn't even know the meaning of the word calculating.' That's what galled her - he was such an open book that Jacqui had just known he was hiding, compensating for something. When it turned out she'd been wrong, it had just turned a mirror onto her own character failings.

'Just how in hell he became a commodore I'll never know. Makes me wonder about the state of our navy,' she muttered to herself.

Craig was silent. He turned away from his wife and followed her stare across the garden.

'And, have you heard?' she went on, oblivious to the hurt silence next to her. 'Those idiots have given him his commission back. He's replacing Malm, who died on the *Hobart*.'

Craig forced a chuckle. 'Aren't you supposed to be relaxing? Next, you'll blame Glen for getting your blood pressure up tonight. Anyway. What's the navy going to do this time, that it hasn't already done?'

Jacqui pursed her lips and let her husband change the subject. She'd suddenly realised she could use the reinstatement of Robertson to her advantage; what if they used it to send a message? One last soft power option before they went completely to a war footing...

Craig had stabbed a couple of bottles of beer into the ice bucket next to Jacqui's wine. He reached across, drew one out and pried the lid off. *Crack-hiss* went the escaping gas, and he brought the bottle to his lips. At that moment, Jacqui levered herself up and walked inside, leaving him alone, and a little confused, in the warm October evening.

Jacqui wandered towards her study. She felt mildly guilty, but she needed to think. Besides, she'd wanted to take her mind of all her troubles, and to be honest, she'd wanted to be alone.

The next day Laffite marched through the halls of Parliament House to yet another meeting. Last night she'd tucked herself away in her study and read for an hour then turned into bed alone. At four-thirty in the morning, she'd woken, dressed, and asked her driver to take her to Parliament house for another meeting.

Futcher, Hammersmith and Air Marshal Cas Castrission all looked up as Laffite, Nick Whittey and Louise Abbott walked in.

'Hello gentlemen,' said Laffite.

'It seems these days we see more of each other than our respective partners. I'm surprised we have time left over to do our jobs,' commented Whittey.

179

'Doesn't leave much time for my wife to do *her* job,' said Hammersmith with a wink.

Abbott gave him a flat stare. 'I'm surprised you're doing anything at all, the way things are panning out on the west coast.'

Hammersmith flared red. 'Events on the west coast are a direct result of decisions politicians have made over the years, Abbott. I won't-'

'I've just had a briefing with Dr Janice Wong,' interrupted Abbott smoothly, 'who runs the Australian Medical Association. She came in to tell me that there's no spare capacity left in the hospital system. Emergency department waiting times are through the roof, and in many city hospitals, we're in a permanent state of triage. We've had to transfer thousands of doctors and nurses to that camp in Geraldton because the refugees are getting off the ships in such poor condition.'

'We're using the term illegal arrivals, not refugee,' said Lafitte.

Abbott blinked. 'Well, whatever they are, they generally need urgent medical care once they arrive. Once we nurse them back to health, a good proportion of them turn to molesting the relatively few women who seem to have made the journey. There's an outbreak of syphilis spreading like wildfire and sexual assault is at emergency levels. Camp security forces are taking draconian measures to combat it, and as a result, we're getting crucified by the press who are accusing us of brutality.'

'Of course they're the victims...' Whittey said caustically.

'As far as I'm concerned,' said Lafitte, anger lacing her tone, 'the security teams must do whatever is necessary to ensure the camp is, if nothing else, safe and secure. I want that situation brought under control immediately. Arthur,' she said, pointing at the Army commander, 'send in more troops and figure out a way to safeguard that camp.' She stabbed the table with a finger. 'I don't care who feels hard done by or what the bleeding-heart press say. Segregate them by sex if you have to.' Hammersmith nodded, and Lafitte turned back to Abbott. 'You were talking about the stretched hospital system...'

'Yes,' said the Foreign Minister. 'The pool of nurses is large at around four hundred thousand, but supply and demand are very evenly matched.' Abbott's voice had taken on a lecturing tone. 'The problem is, we're having to drag staff from suburban hospitals to shore up resources at most city hospitals, because they're being overwhelmed with cases of battery, blunt instrument, and stab wound trauma. Obviously, that's due to the fighting between those ethnic idiots and all the vigilante groups. It's like a warzone.'

'So,' said Laffite, 'the health system is getting-'

'Not only that. Once we bring these violent idiots to hospital, we have to segregate them; not by IQ of course, because they're all as stupid as each other, but by race, because even while we treat them they continue to brawl. Our staff,' she said coldly, 'are in harm's way because they're bringing their hate inside the hospitals. Did you know that last week, these thugs assaulted forty-nine emergency department workers in the course of trying to help these morons?' she finished angrily.

'Louise, please. These conversations are much more constructive if we keep our emotions under control,' Hammersmith said in a placating tone.

'Oh *shut up,* Arthur,' she said witheringly. 'The medical staff are contributing, unlike you and yours.'

'Please!' Laffite raised her hands and started talking before a red-faced Hammersmith could. 'Louise, you raise some good points. We'll also have to increase security in hospitals. Let's make sure it's funded and implemented by the end of the week. Deploying the military to our streets would be unprecedented in our history, and it's not something we can blithely do.' She sighed. 'But...we are considering it. The violence must stop.' She returned her attention to the other people at the table. 'It does, however, demonstrate the urgent requirement that we implement a genuine solution. Now, last I heard there was another boat making the crossing. The *Pong-Sawan*. How do we stop it?'

'There is one way to stop it coming through,' said Hammersmith blandly.

'Tell us,' said Laffite.

'Well, we can sink it.'

'Can we now,' said Abbott coolly.

'Of course we can,' said Hammersmith acerbically.

'He has a point,' said Whittey 'They are taking advantage of our humanity. Despite the *Tamil Nadu,* or maybe because of it, they think we can't afford another PR disaster that sinking a freighter would cause. We should consider taking a harder line.'

'The only way our line could get any harder is if we target the refugee ships as well as the warships.'

Futcher nodded. 'If that's what it takes, then-'

'We're not doing it.' Abbott swatted the idea away with her hand. 'Obviously it's a workable solution, but I'm not interested in being the first Australian leader to order mass murder.' Futcher opened his mouth to speak, but Abbott cut him off. Lafitte watched the exchange carefully - she needed both Abbott and Futcher to agree to her plan. 'I'm not sanctioning it, so forget it...for now. We must find another way,' finished Abbott.

'You politicians have no idea how things work in the real world, do you?' Hammersmith said through gritted teeth. 'None of your policies or speeches have made a difference worth a damn. Nothing that anyone has done has made a difference!'

'That's not entirely true,' said Lafitte finally. 'After Robertson sank the *Tamil Nadu* demand for places dropped off sharply. It only went up again because the Indian Navy stepped in. We bent over backwards apologising, were about to offer

Robertson up to the World Court, but they just saw that as weakness and pressed on. Now...we've had to bring him back to active service. Perhaps we could make use of that.'

'And how is that, Jacqui?' said Abbott.

Lafitte made a show of thinking it through. 'By bringing him back, we could imply that our policy has changed to reflect Arthur's hard-line. Giving him another command is tacit approval of what he did to the *Tamil Nadu*.'

Whittey nodded, catching on. 'At the same time, you can keep making the right noises at a diplomatic level,' he said to Abbott. 'Probably a bit over the head of your average illegal climate refugee but worth a shot,' he said. 'Might give the politicians and Navy types on the take pause for thought.'

Lafitte watched as Abbott thought it through. She needed Abbott to run cover at a diplomatic level, so her buy-in was critical.

'Well,' prompted Whittey. 'What do you think?'

Abbott pursed her lips. 'It does seem like a clever way to take advantage of the navy's decision to put Robertson back on duty,' she said eventually.

'Holloway,' said Lafitte, turning to the spy-boss. 'How've you gone tracking the mastermind of the smuggling operation?'

'We're very close, Jacqui. We've convinced the head of the worker's union at Kolkata docks to flip. He's prepared to tell us everything. But he wants asylum in Australia for himself and his family before he says a word. We're working it out now.'

'How long?'

'A few days at most.'

She thought furiously, the plan coming together like vines on a wall. 'Futcher, Hammersmith, what if we get that SAS team on its way now? Can we update them with target information when Holloway's source has arrived and told us who we're after and where he is?'

The two men nodded at each other. 'If you want covert, you need a submarine. The *Kati-Thanda* is on mission standby at

Fleet Base West as we speak. I believe an SAS squad is on station as well,' said Futcher. Hammersmith nodded the affirmative.

'Ok, good,' said Laffite. 'We'll let this ship through, ostensibly because we're nice but mainly because it's already left. But it's the last one. Meantime, strongly push through unofficial channels that we're changing policy to a rock hard-line spearheaded by Glen Robertson, who got the job because he's a psychopath. We'll have to organise a few strategic media leaks, feed some bullshit to the tabloid journos to get the public speculating. Strongly imply but never acknowledge we're embracing his tactics. Spread it over the news channels to India. Give would-be refugees some food for thought, hopefully put a dent in demand for a while.'

Futcher nodded. 'Meantime, our SAS team transits to Kolkata and decapitates the smuggling operation, sending a very violent message the show is over.'

'Exactly,' said Laffite. 'Minimum collateral damage.' Her colleagues nodded into the silence.

The meeting drifted onto other topics. Laffite went through the motions, trying to pick apart what had just happened. For the first time in a long time, she felt like she had the initiative.

Sure, it was just a giant bluff: Robertson was never going to sink any civilian vessels. But they only needed to buy a little time. It was now down to Holloway's department and the SF team. She prayed they could get the job done.

Chapter 17
Fleet Base West, Western Australia
September 8th, 1600 hours

Glen Robertson stepped out of the MRH-90 Taipan chopper. His boots crunched on the tarmac, and his shirt clung to his chest in the hot sticky air of Fleet Base West. The sun burned his bruised face, and it felt good. He still looked like he'd fallen headfirst onto a painting of a sunset-reds fading to yellow then black, but he could see out of both eyes again, and his jaw worked just fine, so as far as Glen was concerned, things were looking up. He'd been sober for a week and had a vitality about him he hadn't felt since his first command.

After his chat with Swan, a driver had taken him to Garden Island, where he'd received an update on the situation with the *Hobart*. Those hypersonic fragments had shredded *Hobart's* bridge, taking out most of the command personnel and control systems. Fortunately, most of the systems were modular and engineers could replace them relatively easily.

Salty air whipped his hair as the turbines dialled down and the chopper disgorged the other passengers.

Fleet Base West was a narrow strip of bushland, ten clicks long and one wide, of thick scrub, laced by golden beaches. From the air, it looked like a giant, golden necklace lying on grass. At the southern end, the navy had carved a small airstrip into the dunes, and an access road leading to HMAS Stirling skirted the eastern shore. Careening Bay curved away around like a narrow, sandy scythe, topped with the twin moorings of Diamantina Pier. Here was Australia's most significant naval base, and today three Hunter Class frigates were tied to the docks. Two Barracuda class subs hunched blackly in the water behind them. The *Hobart* had also taken her place at the moorings, and technicians worked feverishly to repair the damaged modules. Draped in scaffolding in plastic sheets, to Robertson it looked like a wounded soldier, in stark contrast to the ominous capability represented by the intact vessels surrounding it.

Robertson breathed in the fresh sea air through a still damaged nose and felt for the first time in weeks like he belonged. He drove contentedly past the towering frigates and the sleek submarines that idled in the water and gladly gazed into the bright blue waters of Careening Bay as he made his way to the administration block.

'Beautiful, isn't it,' said the chubby, mono-browed woman sitting next to him. 'I was posted here when I first graduated. Young and innocent. I got to know a sub driver under the jetty at SS Harbour one night...There was a man who knew how to fire a torpedo!' Her stomach shook with laughter. 'You must be the famous Captain Robertson, hiding under all those pretty colours,' she went on, oblivious to his sideways look.

'I can see how you got caught up in the moment,' he said. He remembered his own romantic liaisons under the jetty at Small Ship harbour. It was a popular spot because getting naked anywhere on base, especially near the warships, was against the rules and therefore enticing, but it was not so close to the main warship jetty's that security might shoot you by mistake.

'Who are you?'

'I'm sub-lieutenant Christy Harper; I'm going to be your radar officer on the *Hobart.*'' she beamed, extending a hand that Robertson shook firmly.

'Have you spent any time on *Hobarts,* captain?' she asked.

He nodded. 'I was weapons officer on *Sydney.* They're excellent operating environments. You'll be fundamental to every aspect of surface-up warfare, lieutenant. Radar, fire and weapons control, C&D. It's a well-integrated system.'

'I can't wait to get aboard,' she said as they got out of the car next to the main admin block. 'The closest I ever got to a *Hobart* was the bridge simulators at *Watson.'*

'Don't sound so happy,' growled a technician behind them. 'You're only here because the last bridge crew got wiped out.'

That stifled her enthusiasm. Robertson leaned in, 'Perhaps you could measure your enthusiasm, Harper.' She nodded. 'Sorry, sir,' she said, abashed. He twitched a smile. 'I do like your attitude though. I'm glad we'll be working together.' He left her there and went to his billet, to unpack and change into his Navy whites. Having some time to kill, he took a walk down to Diamantina Pier to see how repairs were progressing on his new command.

The missile fragments had struck the bridge on the port side, smashing through the thin armour plating there. It had been a fluke shot - it looked like there were some scorch marks on the superstructure under the bridge and a few dents in the AN/SPY-1D radar housing. Other than that, just the bridge.

'Well, well, look who it is!' called a technician, jumping onto the dock from the gangway. The two men shook hands. 'Look at your head! It looks like someone dropped fruit salad…and then drove over it!'

Robertson laughed, then winced as some of the scabs cracked open on his face. 'Sathish, you dodgy bastard, what are you doing to my ship?'

Sathish waved his shifter breezily. 'Your ship? Just integrating your fire control with the septic lines. As soon as your target acquisition radar locks onto an enemy contact, the lines are triggered to blow. Test your focus.'

'Makes me twice as glad you're not on my crew, with your diet,' responded Robertson. 'How's it look up there?'

Sathish made a not-good-but-not-too-bad-either gesture.

'Could've been worse, even in the control room which took most of the impact. We just got to pull out the old units and put in new ones. One of the AN/SPY units got holed, nothing major but we got another one airlifted out of the US. We installed it already.'

Robertson snorted a laugh. 'Nice we can rely on them to sell us weapons systems when we need them.'

'Friends in need indeed. Anyway, once we finish in there,' he jerked a thumb over his shoulder, 'we'll calibrate it, and you'll be good to go.'

'So just an unlucky shot then.'

'Depends how you look at it I guess. Another tenth of a second and the whole missile would have hit the ship at Mach 7. Still, it was pretty ugly when she made it back here. Had to scrape charred bits of meat off the walls with a water blaster.'

Robertson grimaced. Malm had done an excellent job in challenging circumstances. The mess of the *Hobart* and memorials to the sunken *Newcastle* were reminders the Navy was fighting battles for the first time since World War Two.

He said goodbye to Sathish and made his way to the admin building. The base commandant had ringed the building with MP's toting Austeyrs; as he got closer, offset concrete barricades with boom gates and heavy machine guns lined the road. He passed security and noticed a group of civilians amongst all the military uniforms. One caught his eye - a petite, slender woman with dark hair and brown skin.

Oops. He'd thought Alice was coming later.

'Alice!' he called, jogging to catch up. She turned and appraised him with a look at once combining pity, amusement, and contempt.

Suddenly he had nothing to say. 'How...how's it going?'

She stopped. 'Ah. Glen. I thought I'd see you here.' She raised a judgmental eyebrow. 'Wow, it almost looks like you got beaten up.'

'Me? Never. It's my new look. What do you think?'

She appraised him patronisingly. Like she'd come home, and her new puppy had shat on the carpet.

'I think you're consistent. Consistently getting worse since your last cruise. Dashing naval hero to pathetic drunk to bashing victim.' She snorted.

He had to double-time to keep up as she strode towards the amphitheatre, heels clicking loudly. She seemed like she was stabbing the tarmac with her pointed heels. *Probably pretending it's me.*

'Swan told me you'd be here,' he said lamely. 'I'm glad you are.' He berated himself for being so useless.

'Mm-hmm.' She didn't break stride.

'You're here to provide intel assessments for senior command, is that right?'

'Yes Glen, that's correct, well done. I'd have thought perhaps our relationship would take priority over the specifics of my posting. No? Well then. I've moved across to the DIO and had a team from ASIS seconded to me. They're monitoring intel assets, you know,' she said, speaking as if to an imbecile, 'human, satellite, signal intercepts, and so on, covering the Bay of Bengal, information which we'll analyse for the military. Any other operational questions?'

'Uh...'

'Then you should attend the briefing I'm about to deliver. I assume that's why you're going the same direction I am?'

Well now. The problem with smart women, he thought, was they knew exactly how to make you feel like the piece of shit you were.

'I know I'm making a mess of this-'

'Oh, sweetheart, congratulations. I thought such insight was beyond you.'

'Yes...yea,' he said. This was going very poorly. Alice had always kept her emotions on a tight leash, but her nostrils only flared like that when she was incandescent with rage...

'I'd like us to talk about things, Alice,' he persisted. She breathed out loudly and shook her head. 'You've got every right to be angry, but I'm done with that bullshit now.' She kept walking.

One of the reasons he'd fallen in love with her was because she was absurdly stubborn, an untamed spirit that he could entice, never compel. She was truly free.

He cursed it.

189

'But obviously you're not interested in anything I've got to say.'

'It's for your own good; You're talking utter rubbish. Besides, there are consequences to your actions. You should already know that, *Commodore* Robertson.'

He looked at her. She was giving him the cold shoulder, but it was clear she was very, very angry. That anger was his one consolation - there was still hope. Plenty of women had hated his guts over the years - he'd always found you could work your way back from there. It was when they didn't care whether you lived or died; that was when all hope was gone.

Still, he reflected, having your girlfriend hate you wasn't ideal. And she was right. The last few weeks were a blur of hangovers, scummy bars, and drunkenness. And responsibility dodging. It was like he'd descended into a dark hole, and now he was trying to climb out of it he could see how bright his world was with Alice in it, and how dark it would be without her at all. Except the light at the top was getting further away.

'You're right. Look, I didn't realise how bad things had got till Jay had a word to me the other night. In some ways, it was a good thing I got beaten up - it snapped me out of it.'

'Oh, well I'm glad you listened to your mate,' she said nonchalantly, betrayed again only by her nostrils. 'You also had the benefit of my support. Advice, even. Which you ignored. Isn't it amazing that *Jacqui Lafitte* listens to what I say, but you don't?' He noticed the vein throbbing on her forehead, and sighed inwardly. He was already dangerous ground, and the cracks were turning into crevasses.

'I need to clean up, and I've started-'

'You're a fool, Glen.' She accelerated away from him.

He clamped down on a glimmer of anger. 'Alright, Alice. You tell me what you want to do. Where we go from here.'

She glanced at her watch. 'I don't know about you, but I'm going to the admin block to deliver this briefing to senior commanders. Somehow you're part of that group?'

'Well, yea. Obviously. What's it about?'

'You'll have to wait, along with everyone else. Are you suddenly interested in what I have to say again?'

He hoped his combat missions went better than this conversation. The glimmer of anger was fanning into a flame.

'I'm about to be deployed again, Alice. To a war zone. I want to resolve things one way or the other before then. So when you get over your indignation we need to talk.'

She arched an eyebrow. 'I'll let you know.'

She turned and left Robertson standing mawkishly until he followed her into the conference room.

He self-debriefed the conversation. If it had been a naval battle his ship, probably in many small pieces, would just be settling into the soft sand at the bottom of the Indian Ocean. But, he thought maybe she'd been repressing the tiniest smile as she turned away. He didn't want to think about the alternative.

He brought his attention back to the intelligence types milling around the podium, and his eyes settled on the enthralling sight of his girlfriend. There would be no sly messages this time.

A body flopped down beside him; it was Lieutenant Harper. He sighed.

'Getting to know our intel people, eh, captain?'

He looked at her sideways. 'Alice and I have known each other for a while now, Harper.

She sniggered. 'I think you'll be 'knowing' each other in all sorts of ways before we set sail,' she offered.

'Thanks for the insight, Harper.'

'That woman really, *truly* hates you right now, captain,' she said cheerfully. 'Obvious as the nose on your face.'

'Is it that obvious,' he muttered.

'You like her? You like her. You should be happy, captain.'

He snorted looked askance at his radar officer. 'Oh, really?'

191

She shook her head. Men were so stupid! 'Love and hate aren't opposites, Captain. When a woman hates you, it means she hates herself for being attracted to you, because you're an asshole, an idiot, or some combination of the two.'

'Are you saying I'm an asshole, Harper?'

'Well...no, I'm just saying...if she wanted nothing to do with you, she'd just ignore you. But you must be stirring her emotions. We love that! So you've got a chance. SS pier,' she winked and settled into her seat, satisfied.

Robertson looked disapprovingly at the woman next to him. 'Harper, I appreciate you've had all sorts of sordid carnal adventures on this base, and returning here is triggering a wave of joyous memories. However, I suggest you focus less on sexual titillations and more on your new role, and the events that led her in the first place.'

She shifted uncomfortably. 'I didn't mean anything by it-

'Alice Ruiz is my girlfriend, Harper.'

Harper's face turned a mortified shade of red. 'I-I'm sorry sir, I didn't-'

'Flippancy won't be tolerated on my ship. Understand?'

Harper deflated like a lanced boil. 'Yes, sir. Sorry, sir.'

He let her see his wry smile to take the sting out of the words and turned back to the lectern.

Alice strode into the small amphitheatre packed with the country's top politicians and Defence brass. The political and military personnel had split arranged themselves on opposite sides of the room; on the right, when looking from the stage, was Jacqui Laffite, Nick Whittey, Louise Abbott and the rest of the political circus arrayed behind them, huddled together over notepads and tablet screens like students in a lecture. In the front row on the same side of the room, she spied Vice Admiral Jason Futcher. Sitting stiffly next to him wearing khaki was the slender Major General Ryan Harridge, Special Operations Commander and chief Australia's SAS and Commando units. Various frigate, destroyer, submarine captains, and fleet commanders were there; a large chunk of Australia's military leadership was in this room, waiting to hear the intel people speak.

A few rows back Glen was sharing a joke with Jack Jennings, a Wing Commander who ran a few F-35 squadrons.

She sighed. After eight years together, she still marvelled at Glen's ability to laugh at himself when the chips were down, which was why his recent behaviour had been so out of character. When she'd first met him, she could've sworn he was a charismatic incompetent bluffing his way through life. But anyone who had anything to do with him, who knew how he operated, had sworn by him. Especially those who depended on him. First, she'd dismissed him, then become intrigued, then eventually fallen in love with this man whose friends and combat partners thought he was solid gold. He was much like gold, she thought, if gold spotted with rust periodically and needed to be forcibly rubbed back to a shine.

She banished the thoughts. She had a job to do.

She faced the heads of navy, army, air force and intel services, SOCOM, her old boss Cam Holloway and a tired-looking Jacqueline Laffite, who was doing a terrible job of eyeing her impassively instead shooting daggers her way.

Nick Whittey got a nod from Laffite and stood up to kick things off.

'Ladies, gents, we're here because the PM has asked for a background on why this,' he jerked his thumb over his shoulder, presumably in the general direction of whatever he believed to be causing the crisis, 'is happening. By understanding the Indians, what their motives are, we can gauge how strong their will to fight is. 'Know your enemy,' that's the old military proverb, am I right?'

Vice Admiral Futcher, from the Navy and Air Marshall Cas Castrission from Air Force both looked at Lieutenant General Arthur Hammersmith, Chief of Army.

193

Hammersmith gave the room a bemused look, 'Something like that. The full version of that quote is 'if you know your enemies and know yourself, you will not be imperilled in a hundred battles.' Sun Tzu.'

Whittey nodded. 'Exactly. We certainly don't want to be imperilled in a hundred battles. Not least because our loyal allies the United States have informed us we're on our own at this stage. So, the more we know about why the Indians are escorting illegals, the better we can tailor a military solution.'

'Excuse me,' said Robertson. 'Does this mean we're abandoning diplomatic efforts?'

Whittey hesitated a moment.

'Of course not,' called Lafitte from the side. 'But diplomacy isn't getting the result we want; therefore we're also planning for war. Our assessment is that further conflict is unavoidable.'

There was a pregnant pause while the room digested her comment. Then Whittey restarted his monologue.

Alice ignored Whittey, and surreptitiously studied the PM; she was exceptionally good at observing a person's body language, speech patterns, intellect, motivations, their insecurities, and accurately judge their competence...In technical terms, it made Alice an incisive analyst, because she could connect the dots and get a feel for what was going on with limited information.

In non-technical terms, it made her an excellent judge of character.

'...this is a good chance to get into the heads of the Indians. It may, and I stress *may* enable us to make some targeted decisions...' Whittey dribbled on, enjoying his audience. Alice cast another furtive glance at the PM. She thought she could connect the PM's dots, but like Glen, there'd always been a layer to Jacqui Laffite that she just hadn't seen coming. She knew behind Laffite's mask of cool competence was a brilliant mind, weighing and measuring, but she could sense some insecurities under the surface, deeply hidden. Unlike Whittey, who didn't bother hiding what he thought of anything, which is how everyone knew he didn't think deeply at all.

'Thanks, Nick,' said Cam Holloway when Whittey finally ran out of steam. 'Moving forward, ASIS will directly support the military response by providing tactical and strategic intelligence to military commanders. We begin today by providing a strategic overview of the genesis of this crisis. Most of you know Alice Ruiz. ASIS has transferred her to the Defense Intelligence Organisation and her team seconded to Operational Command. They will assess HUMINT, SIGINT and other sources of intelligence and disseminate those findings to military planners operating out of Fleet Base West.'

Alice stood up. 'Today I'll answer the question; why is the Indian government aiding and abetting people smugglers in such an unprecedented way?' She gave Whittey a wry smile. 'In other words, know thy enemy. This crisis is a symptom of the huge internal stress afflicting India. There are dozens of small to medium-sized conflicts and massive population shifts. The Indian sub-continent is incredibly unstable, and the Indian government is desperately trying to hold things together.'

The screen on the wall lit up and the Punjab region in northwest India, bordering Pakistan, glowed orange.

'Most of these conflicts have been simmering away for decades. The underlying social and environmental circumstances have now changed for the worst, pushing historical tensions into wars. I'll provide a short example to illustrate the point.'

'In the northwest,' she said, as the Punjabi and neighbouring Faisalabad region in Pakistan began to flicker on the map behind her, 'a couple of factors have merged, leading to civil war. One: the increase in world temperature actually increased crop yields in this part of India and small parts of Pakistan, for a time. Higher temperatures were beneficial for crop germination, and also led higher-than-average meltwater-which the locals used for irrigation-from glacier-fed rivers

195

flowing through the area.' A string of rivers, starting in the Himalayas and carving down to the Indian Ocean, appeared on the map.

'How's that a problem?' asked Futcher. 'Aren't increasing yields a good thing?'

'They were, for a while,' answered Alice. 'But higher yields caused a massive population-shift from central India, which had turned to a dust bowl, to the greener, northwestern areas. We estimate close to thirty million people crowded in. The same thing happened from the west. Faisalabad suddenly became very popular, and with demand from other areas boosting profits, crop production went through the roof. Millions of Pakistani Muslims crossed the border and competed with Indians in Punjab to grow food.'

'Why do people have to live where the food's grown?' asked Abbott. 'Our farmers are thousands of kilometres from our population centres.'

'Indian farms are nowhere near as productive as ours. The last fifty years they've industrialised, but there are still nearly a billion people at or near subsistence level, which is something like a hundred million farms under two hectares. Big enough to feed the people who work them, maybe allow for some barter-driven trade, but that's about it. There just wasn't that much spare capacity. So, when crop yields dropped everywhere else, the country had to import food. Prices went up by insane amounts.'

'She's right,' said Louise Abbott. 'Food exports to Asia are up two-hundred per cent in the last decade.'

'So, the Punjab is majority Sikh, and millions of Hindus and Muslims arriving didn't go down well with the locals. We can trace the genesis of the current crisis back to the rape and murder of a local Sikh girl. The local Punjabis blamed new Muslim immigrants, and a mob beat some Muslim men to death; one thing led to another, and a month later, three thousand people are dead.'

196

'To that point, the Indian government still had a grip on the situation. Last summer, the rivers irrigating the crops dried up, because the Himalayan glaciers feeding them melted down to nothing. Their flow stopped, production plummeted, and it literally became life-and-death as people began to starve. Militias formed on religious and ethnic lines; Muslims, Sikhs and Hindus viciously fighting each other for water; and when the national government couldn't solve their problems, they turned on the government as well.'

'Climate change is like HIV for nations,' said Holloway from the panel. 'It weakens the state so that otherwise controllable malignancies escalate out of control.'

'So, the government decided to support Indian climate asylum seekers, knowing it'd provoke us into a fight, to distract everyone from the bigger issues they've got at home,' said Laffite.

'Pretty much. Our assessment is that high-level individuals are in the pocket of the people smugglers, which incentivised this course of action even more.' Alice shrugged.

'They also correctly picked that the US wouldn't step in. They outmaneuvered us.' She paused to think. 'How close are you to finding out who's running the smuggling business?'

'We're pursuing two avenues. We've got an asset in Kolkata who is selling places on the ships. We can't be too pushy though, because anybody they suspect is talking to intel teams gets 'disappeared' rather quickly.'

'Can't we incentivise him to talk?'

The intel people glanced at each other.

'Hmm?' prodded the PM. 'Stop pretending to be squeamish. If this guy in Kolkata knows something and you need to tickle him to make him sing, get tickling.'

'You can't just walk into Kolkata and clamp electrodes on someone's nipples,' said Holloway.

'Why not?'

'Well, ah…it's a fairly specialised job. All of our experienced interrogators will stand out in downtown Kolkata, and we don't have any facilities there. An extraction would be better.'

'Explain for the benefit of the room what else you're doing?' said Laffite.

'Following the money trail,' continued Alice. 'We're trying to hack the accounts of the ship-breaking yards, see who's been sending them big chunks of change lately. Unfortunately, it's more complicated than that, because the funds are no doubt sent by some form of peer-to-peer currency, so it's hard to track.'

'What makes it so hard to track?' called an airforce major.

'Legitimate transactions occur using a bank as an intermediary,' said Holloway, 'so it's easy to track transactions. You ask, or subpoena the bank, to tell you who sent what where, and who received it. Or we can hack in ourselves.' He shrugged. 'Criminals usually use peer-to-peer networks for transactions that eliminate the middle-man and use virtual currencies they can exchange for real currency at a later time.'

'I read somewhere that the transactions have to go to a specific web address, so wouldn't you be able to track them that way?' probed Laffite.

Holloway gave Laffite a speculative look. 'Their identities are hidden behind public-private key encryption pairs; you can't track account holders by tracking transactions. On top of that, even though the system records transactions, they are also sent to every other user in the system, to make sure the numbers always stack up. When you don't have a banking middleman to do the maths and make sure it all adds up, you need to keep everyone informed of every transaction; so, a colossal amount of data hides the transactions we're looking for.'

'How do they turn that into real-world currency, can you track that?'

Holloway turned up his palms and shrugged. 'That's the problem. They probably don't even need to convert it to hard currencies. You can buy anything you want with it, except, maybe your groceries. By the time the money used to, say, buy a couple of junked coal carriers gets back to the real world it's so far removed from the original transaction it's clean as hospital sheets.'

'Hmm. Is it a question of resources?' Laffite asked.

Holloway glanced at Alice, who nodded, 'It's a very specialised area, but we could recruit systems experts from universities, and research organisations and hopefully yield results.'

'Let's do that then,' said Laffite. She eyeballed Alice. 'I'm counting on you to figure out who's behind this new travel business. If we can ID him, we can take him out.' She turned her gaze to Futcher and Harridge, head of Special Forces. 'And that, gentlemen, is where you come in. Tell me, Admiral Futcher, how close can one of our submarines get to Kolkata docks?'

Fleet Base West
2100 hours

Later than evening, Robertson trod across the dunes of Bauche Bay, on the western edge of Garden Island. Chalky sand crunched under his feet and flowed between his toes. He'd rolled his trousers above his ankles, and his shirtsleeves flapped above his wrists in the gentle breeze. Under a full moon, the Indian Ocean glinted silver as waves tumbled upon the sand which radiated the most subtle hint of muted gold, like an amber long taken from the fire and left to cool in a dark room.

Tangled shrubs silhouetted into dark shadows opposite the break. It was hauntingly desolate, but the words of the woman striding next to him entirely occupied his attention.

'I'm not angry, Glen. I'm disappointed. You've turned into what you were before we got together, an angry drunk.' She shrugged. 'I wasn't interested in that guy then, and I'm not interested in him now.'

A larger-than-usual wave swept up the sand, forcing them to skip up the dunes to stay dry.

She didn't sound emotional or upset; she seemed calm and rational as though she was delivering a briefing. It worried him.

After the briefing, he'd gone to her billet and told her he'd wait for her at the southern end of the beach at sunset to talk things through.

She'd kept him waiting thirty minutes, but she'd shown. That was all that mattered.

'At first, I assumed you'd come around in a few days, or weeks, even. Obviously, what happened was awful, and I didn't expect you to be one hundred per cent, but you pushed me away when I wanted to help, or at least be there for you if you needed me.'

The thing was, he felt good. Great even. Better than he'd felt in a long, long time. Glen had hit bottom and scraped along for a while. Now, he'd levered himself up and was riding the resolve of someone who'd figured out how never to hit rock bottom again.

But he couldn't just tell her that, because she'd look at him like he was a fraud, and frankly, he had no evidence that he wasn't. So, he was going to let her talk, and hopefully, when she'd finished telling him how she felt, she'd agree to give him another chance.

The silence stretched. Glen guessed it was his cue and cleared his throat.

'You're right. I'm not proud of what I've been doing the last few months. I don't make excuses, but I have to be honest, I found it incredibly difficult to process. Not just what happened to that ship. But what happened after, with the Navy...' he wanted to mention how they'd hung him out to dry, but it was another excuse. It was just something that had happened now. '...I just found it a bit tough.' He touched her elbow, so she looked at him. 'But you're right.' He searched. 'I did push you away. He groped mentally for the right way to express himself. 'I've never really had such a crisis of confidence before, you know? Even after the *Bau Anjing.* In any other situation, I would've turned to you first. Should've been the same this time. I took it really hard.' He fumbled for the right words to express himself. 'There's not much else I can say,' he finished lamely.

She crouched and picked up a shell, tilting her head, so her hair fell to one side. So effortlessly graceful. She caught him looking as she stood up again.

'Glen, I know you're going through hell. But, seriously, what were you thinking? I don't expect anything from you at the moment, but I won't accept a stranger. But, if that's what you want, you'll get it.'

A wry laugh emanated from deep in his chest. 'Oh, I know, I hear you loud and clear. That ship kept sinking over and over in my mind, you know? It's like your eyelids are pinned open and it's on replay unless you're blind drunk or passed out. I didn't want to tell you about it, cos I didn't want it to be your problem. It was my responsibility to deal with, and mine alone. So that's what I did. I mean, the movie was still playing, those people kept drowning, but at least it wasn't your problem. I wanted to protect you from the impact it was having. Obviously, I made it worse.'

He stopped and caught her elbow, and they faced each other. 'After I sank that ship, I didn't care about myself anymore, and it was crushing. So I just went, fuck it, I give up. And then I hated myself for that, too. So yea, I wanted to get away from all these things. I should've told you what was going on in my head. I trust your judgment more than anyone else. I know we could've figured something out together.'

They turned and started walking back towards the base.

'Sounds like you've been rehearsing that for a while...' There was a lightness in her voice that softened the words.

'The other night, Jay told me the same thing you just did. I was going to come to you then, but we got in trouble, and I would've felt ridiculous apologising with bruises all over my face.'

'It's not stopping you now. Besides, getting beaten up is the least ridiculous thing you've done this month,' Alice said wryly.

'Yep. I know. The next morning when I got your message, it was clarity washing through my mind. I even threw out the painkillers so I could hang onto it. Then that prick Swan got on the line and told me I was shipping out here, and I knew we'd get to see each other...and here we are. Anyway. I'm done talking about what a reformed man I am. What I need from you is the chance to prove it.'

She strode on in silence for a while. Then Glen felt Alice's hand slide into his and his chest exploded with relief and warmth. He set his jaw against the sudden wet burning in eyes. He had a clarity of purpose, for his country and this woman. He would never compromise himself like that again.

They were now at the southern end of the stretch of sand. Lights and music emanated from a bar camped in the scrub, with a jetty leading across the sand and extending over the water.

Robertson and Alice climbed up onto the wooden structure and walked to the end, where the water washed past the seaweed-wrapped pylons. They dangled their feet over the edge, and sometimes, with the largest waves, tentacles of cool seawater would reach up and splash their toes. Behind them, they could hear the low murmur of conversation.

'Hey America! Thanks for nothing, assholes!' shouted someone in the bar with a broad Australian accent. 'You useless pussies!'

Robertson shared a look with Alice, who was looking at him knowingly. He gave her an *it's not my fault* look.

'The USS *New Jersey* is in town. We're not so friendly with the yanks anymore.'

Alice just chuckled.

The bar suddenly erupted into an all-in brawl. Robertson and Alice craned their heads to watch.

'Aren't you going to do something' Alice asked.

'Hmm…no. They're sorting it out in their own way.'

A sailor, probably American, was flung out of the fight and sprawled on the jetty in front of them.

'Apologies ma'am…sir!' he said scrambling to his feet. He tipped them a salute and charged back inside.

'I think you should do something,' said Alice. 'What if someone gets hurt?'

He burst out laughing. 'I think that's the point. It'll wind down shortly, there's not much I can do. Besides, it's good for morale.'

She snorted and slapped him on the shoulder. 'You're just worried you'll get the wrong end of it again.'

'No.' He put his arm around her shoulders. 'I got everything I need right here.'

Chapter 18
Internment Camp - Geraldton
September 9th

A fresh, dry breeze washed across Fadi's skin. He was on his cot, lying on his back, hands behind his head. The gusts cooled the sweat which made his shirt cling to his front, and blew away the *Tamil-Nadu*-esque, almost chewable odour of the camp septic tanks. He closed his eyes. Dusk was his favourite time of the day. The sun had just winked out, the searing heat finally absent, only the warmth radiating from the creaking and popping corrugated iron roof was evidence of the sun's long onslaught. Fortunately for Fadi, warm light still reflected off the atmosphere even as stars twinkled in the blue-black sky.

He'd come out here to escape the meat grinder that was life in the sheds. There was plenty of food and health care in the camp, but that didn't stop gangs of men forming to secure those necessities of life where demand always exceeds supply. Alcohol, drugs, and sex were the most valuable commodities in the camp now. It reminded him of the Sonagachi, except it had a below-the-surface feel to it, like watching fish six feet deep, because of the heavily regulated environment. Fadi knew of several women and girls who'd been cornered and attacked, and he'd even caught a few men eyeing him surreptitiously if he wandered around late at night.

He shoved his worries from his mind and took in his surroundings. The camp was set up in a clumpy dustbowl next to a gravelly highway. During the day, the breeze dried your skin and whipped across the ground picking up grit to fling in your eyes.

But at dusk, the crushing heat of the day faded, and the penetrating chill of the desert nighttime was yet to settle. The sea-breeze wicked sweat off his skin and Fadi felt energised, relaxed. The giant sheds came alive at dusk. He sighed.

Despite being a prisoner, he found this place, this land, truly breath-taking.

He'd dragged his cot outside and behind the main wall of his shed. There was nothing between him and the chain-link fence that kept the world at bay.

He'd come out here, because sometimes if you were lucky, you could get some privacy, and he liked to be alone with his thoughts as the sun went down. He spent it dedicating some time to remember his mother and Jay. His father, and his abandoned home in Kolkata. Fadi didn't mourn anymore, but it was where he was from, and who he was, from the dusty souls of his feet to the depths of his imagination. Now that he'd lost so much, he loved where he was from with a ferocity he'd never had before. *Even though,* he thought wryly to himself, *you sacrificed everything to get away.*

Perhaps because of this appreciation of where he'd come from, there was an openness, a desire to let this new land into his imagination too. Not just because he had nowhere else to go either, but from the little he could see from behind the wire, this country was starkly, majestically beautiful, as only a truly ancient landscape can be.

He wasn't here to cause problems. All he wanted was a safe place he could call home. Pretty humble aspirations, he thought. Surely somewhere in this giant land, there was somewhere he could call his own?

'There you are! I've been looking everywhere for you. Should've known you were out here, avoiding people. Daydreaming again, are we? Where are you off to this time, Fadi?' said a twinkling, melodious voice, interrupting his thoughts.

He pretended to be asleep. The thin mattress on his cot shifted slightly as the owner of the voice leaned close to him.

Eyes still closed, he smiled in spite of himself. 'What makes you think I'm daydreaming, Khandi?'

205

'Because, Fadi my dear, you're smiling, and there's no reason to smile unless you're pretending to be somewhere else.' He felt he shift again, and when she spoke next, it was close to his ear, in a conspiratorial whisper. 'Take me with you Fadi, wherever you are,'

His smile widened into a chuckle. 'Oh Khandi, how could I refuse you? Come with me, I'll take you wherever you wish to go.'

'Ha!' she jammed her hands into his ribs. 'I've heard that before! You men are all the same!' she said as she pinned him to the cot, squealing with laughter and thrashing like a fish on a hook.

She eventually let him go, and he lay there, panting, mock outraged.

'Oh, you'll pay for that! Tonight, when you least expect it, I'll…' and he gaped, blushing, and out of inspiration.

'You'll what, Fadi?' she teased, eyebrow arched.

'I'll put one of those giant moths in your mouth while you sleep,' he finished lamely.

'Pfft,' she snorted derisively. 'I sleep with my mouth closed, like a lady.'

'Not likely. Your gums flap when you snore like curtains out of a broken window in a gale -ow!' Fadi yelled as her sandal crashed into the side of his head.

'I work very hard to maintain my image, and I won't have a heathen such as yourself falsely blacken it,' Khandi said primly, a smile dancing around the edges of her mouth.

'Or else risk being the victim of very un-ladylike violence,' he grumbled.

'Obviously.' She arranged her sheets on her mattress. Sometimes she brought her bedding out here, and they slept outside together, talking a little but mostly watching the stars.

She tilted her head towards him, eyes twinkling with thought. 'I don't know how you do it, Fadi,' she said eventually.

'Do what?'

'How do you maintain your humanity in a place like this? It's the law of the jungle in there, strong picking on weak. You seem to separate yourself from it all. You alone seem to have mastered your animal instincts.' He looked at her, abashed. 'I guess what I'm saying is, I feel safe around you.' She shrugged.

Fadi nodded slowly. He fought back a sudden pang of dizziness washing through him, like water through a fine sieve. *He hadn't kept his mother safe, or his brother. He didn't feel safe in this place.*

The moment passed. Fortunately, Khandi was studying the scrub beyond the fence and hadn't noticed anything. Khandi, eight years older than him, and, like him, alone. He was sure everyone with common sense who met Khandi was at least a little bit in love with her. He mainly loved her because she was a beautiful human, a tiny flickering candle of hope in this dark place. She reminded him so much of his mother. He swallowed the traitorous lump that was growing in his throat.

He must have dozed off because he woke with a start; something must have disturbed him. Cicadas buzzed loudly. He propped himself up groggily and peered around. It was pretty dark out here, that's why he liked it actually; he'd never seen such a busy sky.

Khandi's bed was empty. *She's probably gone to the toilet.* He looked closer - for some reason she'd thrown the sheets far off the bed and onto the dirt. One trailed away a few metres. He frowned. Not like Khandi to be so...messy. She wouldn't have bothered going inside, more likely she'd just gone up the wall a bit for privacy.

After a few minutes, she hadn't returned, and he frowned to himself. On balance, he thought, he'd feel better about disturbing Khandi while she was taking a squat, than doing nothing and finding out some of the marauding men had cornered her. *She's relying on you for her safety. She literally just told you exactly that.* Mind made up, he got up and trotted down the length of the wall towards the bulk of one of the septic tanks. The giant waste processing plant jutted out from the shed wall, forming a blunt T that caught the light and cast deep shadows the size of half a tennis court where the two structures met. He peered in. 'Khandi,' he called. 'You in there?'

Nothing. Fadi moved around the tank, feeling a little foolish. She was probably back at their cots, wondering what had happened to *him.*

He froze. Scratching, scrabbling sounds were coming from the other side of the tank. A loud *slap* and they ceased as suddenly as they'd started. His heart thumped in his chest, and he continued to edge around the tank. 'Khandi,' he called hoarsely into the dark pools on the other side.

A dark shape quickly flashed in front of him, and a bony man jammed a greasy, reeking cloth into his mouth. Something blunt crashed into his head and he slumped. He felt the man straddle him from behind and something hard crush against his throat. He grabbed it and pulled with all his strength, but it didn't budge.

Beside him, he was suddenly aware of Khandi, groaning, struggling with her attackers, then a harsh whisper in the darkness. 'Make a sound, pretty flower, and your boyfriend will die, and then so will you, and we'll fuck you anyway.'

Khandi whimpered once and was silent. Groggy from the blow to the head and faint from lack of air through the gag, all he could see were Khandi's enormous eyes, locked on his, white with panic, tears reflecting terror in the moonlight.

One of the men peeled off her jeans off, jerking them down her legs. Two more were kneeling, one either side of her chest, a knee pinning her shoulders to the sand. They'd jammed a rag into her mouth and her head compressed into the sand. One of them pulled her shirt up under her chin, and her breasts fell to either side of her chest.

Fadi had often wondered what they looked like, but never like this. He felt so ashamed and weak that he wanted to vomit.

The other man reached out and put his hand between her legs, slapping lightly.

Khandi struggled then. She kicked and bucked violently, almost threw one of the men off her. She started screaming, but it only came out as a distant, muffled squeal. The man who'd nearly come off her recovered and punched her hard in the face, twice. Her head, jammed into the ground, took the full force of the blows. Fadi heard her nose shatter, and as his eyes adjusted to the dark, he saw blood squirt and wash into one eye. He saw the gap appear in her lip where her teeth had pierced it, and he heard the man swear low, and angrily.

'Bitch! Look what she did to my hand - I got her teeth stuck in my knuckles!'

Fadi went berserk. He threw his head back as hard as he could and felt it impact a face.

A muffled cry and the man holding him spun away. Fadi launched himself on the men holding Khandi. No plan, just an insane, animal desire to kill. Knocked one away, found an eye socket and dug a nail into it. The man grabbed his wrist and Fadi was about to drill down into the motherfucker's brain when the guy with the baton came out of nowhere and swatted him in the face with it. Hard. Something broke, and a white light flashed through his head. Tingles shot down his arms, then they stopped working. Come on, die you fucking cunt, he thought as he tried to drill his hand into the guy's skull, but his body wouldn't respond. The man with the bat struck again, and again, and eventually, Fadi rolled off the man he desperately wanted to kill and collapsed on the ground, broken.

Still the blows came, and through it all, Fadi could feel parts of his body snapping, crushing, and rupturing. A gurgling, spasming sound caught Fadi's attention and he realised Khandi was choking to death on her own blood.

He jabbed a finger weakly at his dying friend, and one of the men eventually realised what was going on.

'Look! We'll have to take the gag out so she can breathe!' he whispered frantically.

Fadi couldn't move. He felt like a car that had crashed into a tree but was still crabbing down the road. Khandi was still choking to death and these murderous bastards had subdued him utterly.

'I'm gonna take this rag out so you can breathe,' the man with the baton said to Khandi, whose arms were somehow still pinned by one of the men. 'But, if you make a sound we'll finish that little prick over there off, get it?' Her eyes rolled spastically, one drowning in blood, and her head flopped in a nod.

He slowly pulled the rag out of her mouth, and she ripped a gasp of air, filling her lungs with the most desperate, heart-rending sound of salvation Fadi had ever heard.

Khandi's breathing had slowed down a little now, and she managed to tilt her head at Fadi, who himself was sucking air through what felt like a broken nose.

Once again, he lunged towards her, but he was too weak, too damaged, and the man holding him wrenched him back and slapped him hard on the side of the head.

'It's ok, Fadi. Don't get hurt for me.' She smiled then, her torn lips peeling back over her shattered teeth, one eye glistening red. 'I'll just have to be like you. I can pretend to be somewhere else.'

Khandi lay down. She didn't struggle anymore, and the men took her, one after the other, in front of Fadi who could do nothing. He looked away, but he knew the sounds of the men panting, the wet slap of skin on skin, and Khandi's soft whimpers would haunt him forever.

The last man finished, and they left with dire warnings about what would happen if they tried to report it.

Soon it was once again just Fadi and Khandi, and the haunting, beautiful southern sky.

Khandi didn't speak to anyone after that. Nor did she let any of the nurses treat her.

On the first day, Fadi tracked her down. He sat down next to her and gently said hi. She'd just looked right through him when he tried to speak with her, then turned and faced the other way. He stared at her back, broken mouth working like a fish out of water. After a while, people started looking at him strangely. He went away.

On the second day, he'd found her again, curled up foetal in her cot like a child. At first, he thought she was asleep but her eyes, black and blue bruised now, were open, unblinking like she could see things that weren't there. He'd tried to speak to her. Without looking at him or blinking, she'd told him to go away. Her mouth couldn't form the words properly for the missing teeth and giant gash in her top lip.

Khandi had retreated into her broken, catatonic body and while her eyes were open, Fadi could tell she was looking in and reliving the memories.

On the third day, Fadi left her alone. He couldn't face her - he'd failed to protect her, just as he'd failed his mother and his brother. What use would a woman like Khandi have for such a pathetic creature who couldn't even keep her safe? People needed to be safe. He couldn't keep the women in his life safe. He wanted to scream.

He wanted to kill.

On the fourth day, he wandered around aimlessly, hoping he'd catch sight of her somewhere. Eventually, he took his mattress and went outside, behind the main shed. He found her then - she was sitting on the ground, back against the shed wall in the spot where it had happened. She looked asleep. He edged closer, not sure how to approach her.

Then he saw.

She'd taken a plastic bottle and used a sharp rock to cut it in half. Then she'd taken the jagged plastic edges and sawn through the skin in her forearms.

She'd bled out in the afternoon sun, and by the time Fadi found her, the sea-breeze had dried the rivers of blood in the dirt around her to a fractured black clay, already crawling with ants.

Chapter 19
HMAS Stirling
September 10th, 2200 hours

Commander Jack Phillips rested his elbows on the bulkhead of the HMAS *Kati-Thanda's* conning tower and licked his salty lips. A nasty wind flung spray off the rolling whitecaps and peppered his face. He squinted to starboard; the Australian mainland was a vague grey shape squatting behind the squall.

'Doesn't get much more disappointing than this,' muttered his XO, Dean Albrecht.

'What do you mean?' Phillips asked, blinking salty water from his eyes.

'What do you mean, what do I mean? I was hoping for a final dose of UV before zipping up inside the can for the next two months.' The submarine heaved on the swell and Albrecht used the motion to shift across the tower. 'Can't even see Pig Trough Bay. Never deployed without a final longing gaze at the golden sands of Pig Trough Bay, Jack.'

'You think it means something?'

'How can it not? Appalling weather ruining my *Feng Shui* and that ugly dry-dock shelter bolted to *Katie's* perfect ass.' He sighed. 'Not to mention the eight SAS guys clogging up weapons stowage.' He flubbed his lips. 'It's gonna be an unpleasant few months.'

Phillips chuckled. Among Albrecht's many talents was seeing the negative in every situation. Jack didn't mind; it ensured his plans were properly stress tested.

'This weather's a *good* omen, not a bad one,' said Phillips as a wave crashed into the tower.

'Enlighten me,' laughed the XO.

'Have a look around. You could be a destroyer jock, stuck in this putrid weather for all time. Instead, you get a warm, cosy control room full of sweet-smelling sailors for six weeks straight.'

'Ah! Motivation levels rising as we speak! Do you think our special forces guests are green yet?'

'I hope so, why else do you think we haven't dived yet? We could stay up longer to extend your appreciation of your environment when we dive if you like.'

'That won't be necessary, Jack. You know me; nobody on this boat is as capable of being so thankful, for so little, as I am.'

A smile played on Phillips' lips. He turned to the officer of the watch. 'Sound the dive alarm, Hogan. Close her up and take her down to snorkel depth. Course bearing three-one-zero, speed ten knots, making way under snorkel.' He gestured to the ladder leading down into the heart of the submarine. 'After you, gentlemen.'

Twenty minutes later, Phillips, Hogan, Albrecht and Sergeant Will Marriott, SAS, sat around the fold-out laminate table in the officer's mess. If the heaving seas had had an impact on the army man, it wasn't showing. His face was as weathered and pitted as a sandstone building after a firefight; and as impassive as he listened to Phillips speak.

'Gentlemen. You're all aware, to some degree, of what our objective is on this mission. This briefing is to clarify expectations. In summary, Command has tasked us with ferrying Sergeant Marriott's squad to the mouth of the Hoolie River, where they'll load into the swimmer delivery vehicle housed in the Dry Deck Shelter attached to our rear. They will carry out their mission, during which time the SDV will return to *Katie.* We will egress the area and rendezvous with Marriott and his team further out to sea.' He spooned some beef stroganoff into his mouth. *Delicious* beef stroganoff, he corrected himself. Praterman, the cook, truly was a genius.

There were no questions.

'Nothing is ever simple, however, and the Indians have a string of underwater acoustic sensors to warn of submarines in their ocean approaches. They run a combination of US, Russian and indigenous systems which makes it hard to know their

214

precise capabilities. Our analysts tell us the most likely scenario is that their technology level is about the same as ours.'

'Are your navy analysts any good?' asked Marriott.

Phillips shrugged. 'Sometimes yes, sometimes no. Depends on how many gaps they have to fill. I'm inclined to believe them this time, because they bought the same baseline sensor technology we did, to protect our approaches. In fact, the same guys from Alcatel-Lucent who trained up our Signals Directorate people were the implementation managers for the Indian rollout. They've got similar hierarchy alert algorithms, and we should assume they've been dialled up to maximum sensitivity.'

'What does that mean out here in the real world?' rumbled Marriott, a boulder sitting in Phillips' mess.

'It means that every time a fish farts within detection range of the net, it'll get flagged up for closer analysis. The real question is, how much processing capability do they have? They'll be combing a lot of data. I'm not kidding,' said Hogan seriously when Marriott grunted, unconvinced.

'If they can detect a fish fart, how are we supposed to evade this net?' If the news about the Indian sensors bothered him, it certainly didn't show; the man was methodically mopping up the sauce on his plate with a slice of bread.

'That's the trick. We're going to cruise for a few days at snorkel depth. Then we'll dive and play hide and seek with Glen Robertson's task force; they're going to see if this DDS makes us easier to detect while he does a shakedown on his new crew and systems.'

'Glen Robertson's up there?' said Marriott, who looked mildly impressed. 'Is he any good?'

The sailors glanced smiles at each other. 'If Glen Robertson can't find us, then neither will the Indians,' said Phillips. 'Of that, I'm absolutely certain. After he's painted our new acoustic signature, we'll continue north to the realistic outer limit of their net. Then we'll dive and go into quiet mode.' He

215

swallowed the mouthful of food he'd been talking around. 'In practice, gentlemen, as far as the rest of the world is concerned, we're going to disappear.'

The next day, the *Hobart* eased away from Diamantina peer, pilot pointing her north to the open ocean. Robertson stood on the bridge, embracing the minute shifting of the deck beneath his feet.

'*Ahead slow,*' he ordered. The newly repaired warship steamed through Cockburn Sound, tracking the path of the *Kati-Thanda* the day before. Today, the weather was perfect, and the *Hobart* cut through the ultramarine sea with no more noise than the muted *thrumming* coming from the turbines down in engineering.

When it caught them up, the *Hobart* would be the lead ship in a taskforce consisting of another destroyer, the *Sydney*, and two frigates.

Swan had caught up with him before he'd left. Offered painful congratulations on being appointed task force commander and told him he was free to engage Indian naval assets with extreme prejudice but to leave the tankers alone. He'd handed Robertson his briefing pack, told him not to fuck things up, again, and turned on his heel. Robertson had shrugged.

Swan was a cock.

'XO, we have seventy-two hours until we intercept the Indian illegals' ship *Pong-Sawan,*' Robertson said to Palmer, his second in command. 'In the meantime, I want us running air-defence drills continuously. I want any kinks in the hardware or chain of command identified and rectified before we're in range of those Brahmos.'

'Sir.'

'What do the latest diagnostics tell us?'

'Most systems are ok. There is one significant issue to resolve still; the navigation sensors aren't integrating properly. The data's coming in, but it's not displaying coherently.'

'Who's working on it?'

'Jansen's in the control room playing with circuits now.'

Robertson motioned Palmer to follow him and slid down the gangway from the bridge to the control room. A young sailor was peering intently at a console, fingers tapping code.

Robertson crouched down to Jansen's level and studied the screen for a moment. 'What are we looking at here, Jansen?

Jansen swivelled his head. His fingers didn't stop. 'Ah, the sensors are all reading good numbers, sir, but someone, probably the contractor, didn't check it was set up properly before green-lighting it as ok. He checked the feed but didn't check they were talking to each other.'

'You got it under control?'

'I dunno, sir, It's not really my field of expertise, I'm just the operator. The contractor was meant to-'

'Jansen, sometimes in war, as in life, things don't go your way. The contractor isn't here so he can't fix it. I want solutions, not problems.'

'Oh.' Jansen swallowed. 'Well, I gotta get the radar, fire control, and comms feeds to talk to each other. They're all functioning fine, so I just have to reintegrate them.'

'Is there anybody on board who understands these systems, or could otherwise help?'

Jansen thought for a moment. 'Morieira is pretty handy with this stuff. If he helped, it would speed things up.'

Robertson turned to Palmer. 'Get Morieira up here asap.'

To Jansen, he said, 'How long are we talking, Jansen?'

'Um...three or four hours? Give or take?'

Robertson checked the digital clock on the wall. 'Up and running in three hours. That's...ten-hundred hours. He fixed Jansen with a smile, his eyes kind but also, Jansen noticed, burning with a focused intensity that conveyed both confidence and a clear expectation of results from Jansen. 'Make it so,' said Robertson. He moved to a console on the

217

wall and picked up the 1MC handset, the ship-wide communicator.

'All hands, this is your captain. Be advised that in the absence of standard shakedown timescales we'll be running continuous ASW, AAW, and damage-control drills for this short deployment. As you are aware, Taskforce *Broomhandle's* mission is to escort the bulker *Pong-Sawan* into shore. In the meantime, we will be preparing for any eventuality. All systems and procedures will be locked down post-haste, and our drill schedule will reflect this necessity. Out.'

He clapped Palmer on the shoulder and headed for the exit. 'Jansen!'

'Yes, sir,' mumbled Jansen, attention on his console.

'Those drills are running whether the nav display is operational or not. This is your time to shine, sailor.'

'Aye sir, I'm on it.'

'Glad to hear it.' Robertson pointed to Palmer who flicked a switch on the console behind him. A ship-wide klaxon sounded; a swarm of hypersonic cruise missiles was cutting towards the ship in a simulated attack.

'Bastard,' muttered Jansen as he, and the rest of the ops room crew, leapt to battle stations.

Five days later and two-thousand kilometres northwest later *Katie* pushed quietly through the water. Only her snorkel, feeding air to the diesel engines, was visible from the surface. Inside, Darwin, the navigator, was speaking to the group of men gathered around the luminous table screen which at this moment was displaying a bathymetric map of the Indian Ocean floor.

'So, if we look at the ocean floor to the west of Australia, the Ninety East Ridge runs pretty much north-south for five and a half thousand clicks, basically from the same longitude as Perth, straight as a die, all the way up to just off the coast of Aceh here, in Indonesia.' The underwater mountain range, displayed in different shades of blue to denote depth, pierced all the way up to the south-eastern reaches of the Bay of Bengal. He popped some gum into his mouth and chewed exactly four times to release the flavour, then went on.

'Since we're in a hurry, we've got to take the shortest, most practicable route; which means straight up, cutting between Indonesia on the east, and the NER on the west.'

Katie appeared on the map, fifteen hundred kilometres north-west of Perth, equidistant between home-port and the closest reaches of the drowned mountain range.

'The quickest way to Kolkata is through this gap here,' he said, and a portion of the map began throbbing a soft yellow. 'You'll notice that this forms a sort of natural chokepoint, with the north end of the NER forming the western edge, the Andaman Sea in the middle, with Aceh and the Andaman Islands, to the east.'

'That chokepoint is a hundred-kilometres wide and...' said Albrecht, rubbing his chin, which was starting to itch under his stubble, leaving his audience on tenterhooks 'the NER at that point is over two clicks deep. It's a choke-point in theory only, or am I missing something?'

'Indeed, you are. The Indians have installed a two-thousand-click line of sensors, anchored to the ridge, starting at the top here. Two-clicks sounds deep, but the ocean on either side averages about five clicks down. It's north-south facing because it was designed to keep the Chinese out, who'd be attacking through the Straits of Malacca, not us; but it's so long, it's walled us in any way. It's basically the Maginot Line of underwater detection.'

'Right, so all of a sudden a hundred-kilometre gap becomes a lot smaller than it sounds because you'd have surface assets plugging the choke point,' said Phillips. 'What's the disposition of their assets?'

Darwin pressed a button, and Indian warships suddenly dotted the map.

'This info is twelve hours old, but you're right, sir. There is what looks like an anti-sub taskforce just west of the Andaman Islands. *Shivalik* class frigates.'

Phillips broke the ensuing silence. 'OK, Darwin. Good background. Any suggestions on breaking through this picket?'

'Well sir, I was chatting to Malik over here about this, because I'm just interested in this stuff, but Chinese sub capabilities have come a long way in the last twenty years and their conventional stand-off weapons, in particular, are pretty advanced. Hypersonic cruise missiles and what have you, so, obviously, if we're talking ballistic missiles subs this is all moot cos they deploy for months and sit off strategic targets-'

He stopped suddenly; it had suddenly occurred to Darwin that everybody in the room already knew this stuff.

'Anyway, Malik made the point that since this net was put there to stop Chinese nuclear attack subs from getting close enough to launch cruise missiles or disrupt their staging areas, their net will be calibrated to prioritise the noise signature of Chinese nuclear attack subs, not an Australian diesel sub, especially since we're meant to be allies.' He brought up a schematic on the screen. 'It was Malik's idea though, so I'll let him talk it through.'

Chief Sonar Officer Hakim Malik stood up. The short, stocky man took over administration of the console and changed the display.

'This, ladies and gentlemen, is a Type Oh-Nine-Five Chinese nuclear attack sub, otherwise known as a Qin class. In the grand tradition of the Chinese military, it's essentially just a new and 'improved' version of the Akula III class the Rusky's developed in the mid-nineties.' He bobbed his head and shrugged his shoulders. 'We've actually got a pretty good handle on what Qin class acoustics look like, partly through data sharing with the Indians, ironically enough. So, what we can do, is overlay what we know about their broadband/narrowband noise signature with what we know about *Katie's*.'

Phillips nodded. 'That makes the info we discovered in our exercises with Robertson on the way up here even more valuable. The DDS will have changed our acoustics somewhat.'

'Silver lining of that clever bastard Robertson getting a bead on us,' muttered Albrecht. During the short anti-submarine exercises they'd conducted, Robertson and his task force of frigates and destroyers had managed to track *Katie* for all of a few seconds before she disappeared; long enough for someone to get off a shot if it had been real.

'That genius Robertson,' said Phillips. 'Be glad he's on our side.' Phillips had been fuming at the time, but Robertson had sent a data packet with the anomalies that had given *Katie* away. It had arrived with a crude cartoon animation of a submarine breaking in half and sinking which *Katie's* crew had met with strained smiles and clenched jaws. Then appeared white letters on a black page spelling the message: *Stay low, go slow, shoot first, one shot, one kill, no luck, all skill. Hobart wishes you luck, Katie.*

'Cheeky bastards,' Albrecht had said at the time. Apart from the good-natured gloating, the data packet had shown how the DDS changed the submarines' flow through the water as it drifted through the depths, and now they could incorporate that into Katie's established flow regimes. Tracking a Barracuda class diesel on silent mode was virtually impossible; Albrecht was glad Robertson was on their side.

'What's all this mean, Malik?' asked Phillips.

'Well the Chinese subs are noisier than us in general, cos they're Russian knock-offs made-in-China, but their actual profile is pretty much the same except for this little bit here,' he said pointing to a spike in the Chinese subs noise signature at around the forty-hertz range. 'We think this is their cooling system for the reactor-pumps, pressurizer, and so on. You can see their noise profile is different from ours in that respect and if I was searching for Chinese attack boats, I'd dial in my sensors to be looking for that noise profile.'

'So, you're saying we should try to sneak past their sensors instead of under that picket?' suggested Phillips.

'Yes, sir. We're quieter in all the frequencies the Indians are dialled in to search for; they won't be listening in at the one frequency range we're louder. The catch is, we need to stay under five knots because the DDS ruins our flow above that.'

'Ok.' Phillips nodded. 'We'll get up to about here,' the map reappeared, and he tapped a sheath of ocean, west of the northern tip of Sumatra. 'Before we reach the picket, we'll dive, turn left and slip past their sensors, straight into the Bay, where we'll resurface to recharge the batteries. From there it's plain sailing all the way to Kolkata.'

September 15th
HMAS *Hobart*, 1945 hours

'Results please, XO,' said Robertson. He already knew the results; he just wanted them announced to the ops room personnel.

'The scenario simulated a forty-five-missile attack on a four-ship taskforce, C&C centred on the *Hobart*,' said his XO. 'Twenty-six were successfully engaged beyond visual range by the SM-6 screen, a further thirteen within visual range by Sea Sparrows. Three taken out by Phalanx, one missile drawn off by countermeasures.' He paused. 'Two found homes, including one on the bridge of the *Hobart*.'

Robertson frowned. That kept happening. 'Systems report.'

'All systems are now fully functional and integrated. Technicians have resolved the cooling problems with the new radar panel and Jansen has properly integrated the navigation feed.'

'Non-combat systems?'

XO gave a frowning nod, 'All departments report full operational capability,' he said with a shrug. 'Although, maintenance reports an intermittent problem with the plumbing.'

Robertson started. 'What problems with the plumbing?'

'Well, it seems the toilets are backing up every now and then, something to do with overpressure in the plumbing when we go to flank speed. It's no big deal, just a case of a one-way valve not working properly. It's a quick fix.'

Maybe Sathish really had booby-trapped his toilets instead of integrating his systems properly.

All-in-all however, he was satisfied with the way the crew was performing, the new bridge crew in particular. For the past five days, he'd drilled his crew mercilessly, including the thirty-six hours they'd spent hunting *Katie*. Jack Phillips was a crafty, sly operator and had nearly evaded him. That said, he was proud his crew had found the submarine - it was no small achievement, even with the DDS making it louder; Katie was *quiet*. He'd been pleased with his crew and had let them know. They were starting to see results in the anti-air drills too. They were rapidly becoming a team, integrating with each other and their systems. They were also getting tired. He was tired; he'd been harder on himself than anyone. He knew all the *Hobart's* systems back to front, having served on her before, but he'd never commanded the ship and wanted to understand how man and machine worked under pressure.

He retired to his cabin and set up a line to Swan, back at Garden Island. His CO's weather-beaten head appeared on the screen.

'Sir, I'm satisfied that the *Hobart* is now at operational capability. We've run extensive combat drills and simulations, and all combat and essential systems are one-hundred per cent.'

Swan frowned. 'Very fast indeed, Captain. Are you sure you're not rushing the *Hobart* back to operational status?

'Yes, sir. There's always room for improvement, but the crew has done an exceptional job bringing her back to fighting shape. They're proud of their ship, sir, and are angry about what happened to her.'

'Hmm,' grunted Swan. 'Send the status report over.' He peered down the comms link. 'I hope you're right about your combat status, Robertson.'

'I'm confident, sir.'

'Good. Because five days ago, three more bulkers left Kolkata. There's only one escort; it looks like the INS vessels which escorted the *Pong Sawan* are circling back to meet them halfway. Your job is to stop them from getting through.'

Robertson frowned. 'I don't understand, has the mission changed? A couple of our patrol boats are shepherding *Pong Sawan* into Geraldton, isn't that what we're doing with all the ships?

'No, that was the last ship to get through. Word from up-high is that they were hoping your notoriety would stop any more ships leaving before we had to do something drastic.' He shrugged. 'Didn't work, so now you have to stop them.'

'How am I supposed to do that?'

Swan shrugged. 'Your command, your call. Board, sink, or charm; I'm sure you'll figure it out. You have full discretion to deal with INS vessels, and now you have the same regarding the refugee ships. But they are *not* to reach our shores. This is from the top, Jacqui Laffite. We're drawing a hard line in the sand from here on in.'

'Yes, sir. I must point out that there will be no repeat of the *Tamil Nadu*.'

'Nobody cares how you do it, Robertson. Just make sure it happens.'

There was an uncomfortable pause.

'Robertson.'

'Yes, sir?'

'Good luck.'

Swan cut the link before he could see Robertson's concerned frown transmit down the line.

Chapter 20
September 16th
Internment Camp, Geraldton

Fadi swept the metal rod gently across the concrete, back and forth, soft *swish-swish* barely registering against the background hum of the camp. He sat where Khandi had died, back against the shed, his ass on the same rough concrete on which he was honing his makeshift knife. His cot inside was pushed up against a wall, and he'd worked a leg loose and propped up the end next to the wall with spare blankets. Nobody noticed his bed was missing a corner.

He'd caught Khandi's rapists looking at him sometimes. He knew who they were, and they knew he knew. They'd made subtle gestures implying gruesome consequences if he told anybody. A finger drawn across a throat, or a contemptuous sneer. He'd committed their faces to memory, then just nodded and looked away.

Since Khandi died, he'd only done four things; eat, sleep, hone his makeshift spear, and plan. He'd followed them to their cots and knew where they liked to sit in the dining room. He'd made sure to catch their attention a few times. He'd made sure that in their minds, he was a loose end.

He had always been, he reflected, somewhat reactive in life. Things happened to him. He didn't happen to things. His dad had left him. His mother had booked them passage on the *Tamil Nadu.* The Australians had sunk it and killed his mother and brother. He'd been put in a camp, against his will, then lain there, as useless as ever, and let those men brutalise the last person on earth he cared about. He hadn't realised that it was on him to be there for her, especially when she wasn't there for herself. When she'd killed herself, he'd been somewhere else, ineffective as ever.

He'd decided, in the days since Khandi's death, that he would not be something that life happened to anymore. It hadn't been a conscious choice. It was just a feeling that had settled over him, seeping in through his skin, burrowing down to his bone marrow and the pit of his stomach, deep in his guts. It was more of a fundamental change in personality than a conscious choice.

He would set the agenda and deal with the consequences as they came.

Swish-swish went the knife. Slowly, patiently, over a week, he'd worked the end of the hollow tin pipe into a workable weapon. He tested the point with his finger. Sharp. He licked the blood off his fingertip. *Sharp enough.*

His quarry was usually in the mess hall late, after ten in the evening. He was looking for three men. He slipped the spear-tip down his pants and pulled the drawstring tight so it would stay in place. Couldn't have it dropped out of his pants leg. He made his way to the mess hall, grabbed some fruit and found a corner, back to the wall and waited. Half an hour passed, and he hadn't seen them. He'd have to leave soon because if he kept scanning the room furtively, he'd draw attention from the security teams.

His brain registered a familiar gait in his peripheral vision, and a surge of adrenal flushed into his system - it was Surya, one of Khandi's killers. That's how he thought of them. They'd hadn't cut her open, but they'd taken her to a place emotionally she'd never have got to on her own. *They were killers.*

The man was slender and short, not much taller than Fadi, and had a pockmarked, bulbous nose. Greasy locks of hair partially obscured his eyes, and he twitched his head in an oddly effeminate way to clear his vision; it contrasted strangely with his jutting jaw and hard eyes. Ugly, and easy to dislike. He was with a very handsome, slender man whose name Fadi had learned was Sharma. The man had thick, straight hair and his facial proportions were perfect - in contrast to Surya people were compelled to like him because of his pretty looks and smiling demeanour. His pleasant disposition seemed like

227

camouflage to Fadi, a deceit that made him even more despicable. There was no sign of the third member of the trio who'd been there that night. He considered waiting until they were all together but quickly dismissed the idea. Although he had a new resolve, he had still had to psych himself into what he was about to do. *Tonight's the night, two will do,* he thought.

He stood up and walked past them, made sure they noticed him. Surya nudged Sharma, who was lounging next to another man and shovelling food into his mouth. They both paused and gave him cold, blank looks. He pretended to be nervous and made a beeline to the nearest security guard.

Surya and Sharma stopped what they were doing and fixed him with their full attention. Fadi approached a security contractor leaning against a bench, a stumpy woman who'd hitched her thumbs into her belt.

'Excuse me,' he said, glancing back. Surya and Sharma had fixed him with dangerously blank stares.

'Yes?' the guard grunted.

'Do you know if they'll be serving any other fruit except bananas and apples?' he asked, pointing in the general direction of his the men. He hoped it looked like he was talking about them.

She snorted. 'Do I look like a caterer, kid? Don't know, don't care.'

He absolutely, positively had their attention now. 'Ok, thanks,' he said, and shooting nervous looks behind him, edged towards the exit. In his peripheral vision, he noticed Sharma and Surya had stood up.

He moved slowly through the roofless corridors of the giant shed, never looking back but feeling rather than seeing them following, always just on the edge of vision. He left the enclosed space, and felt the familiar transition out of the stifling odour of humans and heat, and savoured the eucalypt-scented air as it cleansed his lungs.

He edged his way down the side of the building, not going slow, but providing ample opportunity for Surya and Sharma to keep him in sight.

He reached the septic tanks. On this night as most others, the moon was a beacon bright enough to cast shadows. He kicked a pebble into the metal wall. It clanged loudly in the desert evening, and he heard a rustle farther up the wall - Sharma and Surya following.

He rounded the tank, putting it between himself his pursuers, and pulled into a dark crevice which he knew would be obscured by shadow. He could see out, but they couldn't see in. He eased the foot-long length of steel out of his pants and gripped it tightly in his right fist. He breathed as slowly and silently as his thudding heart would permit and strained his ears. The men weren't noisy, but neither were they making a special effort at silence. Fadi heard them come within metres of his hiding place.

These men are here to kill you, Fadi, he thought to himself. *There's no going back now.*

Sharma edged into view. He was looking over his shoulder - on the verge of speaking by the look of it. Fadi stepped forward to strike, consciously telling himself to drive his spear into Sharma's throat, but a vestige of his old self made him hesitate. Sharma's head whipped around, pretty features contorted ugly in rage and he launched himself at Fadi.

Fadi flinched backward, a stabbing terror paralysing him. He whiffed Sharma's body odour a split second before the man was on him. He remembered that smell; it had smothered him the night he watched the men rape Khandi. The recollection jarred him into action and without aiming, he thrust the spear-tip as hard as he could at the onrushing man. Sharma crashed into him, and the metal slid painfully in his hand. Sharma gasped, eyes white as the moon and almost as wide. He sucked a gurgling breath, and suddenly the force went out of his charge and he went limp, staggering Fadi who was still desperately clinging to the bed leg. He twisted out of the way as Sharma collapsed, pulling up as the man fell, the spear tip pulling free. It had pierced Sharma right through the heart. The length glistened wetly in the moonlight.

'Sharma what are you doing -' Surya had edged cautiously around the corner, and Fadi had lost the element of surprise. He launched himself at Surya, who shied away at the last minute and parried with his arms. Fadi felt himself over-shooting and flailed wildly, slashing across Surya's neck. The tip of the blade caught the mans neck, but instead of slicing through, dug in and gouged a chunk of flesh out.

'Ahhh!' Surya bellowed, pain and shock in equal measure. He was between Fadi and the wall of the shed. Fadi had him pinned.

Fadi flexed his grip on the weapon. The rage, the intent, was rushing out of him, like a bath with the plug pulled and he knew he had to act now, or his nerve would fail.

He edged closer to Surya, who was clutching his hand to his neck. Blood was pulsing between his fingers, and they glistened blackly in the ghostly light. Fadi moved in, again not quite sure how to finish the job.

Suddenly Surya jinked left then rushed the other way, trying to shoulder past Fadi who had been fooled by the original feint. Again Fadi slashed wildly, no real aim other than in the general direction of the man's head, yet again he caught flesh. This time it was a little nick, he barely registered the pull as it caught something.

You missed! He thought frantically as Surya cleared past him, then he stumbled to the ground, clutching his face. Then he screamed, the most horrifying sound Fadi had ever heard, and he writhed on the ground clutching his eye. Fadi had caught his eye with his wild swing, slicing through the cornea and into the vitreous body.

Fadi jumped on him, stabbing wildly, piercing chest, shoulder, and neck. Surya flailed with his arms, but he was fighting blind

230

and the shots had little impact because Surya's shrieking filled him with a new terror; the sound would surely draw attention.

In, out, in, out he plunged the bed leg until the man's flailing had slowed to a twitching rattle, and the man seemed to shrink and curl up like a leaf in the summer sun. He wrenched the pole free a final time, wiped it on Surya's pants leg and dashed back to the dark crevice where Sharma was lying, face down and twisted at a weird angle.

Anticipating bloodied clothes, he grabbed the long-sleeved shirt and loose trousers he'd stashed there and pulled them on, concealing the worst of it.

He paused and looked down at the bodies. He felt no sense of joy or even satisfaction. But he felt no guilt either, apart from a distant voice in his head lamenting what he had become. He stuck the blade back down his pants then dashed away silently, the opposite way he'd come.

September 18th
HMAS *Hobart*

Robertson leaned back in the captain's chair and sipped coffee. Like every other system on the *Hobart,* the coffee machine left the one on the *Melbourne* for dead.

A good thing too; he'd barely slept the last week as they'd been practising AAW drills non-stop. His gut told him things would heat up with the Indian escorts.

After his call with Swan, his squadron had followed the Indian ships as they retreated out of Australian waters. They'd slowly built a gap as Robertson hung back, waiting to see what happened when they reached the incoming bulkers. Another destroyer, *Sydney,* was a few clicks off their starboard bow. Behind that, the frigates *Anzac* and *Arunta* were dots on the horizon.

Futcher had tasked P-8 maritime patrol aircraft flying out of RAAF Pearce with tracking both the inbound bulkers and outbound warships; nobody was surprised when they'd reported that the INS vessels had reversed course once the bulkers had reached them. The P-8s fed Robertson a stream of positional updates allowing him to maneuver his taskforce into the path of the oncoming ships. Right now, though, there was a gap in their air cover.

'Get the choppers up,' he said to Palmer. 'I want to know exactly where they are. There is a real risk they'll seize the initiative and attack while we have no air support.'

Robertson leaned on the nav-display. 'Alright, Palmer, let's talk this through. Last known location of enemy vessels was here,' he tapped the screen about five-hundred clicks west of their current location, as the helicopter, which had been on standby, whumped past the bridge. Seahawks from *Sydney,* and the two frigates lifted off their respective ships in the distance. Robertson watched them move silently into the sky.

'If not already, we'll soon be in range of their BrahMos 2s,' said Harper, the weapons officer.

'So, we've got two *Kolkata* class destroyers totalling thirty-two BrahMos 2s and two *Talwar* frigates with another eight each.' He turned to Harper. 'What's happening with those P-8s, when can we expect air support? Be nice to drop a few LRASMs on them and be done with it.'

'Sir, uh, one just left station and the replacement out of Pearce has mechanical issues, they expect it will be here in a few hours.'

Useless, he thought. Aloud, he said; 'Well, if I was an Indian commander I'd attack now when we've got no air support to tip things in our favour. We're going to pull back, out of missile range and stay their hand. When the P-8s are back on station they can send a few ASMs at them before we engage.'

'Sir,' the Tactical Action Officer interjected, 'we're getting radar returns indicating enemy helicopters at the edge of detection range.'

Robertson grunted. So much for that plan. The Indians were going offensive.

232

He raised his voice. 'This is the real deal, ladies and gentlemen. In short order there will be forty-eight BrahMos 2s heading our way. Harper, get our ASMs in the air immediately. We have the latest coordinates from the P-8, they know the general area and the ASMs are self-guiding. We need the choppers to guide our SM-6s onto their inbounds.'

'How should we disperse the flight?'

'Six each on the destroyers. I want to take them out of the fight; we can pick off the frigates later.'

'Yes, sir,' said Harper and issued the command to the *Sydney, Anzac and Arunta.* The three other ships had four LRASMs each, stealthy anti-ship missiles, and the rockets blasted off, piggybacking off *Hobart's* guidance systems, which in turn would rely on the helicopters when they lit up the INS warships with their radars.

'Missiles in the air,' reported Harper.

'Get 2 SM-6s onto each of those Rudras; I want those BrahMos' flying blind.'

The *whoosh-suck* of the missile launch had barely subsided when the TAO spoke again. 'Aircrews are reporting returns indicating multiple launches from all Indian vessels,' he said breathlessly, an edge of panic in his voice.

'Relax, Aiden, we knew this was coming. It's what we trained for.' Robertson studied the chart. The SM-6s were racing to intercept the Rudras which had ducked back below the radar horizon; they'd painted the Australian taskforce for a BrahMos launch and were hightailing it back to their ships.

The Indian ships had far fewer missiles than the Australians, but they had much more powerful offensive weapons, and it's harder to shoot down a hypersonic missile than hit a ship. The Indians had one play, and they'd already made it. If Robertson could survive, he'd be able to pick off the Indians with his leftover SM-6s at will. If he had any.

Or, he thought, *I could go full defensive, soak up their attack, and wait for the P-8s to come back.*

233

'Ten seconds before those BrahMos' are scheduled to pop over the horizon, launch first SM-6 salvo. We'll acquire them and provide targeting en-route. Fire the Sea Sparrows immediately on target acquisition by radar.'

'Two Rudras intercepted,' reported Aiden. 'One managed to get out of range.

Robertson shrugged. A decent start. The BrahMos 2s wouldn't be in radar range for a few minutes. Thirty seconds after they were, they'd either be in the box seat or very, very dead. He settled back in his chair. 'Stay sharp and remember your training,' he said to the bridge. 'Do that, and we'll be perfectly fine.' He forced his jaw to unclench and took another sip of his now cold coffee. He looked at it in disgust.

'Fire SM6s' ordered Robertson, and seconds later the foredeck exploded with pillars of smoke in a cathedral of fire, then curved aggressively towards the inbounds. Seconds later, the BrahMos' sped over the horizon and the radar lit them up.

'We've got twenty vectored on us and *Sydney*, four on the frigates,' said the TAO nervously.

'Thank you, Aiden,' said Robertson.

'Twenty seconds till impact,' said Harper, voice low. She glanced at Robertson. He who was peering at his coffee like it was his biggest problem.

'Look at that crazy fucking bastard,' Aiden muttered to her. She had a sudden urge to laugh hysterically.

The SM6s reached the top of the parabola and began a screaming dive, still accelerating. They would intercept the BrahMos' fifteen kilometres and ten seconds out.

'Sea Sparrows launched,' she said. The BrahMos' started jinking, up and down, and the SM6s rained down like spears from God.

Robertson had another sip. *Alice, I love you,* he thought.

'Launch the Nulka,' he commanded.

Robertson watched the little puffs of smoke and fire turn into a giant, shrapnel-filled cloud when the two flights merged. Radar returns went fuzzy for a moment, then;

'Seven still inbound!' shouted Harper. 'Sea Sparrows in three, two, one...' and the short-range missiles exploded among the big bullets. Flashes of light and puffs of smoke popped like fireworks as they found homes.

'Four, three, make that two inbound,' she shouted. One peeled off towards the Nulka as she spoke.

Fuck, breathed Robertson to himself. One had always got through in their simulations. He stood up and stared hard out the window. He wasn't going to die on his ass.

The Phalanx CIWS whirred, and the chain gun swivelled with mindless robotic intent. The radar locked on. *This was how Malm died,* he thought. The world's most ferocious buzz saw cut through the bridge and the chain gun spat a solid stream of lead. The truck-sized missile and the tracers merged, and for a second, nothing happened. Robertson frowned quizzically, then the warhead exploded. A fraction of a second after the missile disintegrated, tiny fragments peppered into the *Hobart,* a giant shotgun blast pinging off the hull.

But it was smalls-arms fire, and the *Hobart* shrugged it off.

He took a deep breath. In the distance, *Sydney* and *Arunta* looked like they had come through unscathed. The *Anzac* was a billowing pall of smoke. A BrahMos had broken her silhouette like a toy smashed on the floor.

'TAO, report on the rest of the task force, please.'

'Sir, *Sydney* reports superficial damage, *Arunta* unscathed. I can't raise the *Anzac.'*

'Make way to the *Anzac,* when we're there, launch the RHIBs.'

He picked up his mug. Empty. Probably a good thing; his hand was shaking.

'Harper, where are those ASMs? And someone tell me how many missiles we've got left. If those ASMs miss I want to unload the rest of the SM-6s at these bastards.'

'They'll be on target in five minutes, sir.'

Robertson smiled. After a missile launch, there was nothing worse than the waiting. Waiting to die or waiting to live. He didn't envy the Indians.

Aiden nudged Harper who was staring at Robertson with barely disguised awe.

'Look at that lunatic,' he muttered. 'Looks like he's just come home to a hot meal and a horny wife.'

A few minutes later, the anti-ship missiles had closed to strike distance on the Indian ships. 'Ten seconds to first impact,' called Harper. The hysteria had gone from her voice, replaced by steely calm.

Robertson waited impassively. They'd closed on the wreck of the *Anzac* and were looking for survivors; they'd found none so far.

'We've lost signal on four, five, make that six outbounds,' called Harper.

'Twin impact on target one…Impact on target two…' and the two *Kolkata* destroyers blinked red on the battlespace schematic.

'Partial impact on target three.' She bit her lips. 'Target four has evaded the salvo.'

'Send a chopper to investigate the *Kolkatas;* I want confirmation they're out of the fight.' He suspected they were splinters now; the LRASM had a thousand-pound warhead. 'Get a helicopter in targeting range of target four. As soon as we have a firing solution put the rest of the SM6s down its funnel.'

Chapter 21
September 21, 0200 hours
HMAS *Kati-Thanda*

Katie had snorkelled nearly four thousand kilometres to just west of Aceh when Phillips ordered her into quiet mode and took her down. The snorkel retracted into the sail, and non-essential systems were turned off. Diesel generators went silent, and banks of lithium-ion batteries powered the pump-jet, so the sub made an easy five knots, a hundred metres below the surface.

In the control room, Phillips leant on the table screen, reading a short message off a piece of paper. The depth indicator lines of the NER map on the display glowed a soft green and gave his frown a pallid caste.

'Good news, then?' said Albrecht.

'Of course.' He handed the ULF FLASH TRAFFIC note to his XO. 'Looks like we're not taking on the sensor net after all. The Indians have reprogrammed their sensors; changed the frequency sensitivities.'

'Changed them to what?' asked Darwin.

'They're searching for us now, not the Chinese. Not only that, HQ says two more frigates are en-route to the choke point.'

Phillips yawned. 'OK, Albrecht. What are our options?'

'We could try to sneak through the sensors as planned, or, take on the picket. My bet is their sailors aren't as switched on as the systems monitoring this net. I recommend we take on the picket before those two frigates arrive.'

'We have to assume they know we're coming,' said Phillips. 'Can we drift through the target box?'

Darwin shook his head. 'No can do. This time of year, the currents run the opposite direction we're heading. They'd send us down the Malacca Straits.'

'Ok. Do we know where the northernmost array is?'

Darwin made a *sort-of* gesture. 'We have a pretty good idea. They anchor their phones to the top of the ridge, so their coverage ends where the ridge does, give or take the detection range.'

Phillips paused. Get this wrong, and they may never see the surface again.

'Here's what we're going to do,' he said. 'We'll skirt the tip of their coverage, and slowly make heading two-eighty-degrees, keeping a minimum thirty kays between us and our best guess at where the last array is. If the pickets are focusing on the rest of the choke-point, there may just be a little gap we can sail through.' He turned to Albrecht. 'Thoughts?'

'The only alternative is to run the gauntlet under their choppers.' He shrugged fatalistically. 'Your way at least, we might miss the gauntlet altogether.' He nodded. 'It's the least-worst choice.'

'Good as it's going to get. Helmsman, take us wide. Around...' he peered at the underwater mountain range on the display, then reached down and tapped a spot on the northern edge of the NER, on the final downward slope to the ocean plane of the Bay. 'These coordinates, to a heading of two-eight-zero.'

Ninety minutes later, *Katie* was easing around what the Australians hoped was the final array on the NER and had begun her wide swing to the left. Captain Phillips and Albrecht were in the control room, watching the map update their position. The enemy picket ships were blinking red, as were the arrays, the intermittence indicating their exact location was unknown. Phillips hoped things stayed that way: If *Katie* couldn't see them, they almost certainly couldn't see her.

HMAS *Kati-Thanda*
1100 hours

'Captain, I got a contact bearing six-zero degrees, sounds like a SeaKing chopper off one of their escorts,' said Malik, hunched over the sonar display.

Phillips slid his hand into his open shirt and scratched his hairy chest. His hand came out damp due to it being well within the high thirties in the control room; the dialled down ventilation systems weren't coping.

'Vector and range?' he asked.

'Best guess, around forty clicks, heading towards us at a hundred knots.'

Phillips pulled a face. 'Must've turned too early and clipped the edge of one of their sensors…Planesman, set your depth to four-hundred-metres. Reduce speed to steerage; the DDS must've alerted them.' In which case, slowing down should help. 'Any more bad news for us, Malik?'

'No sir, but maybe some good. There's a fair bit of tanker traffic coming outta the Straits of Malacca. They're loud bastards; if we can shadow one it'll probably drown any returns from that picket.'

'Alright. Track all tankers, let's find one and see if we can hitch a ride.'

MV Achilleas
1130 hours

On the bridge of the MV *Achilleas,* a three-hundred-thousand-tonne super tanker registered out of Liberia, Captain Sandy Savage surveyed the horizon with lidded eyes. They were travelling west, back to Bandar Abbas after unloading a cargo of oil in Guanzhou. The sun glistened out of a deep blue sky, but his barometer was steadily dropping, and the blue ended abruptly in mountains of billowing black clouds.

'A cyclone in front of us and Indian frigates behind us,' he mused to his navigator, Jack Lewis. 'Aren't they supposed to be at war?'

The INS had sent a data packet tersely instructing them to circle north, skirting Burma then turning into the Bay. Sandy had ignored it. He had a timetable to keep.

The radio buzzed, and Savage opened the channel.

'To the Captain of MV *Achilleas*, this is Captain Korpal of the INS *Chennai*. Please report.'

'Sandy Savage here, captain of the MV *Achilleas*. What can we do for you today, Captain Korpal?'

'This stretch of ocean has been militarised and closed to all civilian traffic. You have previously been instructed to exit the Straits and track north to enter the Bay with the Andaman Islands to your west. Please adjust your course to the north.'

Were these people stupid? 'Thank you, Captain, for the update. I can't speak for the Indian Navy, but I don't have the luxury of drifting around in circles or touring the coast of Myanmar. Time is money in the tanker business, so unless you guys plan to reimburse me for a two-day detour, we're taking the direct route.'

There was a pause. Somebody on the other end clicked the radio on for a moment. Sandy heard voices conferring before they realised and clicked it off again.

'Very well. But you've been slowing down. Please make all speed to the west and exit the area immediately.'

Savage put his foot up. 'I dunno if your sensors are functional Mr. Korpal, but I've got an air pressure reading of nine-sixty millibars and the closer we get to that storm up there the lower it gets. Now, fortunately, that big ugly storm is going in the same direction we are, so if it's all the same to you, I'm just going to let that storm race on ahead of us. I'll speed up when it's far enough out.'

More silence from the Indians. Jack got the impression they were arguing furiously on the bridge of the *Chennai*. Then, finally:

'Very well, *Achilleas*. We are sending the *Sahyadri* to ensure you exit as quickly as possible. Please follow instructions or we will send a boarding party to ensure you comply with requests.'

'Mr. Korpal, if you want to escort us where we're going anyway, that's mighty generous of you. Be my guest.'

'I think they're serious about that boarding party,' said Jack, motioning to the radar. A helicopter had detached from the frigate symbol and was moving directly towards them at over a hundred knots.

'No.' He scratched the side of his head. 'That can't be for us. They would've had to launch it before they even made contact.' He frowned. 'I wonder, just what the hell is going on?'

HMAS *Kati-Thanda*
1145 hours

'Bombs away,' said Malik quietly. 'We've got a probable sonobuoy in the water, bearing: thirty-seven degrees, range fifteen clicks. The Seahawks continuing to head west.' He pointed to the nav-display, which had marked the location of the sonobuoy impact. 'If I was him, I'd continue tracking west then double back to the south; try to box us in.'

Phillips silently agreed with his sonarman. There was a tanker a few clicks north-east of their position, moving west slowly.

'They're going to drop multiple buoys and start pinging,' said Albrecht. 'Once they get the returns, they'll be able to triangulate our position.' He thought furiously. 'According to Robertson's data, they couldn't pick us up under four knots. Captain, what if we run the numbers and see if we can merge with that tanker without breaking four knots?'

Phillips nodded. 'Do it,' he said to Phillips. 'Head on a bearing of...' he waited until the nav system flashed up a vector that would cause the tanker to float over the top of them, 'three-fifteen degrees at five knots.'

Albrecht's mouth worked but Phillips pre-empted him.

'Yea, I know, it's over the detection speed. We need to hope their anti-sub tactics aren't as good as Robertson's. Because we'll miss the tanker otherwise.'

'We'll be under the thermocline until we come up under the tanker,' said Malik. 'If they ping from the surface, we should be ok,' he said.

'And if they go deep and active with their buoys...' began Albrecht.

'We're in deep shit,' finished Malik.

'We'll be fine,' said Phillips, turning to the planesman. 'Once we match location and vector with that ship, bring us to a depth of fifteen-metres as fast as possible; I want to be stuck to its keel, like shit to a blanket, as it sails into that cyclone.'

Indian Navy SeaKing
1147 hours

Harbajan Singh, pilot of the S-70B SeaKing, peered over the instrument panel as he banked the big rotorcraft to the left. He'd just dropped his first passive/active sono-buoy and was maneuvering to lay a grid of the sensors. The intel people back on the dock had dialed in the probable location and vector of an 'acoustic anomaly' close to their position, and he'd been scrambled to check it out. It was probably nothing, but it was probably nothing that just happened to be where an enemy sub would try to sneak through their sensor/picket net.

That big fucking tanker halfway to the horizon was right in the middle of their search area. Clanking machinery noises crashed through the hull like a giant pile of scrap throbbing and collapsing at the same time. The massive propeller slashed the water and the hull itself creaked painfully as the girders holding its three-hundred-metre length resisted the massive rotational torque of the vessel rolling over waves. Singh shook his head. If there was anything down there, and they got into the noise-shadow of that sound factory they'd be impossible to detect.

'Drop two,' he said. The second metre-long tube dropped out of the helicopter and parachuted towards the ocean below.

His co-pilot tapped the magnetic anomaly detector graphic with his forefinger. 'Useless. That giant lump of iron is ruining any returns. If we get something from the sono-buoys I'll do a targeted sweep.'

Singh nodded and straightened up the SeaKing. It was time to drop the third buoy.

HMAS *Kati-Thanda*

Hakeem Malik hadn't slept in twenty-four hours, but his eyes were pinned open, listening to the Indian chopper cut a grid above them, periodically dropping sonobuoys. He was actually enjoying himself. A little corner of his mind was looking at him in consternation, wondering what sort of madman would get off on being hunted by an enemy intent on torpedoing him into oblivion.

'I've got four buoys in the water,' he said quietly. He updated their location on the nav-display, revealed by the splash they made when they hit the ocean. On the wedge of ocean/earth/atmosphere representing their general position, little hydrophone icons flashing black denoted the Indian sensors. They formed the shape of an L laid on its side, with both Katie and the tanker in the crook of the layout.

'If they go under the thermocline and ping us now, we're finished,' said Albrecht.

'If.' echoed Phillips. 'They don't know for sure we're down here. They probably got a minute return on the sensor array and are doing a pro-forma investigation,' He looked at the display. Ninety seconds till they were literally underneath the oil carrier. 'It may just buy us the time we need to get under that crude carrier. Planesman, be ready to increase depth on merge.'

Indian Navy SeaKing

Singh toggled the co-pilot switch on his comms unit. 'Passive sensors aren't going to reveal jack. If there's anything down there, it's hiding in the pollution of the tanker.' He changed the line to the operations room on the Sahyadri. 'Permission to go active - can't hear a thing, there's too much interference.' He waited impassively.

'Give it one ping. If you get nothing, go passive again.' came the reply. 'If there's something down there, it's probably hiding under the thermocline anyway.'

The co-pilot activated the buoys' sonars and they waited. Nothing.

HMAS *Kati-Thanda*

Katie closed interminably on the tanker.

Twenty seconds, glowed the timer, showing how long until they matched location and vectors. Until it reached zero, they would hide under the thermocline but, in scant seconds they would rise above the boundary layer and the only thing that would prevent them from being discovered, until they were safely under the tanker, would be the Indian decision not to activate their buoys. Phillips had glued his eyes to the depth marker.

'Depth three-fifty-metres,' said the planesman.

'Rising above the thermocline now,' Malik responded quietly.

'If they ping,' said Phillips softly, 'shut down all systems and crash stop to steerage only.' It was their best hope of disappearing like a ghost.

There was silence in the control room. *Katie* was completely open, and her crew trusted against hope that the Indians didn't go live.

Deep in the Indian Ocean, Phillips had never felt so exposed in his life.

Indian Navy SeaKing

Singh checked his instrument panel. All the buoys were at their preprogrammed depths, a few under the thermocline, most above it. 'Ready to go active,' he said loudly over the radio. 'No point wasting time, gents, they'll be turning into a black hole while we mess around up here.'

'Easy, Khiladi,' said the comms guy in the *Sahyadri*. 'We'll go live in sixty seconds. We've got to stop that tanker anyway to clean up the ambient noise.'

Singh clenched his jaw. 'Khiladi' was an impulsive Indian action-hero; Singh didn't see the humour. He had a sneaking suspicion that they were taking too long.

MV *Achilleas*

On the bridge of the MV *Achilleas*, Sandy Savage slapped his coleslaw sandwich down on the plate and regarded the bleeping radio with disgust. What did those Indian pricks want now? He toggled it on.

'Greetings again *Chennai*, what can I do for you now?' he asked with a pleasantness he didn't feel.

'MV *Achilleas*, we require you to switch off your machinery and all-stop. This is a war zone, and you're cluttering up our sensors. Comply immediately.'

'That's a negative, *Chennai*, we won't be stopping. We'll maintain current speed and heading; we have a schedule, and your war is not our problem. *Achilleas* out.'

He caught Jack's look of dismay. 'What?' he shrugged. 'They can't touch us.' Ha barked out a scornful laugh. 'The only thing that stops something this big is her crew.' He paused. 'Or the bottom, if you run into it.'

'Yea,' muttered Jack. 'Or a heavyweight torpedo.'

HMAS *Kati-Thanda*

'Depth, one-hundred-metres,' said the planesman, who was focusing on his data with manic intensity. 'Twenty seconds till we're at target depth of twenty-two metres.'

Getting the target depth was one thing but ensuring they didn't deviate from it was critical; they had to stay as close as possible to the tanker to avoid detection; any misjudgment and they'd collide, damaging the sub, and, more importantly, make a lot of noise.

Indian Navy SeaKing

'Ok Singh, the tanker is non-compliant with our all-stop order. It's time to go live. Hit the switch and take a look.'

'About time,' breathed Singh, and he activated the grid of eight sonobuoys, that had, until now, been listening quietly. On his command, they started pinging, sending pulses of sound into the ocean, both above and below the thermocline. Any sub that was down there would reflect the soundwaves back to the buoys, and they could then triangulate its position.

HMAS *Kati-Thanda*

Even at the relatively low speed of 5 knots, it takes a big generator-set to move three-hundred thousand tonnes through the water. Big engines make a lot of noise, and because there was silence in the operations room, the distant thrum of the supertanker's massive machinery, scant metres above the *Kati-Thanda*, permeated the submarines hull. The sound was barely audible, more a subharmonic vibration.

'Target depth reached,' breathed the planesman.

'We're directly underneath the tanker,' said Phipps. 'Smack in the middle of it, three-metres below the keel, if our figures on its draught are correct.'

'Very good. Maintain this relative position,' said Phillips.

'Sir,' whispered the planesman.

Just then, a ghostly ping-g-g-g echoed softly through the hull. Every man in the operations room held his breath. The Indians had opened their eyes.

Indian Navy SeaKing

Singh frowned. No returns. He felt some sort of dissonance. His gut had told him there was something there, but his state-of-the-art equipment told him otherwise. His jaw muscles worked as he tried to figure out if there was a submarine down there. Maybe hiding under that tanker?

'Let's see if we can get a MAD signal under that ship,' he said to his co-pilot. The man nodded and configured the array to focus on a segment beneath the oil freighter.

He quickly shook his head. 'Too much iron in the way. It's completely blinding us. MAD is no good, and neither is sonar anywhere near that thing.'

'Shit.'

MV *Achilleas*

Sandy Savage looked at his synoptic weather chart. The cyclone that was forming ahead had begun tracking north. Maybe he could turn south a bit and go back to cruise speed. He'd caught some of Jack's pessimism; it was fun antagonising the Indians, but they were hostile warships; no point pushing it too far. Time to get out of here.

'Take her up to sixteen knots,' he said to the pilot. 'Ease south bearing two-fifty degrees, get us out of this so-called war zone and take us under that typhoon.'

HMAS *Kati-Thanda*

In *Katie's* operations room, the men were already on a knife-edge when thudding sounding through the hull suddenly doubled in volume.

Phillips stared up through the hull. 'What's going on? Report on that noise!'

Malik gripped his headphones to his ears. 'Sir! It's the tanker; she's increased revolutions! The extra noise is more of the same, her engineering clattering through our hull.'

'Increase speed and maintain relative position,' said Phillips. 'This is our lucky break. If they haven't found us yet, it'll be even harder detecting us over all that racket.'

Chapter 22
Geraldton Internment Camp
September 22nd, 1300 hours

Fadi had kept to himself after the killings. He'd always done so anyway, especially since Khandi's death, and he figured maintaining the same routine would help him avoid additional suspicion. He'd slipped the makeshift spear into one of the big skip bins lining the perimeter of the camp, and noted with satisfaction when the trucks came and carted it away with tonnes of other rubbish. They'd never be able to pin the weapon to him.

That said, it was no secret that he spent a lot of time out the back of the sheds, on his own. People also knew that he and Khandi were close, even as they kept to themselves. And it was widely known that *something* had happened to her. Rape, it seemed, was a feature of the camp, not a bug, and was therefore not so noteworthy as to attract a comprehensive investigation, not least because the victims rarely did anything about it.

Violent murder, on the other hand, was a bridge too far for the camp authorities, and they brought in military police to investigate the crime.

'Let's recap, shall we,' said one, a burly man whose rolled-up sleeves displayed pumped up, vascular forearms. *Benedetti* said the name patch on his left breast pocket. He was sitting opposite Fadi in the administration office. Between them was a tin-topped fold-out table. The plastic chairs were refreshingly cool on the back of his legs, and the air-con wicked the sweat from his neck. The pleasant environment did nothing to distract him from the fact he was in deep shit, and he had absolutely nobody in the world who could help.

You knew this was a possibility, he told himself. *Present Fadi is paying past Fadi's dues.* Well, he'd been adamant he had to take action. He was glad he'd done what he did. It helped with the trepidation making him lose his train of thought.

The MP held up a thick finger. 'You were not in your cot at the time of the murders.' He grabbed another finger. 'You are known to have spent significant amounts of time at the murder location, so you'd know the ground well. According to camp gossip, these men raped your friend, who later committed suicide. So, you have a motive.' His fingers were bunched like sausages now.

'Well,' he started cautiously, trying to get his brain in gear. 'That doesn't mean I did it. Could have been anyone. Everyone hated those guys.'

The big man looked at his counterpart, who was leaning back on the chair next to him. 'Not the most vehement denial we've heard,' he drawled.

'A good legal argument,' said Hogge, the recliner. 'But this isn't a court. We're not going to waste time listening to and presenting arguments. The question is, do you have an alibi for the period between eleven-fifteen and eleven twenty-seven, when you were not in your cot?'

Fadi licked dry lips with a dry tongue. 'I was in the bathroom,' he ventured hollowly.

'Doing what?' asked Benedetti, eyebrow raised.

Was that a trick question? 'I was pulling my dick.' They didn't react. 'A shit,' he eventually spluttered in the face of their impassivity. 'I was doing a shit.'

The two men shared a disappointed glance. 'Fadi, we have several witnesses saying you walked out the front of the sheds at…' he consulted the folder in front of him, 'eleven-eighteen.' The two men just sat there, studying him.

Fadi felt like he could have been wholly innocent and still felt guilty under their gaze. He gripped the edge of his shorts. 'What are you going to do to me?' he said, eyes darting between them. He couldn't stop licking his lips.

Benedetti's face softened a fraction. 'From what we can tell, Fadi, those guys got what they deserved. But it's not your job to deal justice. We can't have vigilantes in the camp. So, the good news, we're gonna take you out of here. The bad news, is we're taking you to the lock-up in Geraldton, where the WA Police will try you for murder.'

How are your principles now, taunted a voice in his head. He wanted to cry, but nobody would see his tears. Certainly, nobody who cared. Instead, he stood up and let the MP's handcuff him. They led him to their car, and half an hour later he was in a bare cell in Geraldton Police Station. Alone. It was the same, he reflected, as when that people smuggler had locked him up on the *Tamil-Nadu,* just before that torpedo had blown the door open.

Chapter 23
Rati's Emporium
September 23rd, 2200 hours

Adnan Abdullakutty, Indian Defence Minister, disentangled himself from Izhar Khan's sincere and sweaty embrace.

'Welcome Adnan, so good to see you again!' cried Khan, stumbling slightly as Abdullakutty stepped to safety. 'I'm glad you're here,' he said with a conspiratorial wink that left him somewhat cross-eyed. 'We can finally get this show on the road!'

Abdullakutty had come in through *Rita's* back door, through an upmarket bakery doubling as an entrance for respectable clients. Men who mattered, like himself, preferred to be discreet about their association with Izhar Khan.

A man who, Abdullakutty conceded, was quite a fascinating character to spend time with, in small doses. Whenever Khan made a 'political' donation, he would insist on sharing a few bottles of expensive wine before he transferred anything to Abdullakutty's Uruguayan bank account. One thing always led to another, and he had always found himself invited upstairs.

'Where's Chakradev? Isn't he supposed to be here too?'

Khan raised his eyebrows; his eyelids stayed at the same level. *How does the man do it to himself*, thought Abdullakutty with admiration. He'd never seen Khan even close to sober.

'He sends his sincerest apologies! But he's away on urgent business. He says he'll join us at our next soiree. Not to worry! There's more of everything for the rest of us fine fellows!' he finished, loudly slapping the ass of the tall blonde draped on his shoulder.

HMAS *Kati-Thanda*
2300 hours

The *Kati-Thanda* rested on a carpet of sunken garbage and silt that formed the bottom of the junction between the Hoolie and Rupnarayan Rivers at Noorpur. Two minutes to go time. Kolkata docks were too far up the Hoolie to take a two-billion-dollar submarine; the river was too small, and there was nowhere to go if they were spotted.

So, *Katie* had taken them most of the way there. The diver delivery vehicle, *Mini-Kat*, would take them the rest of the way.

In the control room, Phillips keyed his communicator, and the speakers in the miniature submarine piggybacking on *Katie* spoke.

'Equalise the DDS,' he ordered.

The diving officer pressed his screen. A valve opened in the dry-dock shelter and water poured in, displacing air which was sucked out through another valve at the top.

The water sloshed into the small space and quickly washed-up past their faces. Marriott felt, and resisted, an instinctive urge to gasp through his breathing hose. Soon, the compartment was full.

'DDS equalised,' called the diving officer.

Phillips nodded. 'Open the shelter door.'

The rearward edge of the DDS swung up slowly and silently in the murky water and the rails the mini-sub was attached to telescoped out of the cylinder.

'Release on my mark,' said Phillips. *Mini-Kat's* screw began to spin.

Sub-lieutenant Gray, *Mini-Kat's* pilot, radioed from the sealed front compartment, 'ready for release.'

'Release,' said Phillips and the clamps holding the submarine onto the rails wound back.

Mini-Kat rocked left, then right as she caught the current, levitated off *Katie's* back and began to rise through the murky, turbid water. Steadying in space, Gray turned the mini-sub up the Hoolie, towards Kolkata docks, fifty-kilometres away.

This was the riskiest part of the mission. The Hoolie was unusually deep so they'd had plenty of water to hide in, and it was so filthy, visibility from the surface was almost zero. But now they were leaving the safety of the river bed behind. All it would take is a pair of eyes to spot them.

Four hours later, Gray's voice piped in over the comms net.

'Tour's over, gentlemen. Welcome to Kolkata docks.' It was two minutes to three in the morning - the trip from *Katie* had taken precisely four hours.

'I'm going to bring her up to a depth of five metres. Leave *Mini-Kat* on my mark and swim to starboard. We're dead level with the insertion point, only fifty metres to shore. Once the last of you are out, I turn around and go home. Understood?'

'Understood,' said Marriott. 'Thanks for the ride.'

Gray nodded and eased the boat up to the surface. Moments later, they were at insertion depth.

'Time to rock, gentlemen. Good luck,' subbed Gray.

'Acknowledged,' subbed back Marriott. He unplugged his oxygen hose from his mask and pushed off the little sub, straight up through the gap in the roof. He felt, rather than saw, his squad following him. The eight-man SAS fire-team floated, wraith-like, to the surface.

Marriott got there first. He broke the water carefully while the others swam suspended beneath him. He did a full scan of the river; nothing was coming in either direction and no activity on either bank. He motioned his squad-mates to the surface and they breast-stroked to shore.

The was a ferry-stop on the eastern bank of the river, consisting of a rusty iron pontoon tethered to a couple of pylons set in concrete. A set of broad, slimy steps descended into the water. At the top of the stairs and stretching each direction up and down the bank were semi-permanent market stalls.

Imran Magar owned one such stall. One day, during a storm, the river had risen up and plucked his family away. So now, every day after dusk, he sat on the *ghat* in front of his shop, chewing paan and drinking bootleg *bangla*, keeping a silent vigil for his family. He hoped that one day, the river that had stolen his family, his life, would show mercy and deliver them back to him.

On this particular night, as on many others, he'd dozed off in the early hours. He was crying in his sleep; his head lolled on his chest, and tears streaked his grubby face. The bottle of *bangla* had rolled a short distance from his unclasped hand.

He woke suddenly and patted around for the bottle. There. Why did he wake? He looked at the river, hope battling with rational thought as dark figures, black glinting on black, emerging silently up the broad steps in front of him. There were...there were five, six...seven! The Gods had listened to his prayers and returned his family!

'Aasmita...' he whispered,

'Shutup,' she hissed, making a shooshing motion.

'Aasmita. Aasmita!' he staggered up, to run down the *ghat* and embrace them, shouting his wife's name as he did so.

His beautiful wife pointed something at him. Three times it made a muffled popping sound, and something punched him in the chest. He sat down. It was hard to breathe, and he couldn't stand up anymore. That's OK, he thought; they'd come to him.

'Aasmita...' he mouthed silently as they rushed past him across the iron pontoon. He reached out with his free hand, and then it was as though the darkness of the river overwhelmed the fragile light of hope in his mind because then there was nothing.

'What should we do about the body?' whispered Khawaja as they huddled in the wheelhouse of the small grey river-punt tied alongside the ferry terminal.

'Leave it,' said Marriott. 'By the time someone finds him we'll be on the way back out again anyway and this guy will be the least of our problems.'

The men changed into their operational kit in the tiny wheelhouse. They dressed in rumpled, smart-casual clothes, passing themselves off as drunk businessmen looking for some whores after a long night celebrating a business deal. They should fit in just fine with their target in Sonagatchi.

Under their jackets were silenced Chinese army issue Type 95 carbines, and they each carried two Chinese frags and a smoke grenade.

'Secure comms established with *Kati-Thanda*. From now on, all comms relay through me,' Khawaja issued, fitting an earpiece. He tilted his head, listening. 'Your escort is about to arrive. ETA 90 seconds.'

'Good.' Marriott checked his weapon, then stowed it under his jacket. 'We're outta here,' he said. He checked his own comms; in full working order.

'Your lift just arrived,' said Khawaja. 'See you in two hours.'

The other seven men quickly moved off the punt, onto the ghat and through the shopfront. Marriott glanced at the old guy Carey had put to sleep. Looked like he was dreaming. He'd died with a smile on his face.

Then minutes later, their little driver opened his mouth. 'We're coming into Sonagatchi now,' he announced with forced confidence. The ghostly glow from the streetlamps glistened off the sweat beading on his pockmarked face. He carefully picked his way around a group of people sleeping rough in the gutter.

'What a dump,' muttered Willis.

The driver pulled over. A slat-sided dog slunk out from behind a garbage pile and scampered up the street.

'This is where I've been told to drop you off,' said the driver, wiping his brow.

Marriott checked the time. 'We'll RV in forty minutes at the extraction point. He leaned forward, and the driver flinched when he put his hand on the man's bony shoulder. 'Don't be late,' he said softly, teeth glinting in the lamplight.

Marriott, Willis, Carey, and Edelstein climbed out of the van and wandered up the street. The rest of the squad went the other way; they'd stagger their arrival at Rati's Emporium thirty seconds apart.

At the club, a couple of massive men in suits barred their way with big-man arrogance.

'Evening gentlemen,' said Marriott brightly. 'How's your night going?'

The giant cast a critical eye over Marriott's crumpled clothes.

'I'm sorry. But you've had too much to drink,' said one. 'You can come back later when you've sobered up.'.

Willis sniggered. 'Doesn't matter where we are in the world, boss, nobody wants you in their club.'

A hollow boom echoed through the streets; ASIS had paid off local gangsters to bomb the local electricity sub-station.

Marriott smiled. 'We'll be quick, I promise.' At that instant, every light in a half-mile radius went out.

The four soldiers pulled their rifles free. Two pops each into the bouncers threw them back into the door. The silenced weapons were barely audible over the ambient street noise.

The rest of the squad arrived. In darkness, the seven men stepped over the bodies and into the dimness of *Rati's Emporium*.

Marriott scanned the scene through his night-vision goggles. *Rati's* was a seething hive of confusion and panic. The odd torch or cigarette light flashed long shadows, and drunk men stumbled around, trying to gather their senses in the dark. Girls in skimpy dresses were pawing their way to safety, either the staff room or the bar.

Marriott's half of the squad shouldered their rifles and picked their way through the muddled crowds and up into the lobby of the boutique hotel, following the path memorised from blueprints hackers had lifted from the Kolkata Municipal Government archives. The other four would go to the basement to take out the emergency power supply and the security footage.

An elegant woman was at the reception desk. Hearing their footfalls, she began scrabbling around under the cabinet. Marriott watched with cautious fascination as she raised a small pistol and waved it blindly around the room.

'Stop! Don't come any closer or I'll shoo-' *thwack thwack* sounded wetly, and she reeled over backwards.

The team quickly dispersed down the corridor. A door opened and an overweight man, holding a bathrobe over himself, groped his way into the hallway.

'Vēśyā kamabakhta kamīnom!' he screamed. 'What bastard is responsible? I might as well stick my dick in a pudding if I can't see what I'm-' *thwack, thwack-thwack.* He slid wetly down the wall, mouth gaping.

Marriott ticked off the doors as they swept past. *Third door on the right. Banka-Mundi room.* He crouched silently and gave the doorknob a gentle tug. *Locked.*

Edelstein placed a small shaped charge of plastique explosive over the lock. The men hugged the wall and Edelstein blew the door of its hinges. Edelstein took point, Marriott, Carey and Willis rushed through in a crouch, weapons over his shoulder.

Banka-Mundi room
1755 hours

Izhar Khan scratched his belly idly. He'd developed a patchy rash, a rather unattractive scaly redness under his thick stomach hair, which he suspected was some sort of fungus. Khan had no idea how he'd get such a thing, did he not treat his body like a Dravidian temple? He sniggered.

He glanced down at the blonde woman nestled on his chest. *Aha*...he thought lazily. *Maybe she is responsible for my fungus?* Lina had become his sort of de facto...not girlfriend. Favoured concubine? That implied he had a harem, and as such was a king or at least a leader of men. He liked that. Yes, Lina was his favoured concubine, a beautiful, seductive, and attentive satin-skinned blonde who somehow knew precisely when to gently tease him (rarely), when to challenge him (seldom) and when to fawn coquettishly (the rest of the time).

At the end of the day though, she was still a whore, and probably an incredibly cold and calculating little bitch at that, the more so since she'd almost convinced him that she felt something for him.

Anyway, even the most fastidiously hygienic whore was a potential vector for disease, including fungus. He resolved to discuss the matter with her. Now was not the time, however.

His head lolled to the side. What a wonderful sight. Here he was, satiated by the woman he loved (he sniggered at that one), and over there was Defense Minister Adnan Abdullakutty, receiving a deep-tissue massage from some of Lina's friends. The Attorney General, Virendra Mudaliar was behind that rice-paper partition, and shadows outlined the movement of bodies. The man rumbled some witticism, eliciting stifled giggles from the girls hiding there with him.

'Lina dearest,' he murmured, and she cupped his testicles.

'Oooh...mmmm. I've discovered,' Khan said once he'd regained his composure, 'the meaning of life. Do you want to know what it is?'

Lina's mouth twitched slightly. Sometimes he got the impression she was secretly laughing at him.

'I'd love to know the meaning of life,' she whispered into his chest. Straight faced.

'Happiness. Happiness is the meaning of life. To be happy.' He glanced down. She looked a little nonplussed. He elaborated. 'Happiness requires freedom, and freedom requires courage.'

'You're very brave, Izhar,' she said around his ear lobe.

'Indeed. Courage to pursue a man's dreams is what's important. Can you guess what my dreams are, my darling?'

'Why don't you tell me,' she whispered into his ear.

'Lina, my dear, professional satisfaction, good personal relationships, and good health are the goals I aspire to.'

259

'I think you might be right,' she said, snuggling into his chest. 'Are you happy, Izhar?'

'Well, nobody could claim I'm healthy! But business is booming, and look at my business partners! They're having such a wonderful time. I've got dirt on half the politicians in the Lok Sabha. And...' he said, caressing her silky hair, 'I've got a good woman beside me. Two out of three, as they say, ain't so bad, is it!'

Lina snuggled deeper into his chest and nuzzled his neck. Gave his balls a good squeeze and let the verbal diarrhea wash over her. She just hoped he didn't figure out where he'd got that rash from.

Suddenly the lights went out, and blackness descended. Confused noises broke out from the rest of the room.

'What's going on, Khan?' bellowed Abdullakutty. 'Is this some sort of game?'

'I can't see. I'm missing out on quite a show!' grumbled Mudaliar.

'Just relax, everybody,' called out Khan. 'It's probably just a local transformer blown. It happens sometimes; unscrupulous people patch into the power grid illegally and overload it. Don't worry, our emergency generators will be online very shortly.' That seemed to mollify them. A slap and another round of giggles emanated from behind the screen.

A low growl escaped from Khan's lips. 'Don't you stop, Lina dearest,' he said. 'What you're doing is perfect.' He gave her a squeeze. 'I'm so lucky to have you...' he closed his eyes and drifted away...

Scant moments later, an almighty bang and a bright flash crashed through Khan's dopamine bubble, and Lina let go of his balls, withdrawing her hand painfully. 'Ow!' he shoved her away. 'Stupid bitch! What is the meaning of this?'

Streaks of light silhouetted large shapes moving purposefully into the room. Indignation turned quickly to fear. Khan's erection shrivelled and he suddenly felt vulnerable in his nakedness.

The shapes fanned out. They made little pops and *thwacking* noises, like slapping a table covered in water. From behind the rice-paper screen, he heard a short scream, then a *thwack*, and silence.

'Which one of you is Izhar Khan?' intoned one of the voices. Low sobbing and wet, sucking noises permeated the room.

In the dim light, Khan could just make out the shape of Lina backing away, one hand over her mouth, the other pointing to him.

'We have a gift for you, Izhar. From the people of Australia.'

Khan looked at the speaker. He could see the vague outline of a powerful man, and Khan wondered if he'd get to see this man's face. Instead, all he could make was a black, boxy shadow where the head should have been. The man, who had been scanning the room left and right, turned his head to regard Khan directly.

The weight of his gaze immobilised him, but all he could see, where the eyes should have been, was a soft green glow. He was pinned, like an insect on a page. Utterly at the mercy of a man who Khan knew had no mercy to spare.

He looked at Lina. *So, this is what it feels like, to be trapped. Out of options. Like a whore.* A sudden surge of confusion surged through him.

Thwack, thwack-thwack.

Marriott and his team exited the building quickly. They'd been surprised by the number of people in the room with Khan. Operational prerogatives had taken over, and they'd had to sanitise the lot of them. Marriot Sr. had always told him that you could judge a man by his friends, so Marriott figured they'd all got what they deserved.

The two groups of men had shed their weapons and filed out of Rati's Emporium acting confused and bewildered like the

261

rest of the clientele. Ignoring each other, they rendezvoused two blocks away.

There was another van waiting for them. A different one. The men filed in, took their seats and Marriott tapped the driver on his shoulder, 'Let's go.'

The man stammered a nod, and the van moved up the road. It was the same man who'd driven them in. He was pretending to be nonchalant, but Marriott could see his breath coming in rapid little gasps.

The van picked its way through early Kolkata traffic. The team was silent, mission comedown jitters mixed with apprehension; they weren't in the clear yet.

They'd quickly left the blackout zone behind and were ostensibly on their way to the Sumbbdlat Hotel in Kalinagar, a few streets from their RV with Khawaja.

Marriott realised how flimsy their cover story was as shiny office towers quickly gave way to brown slums in green fields of rubbish. The driver was taking them to a rural slum, an unlikely destination for eight Western businessmen.

He shrugged. They'd shoot anyone who pulled them over.

Two hours later, with mute-grey light fogging the sky, the van pulled off National Highway 117 and into Kalinagar. Weeds lined the gravel road. Shanties and garbage piles dotted the fields like crumbs on a table, the locals' lacklustre attempt at cropping was overpowered by spreading scrub.

The driver guided the van to a crunching halt next to a forlorn building; some type of abandoned shop. Behind it, the Hoolie stretched bleakly to open ocean, a miserable tear to match the sky.

The driver spoke. 'This is where we stop, like that.' He managed a tight smile. You think good, not bad driving, I hope. I suppose I see you later then.'

Marriott raised an eyebrow at the man's inane babbling as the squad levered themselves out of the van and trotted over to the dock. Khawaja was waiting for them in the junk.

262

'Take us home, Khawaja,' Marriott ordered.

The little craft puttered to sea, where the *Kati-Thanda* waited for them silently.

Chapter 24
September 23rd, 0400 hours
Canberra

Jacqui Laffite rolled over and banged the 'transmit' button on the comms unit bleeping beside her bed. Anything to shut the damned thing up.

She massaged her temples, eyes closed. The message began.

'Mrs Laffite, sorry to disturb you so late but we've got an emergency developing in Geraldton.'

Of course there was. 'What's that supposed to mean?' Jacqui muttered.

'Well, ah, it seems the *Pong-Sawan* was full of armed men. When they landed, they killed local security. They've commandeered local vehicles and are spreading throughout the town taking hostages. Some of them assaulted the detention centre and overwhelmed security there - illegals are flooding back into town.'

'Jesus Christ.' Her stomach seemed to be launching off the top of a cliff, vertigo increasing at ever-increasing velocities.' She levered herself upright and turned on the bedside lamp. 'Andrew,' she said to the aide. 'Are you telling me a shipload of armed refugees has invaded us?' She avoided Craig's concerned gaze. She felt like vomiting.

'Well...in fact, yes. It seems the last ship was as much of an invasion force as a refugee ship. When they landed, they just streamed off, shooting anyone in their way. Prime Minister, I'm afraid twenty thousand armed men are running around the streets of Geraldton as we speak. Not to mention two hundred and fifty thousand illegals.'

She turned to Craig, aghast.

'What is it?'

'It looks like we've lost Geraldton,' she breathed.

Twenty minutes later she was in her office in Parliament House. 'Jacqui, I know this isn't an easy call to make. But we

264

have no choice. We have to authorise the military to target the tankers.' Whittey's voice had an edge of panic. 'We've just been invaded!'

Laffite touched a hand to her temple. She had such a splitting headache; she could barely think.

'Jacqui, even before the breakout there was an epidemic of rape and assault in that camp,' pushed Whittey. 'The place was out of control. Even before this happened,' he weaved his finger at the air, 'we had to stop more coming. And now those monsters are loose on our streets. What do you think they're going to do to local families?' he demanded.

Laffite was barely awake. Events were racing ahead of her ability to grasp them. She felt disconnected to what was happening and buffeted by everyone who thought they knew what to do but didn't have to make the call.

She had to make a decision and she was terrified it was the wrong one. But the wrong choice is often better than none…

'It's time we removed all ambiguity from our response,' said Jacqui, a kind of relief replacing vertigo now that she'd made a decision. 'I'm going to authorise, no, command Defence to target these ships with extreme prejudice. Who's in command out there?' she asked.

'Glen Robertson,' responded Whittey.

She nodded. It wouldn't be an easy command to follow, but if anyone could do it, Glen could.

'I'll make the call now.'

September 23rd, 0600 hours
HMAS *Hobart*

Thump thump thump thump…

'Go to hell…' muttered Robertson under his breath, then rolled upright and flicked the lights on. He'd handed the bridge over to Palmer after the battle and was trying for some shut-eye. He rubbed grit from his eyes as he shambled across the stateroom.

He cracked the door. 'What's up, Aiden,' he growled at the midshipman.

'Sir, Commodore Swan has been trying to raise you for five minutes. You weren't answering your comms call, so XO asked me to wake you up.'

He grunted. 'Five minutes? Hmm.' He scratched his stubble. He went to the bathroom and splashed some water on his face, shrugged into his uniform shirt and activated the video.

A very angry looking Leighton Swan appeared.

Asshole thought Robertson spontaneously.

He felt as bleary as the disembodied head of his senior commander looked.

Swan dispensed with any preamble. 'Congratulations on your victory Robertson, but events are moving fast, and there's no time to bask in glory. The *Pong-Sawan* landed in Geraldton at oh-three-thirty this morning, as expected. What we didn't expect was that it was full of armed insurgents who shot the welcoming committee and have moved through the town. Many have stolen vehicles and are using them to disperse through the country, and many more have invaded homes and are holding hostages. We're already getting word that these bastards have executed some families.'

Robertson stared in confounded amazement. Anger started boiling in his stomach; no nation had ever landed an invasion force on Australian soil.

'At the same time, some of them, with the help of ethnic Indian-Australians, rolled up the road to the internment camp, shot the security guards and opened the gates... The few army units already in the area have moved into the camp. It is all but empty. We've got nearly three hundred thousand illegals roaming through Geraldton, around ten per cent have light arms. The army is moving in and has orders to round them up.'

'How will the army differentiate between refugees and...the invaders?' asked Robertson.

'They won't. Anyone with brown skin will be commanded to lie face down on the ground to be arrested and removed to custody. They have orders to shoot anybody who doesn't immediately comply. Which brings me to the point of this discussion.'

Robertson could guess what was coming. Hoped he was wrong.

Swan eyeballed Robertson. 'You won a good victory today, Robertson, but the battle isn't over. You are to aggressively seek, engage and destroy the remaining vessels travelling from India.'

He nodded slowly, mulling the order. 'Are you saying we're now operating on the assumption that they're all carrying armed insurgents? Do we even know if these ships have armed men on board?'

Swan shrugged. 'We don't. It doesn't matter. We're now operating on the assumption they are. To do otherwise is to invite another armed force onto our soil.'

'Sir,' he began slowly, buying time to think. 'I was reinstated to bluff the Indians into believing that I'm a mass killer who'll sink their ships on a whim, not to actually do it.' The pieces were clicking into place. A small portion of his rage against the Indians was diverting to his political masters. A vision of Alice appeared in his mind. *What happens next is going to be pinned on you, Glen. So you better take control of the situation, fast.*

'Are you listening, Robertson?'

He snapped back to the present. 'Yep...yes, sir. Before I go and murder fifty thousand people, I was wondering if there's a shred of evidence these ships are carrying weapons?'

'All the evidence you need is running around Geraldton, looting, raping and pillaging as we speak. Robertson, this isn't a discussion. We've been saying for months that they can't come and that we'll take all measures to prevent illegal arrivals. We've been pussy-footing around, and they've been laughing at us all the way to the UN. This time they've given us ample reason to finally make good on that threat.'

Sometimes he wished he saw the world in black and white like the man in front of him. How much simpler it would be. But there was *no way in hell* he was sinking those ships. He just had to find a reason to stall until he figured something else out.

'Sir, I didn't enjoy sinking the *Tamil Nadu,* so if that's why you think I'm the man for the job-'

'Why do you think we put you in charge?' barked Swan. 'Precisely because you've done this before. You got what it takes to do what needs doing. This is coming from the top, Robertson. Laffite gave the order this morning.' He fixed Robertson with a hostile glare. 'Now get on with it.'

It felt like iron bands were constricting his chest. He knew what he had to do; it was simple. But he'd never thought he'd have to make this decision again. Well, the first thing he needed to do was buy some time. He spoke slowly and carefully. 'Hear you loud and clear, sir,' he said and cut the line.

He stared blankly at the screen; behind his eyes, his mind worked at full revs. His anger had subsided, replaced by an almost amused contempt for his superiors. Thinking they could use him like this. Fuck Admiral Futcher, and fuck Jacqui Lafitte. *That scalpel-hearted bitch,* he thought. He had no particular love for the Indian refugees either, but they'd have to shoot him before he needlessly killed so many again. Of course, if the ship *was* full of weapons, that was different. He had to find a reason not to massacre those people, fast.

He had to find out for himself what was on those ships.

Five minutes later, he was on the bridge. 'Get the helo fueled up and an armed boarding party ready to embark onto the nearest freighter,' he called down the 3MC to the team in the helicopter hanger. He turned to Bevan, the communications officer. 'Raise the bridge of those freighters. Do what you have to do to get their attention. Tell them if they don't respond after three hails, we'll put a five-inch shell into the top of the superstructure, and work our way down at thirty-second intervals until we've levelled it or they respond.'

'Uh, yes, sir,' a bemused Bevan replied and got to work on the radio.

'The rest of you. Listen up.' Aiden and Harper sat back from their consoles, swivelling their heads to face Glen. Palmer straightened up from the radar display he'd been studying. In short order, he was satisfied all eyes were on him.

'I've just been briefed by command. The last freighter to land, the *Pong-Sawan,* was full of illegals with guns. They've overrun Geraldton. We now have orders to sink, on sight, the rest of these freighters.' He paused, let the implications of the order sink in. His comments were met with silence, accentuated by the soft hum of the air-conditioning.

Now to drive his point home. 'If we comply with this order, each of us on this ship will be responsible for the deaths of tens of thousands of people.' He paused again. Aiden seemed to shrink in his seat. Harper looked aghast like she was about to cry.

'Here's what we're going to do. We're going to land boarding parties on those ships to verify if there are weapons on board. If there are not, no ship under my command will be firing on those vessels. If there are, we'll think of another plan then.'

Palmer found his voice. 'Sir, what if they resist the boarding party, like last time you tried something like this?'

'I sank the *Tamil-Nadu,* Palmer. Would *you* call my bluff?' Palmer nodded. Point taken.

'Sir, I can't raise them,' said Bevan.

'Aiden, put a five-inch shell through the top level of the superstructure of the lead ship.'

'Yes, sir,' said the TAO. The naval cannon at the front of the ship rotated and moments later barked once, spurting a little puff of smoke, and a few seconds later the top of the superstructure exploded in a cloud of grey dust.

'Repeat in thirty seconds,' he said.

Fifteen seconds passed. Then the radio crackled. 'Sir, we have the captain of the *Maya* on the line,' said Bevan. Robertson gestured for him to pass the radio console.

'This is Commodore Glen Robertson of the HMAS *Hobart*. To whom am I speaking?'

There was a short pause, then, 'My name is Virat Saanvi. We are a refugee ship. Why are you firing on us?'

'Virat, we are going to land a boarding party on your ship. They are going to search the crew and passengers for weapons. You *will* comply with all our commands. Do you understand?'

'Weapons? We are carrying no weapons! There is no need for your boarding party.' There was a short pause. 'They will turn the ship around, which we can't allow. The passengers will riot; there will be chaos if they don't reach Western Australia.'

'Virat. I am the officer responsible for sinking the *Tamil Nadu*. The operatives on that ship shot down the helicopter carrying the boarding party, so I ordered my crew to torpedo the ship, which subsequently sank with the loss of twenty-five thousand Indian lives. If you repeat their mistake, I will repeat my orders, and you will suffer the same fate. Do I make myself clear?'

There was a long silence. 'Aiden. Fire the cannon again. Hit a peripheral area; we can't negotiate with them if they're dead.'

The shell detonated on the jutting wing, part of the bridge that was only used to help the ship dock.

He fingered the radio again. 'Virat, we can do this all day. Do you comply?'

The radio crackled. 'We comply.'

The helo whoomped off the rear deck, and Robertson got back on the radio. 'Virat,' he called once he'd got the Indian captain back on the line. 'In the event of any non-compliance, my team has direct orders to shoot first and ask questions later. Nobody wants a repeat of the *Tamil Nadu*. Not me and definitely not you. So, treat them nice and if you got nothing to hide everything will be fine. If anything happens to them, I *will* sink you. Understood?'

A short pause, then; 'We'll comply with their wishes. Please ensure they are not too heavy-handed. There are a lot of very sick people on board.'

'I'll pass it on,' said Robertson, and cut the line.

Four hours later, he was back on the radio, this time with the commander of the boarding party who was reporting in.

'Sir, we've swept the ship. I wouldn't say it was thorough, but there is no evidence of a large cache of weapons. Not enough to arm everyone on board.'

Robertson nodded. *Thank God for that,* he thought, breathing a long sigh of relief before he replied. 'Did you find anything else of interest?'

'This ship is full of sick and dying people, shit, piss and the most appalling smell I've ever come across. Nothing I'd call interesting from a military perspective, sir.'

He'd heard in detail about the conditions on those ships and didn't envy the boarding team one bit. 'OK, good job. Now secure yourselves in the engineering spaces and shut the engines down. I'll send another team to reinforce you and additional weapons immediately.'

September 23rd, 1400
Parliament House, Canberra

A muscle in Lafitte's jaw was spasming. She clenched her teeth and seemed to short circuit the twitching, for now.

'What's he done this time,' she said thinly.

'He managed to get a boarding party on board. They did a sweep. Apparently, there are no weapons aboard,' reported Futcher.

'Why did he do that?' she demanded. 'So that he has a reason not to sink that ship?'

'He says there's no reason to sink it because they're unarmed. They can't do any harm, according to Robertson.'

271

'Fucking hell. It's never simple is it,' she muttered to herself. She realised she'd stood up. Took a deep breath, and sat down again.

'He's right,' said Abbott, pointing at Lafitte. 'We can *not* fire on that ship if we know they're unarmed.' Lafitte ignored Abbott's finger. 'What are they playing at, sending one with guns and the next without...' She bunched her face, confounded.

'It's smart from him,' said Abbott. 'It's hard enough to order that sort of thing, but only a psychopath would follow through.'

'It's insubordination,' said Futcher blandly. 'We'll stand him down and get someone else to do it if necessary.'

'Frankly, I don't blame him,' Abbott said, glaring at the Admiral. 'It doesn't sound like your pilots want to do it either.' Futcher shifted uncomfortably. The P-8 pilots had not refused the command directly, but a slew of mechanical issues had suddenly grounded the fleet of brand-new planes. 'Seems like Robertson isn't the only maverick in the Navy, Admiral.'

The door opened, and Cam Holloway strode in. Without preamble, he said 'The Indians are loading up another *five* ships out of Kolkata, he said, throwing satellite photographs onto the table. Two rows of two ships lashed together, with a fifth behind them. The crowd was like an ink-stain on a table cloth, spreading across the docks and down the streets around them.

'What's that, a hundred and fifty thousand people?' said Lafitte, deflating slightly.

'About that, yes. The ships will be ready to go in twenty-four hours,' said Holloway. He dropped more satellite shots on the table. 'And here are the warships that are on station to escort them.' Lafitte scanned one; *Kolkata class block II guided-missile destroyer, 7500t, capability level: peer*. There were seven of them.

'While Robertson fucks around pointlessly searching these ships can we get someone else to sink it?' Lafitte asked the room. 'I mean, the requirement is the same, we still have the same requirement, with the added urgency of sinking the *Maya* before this next flotilla gets to sea. We have to see this to the end. What can you suggest, Air Marshall?'

Cas Castrission shared a glance with Futcher before answering, then chose his words carefully.

'They're too far out for the F-35s to hit without tanker support. We don't have any tankers on station right now. I can order some up to Pearce, but it would be days before we're ready to deploy.'

'Days?' she snapped. 'We don't have days. We've got twenty-four hours. You heard the man,' she said nodding at Holloway. 'They,' she pointed at the spy-sat photos at Kolkata docks, 'will have left in days, 'and *Maya* will be on the beach by then.' Lafitte slapped the table. 'Your branches are either incompetent or deliberately subverting orders. It's a disgrace.'

'I think,' started Abbott slowly, 'that it makes more sense to meet them with the army-' Whittey and Futcher had opened their mouths to object, but they were all cut-off by the sharp report of Lafitte's hand slapping the table again. 'Absolutely not,' she glared at her colleagues. She wasn't really angry with them, she knew. She was angry she was in this position at all, having to order the deaths of thousands of probably innocent people so that millions more didn't come streaming onto their beaches. She would do what needed to be done; she would *always* do what needed to be done, no matter the personal cost. But she was terrified she'd lose her nerve entirely and she wanted to *bloody well get on with it* before she let her country, and herself, down.

She felt like a truck crossing a flooding river. Too late to turn around, and stopping not an option. She *must* plough on.

'Futcher, can we get Robertson on the line now? I want to tell him the situation directly.' Her tone softened. 'Maybe that will motivate him to act,' she said to the wall.

Futcher nodded and made a phone call. A few minutes of ID checks later, he'd been patched through to the bridge of the *Hobart*.

'Admiral Futcher!' Glen's voice boomed through the speaker on the desk. 'To what do I owe the pleasure?'

Futcher cocked an eyebrow, thoroughly unimpressed. Lafitte found herself staring earnestly at the speaker. 'Commodore, I'm here with the Prime Minister and her inner cabinet of advisers, as well as the head of Army and Air Force.'

'How can I help, sir,' Robertson said briskly.

Lafitte raised a finger; she wanted to speak. Futcher nodded in the direction of the phone, and she took a deep breath.

She hadn't spoken to Glen like this in years. The faintest flutter of butterflies twinged in her stomach. She frowned at the utterly inappropriate sensation.

'Glen, it's Jacqui...You've done the Australian Navy proud. That victory has improved our negotiating position with the Indians and lifted the national mood.' She'd planned to start massaging his ego but found that she meant what she was saying. After all, it was true, wasn't it?

'Thank you, Prime Minister,' he responded. Was there a hint of humour in his voice? 'The men and women under my command have indeed done us proud.' It *was* humour - she could hear him smiling wryly down the connection. She remembered that tone, like he knew something that she didn't. A wave of nostalgia washed over her, and she felt the ridiculous urge to engage in idle chit-chat with him. Even stronger, she suddenly felt wary. What did he have up his sleeve today? She started cautiously.

'Glen, I know you've established that there may not be weapons on the *Maya*. Despite this-'

'That's correct, Prime Minister. No weapons,' he interrupted, voice now granite hard. 'Therefore, no need to sink that ship.'

She responded in kind. 'Wrong, Glen. There are five freighters with a hundred and fifty thousand people loading as we speak in Kolkata. If you sink that ship they *will not leave for Australia.* Therefore your orders remain the same. It's about sending a clear message.'

There was a long pause. 'Robertson, please report,' said Futcher.

'Admiral, Prime Minister, I've thought about this,' said Robertson, resolve tinged with resignation emanating from the speaker. 'I cannot comply with that order. This is cold-blooded murder. We're soldiers, not butchers, sir.'

Jacqui clenched her fists and banged on the mute button. 'Always was such a *fucking...*' she reached for the right word- he'd always been exasperating, but that didn't cut it. 'Bastard,' she finished lamely.

'Prime Minister, Admiral,' Robertson called confidently and clearly. 'I don't envy you the decisions you have to make. I do understand the why of what you're asking. Climate change is tearing the subcontinent to pieces, and there's an unlimited supply of refugees who will swamp us if we let them. That notwithstanding, the *Maya* is the wrong ship to make an example of, and I will not fire upon it without just cause. I understand there will be consequences for my actions today and accept them completely.'

Jacqui grimaced and felt her mind flitting back to her time with Glen. Whenever they'd had intractable arguments he'd said much the same thing then. Carrots to entice or sticks to threaten had had the same impact, *I respect your opinion but I don't share it, and I'm not changing my mind regardless of the consequences,* his voice echoed in her head.

'Jacqui, if he won't do it, we'll just find someone else who will,' said Futcher, normally gruff voice now sounding like he was milling rocks in his throat. She nodded assent. She knew how this conversation would go.

'Commodore,' Futcher said gravelly, command voice suddenly radiating throughout the room. 'You will comply with your orders, or you'll be relieved of command, and Captain Palmer will carry them out in your stead. You will then face court-martial for insubordination.'

'Palmer sees things my way, sir,' responded Robertson instantly. 'Besides, I will make it known that I will fire upon any ship that fires on the *Maya.*' Futcher, Lafitte, and Whittey shared horrified looks with each other. Abbott was peering at the speaker, squinting, as if in pain. 'Furthermore, I have instructed the boarding party to secure themselves in the engineering spaces of the *Maya.* Any attempt on that ship is an attempt on their lives as well.'

'This is a disgrace,' Lafitte said in disbelief at Futcher. *How can you have so little control over one of your top officers,* her expression said clearly.

Futcher's jaw worked, his face had taken on a dark purple hue, and his head seemed to be throbbing. He suddenly looked older. 'Stand by for further orders, Robertson,' he said and cut the line.

Silence lay heavy on the conference room as they digested what had just happened.

Jacqui pieced it together in her mind. 'So, we have twenty-four hours to prevent those five freighters from leaving, and the only way to do that is to sink the *Maya.* And the only capability we have that can act soon enough is that navy squadron that Robertson is hamstringing.'

'That's how I read it,' said Whittey.

Cam Holloway cleared his throat. 'There are...measures...we can take to motivate the crews of our ships to carry out their orders. Would you care to discuss them?'

'No,' snapped Lafitte. 'If you have a solution, implement it. Do what you can to motivate that asshole to sink the *Maya,* while Futcher figures out how to get someone else to do it. We've wasted enough time.'

Holloway looked at Abbott, who gave a tired shrug.

'Do what needs doing, Cam.'

The old spymaster nodded. 'I'll make a few calls.' He pulled his phone out of his pocket and left the room.

HMAS *Hobart*

Glen carefully clicked the radio handset back into place. His hand was shaking. *Like an alcoholic in remission,* he thought. He needed to gasp like he'd just finished a four hundred metre sprint. He wondered how long they'd lock him up for, for this. Palmer was standing upright, staring straight out the window, watching his career disappear across the waves.

There was a funereal silence on the bridge. Each individual was in deep consultation with their thoughts.

'Alright, Robertson. You sold us on not sinking the *Maya.'* Palmer said eventually. 'Now we get to find out at what personal cost bought the lives of those illegals.' Glen rubbed the stubble forming on his chin, the roughness reassuringly real. *You're still here, Robertson.* 'We've done the right thing. No matter what happens, next, *we've* done the right thing.' Nobody replied. It was the exact opposite circumstances, but the atmosphere on the bridge felt identical to his command on the day the *Tamil Nadu* had sunk under the waves. He took a swig of coffee. 'Listen up,' he snarled. 'We're damned if we do, damned if we don't. So, we might as well stick to our principles. Because I'll tell you from experience. In situations like this, they're all you've got left.'

Chapter 25
Geraldton Police Lockup
September 23rd, 1800 hours

Fadi stretched on tiptoes to peer out the grated slit passing for a window in his cell. He wanted to see what was happening outside. It looked like things had calmed down a bit; he'd barely been inside twelve hours when a stream of his country-men had rampaged through the town. At first, he'd wondered what the hell was going on; then he'd shouted through the slit like a madman, screaming at them to let him out. A couple had veered off and jogged over to the lockup. The police had abandoned their posts, and the men had walked in unmolested. Fadi had gaped in astonishment as they explained that everyone on the *Pong-Sawan* had been given a rifle just before they arrived at Geraldton. They told him they were going to the camp to free the refugees there, but their top priority was to find vehicles so they could disperse around Australia, and link up with the vast Indian diaspora, many of whom were determined to hide them throughout Australian cities.

They'd done a cursory look for the keys to Fadi's cell but had found nothing. They'd shrugged apologetically to Fadi and walked out. 'Sorry!' one called. 'Did our best...good luck!'

He pissed into the little pan they'd given him, and sat down, despondent. Nobody had passed for hours. And nobody had keys anyway. For a few hours, he'd berated himself for killing Surya and Sharma, then for not covering his tracks a bit better, because if the cops hadn't caught up with him for twelve more hours, he'd be running around the Australian desert, a free man. Then he'd seen the Australian army roll in, and the frequent sound of shouting, and the less frequent but still regular sound of gunshot, and wondered if hadn't panned out ok, given the circumstances.

The lockup door creaked open, and he snapped his head around. A bulky woman in dark trousers and a blue work shirt materialised from the darkness. Her mousy hair was pulled back in a severe ponytail and her heavy jaw flexed. She was chewing gum, really mashing it between her molars. Hanging back was a stocky man dressed the same. He rested his elbows on his pistol holsters.

She peered at him through the bars. 'What do you want?' he asked warily.

'I want to know your name,' she said, jangling a set of keys. 'Answer right, and you get out of here.'

He eyed the keys hungrily. He contemplated making up some bullshit name, then dismissed it. They were obviously expecting a specific response, or they wouldn't be offering to let him out if he replied correctly.

'Fadi Manoj,' he said warily. 'My name is Fadi Manoj.

'Fadi Manoj.' She nodded like she'd been expecting it. She rolled the name around her mouth like she was tasting it. 'Sounds like an infection of the colon. Perhaps his parents had a premonition,' she said to the guy behind her, then stuck the key in the lock. 'You can call me Patterson,' said the woman. 'This is my partner. You can call him Whyte. Don't ask any questions Fadi; we're in a hurry.'

A little while later, he was in the back of a beat-up old four-wheel drive, jolting over some outback roads. There was a thick Perspex screen between them and the front seats which blocked all sound. Another refugee sat next to him. A powerfully compact man, he exuded strength his diminutive stature did nothing to detract from. His shirt clung to his thick chest in the sticky heat, and his stoop-shouldered slouch accentuated the ridge between his pecs. The ring finger on his left hand was missing, and he rubbed the stump absent-mindedly. He periodically thrust his jaw in Fadi's direction and assessed him like a tree stump that needed chopping down.

279

Despite this, he didn't appear to be particularly malevolent. He wondered what they had in common?

The jolting stopped, and suddenly they were on smooth tarmac. The windows in the back were tinted almost black and reduced oncoming headlights to little pinpricks of white; Fadi could see nothing of the outside world. But the tyres buzzed in a high-pitched whir indicating they were speeding down the road well over the standard limit. There was a small sliding window between the driver's cabin and the two prisoners. It slid open with a snap, and Patterson's face appeared. She twisted around backwards, squinting uncomfortably through the gap.

'Listen up, you two. Fadi and Akshay.' Fadi glanced at his companion. So that was his name. 'First of all, let me assure you, you're both in very deep shit. But, we have a little problem, and even though you're good for almost nothing, you might be able to help. Have either of you ever heard of Commodore Glen Robertson?'

Fadi risked a glance at Akshay, who'd levered himself upright. It was common knowledge that Robertson had sunk the *Tamil Nadu.* Fadi had a recurring fantasy that involved watching Robertson's ship explode in a fireball, with Robertson miraculously surviving the blast only to be trapped on the bridge as it sunk under the waves.

'Well?' prompted Patterson.

'I know who he is,' said Akshay. Patterson looked at Fadi, who nodded.

'He's the guy who sank the *Tamil Nadu.* Killed twenty-five thousand Indians. Just like you,' she said, tapping the glass. 'Now, he's in charge of a squadron of ships tasked with stopping the next shipload of illegals.' She sucked saliva between her teeth. 'It appears he's just lost his mind. He kicked your tin can Navy's ass, which is no surprise, given the quality of human being operating those vessels, and of course, we're glad about that. But he's gone rogue, and he's telling us he's going to sink that ship, the *Maya.* He's co-opted his crew and the other ships in his command.' Patterson sighed dramatically. 'We believe there's another thirty thousand of you illegals on that ship.'

Fadi was panting like a dog on a hot day. He was searching for something to say when Akshay spoke. 'What's the problem, isn't that what you people want?' he said laconically.

'Absolutely it's what I want,' said Patterson enthusiastically. Fadi stiffened but said nothing. He was used to people baiting him these days. She'd turned side-on a little, and the slit only afforded them a view of her slab-sided cheeks hanging off sharp cheekbones, and her lips, which she'd twisted cruelly. 'But our government doesn't share that view. They don't want another mass sinking at sea.' Patterson sighed dramatically, her lips pursing. He noticed they were cracked and dry. And very thin. 'That's what happens when you put a woman in charge.'

Was that a joke? Must be why you're overcompensating, he thought. He found his voice. 'What do you want with us? Call him up on the radio, ask him nicely to stop?'

The lips moved before she spoke, as though she was chewing on the answer before it exited her mouth. 'We need to incentivise Robertson to stand down. To want to come home. He's not listening to orders.' Patterson edged her face closer through the gap and dropped her voice. 'We're going to take you to his girlfriend's house. You're going take her hostage. You're going to demand that Robertson comes home, and if he doesn't, you'll kill her.' Her face looked pale and bloodless in the shadows cast by the passing cars. *Dead,* he thought, *with just some mechanical bits moving and making noise. This woman is dead inside.*

'You want us to kill an innocent woman in cold blood,' he sneered. He appealed to Akshay with a look - surely he would agree this was impossible! The man just frowned, nodding

281

slowly. He didn't like, but clearly understood what he was hearing.

'What makes you think we'd do that?'

'You're both killers.'

Akshay and Fadi looked at each other again. Akshay was nodding again, looking at Fadi with a mix of surprise and, respect? Fadi noticed gold flecks in the man's eyes. They were different from Sharma's eyes, and Surya's. The man looked powerful and dangerous but not like a murderer. Fadi hoped desperately the panic wasn't showing on his face.

'What happens to us after?' asked Akshay.

'Oh, we'll send you back to internment,' said Patterson breezily. 'Maybe get them to look at your application for refugee status a bit more seriously for being so patriotic. How's that sound?'

'Sound like a load of shit,' replied Akshay blandly.

Patterson shrugged. 'Yea...it is. But if you refuse, we'll find someone who won't, and you'll be dead on the side of the road.' Pattersons jawed clenched and unclenched, the muscles flitting black and white in the dim light. 'Not only that, if you get him to stand down, you'll have saved thirty thousand Indian lives.' She sounded like one of the bric-a-brac sellers in the markets back home, lying about the quality of the stolen goods they were vending.

'So you take us to her house, give us some weapons to take her hostage with and what, she calls up her boyfriend and tells him if he doesn't stand down we'll kill her?' Fadi asked, voice dripping with scepticism.'

'That's right. You're helping us, and you're helping other Indians. Win-win.'

'And if he doesn't stand down?' Fadi asked.

'Then you rough her up. Cut off her toes, whatever you like. Get him to stand down, no matter what. If he doesn't, your countrymen die, and so do you.'

Fadi sat back, a little shocked.

'And afterwards, you fast-track our refugee application?' Akshay said, as casually as if he was at the post office asking for a priority post stamp.

Patterson chewed the words then enunciated them. 'You got it.'

'Let's do it,' shrugged Akshay. 'Not like we have a choice anyway.' Like he'd been told there were no priority stamps. *Oh well, standard post will do.* Fadi almost laughed, he'd never met anyone so fatalistic.

Patterson tapped the Perspex with her knuckles. 'What do you say, little buddy?' she directed at Fadi.

He shrugged too. Fatalism seemed to be appropriate, given his current situation. 'I'm in.'

'Good.' Patterson snapped the Perspex slide shut. Akshay leaned in towards Fadi, gestured him closer. He wanted to speak without shouting too loudly.

A bemused smile played on his lips. 'You don't look like a killer,' he said appraisingly, just over the sound of the tyres. Fadi strained to hear. 'You look like a scared shitless kid. Did they get the right person?'

'I'm not a killer,' he snapped. 'I mean, I've killed. I killed two men. They raped my friend, so I stabbed them. But it's not who I am,' he finished.

Akshay threw his head back and burst out laughing. 'I had a friend once. He had a wife and three kids. Bummed men every chance he got. Wasn't gay though, according to him.'

Fadi frowned. 'What are you on about,' he asked quizzically.

'You are what you do, kid,' Akshay smiled wryly. He had kind, sad lines around his eyes, Fadi noticed. Suddenly the smile disappeared, and the hard blankness was back.

'They're gonna kill us. You know that, right?' Akshay said. He was leaning forward again, eyes boring into Fadi's. 'They're gonna kill her and say it was us, and leave us dead at the scene. Or kill us later, when it suits them.'

He thought for a moment, then nodded slowly, understanding. 'If we're alive we can talk, tell people they,' he jabbed a finger at the driver's cabin, 'put us up to it killing an innocent woman.'

'Yea. Even if that load of Dharavi diarrhea she just told us is true, we're dead. So when we get out of this van, we have to get away from those assholes somehow. And we still have to kidnap Robertson's wife. Otherwise, they'll hunt us down and shoot us on sight.'

Fadi bit his lip. He couldn't see how Akshay was wrong. The man waited patiently while he thought it through. 'How we gonna do this?' he asked eventually.

'At some stage, they'll have to tell us what house is hers. Once we know that, we need to wait until they're close enough that we can rush them. We have to get their weapons. The signal is *Kolkata.* When I say that, we attack them. Meantime, keep acting like you're about to shit your pants. It may make them overconfident.'

'It's not an act,' he said, shaking his head. That pit of fear in his guts was opening up already; he could feel his bowels loosening as they spoke.

Akshay beckoned him close. Their heads almost touched in the middle of the space, and they swayed as the car sped down the road. Akshay put his hand on Fadi's shoulder and looked at him with kind eyes turned hard. 'Remember who you are, kid, or you'll be dead in four hours.' His hand clamped hard on Fadi's shoulder, a rock-solid grip on the verge of pain.

'You are a killer.'

Fadi met his gaze. Then he nodded. He wasn't a killer, but he could kill.

South Perth
September 23rd, 2130 hours

About two hours later, the car slowed, and Fadi could feel them picking their way through suburban streets. He looked at

Akshay, wrapped in thick slabs of meat. Fadi looked at his own slender arms. Wiry, lean muscle. But not much of it.

'Hey, kid,' said Akshay, noticing the consternation on his face. 'You can do this. You did it before, and you'll do it again.'

'Yea, but I had a weapon. And I surprised them,' he muttered back. He wiped clammy hands on his shorts for the thousandth time.

'We're still gonna surprise them,' Akshay said sharply in a low voice. 'And this time you've got me,' he thumbed himself in the chest. His stocky bulk was reassuring. 'Remember; as soon as we know what house, I'll say the word and we attack.'

Fadi nodded stiffly. Every time they stopped at an intersection, Fadi worried they had finished the journey. Then it would accelerate, and the tension would boil off a little. The constant anxiety was driving him mad. 'I wish we could just get this over with,' he said to Akshay. The man nodded tersely. For all his calming demeanour, he was on edge too.

Eventually, the car stopped and didn't move again. The engine shut down. There was silence.

'*I'm so fucking scared*,' he whispered. The front doors unlatched, the car swayed minutely as Patterson and her partner got out. The doors slammed shut. Boots scraped on tarmac, moving down the vehicle.

'Fadi,' hissed Akshay. Fadi shot him a wide-eyed look. The man gave him two thumbs up, dipped his head meaningfully. *You've got this.*

Time to do or die, Fadi, he cajoled himself. That little traitor in consciousness piped up. *Probably to die.* He felt a spike of rage at the self-doubt, and it abated a little.

The door clicked open and fresh cool air rushed into the back row. The two Australians pointed silenced pistols at the Indians. 'Shh,' said Patterson, finger to lips. She waved them outside with her gun. A dark sky beckoned them, and Fadi stepped down into a completely alien environment.

The street was wide, smooth tarmac, lined with high gutters of white cement. The gutters gave way to thick, even grass, then a spacious footpath, then the front yards of the houses.

He gawped, forgetting why he was here. Some houses had picket fences out front, others bricks. Others had manicured hedges, or just lawns running down to the road. Each house, he calculated, took up enough frontage to fit about twenty of his slum homes in. And each one was different! The variety of building materials - brick, wood, render - captivated him. He shook his head. *You could fit ten families in* one *of those houses.*

'Is each of those houses for just one family?' he asked before he could stop himself.

Patterson shot him daggers. She trained her gun at Fadi's head. Pulled a large knife from behind her belt and threw it on the ground a few metres away.

'That house is where you'll find Robertson's woman,' she hissed, pointing to a cement-rendered bungalow twenty metres away. It glinted creamy white in the moonlight. *It has a corrugated iron roof. Just like back home.*

'Pick up the knife on your way there. Tell her to get on the phone to her husband, and for him to stand down, or she's a dead woman.'

Akshay took a step back to the four-wheel drive. 'I need to piss,' he shrugged apologetically and had his dick out before Patterson object. 'Hurry up,' she hissed. Fadi edged closer to Whyte, who was carrying his weapon by his side.

Akshay took forever to start urinating and he finished after a little splash on the back wheel of the car.

'Ah shit,' he said, fiddling with his fly. 'Fuck! I've caught my dick in my fly!' and he doubled over in pain. 'You're not serious,' a thoroughly pissed Patterson said, peering around him to get a look. 'It really hurts. Here,' Akshay said edging closer to Patterson, 'Help me out, I can't see how it's stuck.' She cautiously approached Akshay who was clutching his crotch. She came within an arms-length. Akshay looked directly at Fadi. '*Kolkata,*' he bellowed, then dove onto Patterson.

Patterson had the gun in her trailing hand, and as she fell backwards with Akshay on top of her, she struck a glancing blow to his head. She landed on her back with Akshay on top, and he quickly rolled to the side, putting her between Whyte who was trying to get a shot off. The silencer made it hard for her to get the angle she needed at such close range, and she was effectively fighting one-handed. Akshay gripped her wrist and held the gun away with one hand. With the other, he jammed his fingers into her throat, right around her jugular, and squeezed with all his strength.

A dry gurgling scream emitted from Patterson, like a live animal fed into a garbage compactor. She dropped the gun and scratched frantically at Akshay's grip.

Fadi froze; should he rush the guy with the gun - *hell no you shouldn't* - or should he try to help Akshay? Patterson was scrabbling frantically now, and her face was swelling up like a rotten fruit. Whyte solved the problem for him; he fired once, twice at the tangled bodies on the ground, little popping sounds punctuating the quiet street. Patterson spasmed so hard she wrenched herself out of Akshay's grip, then was still. '*Shit!*' grated Whyte, high-pitched panic in his voice. He edged closer, weapon trained on the two bodies on the ground. Akshay tried to shrink under Patterson's body. It was scant cover.

Fadi had to buy time for Akshay to get that gun, without getting his head blown off. His mind raced. No weapon, too far to rush Whyte, nothing to throw. He did the only thing he could. 'Now listen, I think there's been a bit of a misunderstanding-'

'Shut up and get on the ground,' growled Whyte, not deviating from Akshay.

'Ok, I'm just gonna do it over here, away from all the guns,' he said, walking perpendicular to Whyte and away from Akshay.

Whyte whipped his aim to Fadi. The gun looked small in Whyte's giant hand. Small and deadly. 'Drop, or you're dead,' Whyte growled. 'I'm dropping! Don't shoot,' Fadi squeaked, not having to feign the terror in his voice. He dropped slowly, watching the barrel of the gun all the way down. *Come on Akshay, do something!*

Right then, Akshay threw Patterson's deadweight off, and rolled frantically, grabbing the gun as he did. He fired without aiming, as Whyte swiveled and fired simultaneously, three shots in a row, Akshay jolting like the bullets were heavyweight punches impacting.

'Argh!' shouted Whyte, collapsing at a knee-wrenching angle

Fadi still hadn't moved. He stared at Akshay. He was curled on the ground, gasping. His breath came in shallow gasps, and his eyes were lidded. He looked like a man who'd fallen over and was too tired to get up. But the pistol was still tight in his grip. Fadi whipped his head back to Whyte, expecting bullets to impact him at any moment. But Whyte was rolling around in agony, moaning through gritted teeth and clutching his leg - it looked like his kneecap was blown off.

Fadi scampered to Akshay and pried the pistol from his hand. Their eyes met and Akshay gave him a tired nod. Fadi walked towards Whyte, gun aimed right at his head. He picked up the discarded pistol and jammed it in his belt.

'Stop whining, Whyte. You don't know real pain, but I'll show you if you don't shut up.' Whyte nodded, eyes as large and white as the moon, and he bit down on the groans emanating from his throat.

If you run away, you're a fugitive who shot some cops, and they'll shoot you on sight, he thought. *If you take someone hostage, you may be able to negotiate a settlement. But probably not.* He looked around the quiet street. Unbelievably nobody had come out yet, but he had to figure out his next move, fast. *If you take Robertson's woman hostage, you'll probably still end up shot, but you may save those people's lives.*

He ran back to Akshay. He'd closed his eyes but his breath still came, little gasps that scarcely seemed to pump enough oxygen to sustain him. He levered stuck the second gun in his belt next to the first one and dragged the man upright by his arm. Got him vertical, then hugged him close, slipping under him till he was over his shoulder. He forced himself to his feet and staggered towards Robertson's house. Whyte watched silently as he passed, and out of the corner of his eye saw the man inching towards Patterson's body.

Moments later, he was at Alice's door. He dropped Akshay as tenderly as he could, pulled out a gun, and rang the doorbell before he realised just how ridiculous that was. Surely he should've climbed through a window or something. He craned his neck around the side of the porch, trying to pick an entrance. Then it was too late because a light switched on inside, and soft footsteps approached the door. For the thirtieth time that day, terror overcame him. Again, he steeled himself.

The door unlatched and swung open. Alice Ruiz was wearing gym tights, hair tied up in a hasty bun. There was a smudge of flour on her cheek, and she was cleaning her hands in a tea towel. She frowned at him, then she looked down at Akshay and gasped.

Fadi swallowed. They had absolutely nothing in common, but right then, Alice reminded him of Khandi; They were both victims of violent men. His heart reached out to this woman. Then he pointed the gun at her face. 'Let me in.'

'Sir, we've looked over the engines. They're pretty beaten up. To be honest, the engineers on board have done a good job keeping them running this long.'

Robertson rubbed his grainy eyes and inhaled a deep breath. He was leaning on the centre console on the bridge of *Hobart,* coffee mug in one hand, radio handset in the other.

'Could it make the return trip to Kolkata?' he queried. There was a moment's delay while the boarding team conferred. 'Probably,' said the team lead slowly. 'But it'd need support. The lube oil pumps are all shot, and the engine seals are holed. Pissing lubricant everywhere. Only one generator is online. She could maybe creep along at a few knots, above that and it'd seize, or the last genset would go and same result. Dead in the water.'

'Ok, Good job. I'll see if I can get an engineering crew out here. *Hobart* out,' he said, closing the channel.

'Sir, Admiral Futcher is on channel four. Says it's urgent,' Aiden called. Robertson picked up the handset again and waved the call through.

'Robertson reporting,' he said without preamble. He swirled the coffee mug, then handed it off to a midshipman to refill.

'Robertson, this is Futcher. If you're on the bridge, please go to your quarters to take this call. It's of a personal nature.' He frowned. 'One moment, sir,' he said. 'Palmer, you're in charge,' he said as he made his way aft.

In his stateroom, he picked up the channel. 'Admiral Futcher, how can I help?'

'Robertson, I have some bad news. An illegal, escaped from the camp in Geraldton, has somehow found out where you lived. He armed himself and is holding Alice hostage. He demands that you stand down immediately or...she'll come to harm.'

The floor of his cabin seemed to drop away, down the chute of a rollercoaster at increasing speed. 'Sir, is she ok?' he managed. 'How did they find out where we live?' he asked.

'She's fine,' Futcher replied. 'So far. We've surrounded the house with police, and we have an SAS team from Campbell Barracks en route.'

'Jesus Christ,' muttered Robertson. 'Keep those fucking madmen away from my girlfriend. They'll shoot everything that moves if you send them in.' He frowned. 'You said there's only one. What's the problem? Can't you wait till he falls asleep then send in the shooters?'

'Not this time. Robertson, there's a recorded message from Alice that you need to hear. We can discuss your questions afterwards. Are you ready?'

There was a little framed picture of Alice and Glen stuck to his desktop. He was in his Navy whites, and his arm was around her shoulders. She'd nestled her head into the crook of his neck. Her left arm was clamped tight around his waist, her right hand resting on his chest. She was wearing a red patterned dress and her thick dark hair cascaded over her bare shoulder. But it was her eyes that he studied. The eyes don't lie, he thought. Her eyes in that photo told him she was utterly devoted to him. He swallowed and shook his head. The floor was still disappearing from underneath him.

'Yea. I'm ready.'

'Standby,' said Futcher, then Alice's voice filled the little space.

Glen, it's Alice. Firstly, I'm safe. I've been taken hostage by one of the...refugees from Geraldton.' She spoke clearly, firmly. There was no fear in her voice. He was so afraid for her, and at the same time, so *proud.* Hot tears burned in his eyes. *'His name is Fadi Manoj, and he says his family went down with the* Tamil Nadu. *He wanted me to tell you that you are a murderer*

291

and that you are not to be trusted to deal with the other refugee ships. He says that you are to stand down, to hand over command of your ship. He understands that he is going to die, either way, so has nothing to lose and that you have until six a.m. to relinquish command, or he'll put a bullet in my head.'

There was nothing after that, and Glen realised the message was over.

'Sir, you have to get a team in there asap,' he grated. A throbbing had sprung up in his head, like the resonance of a giant engine *whoomping* through his skull. 'When will the special forces guys arrive?' he demanded. This Fadi guy had given him five hours to do something. Suddenly the lunatics from the SAS team seemed like a great option.

'Robertson, listen up. This is a god-awful situation we're all in. Especially you. Because you need to make some very tough choices now.'

Robertson's brow drew down. Where was this going?

'You have standing orders to sink the *Maya.* You know why, yet you refuse, and you've co-opted your crew somehow. Make no mistake, we want to do everything we can to safeguard Alice. But all responders, including the SAS when they arrive, are under strict instructions *to do nothing* until specifically ordered otherwise.'

'Just what the fuck are you talking about, Futcher? Are you trying to blackmail me into committing mass murder with the life of my girlfriend, you piece of shit?' Robertson shouted.

'Follow your fucking orders, Robertson,' Futcher snapped back. 'Follow your orders, and you'll get your girlfriend back,' he repeated, regaining some composure. 'You win, we win. Refuse, and that little terrorist, of whom there's now a quarter of a million running around WA, will blow Alice's brains out.' Futcher's voice dropped in tone and became even rougher. 'And it will be on *your* head, Robertson.'

'That's bullshit Futcher, does the kidnapper even know what's happening out here? I don't even want to sink that fucking ship; he should be glad I'm in charge. But if anything happens to her, I'll pump it full of MK48s... You tell him that.' Futcher didn't respond, so Robertson bulldozed forward. 'As for you, Futcher. Get that counter-terrorism team from Campbell in there and get her out of there, safe, and prove it to me, and I'll step down immediately. You can find someone else to commit your murder for you.'

'Alright, Robertson. I'll see what I can do.' Futcher paused. 'Robertson,' he began uncomfortably. 'Nobody wanted it to be this way; we're all in a very bad situation here...'

'Oh, *shut up* Admiral,' Robertson spat contemptuously. 'Spare me, please. *Alice* is in a really bad situation. Fix that, and we'll talk.'

The line cut. Robertson picked up the little model *Hobart* sitting on his desk and flung it across the room. Paced from the bunk to his desk and back again, two steps each way, over and again in a mad circle, then took a deep, slow breath and got himself under control.

Think, Glen. If you sink the ships, the SAS goes in, shoots the kidnapper and Alice gets out alive. Probably. Hostage raids often ended with the wrong person getting shot. *But, if he finds out what you've done, he kills Alice. Or he finds out you've stepped down and you get Alice back.* 'Unless you step down, and McClennan on the *Sydney* follows orders and sinks the *Maya,* and this terrorist hears about it. Then she's dead anyway,' he finished to himself. He checked the time on the wall. One-thirty in the morning. He had less than five hours to make a decision.

Canberra
September 24ᵗʰ, 0200 hours

Jacqui Lafitte waited impatiently in her Parliamentary office. She kept glancing at her phone as if staring at it would encourage it to ring faster. She dipped her fingers in the ice water on her desk and dabbed under her puffy eyes, the coolness momentarily refreshing. She was mildly concerned if she succumbed to the crushing weight of her eyelids and let them shut, she wouldn't get them open again. Cam Holloway sat on the couch opposite. The lines on his long face resembled ravines tonight, his thick leathery skin collapsing on itself in exhaustion.

'Cam,' she said coldly, 'This is one hell of a situation you've put us in. Aiding and abetting the kidnap of one of our own citizens, one of *your own staff no less...*' she shook her head. They had to bury this deep in the Simpson Desert or they'd end up in jail, at the very least.

He frowned, at her, ravines turning into canyons. 'You wanted leverage, Jacqui. I gave it to you. This could be what stops those boats.'

She couldn't shake the feeling that Cam Holloway was like a trusted hunting dog that had maybe picked up rabies from somewhere and was starting to froth at the mouth. Very useful indeed, but maybe the safe option would be to shoot it.

'What if this Fadi guy talks to Alice, tells her he doesn't even want to be there and was put up to it by your agents?' She bit her lip as the thought ran its course.

'If Alice hears what happened, she has to be silenced,' said Holloway. 'We've got a few select operatives heading out there now-'

'*Select operatives,*' Laffite scoffed. 'You mean, psychopathic.'

'We have kept the situation from the local police,' Holloway continued smoothly. 'We should be able to contain things.'

She *tsked* angrily. '*Should* doesn't fill me with confidence, Cam. It leaves me devoid of confidence.' She enunciated each word clearly and slowly. For the avoidance of doubt. 'You will clean up *all* the loose ends, Cam. If I go down for this, don't doubt for a second I'll take you down with me.'

Cam regarded her coldly. 'Oh, I don't doubt that at all, Prime Minister. We're all doing what we must.'

The phone rang. It was Futcher. *Finally.* 'How'd it go,' she asked without preamble.

'He said he'd step down if we got her out safe. He also said to tell this Fadi guy he'll sink the *Maya* if he hurts Alice.'

'Hmm,' she grunted. 'So, we have two options to get that ship sunk. How likely to be successful is a rescue attempt?' she asked.

'It's going to be tough. There's an SAS team en-route and the police have ringed the house already. But he's set a very short deadline so we'd have to storm the building and take him out before he can react. Low probability of success. Before we get to that though, your assessment isn't necessarily correct.'

'What do you mean,' she asked, shaking her head a little. *This is already awful, and even this isn't clear cut,* she thought.

'Robertson may be bluffing. He may not sink that ship even if the kid kills his wife. And, he may not stand down even if we get her out.'

She rubbed her temples with her hands. 'What if we tell Glen we got her out safe, will he stand down then?'

'Well, no, because we'd have to prove it, which we can't do.'

'Well, how about we tell him the terrorist killed her, see what he does then? We can still work on getting her out in the meantime,' she said. She was reaching, shooting wildly in the dark, but someone had to come up with a plan.

Futcher grunted. She could tell he was considering it. 'That's not a bad idea. At least it'll flush Glen out, if he's bluffing or not. I'll do it.'

HMAS *Hobart*
September 24th, 0215 hours

The comms unit on the desk in Robertson's stateroom flashed red; Futcher was calling. He snatched it up before the second ring. 'Robertson speaking,' he snapped.

'Commodore, the kidnapper has changed the timeline. I think he understands the longer he waits, the better we can plan a rescue. So he's given you till oh-three hundred hours to stand down.'

'What happens if I don't. He kills her?'

Futcher grunted in affirmative. 'That's what he's saying.'

'Who is this fucking guy anyway? Do you have any info on him? I mean, is he actually capable of doing this?' *It doesn't matter Glen, you have to assume he would...*

'We've done some digging. His name is Fadi Manoj, and he was on the *Tamil Nadu.* His mother and brother went down with the ship. He was in the lockup in Geraldton, local cops were holding him for murdering a couple of other internees. Stabbed them with a sharpened bed leg.'

Dammit, he fretted to himself. That wasn't what he wanted to hear. Once again, he was choosing between someone he cared about and tens of thousands of people he didn't.

'I want to speak to him. Get me a line to him and Alice. I want to speak to them both.'

'Negative,' Futcher responded immediately. 'He has expressly stated there will be no communication with you.'

'Really?' said Robertson, incredulous. 'So he goes all the way to Perth to take my girl hostage to blackmail me, knowing that one way or another this ends with a bullet in his brain, but doesn't want to speak to me except third hand through you?' He shook his head. 'This is all pretty fucking irregular, Futcher. Didn't I kill his mum? Surely he's got something to say.' There was an uncomfortable pause, which Futcher eventually broke.

'Couldn't tell you, Robertson,' he said gruffly. 'Maybe he's just as delusional as you, who knows.' Something in that comment twigged Robertson, and he circled around the thought, trying to pin it down.

He was still wrestling with his choices when Futcher spoke again. 'Stand down, you'll get your woman back, and McLennan will sink the *Maya* anyway. Or you can do what you've been ordered to do, and the SAS boys will go in and get her out. The only way she gets hurt is if you continue to disobey orders. Up to you.'

He glanced at the clock on the wall. Oh-two twenty-eight. Less than half an hour to make a call. He pinched the bridge of his nose, trying to unpick the vague sensation that was trying to coalesce into a coherent thought. *Dammit,* he thought. It was like grasping at air.

He picked up the intercom on the desk. 'Palmer, can you come to my stateroom please,' he called to the bridge. A few minutes later, the XO was sitting in Glen's desk chair. Glen had perched himself on the edge of the bunk. He appraised Palmer of the situation with Alice.

'Jesus,' his XO breathed when Glen finished. 'What are you thinking?'

'Well, the more I think about it, the fishier this smells. This Fadi guy is trying to save the *Maya,* and so are we. If he spoke to me, he'd know our interests were aligned, so there'd be no point threatening Alice, would there?'

Palmer frowned and shook his head. 'No, there wouldn't.'

'But, for some reason, the guy doesn't want to talk to me. I mean, he's got the wrong end of the stick.'

'And our side obviously hasn't set him straight,' said Palmer, 'or he'd stand down, or be making some other demand. Like asylum in exchange for Alice,' he finished.

Robertson pointed at Palmer. 'You're right,' he said, thinking furiously. 'They're not telling him what's really happening out here. So maybe they're not telling me what's really happening back there...'

'You think they're trying to manipulate you into standing down or sinking the *Maya*?' Palmer mused.

'It sure feels like it,' he nodded, then shook his head. 'But I can't gamble with Alice's life on a hunch,' he muttered.

Stand down, Glen. You've stuck your neck out far enough, murmured a reasonable-sounding voice in his head. *You just*

got her back. It's good you've got your balls back, but she can't
appreciate that if she's dead.

He checked the time. It was oh two forty-five.

September 24th
South Perth, 0255 hours

Alice and Fadi sat opposite each other in the living room. There were no windows to the outside world, so he was less vulnerable to a sniper shot. He figured. But, of course, he couldn't see what was going on out there either now. He looked around, at the photos of Glen and Alice peppering the room, the plate with the remains of a salad sandwich on it next to the lounge, the deep tan coloured leather of the lounges themselves, strewn with cushions. The only fly in the ointment was his bloodstained self. Alice herself sat reclined on the lounge opposite him, one leg crossed on the opposite knee. She didn't appear intimidated in the slightest. In fact, she looked perfectly at ease. One of the silenced pistols lay on the lounge next to him; the other was on his lap.

She was looking at him, mouth pursed in a flat line, almost a frown, but her eyes sparkled with...mirth? No. With sympathy.

He'd just told Alice the story of how he'd come to be in her house with two guns and blood all over his clothes. She'd listened intently, face moving through expressions of interest, surprise, amusement then incredulity. Sympathy when he'd told her about Khandi. 'They said they chose me because I killed those two guys - that I'm a killer. But,' he said, sheepishly, 'I'm not, even though it probably doesn't look like it.'

Alice nodded. She sat back on the lounge, one leg crossed over her knee. He realised, with rising embarrassment, that his last sentence had been completely redundant.

'That's an incredible story, Fadi,' she said. 'You've been through a lot.'

'Yea,' he said, not wanting to talk but the words tumbling out of him. She was serious and considered, but she did remind him of Kandi, with her playful confidence. 'So now they're using me to try to get your boyfriend to stand down because he wants to sink the *Maya.* They want me to choose between killing someone in front of me or killing thousands of people I've never met.'

'Fadi, you may not believe this, but when Glen sank the ship you were on, it nearly killed him. I've never seen him so guilt-stricken in his life. Fadi, listen closely. There's *no way* Glen wants to sink that ship. I'm aware of our government position on this. We need to sink the *Maya* to stop any more ships coming; otherwise they'll never stop. Nothing else is stopping the boats from coming.'

'You don't have to sink any boats,' he said angrily. 'I've been in your outback. There's enough land for millions of people to live...'

'Fadi, that's true, but it's not the way we think. And it's not the option our government is going to pursue. So you need to decide if you want to talk about how things should be, or how things are. What's it gonna be?'

'I think your boyfriend killed my mother, my brother, and all those other people,' he said, unconsciously gripping the grip of the pistol tighter.

She gave him a piercing look. 'Should that have happened? Yes, or no? Quickly now, did your mother deserve to die?' Anger flared in him. He could shut this stupid woman up in a heartbeat- 'Yes or no Fadi?'

'Of course it shouldn't have happened!' he grated. He looked at this perfect woman with her perfect life with loathing. *If she keeps disrespecting mother you can always put a bullet in her brain.*

Her tone softened. 'Of course it shouldn't have happened. You shouldn't have had to get on that ship in the first place, and Glen shouldn't have had to choose between his

299

countrymen and yours.' She made a placating gesture with her hands. 'But all those things *did* happen. So we need to look at reality, and reality says our government isn't going to let millions of Indians land and live in the outback.'

He matched her cool gaze with hot eyes. 'So what's your point?'

She settled back into the couch, looking resigned. 'Look Fadi, I don't expect you to believe me. But I think Glen's refusing to sink the *Maya,* and they've put you up to this to get him to follow orders.' She shrugged as if to say *take it or leave it.*

If she's lying, she'd pretty good at it, he thought. 'Look Fadi, if you kill me, they'll tell Glen, and he'll get upset and maybe sink that ship. If I'm lying, and he's not a good guy, then he already wants to sink that ship. And killing me will give him another reason.'

He laughed mirthlessly. 'So if he's a nutcase, keeping you alive may stop him from attacking. If he's a good guy, killing you may give him a reason to sink the *Maya.'* He felt the air expelling from his lungs as realisation dawned. 'Either way, I'm a dead man, aren't I?'

'Fadi, if you kill me, you're *definitely* a dead man,' she said. 'If I live, maybe, *maybe* I can protect you.' She spread her hands and smiled wryly. 'Don't get your hopes up though. They obviously think I'm expendable too,' she finished with a dry tilt of her head.

He licked his teeth, thinking of all the ways she could be bullshitting him. And couldn't find any. 'So what should I do?' he said, exasperation creeping into his voice. For all he had the weapons, it sure felt like this diminutive woman was completely in control of things.

'Well, I'm going to make a cup of tea. Would you like one?' Alice said, getting up. Fadi snatched the gun up and pointed it at her. 'Sit down,' he commanded.

She gave him a disappointed look. 'You're not going to shoot me, Fadi. You're not that man, you said it yourself. Now,' her tone brightened, 'Would you like sugar and milk?' and strolled into the kitchen.

He gawped at her retreating back. 'Er...sugar, please,' he managed eventually.

HMAS *Hobart*
September 24th, 0258 hours

With a shaking hand, Robertson coded in Futcher's direct line. He was hunched over his desk in his stateroom, other hand clutching his temples. Palmer sat on his bed behind him, body rigid with tension. Futcher answered before the first ring expired. 'Robertson. You've got two minutes to save Alice. Talk to me,' he fired down the line.

Glen took a deep breath. His room was revolving around his head like he was in the middle of a grey-walled vortex. The thudding in his temples was now a roar occupying the space behind his eyes. Futcher's voice sounded very, very distant.

'Sir, I won't be standing down. If anything happens to Alice, it will be on your head, not mine.' Silence answered him. He swallowed dryly, licked a cracked bottom lip, and ploughed on before he ground to an interminable halt. 'I will not be responsible for the murder of thirty thousand more people, regardless of the threats you make to my loved ones.'

Hostile silence radiated from the speaker. He swallowed again.

'Robertson out,' he said, cutting the line. He swivelled to Palmer who was searching for something to say, concern etched into his expression. 'Palmer,' said Robertson, a haunted look in his eyes. 'Just what the fuck have I done?'

Palmer reached out and put a hand on Robertson's shoulder. 'Look at me, Glen.' Robertson dragged his eyes off the floor, blinking to stop the tears from shedding. Palmer spoke. 'You've done the right thing, Glen.' Palmer gripped his shoulder harder and shook the message into him. 'Do you hear me?'

301

Glen gave a minute shake of his head. 'It doesn't feel the same as when I sank the *Tamil Nadi,*' he said hoarsely. 'This feels worse.'

South Perth
September 24th, 0315 hours

They had resumed their respective places on the lounges, opposite each other. He'd put the guns on the pillow next to him, and Alice was wringing out teabags into a cup of tea on the coffee table. He brought his cup to his mouth and inhaled the subtle fragrance; it was a herbal tea, with a subtle streak of mint filling his nostrils. He took a careful sip, mindful of the temperature.

'How's your tea?' asked Alice, still stirring. He couldn't help but shake his head ruefully. 'It's the most delicious thing I've tasted since I left India,' he said truthfully.

'I've been thinking Fadi,' Alice said, suddenly all business. She jabbed at the air like she had to puncture something for her idea to take shape. 'You came here to save the *Maya,* knowing you were going to die.' She leaned forward, 'what if we can save the refugees that are already here, and get out of here without any bullet sized puncture wounds in our skin?'

He studied her silently, intently, to the point of slight awkwardness. This woman seemed like a combination of his mother, of Khandi, with the addition of a sophisticated confidence he'd never seen before. The lines of her eyes were crinkled slightly, and she held his gaze confidently, utterly unselfconsciously. He trusted this woman.

'Tell me,' he said eventually, 'but first, this.' He picked up the guns and Alice pulled back, eyes widening. He put them on the table sitting between them. Slowly took his hand away then sat back on the couch, so he was out of reach, and she was within grasping distance. She stared at him, then her face broke into a radiant smile, and she too leaned back on her couch. 'Ready to hear my idea?' she asked.

He nodded. For the first time since Khandi had died, Fadi smiled too.

Canberra
September 24th, 0330 hours

Jacqui Laffite had just hung up the phone to Admiral Futcher who'd relayed the news about Robertson. She hung up the receiver and gave Holloway a despairing look. 'That man,' she muttered. 'I...should have known we couldn't push him around like this,' she said shaking her head in disbelief. The truth was, she felt humbled by his resolve. It was almost scary, how immovable it was, once he'd made up his mind.

Holloway shifted in his seat, then bit his lip. 'Hmm,' he said, a rare show of indecisiveness from the ASIS man. Suddenly his phone rang. He fished it out of his pocket and shot a raised-eyebrow look at Laffite. 'It's Alice,' he said questioningly. She frowned. There were some very obvious reasons for Alice to be calling Cam Holloway right now. 'Answer it,' she snapped.

'Alice,' boomed Holloway confidently. 'Good to hear from you. Are you ok?' he asked, his demeanour changing to match the friendliness of his words.

Jacqui watched with interest, then concern as Holloway's body language changed from feigned bonhomie to guarded caution. 'Alice, that's one hell of a story you've come up with, I have to say I'm surprised you let this guy convince you-' he stopped abruptly. He peered up at Jacqui. 'Yes, she's here with me,' he nodded. To Jacqui, he said, 'She wants to go on speakerphone.'

'OK,' she said uncertainly, anxiety balling in her stomach. Holloway put the phone on her desk.

'Jacqui, Cam, lovely to speak to you both,' called Alice. 'I'm here with Fadi Manoj, who you planned to frame for my murder. We're enjoying tea and biscuits; I hope your evening is as pleasant as ours.'

Jacqui and Holloway shared a wide-eyed look. *Uh-oh.* 'How can we help you, Alice?' she said eventually.

'Look Jacqui, no hard feelings, ok? I get what you're trying to do. But I don't want to die, and unless I'm mistaken, Glen doesn't want to commit an atrocity on your behalf. So here's what's going to happen. I've sent a dead man message to my lawyer, who has instructions to forward it to ten associates of his, and they have similair instructions. Logarithmic multiplication, very difficult to silence everybody, you see. The message is locked and encrypted, but if I die, the key activates. As you can imagine, they will all read about an Australian government plot to kill it's one if it's own citizens.' She paused. It sounded like she was taking a sip of a drink.

'But,' she said, 'we don't need the world to know about the things you do when safeguarding national security. So if you don't kill me, he won't open that document, and I won't say a word about what happened here tonight,' she continued clearly and methodically.

'And why is that, Alice?' Jacqui ventured.

'Because you're going to grant Fadi here Australian citizenship,' Alice replied. 'And you're going to grant the rest of the illegal Indians on Australian soil asylum within the week. Furthermore, you'll let Glen stand down with no repercussions. I know he won't sink that ship, and I won't allow you to sanction him for that. In exchange, we'll take tonight's little episode with us to the grave.'

Holloway and Lafitte stared at each other in disbelief. She corraled her thoughts. 'Can, can we have five minutes to discuss it...please?'

'You may,' said Alice. 'But Jacqui, you'll forgive me for not entirely trusting you. At the expiration of five minutes, I'll call my lawyer with new instructions. The clock is ticking.' The line went dead.

Jacqui stood up. She couldn't maintain her calm façade anymore. 'Ok, shit,' she started. 'This is actually our chance to dig our way out of the giant shithole you landed us in, Cam,' she said. 'Only God knows how we're going to sell this to the Australian public,' she finished sharply.

She jabbed the redial button on the phone. Barely sixty seconds had passed. 'Alice, it's Jacqui,' she said as soon as the line connected. 'We agree completely to your terms. I'll have a representative of the Department of Immigration pick Fadi up tomorrow and start processing his citizenship.'

'Very kind of you, Jacqui,' called Alice. 'Fadi is very pleased.'

'As for the granting of asylum question; I do need some time to figure out how to sell it to the public. A day or two. But we will implement it. I'm sure you've got measures in place to ensure we stick to the agreement,' she finished wryly.

'I do indeed. Jacqui, that's great to hear. Glad to be working together finally.' The false joviality of her tone hardened. 'Now. What are you going to do about Glen?'

'I don't know, Alice. He's disobeyed a direct order and effectively led a mutiny of the Navy on his own ship. It doesn't get much more serious than that. He will be stood down, I know that. What happens next...I'm not sure. I'm sure I can have a word to Futcher such that he's discharged without overly onerous repercussions. That's about it for now.'

'OK, Jacqui. You do that. He's blameless in this, just the same as me, and Fadi. Meantime, I'll wait for the Department of Immigration people to pick up Fadi.' The call ended.

'What next?' Holloway said eventually. Jacqui tapped the desktop. Part of her still in shocked admiration of Glen Robertson's girlfriend. *What a couple they are,* she mused to herself, then she exhaled. 'We'll tell Glen that Alice is safe, and that he's ordered to return to base where we'll give him an honourable discharge,' she waved a hand dismissively, 'or whatever the terminology is.' She frowned, deep in thought, then typed in Futcher's name on her desktop comms unit.

He answered immediately. 'What's the latest?' he asked.

305

'Futcher, didn't you say we have planes that can launch missiles at those ships?' she asked snappily.

'We do,' he said. 'P-8 Poseidons have the range and payload to sink a freighter with torpedoes,' he said. Where was she going with this?

'Tell Robertson to take his squadron back to base. He's too fucking stubborn to cave, even when his girlfriend was threatened. So let's get him out of there. And get the pilots to do the job on the *Maya* for him once he's left the area.' She gave Holloway a withering look. 'Maybe you can kidnap their girlfriends too.'

HMAS *Hobart*
September 24th, 0430 hours
Robertson was back on the bridge. A subdued, morose atmosphere filled the bridge like fine dust, permeating everything and everyone. Each crew member was consumed by anxiety about their future, overcome with fatigue. Robertson leaned back on the central console, one booted foot on the window sill. He stared out the front of the ship, the leading edge of the sunrise staining the eastern sky the palest blue. He scratched some dry skin off his lips and flicked it onto the floor.

'Sir,' said Aiden on the radio. 'I have Admiral Futcher on the line.' Robertson flubbed his lips and looked at his crew apprehensively, then forced a grin. 'Couldn't possibly get any worse, could it,' he muttered.

'Futcher, Robertson here. How is Alice?' he said, more command than question.

'Good news, Commodore. She's fine. She's at home and safe. We have the…kidnapper in custody.'

Robertson clenched a fist. *She's ok…she's ok…you did the right thing…*'She's ok, sir, did you just say that?' he mumbled, not daring to let the tidal wave of relief burst through the dam walls just yet.

'She's one hundred per cent fine,' Futcher said, 'Believe me, she's never been better, Glen,' Futcher said.

Robertson exhaled; he'd been holding his breath without knowing it, and clenched his fist in muted exaltation.

His crew was staring at him, anticipation etched on their faces. He contained his glee for a moment and stood up straight. 'And what happens to us now?' he asked Futcher, the eyes of his crew boring into him like drills.

Futcher sighed. 'You have orders to come back to base. You'll be relieved of command and discharged from the Navy. We won't lay any charges. The rest of your crew will be given pardons due to exceptional circumstances.'

Robertson looked at each of his bridge crew in turn. Harper looked like the hangman had placed a noose around her neck and earnt a last-second reprieve; Aiden's face had split in half his smile was so wide, and he was rocking back and forward in his seat like a man having a seizure. Palmer nodded slowly, a grin widening into open admiration.

'I fucking *told* you,' Robertson said, waggling a finger triumphantly, 'that we were doing the right thing.'

Chapter 27
The Lodge, Canberra
September 27th, 2300 hours

A warm, dry breeze laden with the scent of wattle and eucalyptus wafted through the verandah doors of Jacqui's study. It was past eleven pm, and cicadas chirped outside. It wasn't even October, but it felt like it was going to be another hot summer

She'd always loved the long, hot nights of Australia around Christmas time. The effect compounded itself at the Lodge, where she could sit on a wide verandah, inhale the perfume of the bush, and listen to the gum trees and bottlebrush rustling in the distance like old ladies muttering to themselves.

Tonight, she noticed none of it. One of the Poseidons operating out of Curtin had finally got in the air and sunk the *Maya.* She'd ordered the deaths of thirty thousand people. She repeated that in her mind. *You ordered the deaths of thirty thousand people.* She shook her head. *You also ordered the kidnapping of Alice Ruiz.*

To cap it off, Malhotra hadn't come begging to the negotiating table. Instead, he'd begun marshalling his military and threatening massive retaliation. She needed Malhotra to make the first move, or she'd lose the upper hand. He wasn't playing ball.

She took a deep, shuddering breath. Something was convulsing inside her. An avalanche of guilt and sadness had buried the stress and anxiety of the last few months. When she'd dumped Glen for her ambitions, she'd known how calculating and cynical she was being, but she'd still had a sort of wide-eyed optimism about how her career would pan out. She'd have some difficult decisions to make, she'd lose friends, and she'd disappoint people. But in the wash-up, history would judge her kindly; a woman who'd been tough but capable, a fearless decision-maker, and fair. *History will judge you somewhat more harshly than that, Jacqui.*

She needed the Indians to come to the negotiating table. She needed to figure out where her line was. She didn't want any more people to die.

She heard Craig's slippers whooshing over the grey marble floors. The study door swung open slowly, and dim yellow light from the candelabras in the hall spilled into the room. She didn't look at him as he entered, but she tamped down her emotions as far as possible.

He studied his wife, hunched over a sheaf of papers.

Her head was hanging, motionless like a piece of fruit on a tree. One elbow rested on the tabletop, her hand in a tight fist, thumb in her mouth, chewing her nail by the look of it. He just stood there, waiting for her to look up. She didn't. She seemed to be peering intensely at the papers in front of her, with her mind clearly elsewhere.

He started towards her, but something compelled him to pause. He suddenly felt nervous around his own wife.

'Jacqui, please. You have to stop. You need to come to bed.'

'There's no point, Craig,' she muttered desktop. 'I couldn't sleep anyway.'

His balled his hands into sweaty fists, then, realising what he was doing, forced them open. 'I know, Jacqui. But...you need to try. To do something else. You're eating yourself up.' He had more to say but couldn't bring himself to say it. She wasn't hearing him.

'Full of armed insurgents. It had to be done, Jacqui. You know this. You wouldn't have ordered it otherwise. You're not a psychopath. There are no easy decisions anymore.'

'We used Glen. And Alice,' added in a low, wry voice. 'They didn't play ball though, and neither is Malhotra.' She pursed her lips. 'The longer things continue, the worse they get. And it's my responsibility; it was my decision...'

She finally looked up then. Her eyes were a haggard red, bags he'd never seen before hanging low and dark. Such a beautiful woman, such a wonderful soul. *But not yours*, called a traitorous voice in his mind.

When he spoke, there was no accusation in his tone. More like the sad and gradual revelation of a long-unspoken truth. 'Why are you always running towards something you can never have?' he finally asked.

'I love *you*, Craig.' She shook her head while she spoke. The last thing she needed was to worry about Craig's feelings. She bit her tongue to stop herself from saying just that.

Craig smiled emptily. 'I know.' He walked around the desk and took her head gently in his hands. 'I love you too, Jacqui,' he said and kissed her tenderly on the forehead.

He turned and left, closing the door softly behind him. Jacqui frowned at the closing door. She stopped thinking about him before it latched.

How can I get Malhotra to talk?

Jacqui was quite correct - she wasn't able to sleep. So she'd dressed and walked to Parliament House at two-thirty in the morning. She'd ordered her security team well back and breathed a tiny sigh of relief as she walked through the gates of the Lodge. It suddenly didn't feel like home anymore.

At six-thirty in the morning, she called her advisory group together. Admiral Futcher, General Hammersmith, Cas Castrission from the RAAF all dialled in via video link, and Cam Holloway once again reclining himself on the couch on the corner of her office. Louise Abbott, Foreign Minister and Nick Whittey, Defense Minister were seated in front of her. Whittey's eyes were hanging out of his head with exhaustion, red-flecked white balls squatting on dark bags hanging low on his face. Abbott looked more presentable, but she did have a liberal layer of make-up on, Jacqui noticed.

'We have a problem,' she started without preamble once everyone was present and accounted for. 'The Indians don't seem to be interested in grovelling for peace, and we need to know what their next move is. I mean,' she said with some doubt lacing her words, 'is it possible that *we* should approach *them*?'

Nobody spoke for a moment; the whole point of sinking the *Maya* was to force the Indians hand, get them pushing for peace and give the Australians the upper hand in any settlement.

'Well, it isn't panning out the way we hoped,' Futcher eventually said. 'Malhotra has ordered the activation of all his naval assets in preparation for a strike on our west coast in retaliation for the *Maya*. Including their aircraft carriers and nuclear submarines which have land strike capability.'

'So they're going to invade us?' Abbott asked incredulously.

'Not necessarily,' replied Futcher. 'They may just want to level a few city blocks in Perth for payback. They certainly have the capability.'

'Really?' said Whittey. Surely we could keep them from doing too much damage?'

Futcher sighed down the phone. 'We have to be realistic here. They're hurting, but they still have thirty times the population we do, four times the GDP. And their navy is three times ours. Do we really want to get into a full-blown conflict with them?'

'Malhotra isn't going to shy away from a fight,' said Hammersmith matter-of-factly. 'Nothing would keep him in power better than a war with Australia.'

'Especially one he can sell as completely justified,' said Whittey.

Laffite snorted. 'He doesn't even have to sell it,' she said. 'They're screaming for it over there.'

Abbott and Whittey shared an uncomfortable look because Jacqui was right. The Indian media was full of politicians of all stripes demanding Malhotra avenge the *Maya*.

'It's not just about protecting the refugees anymore, it's about national pride,' said Jacqui.

Holloway stirred on his couch. 'I think it may be time to swallow our pride and sound out Malhotra. We should make him an offer. He may be more interested in peace than it looks in the media.'

'What offer?' said Whittey. 'Offer to keep sinking his ships for him?'

Jacqui gave him an exasperated look. Then glanced at Holloway, who gave her the slightest nod. 'What about we tell Malhotra that we'll give asylum to all the illegals already here. Give pardons to all of them save the ones found to have committed the worst crimes in Geraldton, and residency in time.'

Nobody spoke for a moment while they digested the idea.

'Let's be realistic,' murmured Holloway. 'it's not like we're ever getting rid of them anyway. It is, however, a goodwill gesture that will be hard to refuse.'

'He'll probably say no,' grumbled Whittey to his coffee. Looking around, he spoke louder. 'What if they say no?'

'Then we prepare for war,' said Laffite with calmness and determination completely at odds with the clamouring anxiety in her stomach.

Abbott stood up. 'They started this,' she said, pacing from side to side, 'but we escalated it by sinking those ships. This is our chance to de-escalate things. For once,' she finished glancing meaningfully at Jacqui.

'Are we happy with this approach?' Jacqui asked the room. Nobody spoke. She wanted to wrap this up quickly, while things were going the way she needed them to. 'Good. Since we've expelled the Indian ambassador,' she said snappily, 'I'll call the Kiwis, see if they can set up a call with Malhotra.'

They chatted about other things for a while, and then the meeting ended, and Jacqui was left alone. She pulled a small bottle of scotch whiskey from the bottom drawer of her desk and poured a measure into a crystal tumbler. She took a deep breath and tipped most of it into her mouth, embracing the pungent heat radiating from her throat down to her stomach and up into her nose. It felt like she'd been holding her breath for hours, and she exhaled long and slow. After the debacle with Alice and Fadi, she'd told Holloway to post security around her house twenty-four seven. She smiled at the irony. It was suddenly critical to keep Alice alive, or the sword of Damocles Alice had placed above Jacqui's neck would drop.

Convincing your colleagues was the easy part. Now we got to get Malhotra to buy in, somehow.

She tapped the New Zealand Prime Ministers' details into the touch screen on her desktop.

Mel Tua'afu was the Prime Minister of New Zealand, and he picked up after a few rings. She got along with Mel in normal circumstances. More lately, his incessant prattling about the need for dialogue was doing nothing but cementing his position on the fence, right when she needed him most. There was never anything concrete from the guy unless you counted declarations of support at the UN. Maybe that was something; nobody else was doing it. Still, some warships would have been nice.

She patched him through on the video link.

'Jesus Jacqui. You look like shit. Big night, eh?' He grinned, muscular, tanned face folding into friendly creases.

She forced her lips to bend into a smile. 'Thanks, Mel. You, as ever, look like you don't have a care in the world.' His smile slipped.

'How can I help you, Jacqui,' he said brusquely.

'I need you to send the Indian ambassador across. I'd like him to arrange a call with President Malhotra. We have a peace proposal to put to him.'

Mel nodded without hesitation. 'I'll call him straight away. Will you host him in Canberra?'

313

'If he's amenable to the idea, yes. Mel,' she said, masking her impatience with a smile, 'the sooner we have this conversation, the better.'

'I'm on it, Jacqui. I'll be in touch asap,' he said, signing off.

Chapter 28
September 28th, 1400 hours
Parliament House, Canberra

Eight hours later, Pratesh Patel, Indian ambassador to New Zealand and now de-facto ambassador to Australia, settled into the large couch in the PM's reception room. Jacqui watched him take in his surroundings with a slight frown.

'I admit I am curious as to what the Australian government spends all its money on,' he said, waving his hands at the nondescript furniture. I've been in a more luxurious dentist waiting room back home.'

That pulled a wry grin from Jacqui. 'Currently, we're spending all our money on rounding up illegal Indian immigrants running riot on our west coast,' she responded, 'and preparing our Navy for the invasion force we understand Prime Minister Malhotra has ordered mobilised.'

She'd tried to snatch a few hours' sleep on her office couch since she spoke to Mel, but her mind hadn't slowed down anywhere near enough for that to happen. Instead, she'd loaded up on the caffeine, with a shot or two of whiskey to take the edge off.

'Thank you for seeing me at short notice, Pratesh,' she said over a cup of tea. 'As I mentioned to Prime Minister Tua'afu, I'd like to make a peace proposal to Mr Malhotra. Have you been able to arrange a meeting with him?'

Pratesh Patel's face was a mottled arrangement of brown, dark brown and tan-coloured skin, with black bags sagging under his large, wet brown eyes which he now blinked slowly. 'Firstly, let me say we're very glad you are open to dialogue. We are all very keen to resolve this issue peacefully.' He sipped tea and licked his lips. 'Unfortunately, President Malhotra is preoccupied today. He sends his sincere apologies. I will relay our conversation to him, and he will respond directly, I can

315

assure you,' he finished quickly, perhaps in response to Jacqui's teeth grinding loudly.

That's a real power play, she thought bitterly. *As if there could be anything higher on his agenda than sorting this mess out.*

She swallowed her bitterness and tried to come across as engaging in good faith. 'Well, I'm glad he's open to dialogue,' she said. 'As they have been from day one, we require cessation of all state-sponsored illegal migration.'

'We understand this, Prime Minister. However, Malhotra has his own, domestic, considerations, and the sinking of the *Maya* has put him in a very difficult position.'

'We understand this war has helped unite the factions behind Malhotra. While the state of affairs in India is tragic, it's not our view that Malhotra should sanction the transfer of India's problems to Australia.'

'Of course, I understand.' He hesitated. 'However, the international community has spoken and like us, believes rich countries did largely contribute to our current predicament.'

Jacqui shrugged. 'With respect, Ambassador, the world has had this conversation already. Let us discuss the current situation.'

Patel leaned forward and placed his tea on the table between them, then interlaced his fingers and put his hands on his knees. 'Mrs. Lafitte, between you and me, Prime Minister Malhotra is in a very difficult position. If he doesn't prosecute this war, and in fact escalate it in response to the most recent atrocity your Captain Robertson has performed,' - she bit her tongue - if they thought Robertson was responsible for the *Maya* in some ways it made things simpler. Fewer people to blame, just one hyper-aggressive madman causing chaos- 'he'll lose support of the factions, who control various paramilitaries around the country. If he loses control of them, we plunge back to civil war.'

Not my problem, Jacqui wanted to say, but she knew that it could very well become her problem, a suspicion confirmed in Patel's next utterance.

'Prime Minister, the Mr Malhotra has ordered the activation of all our naval assets in preparation for a strike on your west coast in retaliation for the *Maya.* This includes our aircraft carriers and our nuclear submarines which have land strike capability.'

Even though she knew this information, her world tilted a little, and she gripped her mug tightly which seemed to balance her. Hearing it from the enemy rammed reality home. Steadying herself, she nodded. 'We know, I had an update from our intel people earlier today. We're at a very dangerous moment for both countries, Pratesh.'

Patel licked his lips. He desperately hoped what he would say next had the required effect. It was the first time in his career as a diplomat he'd had butterflies in his stomach. 'I hope you appreciate I am speaking with extreme...candour, and that you understand this is a sincere overture.'

Laffite only nodded.

'Now, Prime Minister Malhotra is not averse to a peace settlement,' he shook his head, 'but your Navy has dangerously escalated the situation...and now he has no choice; he either presents them with a victory for Indian prestige, or continues to push for peace, looks weak, and loses control.' Jacqui was following every word closely. 'Prime Minister Malhotra is your best hope for peace, Jacqui,' he finished emphatically.

Laffite looked out the window, face blank, eventually turning her gaze back to the ambassador. 'I'd like you to take the following proposal to Prime Minister Malhotra straight away.' She waited for him to nod before continuing. 'As you know we require full cessation of all illegal arrivals, and no more Indian navy vessels in our territorial waters.'

317

'And what do we get in exchange for this? Remember, we need a clear victory, Prime Minister, something Malhotra can sell to the factions.'

Jacqui tapped the rim of the coffee mug on her desk. She'd fortified it heavily with brandy. She licked her lips and gave in to the urge to take a full-blooded swig. This was the most important pitch of her life.

'Right now, there're three-hundred and twenty thousand illegal Indians in Australia. Twenty-thousand of them are armed. We're prepared to offer all of them asylum, with residency for those who want it. However, many who were on the *Pong-Sawan* have committed crimes, for which they will be punished. But everyone else, those whose only crime was to come here illegally,' she paused to favour Patel with a wry smile, 'we will allow to settle. This, surely, is a victory for Malhotra.'

The ambassador's eyebrows shot up in surprise, and she felt a spike of hope in her chest. He cleared his throat, and his face quickly resumed it's sadly haggard aspect. But suddenly she dared to believe that the deal was a realistic one.

He blinked owlishly, eyes shining wetly. Jacqui found herself wondering how the moisture stayed suspended on his pupils instead of running down his face. 'I think that proposal *may* be of interest to the Prime Minister,' he replied, pursing his lips. 'Do you have any other items to add to your proposition?'

Jacqui shook her head. 'No, we don't. We think this is a very generous offer, as it will cost billions to settle those people, but certainly cheaper than prosecuting a war with India. And Malhotra can tell everyone he secured the future of all those refugees which surely is enough to satisfy the requirement for a boost to Indian prestige.'

'Will you excuse me?' asked the ambassador. 'I'd like to speak with the Prime Minister.'

'Of course,' she said. Under the table, she balled a fist in triumph. 'I'll ensure I'm available when you need to relay Malhotra's response.'

Barely twenty minutes later, Patel was back in Jacqui's office.

His bulbous eyes were blinking steadily now, which Jacqui interpreted as either excitement or nerves.

'I have some good news, Prime Minister,' he began as soon as he'd sat down. 'Firstly, in response to your proposal, Prime Minister Malhotra believes he can get support to stand the navy down, to stop them from leaving port to retaliate against Australia. Second, he commits to ending the shipment of all refugees, and to wrap up the people smuggling operations out of Kolkata for good.'

Jacqui suppressed a giant sigh of relief, whilst embracing the prickling of adrenalin spreading up her spine.

'That's a very positive development,' said Laffite, understating her emotions by a very large margin.

A curiosity as to the impact of the SAS hit on Izhar Khan suddenly overcame her. It had been an incredibly risky call to make. 'I have it on good authority that a Chinese organised-crime syndicate recently killed the mastermind of the smuggling operation in a brothel he was frequenting,' she asked with all the innocence she could muster.

Patel cocked his head at her as if to say *you have it on good authority because you authorised it*. What he did say, flatly, was, 'Yes, well, *somebody* took him out. Prime Minister Malhotra believes this terrorist attack to be a stroke of good fortune. He thinks there is the opportunity to...reset our respective positions, now that the mastermind of this operation out of the picture.'

She tamped down on the sense of grim satisfaction. Finally, something was going the way they'd planned it. The SAS raid had sent the right message. She took a deep breath. The stick of the SAS and the sinking of the *Maya*, coupled with the carrot of the refugee deal had drawn Malhotra out.

Patel went on. 'But it's a lucrative business and plenty of people will be queueing up to take his place. Only the government and the Navy can truly close it down.'

She wanted to tell the man that if they didn't close the smuggling business down, she'd order the systematic assassination of Indian politicians until they did. But right now, the Indians were pretending it wasn't Australia who'd killed Khan. If that became public, it would make it even harder for Malhotra to settle. And besides, there were many more Indians in Australia than vice versa, and the Indians could always try to respond in kind. She scrapped the thought.

'So we have a deal?' she asked. She wanted to close this down now, while Patel was saying things she wanted to hear..

Patel swallowed nervously 'There is one final condition you need to meet, Prime Minister, in order for peace between us.'

'What would that be?' she asked cautiously.

Patel's voice grew harsh. 'You must agree to hand over Captain Robertson from the RAN to Indian authorities so that we can put him on trial for crimes against humanity. We must make an example of him for all the world to see.'

The sun beat down from a white-hot sky on the home of Glen Robertson and Alice Ruiz. Overlooking the backyard on their newly laid deck, a shirtless, shoeless Glen Robertson gently eased himself onto it the outdoor wicker sofa, the cane creaking as he settled in. Clad only in half thigh-length black board shorts, he gazed contentedly at his yard, the slope of the grass (needed cutting) and the little jetty he'd flung together while trying to distract himself from the events around the *Tamil Nadu.* He pushed into the corner, one leg splayed on the cushion, resting an arm on the sofa back. He took a swig from the almost-frozen bottle of beer in his hand, then placed it on the glass table on the side with a soft *clink.* Thirty metres away, a little punt drifted down the canal, triangular sail grabbing at the soft breeze half-heartedly. Sitting at the rear was the pilot, one hand on the tiller. He flicked his other hand in greeting to Glen. Glen raised his beer in salute. 'Fair wind and a following sea,' he murmured.

'They say talking to yourself is the first sign of madness,' said Alice, emerging from the kitchen. She was wearing a short red summer dress with white polka dots, thin straps over her shoulders and cinched tight around her narrow waist. The dress rode up on athletic brown thighs as she made her way to the sofa, and the sun glistened off her tanned shoulders, and the light sheen of sweat on her cheekbones glinted. She brushed ropes of dark hair over a shoulder and her dark skin drunk the sun hungrily.

'You just figuring that out, babe,' he said laconically as she backed into the curve of his legs. She leaned back on his chest, sliding into the crook of his shoulder on sweaty skin.

'Aren't we lucky,' he said, gesturing with his beer at nothing in particular. 'Aren't *I* lucky,' he muttered reproachfully.

She swivelled a little to almost make eye contact. 'What do you mean?' She knew from the tone of his voice that he had something to get off his chest.

He took a deep breath and exhaled slowly. Noticed for the thousandth time the curve of her ear and the small pearl earrings gracing the lobes. It was just an ear, but it was her ear. And thus something to be admired.

'I had a choice,' Glen said eventually. 'I had to choose between you, and a whole bunch of Indians I never met. I chose the Indians. Admiral Futcher told me that my choice was going to kill you. He said your blood was on my hands.'

Alice twitched a smile and pushed herself into him a little harder. 'So why did you choose to let me die?' He was getting the impression that she knew everything he was about to say. Nevertheless, he wanted to say it.

'Firstly it just didn't make sense, Fadi not wanting to speak to me. If he did he'd know I was on his side, we both wanted the same thing - to not sink the *Maya*. It just seemed like something that Futcher cooked up to manipulate me into doing something I swore I'd never do again.'

'Futcher and Jacqui Laffite, I think you'll find,' said Alice, flat and grim.

'Yea. No doubt,' he said, not noticing the suggestion in her voice. She let it slide.

'What was the other reason?' she asked. He smiled through clenched teeth. It felt like he'd been explaining himself to Alice a lot lately, and none of it for any good reason. He blundered on.

'I know that you wouldn't have wanted me to choose you over those people. You would have been ashamed that I'd spared you at their expense. I know that I would've saved your life, but lost you anyway. And fundamentally, what I did was the right thing to do. That, plus the strong feeling that Futcher was bullshitting me, is why I chose to let you die.' He kissed the back of her head softly. 'It was the hardest decision I ever had to make,' he said simply.

She arched her neck, so her cheek was resting against his. 'I know. Do you know what I was doing while you were agonising over whether to let me live or die?' she asked

He looked askance at her out of the corner of his eye. 'What's that,' he asked suspiciously.

'Fadi and I were drinking tea. He's a lovely young man, actually.'

He swore softly under his breath. If anyone could look after herself, it was Alice Ruiz. He chuckled mirthlessly.

'I was so fucking scared, Alice,' he said quietly once the ironic chuckles had subsided. 'I thought I'd never see you again.' She swivelled her head and searched for his cheek with her lips, then took his arm and draped it across her and he held her tight. Sweat ran down her stomach and pooled in the little dam created by his forearm. 'Glen, you did the right thing. I'm proud of what you did,' she said, gripping his arm tight. 'Even if you'd been wrong, and Fadi did kill me, you did the right thing. What Futcher and Laffite wanted you to do was utterly barbaric. It's not who we are, and it's not why you signed up to serve.'

'When Futcher got on the radio and said you were OK, I felt like a drowning man who finally took a giant breath. But then I realised that you'd not be able to trust me again because I would've let you die.' He stroked some loose strands of hair behind her ear. 'And then I was drowning again.'

She unpeeled herself and turned around, so she was straddling him. He clasped his hands around the small of her back. Her dark skin glistened, and her hair caught the breeze as she settled her thighs on his legs.

'You weren't letting me die, Glen. You were letting those people live. There's a difference.' She pre-empted his next comment by putting her finger on his lips. 'It doesn't matter what happened next, Glen. You chose to let them live, and you did what you could to make it that way.' She stroked his hair back from his face and smiled, simple and open. 'And Glen, I do know how you feel about me,' she said unselfconsciously. 'I can't imagine how hard it must have been for you out there.' To that, Glen had no words, but the unbidden salty sting in his eyes said more than he could have put into words anyway. He stared up at her intensely for a moment; she seemed to be studying him, then she cupped his face in her hands. Her hands gripped his face tight, and while her face betrayed no expression, he saw a rare intensity in her eyes. He gripped her hips hard, kneading her flesh with his fingers, the firm muscle of her back and the soft suppleness of her backside, pulling her against him. His heart thudded painfully in his chest, and he noticed her nostrils were flaring, but this time, she was not angry. They studied each other a moment longer; he resisted the urge to pull her close and instead appreciated the fine details of her face; the thick, dark eyebrows, the curve of full cheeks highlighting her gold-flecked wolf's eyes, then she leaned in and kissed him, her lips pushing hard into his. Her tongue pushed into his mouth searchingly, and he crushed her to him, telling himself that he'd never again tell her goodbye.

September 30th 0900 hours

Parliament House, Canberra

Jacqui paced, barefoot on green carpet, up and down her small Parliamentary office. She'd brought the tumbler out of her bottom drawer, and it dangled from her hand as she walked to-and-fro, tapping the rim and periodically sipping scotch whiskey from it. She was more nervous about her next appointment than she had been with the Indian ambassador.

Stop delaying Jacqui; you're being pathetic, she scolded herself, and taking a deep breath, she slid the tumbler onto the table, sat down, and pressed the intercom to her receptionist outside.

'Send her in please, Karen,' she said, composing herself.

The door opened, and Alice Ruiz strode into Jacqui's office. Dark blue jeans, mulberry business jacket and a white business shirt, three buttons undone, hinting, never revealing. Alice Ruiz looked slightly tired, effortlessly stylish, and utterly formidable. *It's like looking in a mirror,* thought Jacqui, and judging from the wary look of amusement on Alice's face, she was thinking the same thing.

'Alice, please, take a seat,' Jacqui stood up and pointed at the chairs in front of her desk. 'Thank you for coming, at such short notice too. I can imagine that I interrupted an emotional reunion with Glen,' she said a little awkwardly.

Alice nodded. 'Cam Holloway said I was required urgently to look at some new intel,' she said coolly, 'however I suspect that once again, Cam Holloway has lied to me.' Alice glanced at the tumbler and said nothing, but Jacqui felt the judgment.

Jacqui nodded. 'He did, on my request.' She grimaced and suppressed the urge to hide the tumbler in her drawer. 'Alice, Malhotra was threatening to mobilise his entire fleet in retaliation for the *Maya.'*

'Jacqui, the only reason I'm not dead, and you're not in gaol, is because I understand that you're making some very tough decisions on very short notice. That said, it sounds like the *Maya* was a catastrophic error in judgment, and suddenly I get the feeling that once again, Glen and I are going to pay for your mistake.'

Jacqui nodded brusquely. 'Well, you're only half-wrong,' she said delicately. 'Sinking the *Maya* caused him to threaten escalation, but it also opened him up to negotiating. Because of that, we managed to secure an end of hostilities based on satisfying two conditions.'

Alice folded her hands in her lap, like a pre-emptive defensive maneuver. 'OK…' she said eventually. 'And these conditions relate to me, how?'

'Well, we told them we'd grant asylum to all Indian illegals currently on Australian soil if they ceased further shipments.

That was your idea, of course, and they seemed to like it. Of course, we told them we'd continue to sink their freighters if they didn't. They agreed to those terms, with one caveat.'

'And what would that be,' said Alice, suddenly wary.

Jacqui cleared her throat to buy an extra second. 'Alice, the other non-negotiable was that they want us to hand over Glen so they can make an example of him. Malhotra needs him as a victory for his prestige. So, I'm here, asking for your permission. To hand Glen over to the Indians.' There, she'd said it.

'I see,' said Alice icily. 'How considerate of you to ask.' Jacqui noticed the veins on her hands were standing out, and her nostrils were flaring, as though they were weak points where her nascent rage was losing containment.

Jacqui met her judgmental look with a flash of anger. 'Alice, I'm not trying to destroy your life,' she snapped. 'I'm making decisions for the best of the entire country, and yes, I'll say it, you and Glen have been collateral damage. But, frankly, we've almost got the result we need-'

'You've used Glen like a pawn since the *Tamil Nadi,* you and Futcher,' Alice simmered 'He could deal with that, Jacqui, but then you decided to play me into the game, Jacqui. And, I,' her voice dropped dangerously quiet, 'am not as forgiving as Glen.'

'Do what you have to do, Alice,' Jacqui said, edge of anger sharpening her words. 'I'll tell you here and now, I'm comfortable with the decisions I've made, and if you decide to out me and send me to gaol for the rest of my life, I can live with that, because I know, in my heart of hearts, no matter how deplorable some of the things I've done are, they've all been for the greater good of my country.' She grabbed the tumbler defiantly and thrust it at Alice before drinking. 'You have no reason to like me, Alice, and every reason to hate me. I can see in you a very dangerous adversary, but I have to admit, I have nothing but admiration for how you've handled yourself throughout all this. Not many people would have the...control to be in the same room as me right now. But I do have to ask you, Alice, and I need you to think of your country first, as I am.'

Alice's posture hadn't changed, nor had her expression, but some of the frost had melted from her demeanour. 'Ask me what, Jacqui?'

Jacqui sighed in resignation. 'I need you to let me give Glen to the Indians. I swear on my life that as soon as we do, I'll order Futcher and co to come up with a plan to get him back again. But I need you to let me give them Glen and give me enough time to let this peace work, really catch. And then, when the time is right, I'll order his rescue, or do some backroom deal with Malhotra to get him back.'

Alice just sat there for a moment, then sagged into her seat. 'This must have been how Glen felt that night,' she said softly.

'What do you mean?' ventured Jacqui.

'The night he thought he was letting me die to save the people on the *Maya.* He had to choose between the greater good, and me.'

'Alice, the choices I've had, have been just awful, as have Glen's. I never thought I'd have to make these decisions. I don't want sympathy, but I will say that my only defence is that, at least in my mind, I've been doing what needs to be done, and so has Glen. Now, it's your turn.' Alice nodded. Her expression was blank, but there was a sheen of liquid welling in her eyes.

'Jacqui, I have plenty of leverage. Like you, and Glen, I will do what I have to.' She spoke clearly, slowly, unaffected by the tears running down her cheeks. 'But, for now, for the greater good, I will *loan* you back Glen Robertson until the peace is secured.'

'Thank you, Alice,' said Jacqui earnestly. 'If you ever decide I've just abandoned him you've got enough dirt on me to destroy my life. I'm not making idle promises. We *will* get him back,' she said with surprising vehemence.

The women regarded each other, two unwilling allies forced into a working union, no matter how temporary. Alice suddenly seemed to transform, an assassin emerging from the broken woman she'd been for a few moments.

'You're very...pragmatic, Jacqui.' Alice crossed her ankles indolently and leaned back, making the staid government chair look suddenly throne-like. 'He told me that you learned that from him.' She cocked her head; she was speaking to express her mind, not to elicit a response, so Jacqui didn't interrupt. 'He said that you started out quite idealistic and that he showed you how the world really worked. Or maybe,' she said smiling devilishly, 'deep down you knew you needed someone to harden you up so you could achieve your political ambitions. Glen was your mark, and when you'd learned what you needed, you used his pragmatism against him.' Alice pursed her lips as if to say *such a remarkable turn of events.* 'Don't you think it's just a little ironic, that now, you may need someone to help you rediscover who you used to be?'

Jacqui nodded. Alice was correct, and she felt a strange longing sensation, a part of her that burned for who she'd been before she met Glen, before she embarked on this path of whatever-it-took. When she'd been innocent, and idealistic, and could see the merit in putting morals before practicality.

When you didn't have the interests of your country to put before your own, a voice in her head snapped at her, and in measured tones, she said, 'You're right, Alice. Back then, I had the luxury of putting my conscience first. I don't have that luxury anymore, and now, neither do you.'

Alice smiled with darkened eyes, nodding. Doing a deal with the devil.

'Alright, Jacqui. You can have Glen back. Temporarily. But you make this peace work. And you make sure that I get him back in one piece, with no permanent damage, or you know what will happen. And Jacqui,' said Alice, as Jacqui felt one crushing

328

weight of responsibility and guilt lift only to be replaced by a different type of relentless pressure, 'the clock. It's ticking.'

Chapter 30
October 1st, 1600 hours
RAAF Pearce, 45 minutes northwest of Perth

Robertson ducked his head to step out of the AFP van onto the shimmering tarmac of RAAF Pearce. The AFP officer held out a hand to help him down. 'Fuck off, cunt,' said Robertson without looking at him as he jumped down. The man backed away, embarrassed.

'Straight to the back entrance, I see.' He spat, goblet of phlegm landing very close to the AFP man's boot.

The security guards at the entrance of the airfield had waved them through without stopping them, and the van had driven past the general quarters building and the hangars housing the prop engine trainers and the P-8 Poseidons which had been drafted in from the east coast. It had pulled up at the end of the western runway. Like a rendezvous for a drug deal in a shitty Hollywood gangster film, thought Robertson.

They'd pulled up next to a small unmarked jet in white paint, stairs extended. There was a detachment of clearance divers with weapons slung across their chests taking up space on the left wall of the tarmac. They held the weapons, loosely ready, staring with extreme agitation and hostility at a group of civilians opposite. It looked like they were itching to use them.

He scanned across. The civilians were all Indians, dressed in suits. Well built, serious-looking men. They were relaxed, alert, coiled and ready to spring. They were an integrated unit rather than individuals; he recognised the body language of elite soldiers.

Admiral Futcher stood between them with Leighton Swan at his shoulder. He regarded Robertson with what passed for a look of compassion.

'Futcher, you dog. What is this? And who are these assholes?' he jutted his jaw at the Indians, who stiffened.

There was an uncomfortable silence. Glen let it drag.

Eventually, Futcher cleared his throat.

'Glen.' He started, then abruptly ran out of steam. He coughed dryly and took a second to gather himself. Swan was studying the air above Glen's head. 'Glen, due, in large part to your actions, we have been approached by the Indians. They are mobilising their carrier wings and are planning to attack the West Coast in retaliation for...the actions of your squadron. However, they are open to peace, subject to certain conditions being fulfilled.'

Futcher's mouth was incredibly dry, and it wasn't the afternoon sun. He stood stiffly like an ashamed, embarrassed schoolboy caught doing something he instantly regretted.

'The Indian Navy will stand down, on two conditions. One, we grant amnesty to all Indians already on our soil. Two.'

Glen peered at him incredulously. 'Spit it out, mate. Whatever you've got to say is obviously going to be a lot worse for me than you.'

Futcher tried to swallow, it was sawdust, and cleared his throat again, 'You are to be handed over to the Indian government, to be interred and tried, for crimes against humanity, and war crimes,' he recited, as though he'd rehearsed it.

Robertson rested his gaze on the Indians. Looked at each of them in the eye and hated them too. Their acrimony washed over him like a storm.

'And these no-hopers, what are they doing? Welcoming committee, are they?'

'This is a detachment of Indian government representatives. Special Frontier Force, I'm told. They will be transferring you back to India. Upon your arrival, all refugee shipping will cease as will Indian naval-'

Robertson motioned Futcher into silence. 'Whatever Futcher. What happens if I don't want to go? Doesn't seem like I have a choice.' He suddenly feinted to the left, as though he was going to make a break for the open runway. The Indians crouched and one or two lunged towards him. He stopped just as suddenly, laughing bitterly. The Frontier Force members who'd been fooled glaring at him. Futcher motioned beseechingly, the unnatural body language uncomfortable on him. 'Glen, this will go a lot easier-'

'Shut up Futcher. Who's going to tell Alice? I want to speak to her before I go.'

Futcher fidgeted, embarrassed. 'That won't be possible. But we have informed her, and she gave me a note to give to you.' He pulled an unmarked envelope out of his pocket and gave it to Robertson. 'She wanted you to read it straight away.' Futcher dipped his head at the envelope, so Robertson opened it. Inside was a single, unfolded piece of paper. On it, was written: 'For your eyes only…We are coming for you, so stay strong, Glen. Your love, A.' He frowned quizzically for a moment. What the hell did that mean? Why did Alice already know they were sending him to India, and why did she think she could do anything about it? Who was 'we'? He stuck the note in his mouth, chewed it rapidly while the entire contingent, Australian and Indian, looked on bemused. He swallowed dryly.

He had no idea what that message meant, but it seemed Alice knew where he was going and had some plan, however implausible that may seem. The confusion sharpened to anger, and he focused down on it, bottled it up so he could draw on it later. He'd need it to get him through the next few months.

He shot his Admiral a vitriolic look. 'All right, Futcher. Let's get this absolute farce over with.' He walked to the Indians and held out his wrists.

Parliament House Press Hall
October 2nd, 0800 hours
Jacqui flinched away from the make-up artist, who was trying to dab on some eye-shadow. She was about to step in front of

332

the press gallery and announce the peace agreement to the world. This was her moment of triumph.

'Sorry, Mrs. Lafitte,' prattled the artist. 'The lights out there are very bright tonight, and there will be lots of press. We can't have you looking washed out. You have the most beautiful complexion, but the stress is getting to you! You should try to get more sleep. Can you take a holiday? Hold still-'

'Jane.' Laffite growled. 'Get out. Now.'

She studied Holloway with detached curiosity. The spy chief flicked through his phone, ignoring her except when she spoke to him directly. She wondered idly what she could do about him. She felt like a spike of ice. She'd made the difficult decisions; the numbers of the dead were breathtaking. The betrayal had been absolute, and not that she cared, but nobody would ever know her sacrifice. Submerged under it all, was a flickering candle of hope. It was a tremulous thing, trapped in an ice cave in a blizzard, but she clung to it. She'd made her move, and all the Indians had to do was keep their end of the bargain.

The video unit parsed softly. The ID displayed the origin, Sonal Malhotra. The candle flared.

The Indian Prime Minister appeared. He looked tired and strung-out. Not the presidential figure he'd been a few months prior when he was calling India to arms. He looked like she felt. Hollowed-out, with little left to give.

'Jacqueline Laffite, I am here with the respective heads of my armed forces and the senior members of my cabinet. I am calling to inform you that our delegation has landed and that Captain Glen Robertson is under the authority of the Central Bureau of Investigation. They will inter him until a court is convened to try him.'

'Ok, Sonal.' Laffite composed herself. 'After this call, I will announce to Parliament the offer of amnesty for Indian refugees on our shores.' Malhotra nodded. 'Those who we find

333

have committed crimes on Australian soil will be tried, Sonal.' The Indian Prime Minister nodded again. Give and take.

'We are actively monitoring Indian naval activity. Once I announce the amnesty, we need to see evidence of a full de-escalation of the carrier force, withdrawal of all Indian naval forces to Indian territory, and the cessation of smuggling activities out of Kolkata.'

'I'm sure your intelligence people have seen evidence of this already,' said Malhotra. And in fact, he was telling the truth. The Navy was making it obvious the aircraft carriers and their escort vessels were going nowhere. They were tied up alongside, and the Indians had stopped loading them with provisions and armaments while their crews awaited the outcome of these negotiations.

'You are correct. We also hope that ships in Chittagong, or any of the other breaking yards, will remain there.'

He nodded. 'There will be no more refugee missions.'

'Then, it is decided. I will announce the amnesty, and the cease-fire to the public now.'

He nodded again. 'Good luck, Prime Minister,' said the Indian man, and his face disappeared from the table.

Laffite turned to Cam Holloway.

'Where have they taken him?' she demanded.

'We've tracked him to Mumbai Central Prison.'

'Where's that?' she snapped. 'In the middle of Mumbai?'

'No. Far from it, in fact. It's on a peninsula to the south of the main city.' Holloway's expression didn't change, but she could feel him weighing her words, trying to figure out where this was going.

'Why's it called Mumbai Central?'

'I don't know. However, it used to be called Arthur Road Jail. One of the most notorious jails in India.'

'Fine. Good.' She jabbed a red nail at Futcher. 'You and Hammersmith are going to come up with a plan to get him out. Something we can enact at *very* short notice.'

The Admiral's bushy eyebrows shot up. 'I beg your pardon?' He shook his head. 'That's...that's...obviously impossible. We'd be mad to even attempt it!' She cocked her head, and he sputtered. 'Would you seriously risk the peace for one man-'

She cut him off with a dismissive shake of her head. 'We're not going to do it *now;* we'll have to wait till the dust has settled, obviously. But I want options to get him out so we can pull the trigger when the opportunity presents itself.'

Laffite chopped him off with calm savagery. 'Make the order Futcher. Or we'll find somebody who will.' She smiled coldly. 'We're getting very good at persuading people to follow even the most ghastly of orders.' She gathered up her things and left the room.

Futcher and Holloway locked eyes, the Admiral's eyes blazing with anger. The old spy gazed back, calmly inscrutable.

Mumbai Central Prison
November 3rd, 2300 hours

Glen leaned against the stone wall of his holding cell at Mumbai Central Jail, hard coldness seeping into his back.

His lawyer, whose purpose here was unclear to Robertson, given that he had effectively already been found guilty (or else why would he be here?), had accompanied him to his cell, and remonstrated with the prison authorities until they acknowledged that, yes, this was exactly where they'd hold him for the foreseeable future.

Robertson was too dead inside to appreciate the effort, and the lawyer had left, promising him he'd do his best to get him out of here. The man had looked earnestly into his eyes and actually seemed sincere.

Lying bastard, he'd thought, dismissing him with an ungracious *thank you* and been more than pleased when he'd disappeared down the cream-painted corridor.

He juxtaposed the numbness of emotion he felt with the searing agony in his right arm, where the tibia had been snapped in two by a guard.

The guard was ostensibly there for his protection, but Robertson quickly judged him as a man expert at nothing but his own survival. As such, Robertson knew, the man had no moral code, other than the mood of the crowd, which he could assess with rat-level fidelity.

The crowd here wanted to spill Robertson's blood. He'd initially shared a cell with two other men who'd attacked him without preamble on the first night. He'd taken blows to the face, his body, his back, and prisoners around them howled like animals with excitement. He embraced the excuse to lash out and knocked one out with a clean shot to the jaw. Felt teeth splinter as they crunched together. He wrapped the other in a crushing headlock, wrenching his head like a fish on a line, trying to crack the man's skull under the weight of his grip. The

336

man's face went purple, and his eyes flushed red. A trickle of blood started from his nose. On reflection, he probably would've stopped short of killing the guy - after all, he wasn't a murderer, was he? But then the guards rushed in, and one swung full force at his head with a truncheon. He ducked behind his right arm, an act which probably saved him from brain damage or death.

He shoved the scraping burn of his arm out of his head. It was a paltry thing, like a pebble in a shoe when further up the leg, a kneecap has been blown off.

He had a recurring fantasy where he strangled Futcher and Jacqui Lafitte, one after the other. It was always an implacable, impassionate visualization - the anger he'd felt when Futcher had handed him over had dissipated since he'd been at Arthur Road. Seeing the lights go out in their eyes was just something that needed to be done, like mending a fence or mowing the lawn.

Occupying far more of his imagination than murdering Lafitte and Futcher were thoughts of Alice. He would have given anything to have five minutes on the phone with her. He ruminated over what that little note had meant. It had given him hope that he'd get out of this prison fortress alive, which in itself frustrated him because without hope he could have made peace with his situation.

He'd shoved his role in the entire situation out of his head. Intellectually, of course, he knew he'd got the ball rolling on this entire calamitous course of events by sinking the *Tamil Nadu*. But, as Jayden Jones and Alice had said, the world had been sleepwalking towards this for years, and he'd just lit the fuse. He knew a convenient rationalisation when he saw one, but he also knew holding himself to account would be emotionally debilitating, so he'd put that knowledge into a little black box and sealed it up tight in his head.

It seemed like everyone had good intentions, which all told didn't mean a single damn thing.

Fadi had just been trying to do the right thing. Robertson had just been trying to do the right thing. He supposed Jacqui Laffite was doing her best too. Intellectually, he understood the *why* of her decision making. Better he was offered up as a sacrificial lamb than his country plunged into all out war.

He grunted to himself. Putting it that way, he was just another man dying for his country. Well, he sure wasn't the first to do that. Maybe he wasn't so hard done by. The thought was comforting.

He looked forward to a guilty verdict and hoped they wouldn't drag it out too long. He visualised an hourglass, sand streaming through the little gap in the waist. How many did he have left, had the final rush started? He was barrelling straight towards a death sentence, and the only thing in his control was how he dealt with it. He wondered if they'd publicly execute him, hanging maybe. He'd make sure to wave to the crowd before the long drop.

The embryo of a smile flitted at the corner of his eyes. He felt tranquillity like he'd never experienced before.

He inhaled deeply, shifting to ease pressure on his arm. When he exhaled, he closed his eyes, and it felt like a pressure valve releasing. Pent up angst evaporated as he breathed. In the darkness of his mind, Robertson watched impassively as emotions cascaded through his skull.

Chapter 31
Parliament House, Canberra
December 15th, 2330 hours

Distant lightning blinked silently behind the curtains of Jacqui's office, a light show accompanied by the staccato rhythm of heavy rain lashing the window in random waves. Low thunder provided a rumbling baseline, a relaxed, almost laconic counterpoint to the frantic wash of water pelting the glass.

Jacqui had dimmed the lights, so most of the room was cloaked in deep shadow. Her desk lamp cast the one bright circle of light, a yellow pall on her desk, illuminating her touchscreen which she'd stared at for the last few hours, and was now closed, a submission to her lack of productivity. Instead, she'd been dawdling on a cream coloured notepad, baseless iterations of a sequence of events that would lead to her finally defusing the Alice Ruiz timebomb around her neck. It had been a recurring theme the last few months.

Jacqui Lafitte had turned the disaster of the Indian refugee invasion into a political tour de force. The conservative media feted her for pushing a hard line with the Indians, and the liberals held her amnesty for all in-situ refugees as a win for enlightened thinking. The controversy of handing over Glen Robertson had barely registered in the press; the greater good had been catered for and they weren't interested in a little collateral damage. Jacqui Lafitte was the most popular Prime Minister in generations.

As a result, in the last three months, Jacqui had developed persistent, hanging bags under her eyes, and her cheeks, formerly full and round, had developed cavernous shadows, over-pinned by sharp, high cheekbones which now loomed over the lower half of her face like gargoyles.

She took a deep breath, backed her chair away from her desk and slipped off her shoes. Felt the woollen carpet through her

339

stockinged feet. Alice Ruiz was not a heavy-handed woman, and she'd only prodded Jacqui once. Futcher and Hammersmith had thrashed out a rescue plan, but she had no fucking clue when she could justifiably implement it. She picked up her phone and rifled through the messages until she came to one from Alice, dated three weeks prior: *Time is running out, Jacqui. Make your move, or I'll make mine.*

She closed her phone, dumped it on the table and rubbed tired eyes in resignation. Her elbows were still on the desk, knuckles still in her eye sockets when the phone rang. She exhaled slowly and glanced with sudden interest at the caller ID. *Marion Cain, US President.*

She frowned and took a moment to compose herself while wondering what this smug asshole wanted. Punched the connect key and said; 'Hello Marion, to what do I owe this unexpected pleasure?' She kept her voice as neutral as possible.

'Hello, Jacqui!' said the US President, without a trace of embarrassment or humility. 'I'm so glad I caught you! Your people suggested you'd be free now, not interrupting am I..?'

Jacqui bit her tongue, took a deep breath, then answered. 'Not at all, Marion, I was just finishing up. What can I do for you?' *You glad-handing, two-faced sonofabitch.*

'It turns out cyclone Sussan has, ah, caused significant damage up in India. Nobody saw it coming, it spun up well outside the usual cyclone season, I'm told, but that's the world we live in these days.'

She paused in the act of pulling on her heels. 'Thanks for the update, Marion. I am aware of the situation to our north.' She slipped her shoe off and spun her knees back under the desk, suddenly utterly bemused. She waited to see what would happen, and an embarrassed silence emanated from the other end.

'Then you'll know there are hundreds of thousands dead and tens of millions displaced,' snapped Cain eventually.

340

'I do indeed,' said Jacqui, mildly. 'So, what can I do for you today, Marion?'

He cleared his throat and spoke in a milder tone. 'Earlier this year, we agreed that Australia would contribute to any effort in case of any humanitarian disasters in the sub-continent...' Once again, Jacqui let the silence stretch. *He actually expects you to make it easy and re-commit our forces,* she thought to herself. She was on the verge of bursting out laughing.

'Marion,' she started, a devilish smile lighting up her features for the first time in months. 'Are you asking for Australia to provide humanitarian aid to the Indians as a result of cyclone Sussan?' She put a half-hearted effort into keeping the mirth from her voice and failed.

'Fuck Jacqui,' exploded the American President. 'I know what you're thinking, and no, this wasn't an easy call to make. But, you solved your little crisis and came out looking good, and now they're our allies again, and the fact is, they need our help. People are dying up there, and you guys can make a serious difference.' He groped for a moment. 'Don't make this harder than-'

'Marion, we'd be happy to help,' she cut in, tone dripping reasonableness. Hammersmith and Futcher had come up with a plan to get Glen Robertson out, but it needed a plane flying over Indian airspace. So she rolled the dice. 'May I suggest we send our C-17 transport planes up straight away with supplies and medical personnel? Meantime we'll activate the two LHDs. They can integrate into any taskforce once the US Navy arrives and takes control.'

Cain sputtered. 'Ah, yea, that'd be great.' He cleared his throat. 'I'm not sure the Indians will clear your planes in their airspace though, we need to check that. But, um, Jacqui, I know we've had our differences, but...thank you.'

Jacqui pressed the mute button just in time to cut off the snorting laughter that bubbled up from her stomach. She quickly composed herself.

'Not at all, Marion,' she said breezily. 'Friends keep their commitments to each other, of course you know that. Regarding airspace permissions, I suggest you get the Indians to agree to our planes going up there asap, or *what's the point*? People *are* dying, and we *can* help them, as you say...'

Cain cleared his throat. 'I, ah, get your drift. I'll have a word to Malhotra.'

Mumba Central Prison
December 17th, 0930 hours

Clinton Harvey's burgundy leather plimsols echoed loudly on the naked concrete floor of eight/two barrack, one of several double story oblongs lined on either side by cages crammed with the forgotten dregs of Mumbai society. It was early morning at Arthur Road Jail, and the sun had yet to break over the walls. Silence followed Harvey like a wake as he progressed down the dim central passage. The guards led him wordlessly to a wide metal door with a perspex hatch cut in the centre. The guards swung the door open. Waved him inside, where he took a seat on a plastic fold our chair that was chained to the floor. He placed his leather manila folder onto the table and sat down. Glen sat opposite him. He looked like death.

'Jesus Glen. Been staying up late again?'

Robertson chuckled. 'You could say that. What's been happening?'

Harvey couldn't help the laughter that boiled up from his chest. He always had the urge to laugh at inopportune moments. Like when his wife told him she wanted a divorce, or when his brother told him their father had passed away. He didn't actually think anything was funny; it was a more of a manic reaction to something he couldn't process.

It hadn't made his divorce proceedings any easier.

'It absolutely stinks in here. What are the prisoners burning?' he said, wrinkling his nose.

A smirk glinted in Robertson's eye. 'These cells are at triple their design capacity. The toilets don't work, and you have to burn garbage in your cell to cook what food they do distribute.'

'God, that's why it smells like a sewer on fire.' He pointed helplessly at the broken arm. 'Sorry Glen, this wasn't supposed to happen. You're scheduled to move to the Anda solitary confinement cells in a couple of days. You should be safe there.' He pursed his lips. 'They were supposed to ensure you were protected. What happened?'

'Well, there are wardens in the barracks, but mostly, the inmates enforce discipline.'

Harvey frowned. 'How do they decide who's in charge?'

'How do you think? Natural selection. The clever psychopaths rise to the top. The dumb ones enforce the rules. Everyone else finds their level pretty quickly. Law of the jungle.' He leaned back in his chair. 'If you've got money, you pay off the head honchos to be left alone or for favours.' Harvey couldn't help but glance at his shattered arm. 'Well, it's not a perfect system - I'm not your run of the mill rag picker or murderer am I. Doesn't help having white skin either.'

'Travails of the white man,' murmured Harvey dryly. He uncrossed his legs, careful not scrape the sole of one shoe on the gleaming buckle of the other.

'Glen, let me be honest. I'm surprised they let that happen to you,' he pointed at the broken arm, 'because they need you to get to trial looking healthy. They at least need to make a show of respecting international law, due process and all that.'

'I hear you. International law must be obeyed.'

'Yes.' He unclenched his fists and placed his sweaty palms on his trousers. 'Glen, I've got something for you,' he said, reaching into his folder and pulled out a small home-cooked peanut bar. The foil crackled as he placed it gingerly on the desk.

'This is from us at the consulate. It's a small thing, but hopefully, it'll make your time in here a little less onerous.'

Robertson looked at Harvey blankly. The man just gazed back. He didn't even have the grace to look embarrassed. Robertson picked up the bar and regarded it with a bemused expression.

'What am I supposed to do with this?'

'Eat it,' he said with a nod at the bar.

'I don't understand...'

'It would mean a lot to the people at the embassy if you were to enjoy our gift - could you try it and let me know what you think?'

Harvey was still looking at him meaningfully. He'd never liked lawyers, but his antenna had started to twitch...he decided to play along. He unwrapped the bar and bit a chunk out of it. Shards of peanut crumbled in his mouth, and the brittle stuck in his teeth.

'You really want me to eat this, don't you,' frowned Robertson, regarding the bar, then the lawyer with a confused look.

'Yes, Glen, we do.'

'It's very good,' Robertson said around a mouthful. 'Want some?'

Harvey barked a short laugh. 'Er, no, it's all yours.'

Robertson eyeballed Harvey as he chewed.

'Send my thanks to your colleagues at the embassy,' he said.

'Mm-hmm. They'll be very pleased to know you ate it all.'

Glen stared at Harvey a moment, then put the rest in his mouth. Harvey returned his gaze until he swallowed the last mouthful. 'Harvey, you're a little overqualified to be delivering peanut brittle, don't you think?' he said eventually.

Harvey shuffled his papers. 'I'll explain later. I promise.' He banged the papers with his palm. 'The peace is holding, you know,' he said more loudly. 'The shipments of refugees have stopped, and so have the riots in Australia. Things are essentially back to normal.'

'I'm glad to hear it,' Robertson said. He meant it. 'What about the amnesty, for the Indians already in-country?'

'We're honouring it. It's going to take a while to bring them all into the fold, and some have gone rogue, as you know.'

'Yea, I know.' Alice's face flashed before his eyes.

'Want to hear something funny? Lafitte is sending supplies and personnel up on C-17s and the LHDs to help out after the cyclone. Isn't she a good global citizen?'

Glen laughed, a deep, genuine rumble, much to Harvey's surprise. He wouldn't have had such good humour if he was sitting in Glen's chair. 'Jacqui Lafitte, she's a remarkable woman,' he said reflectively. 'An absolute cunt, of course,' he said, glancing up at Harvey, 'but remarkable nonetheless.'

'None of this would've been possible without what you did, Glen,' said the lawyer.

Robertson smiled softly. 'I know, Clinton. It's a shame it came to this, though.'

The lawyer stood up briskly. 'It is. I have to go now, Glen. We'll get you out of here as soon as possible, I promise.'

'Don't stress, Clint. The Anda cells aren't going anywhere.'

The lawyer knocked on the door, and the guard outside unlocked it and swung it open noisily.

'That's not what I meant,' said Clinton Harvey just before the door clanked shut behind him.

December 17th, 2235 hours

Robertson had scavenged some floor space in the crowded barrack. A small fire smoked blackly in front of him. Suspended over the fire on a bent wireframe was his katori, a grime-caked aluminium bowl from which he shovelled watery dal into his mouth. At eight o'clock every evening, wardens wheeled the food carts into the barrack and tossed the sacks with the katoris into the cell, then served the prisoners who lined up in rustling rows. He'd traded his ration of potatoes for some combustible garbage and the means to light it.

There was some rice sloshing around the bottom of the bowl, a family of weevils struggling frantically in the off-white slop. The rice was there to soak up the dahl. Robertson had stopped picking out the weevils - they were the most nutritious part of the meal. The curry itself had separated, and globs of yellow lentils floated like little icebergs in a brown sea. It didn't smell like food. It didn't smell at all. As far as Robertson was concerned, that was a blessing. Even so, it was virtually inedible unless heated up.

The morning's exchange with Harvey didn't make any sense. The man had insisted on the meeting, told him nothing he didn't already know, gave him a ridiculous token of goodwill, and generally acted cagey throughout. He scratched under his broken arm; his armpit was aching. So were his testicles. He must've been belted there and not even realised it, suppressed under the pain from his arm.

He put the bowl down and cupped his hands over the small fire, warming them. His body trembled, shivering. Why was he cold? The place was an oven. A wiry man in tattered cargo shorts and moth-eaten shirt sleeves had squashed in next to him. The man's back was glistening with slimy sweat. When large patches of skin came into contact, the wetness sucked onto Robertson's arm. It was a reeking sauna in here, no reason to feel anything other than oppressively hot.

He shivered again, his appetite gone. He tapped sweaty-back on the shoulder, then passed still-full bowl across. The man nodded thanks. Robertson motioned for the man to make some room. He needed to lie down. Why was he cold? He shook his head in confusion and felt like someone had driven an axe behind his eyes. The worst hungover headache paled compared to this. He lay down, shaking.

The guy he'd just given his dinner to leaned over him.

'What's wrong with you, man?'

Robertson shook his head weakly. 'Been a rough couple of days. Taking its toll.'

The man looked down at the shivering Robertson, then the bowl from which he'd just been slurping dahl. Frowning, he put the bowl down. He wasn't hungry anymore.

Chapter 32
Situation Room, Parliament House, Canberra
December 18th, 2100 hours

Laffite, Hammersmith, Futcher, Abbott, Hayne and various other senior defence officials crowded into Laffite's office at the back of Parliament House in Canberra. The room was electronically hardened, and the signals directorate was piping in a live mission feed from the SAS teams sub-net. Most of the info came from the cameras attached to their gear, which gave the bureaucrats a birds-eye view of what was happening. Laffite had ordered those feeds shrunk down - all it was showing was the inside of a plane now anyway.

'What does that mean?' asked Laffite, indicating a timer which had begun counting seconds on the corner of the screen.

'It's a mission timer. Everything they do is by the clock. It's started because the C-17 has just left Bagram,' said Hammersmith. 'They'll be over the drop-zone in six hours.' He glanced at Futcher. It wasn't too late to stop this madness, but all their objections had been slapped down by the Prime Minister. Such an incredibly stubborn, headstrong woman.

'I can't tell if she's got bigger balls than the rest of us put together or is stupider than the rest of us put together,' he murmured to Futcher, looking at the PM who was sitting, hands clasped on her lap, looking calmly at the info projection.

'It's a fine line,' Futcher replied.

'Yea. And we'll know in less than seven hours.'

RAAF C-17
December 18th, 0230 hours

Will Marriott yawned gratuitously till has jaw cracked, then smacked his lips and put the oxygen hose back in his mouth. He chewed the line. After tonight he was looking forward to doing an operation, from start to finish, at sea level, no oxygen required.

Nobody noticed his yawn; the jump bay of a RAAF C-17 Globemaster III cargo plane is a noisy place. Marriott and his squad were at the back of the aircraft, and the jet wash from the four big turbojets made anything other than shouted communications useless. The vast bay that had been designed to cart main battle tanks or a hundred paratroopers to war was now virtually empty except for Marriott's eight-man squad.

Portside up near the cockpit, the aircrew had strapped a few low-stacked pallets to the deck with green tie-downs; other than that, the metal deck, crisscrossed with grip pads and cargo hooks, was bare. Fluoro lights lined the grey panel walls, and Marriott noted the loadmaster had assiduously scrubbed the surface. It looked clinical, like the pit area of a Formula One team rather than a workhorse military transport flying out of dusty Bagram Air Force Base in Afghanistan.

A door in the bulkhead leading to the forward cabin opened, and Master Sergeant Jolly Hicks, the jumpmaster, climbed through and sauntered towards Marriott's squad.

'You goddamn paratroopers are crazy, I'll give you that!' he shouted, grinning madly.

'What the hell are you talking about,' Marriott shouted back. Nobody knew what they were doing; they'd flown up to Bagram to make it look like they were a US plane, because even though Cain had got permission from Malhotra for the Aussies to fly over India, there was no reason for an Aussie C-17 to be flying over Mumbai when the cyclone had decimated Chennai on the other side of the country. So the RAAF had flown up to Bagram on some ridiculous pretext that had created all sorts of confusion when it landed; the pilot laughing it off while the stocky US base commander squinted at him sideways and told him to park his plane *over there* and wait while he made a few calls to check that all the ducks were lined up and ready for plucking. He'd unexpectedly found himself being told by the Chief of Staff of the US Airforce to 'feed em, fuel em and clear them to fly at 9 pm local time. And colonel,' the CoS had growled down the phone. *This stays out of the flight log. Do you understand?'* The C-17 didn't know why they were flying halfway around the world and had no instruction other than to take the SAS guys along for the ride and to let them jump out at a specific waypoint over Mumbai.

Hicks ignored him. 'You should've seen that yank CO's face when he cleared us for this mission! Looked like he'd woken up naked next to his sister!' he leaned in a little as if eavesdroppers were trying to listen in. 'Isn't that navy guy our government double-crossed staying in Mumbai?'

Marriott checked the straps on his tag line. All as it should be. 'Why are you here, Hicks?'

Hicks roared with laughter. 'You SF boys are all the same!' Checking a datapad on his arm, he got serious.

'This is your stop, boys, time to get off.'

Marriott's squad walked to the rear side exit, switching to their bottled oxygen. Marriott beckoned Hicks closer.

'Last time we did this,' he said with a wink, 'was into a brothel.'

Hicks's eyes shot wide. 'Get outta my plane, you filthy animals!' he roared, shaking his head and then, the white lights in the bay changed to an ominous red. Red lighting for a mission go. 'Two-minute warning, equipment check!' bellowed the jumpmaster.

Marriott's team checked their loadout, running their hands across buckles, straps, and cinches, then doing a visual check on the man in front of them.

The C-17 had taken off from Bagram AFB nearly six hours before. The old transport flew at thirty-five thousand feet and was vectored right over the Royal Western Indian Turf Club in downtown Mumbai. They were just a few miles short of their final destination and would be covering the rest of the distance outside the plane. There was absolutely no margin for error and even though the racecourse, which was their target landing area, was big - over a kilometre long and nearly that wide - they had to time their jump to the second.

Marriott had done HALO jumps before, high-altitude low-opening insertions designed to get a team of elite soldiers into a battlefield without being detected. Too high for the primitive SAMs used in Syria or Afghanistan, it was safer for the planes, and pulling their rip cords as close to the ground as possible, the paratrooper was much harder to detect as well. In the deserts of the Middle East there was always plenty of space; either remote outcrops of sand and rocks or farmland far from any population centre. Nothing to hit and nobody to see you if you blew off course.

This was different. This was, to his knowledge, the most high-risk insertion ever made by a special-forces team. Once they left the plane, they were on their own - no support of any kind, no helicopter extraction, nothing. At least if they were still technically at war, they'd have an excuse for being there. So many things could go wrong - so much needed to go right. Leaving the plane at the right moment was non-negotiable, and then their ballistic arc had to be flown to perfection. Mumbai was a giant, grotty human sardine can and the racecourse was the only empty patch of land in the city. If they missed it, they'd end up in a bustling market, in the middle of a freeway, or, since the racecourse was on the coast, drowning under the weight of their gear in the ocean. Tonight they'd been blessed with good weather and still air - or else the mission would've been a no-go, which, in Marriott's humble opinion, should have been plan A, B, and C.

It was two-thirty am in Mumbai. He leaned out the jump door and peered at the city thirty-five thousand feet below. Mumbai sparkled, black emptiness of ocean giving way to a glittering jewel of city lights. Human endeavour always looked beautiful at night and at this altitude. He suspected the reality on the ground was less romantic, especially if Kolkata was anything to go by. *Good from far, far from good.* They knew the C-17 would've shown up on local radar; the commander at Bagram had logged the flight as a routine patrol with Mumbai air traffic control. They'd flown six-thousand clicks with no issues, and there was no reason for Mumbai radar operators to scrutinise the flight closely.

All they had to do was get to the ground without anyone seeing them.

Parliament House, Canberra
0255 hours

'The C-17 is over Mumbai and thirty seconds from the drop-zone,' said Hammersmith.

'Thank you, Arthur,' said Laffite. Despite the hour, her eyes were clear, uncompromising.

He leaned towards the Prime Minister and licked his lips. 'I can call them off; there's still time-'

'Enough, Arthur!' she snapped. She was sick of his simpering. Then, more gently. 'We're committed, now.'

Hammersmith leaned back in his chair and took his phone out. *Incredibly stupid,* he tapped out to Futcher.

Incredibly brave, Futcher fired back.

RAAF C-17
0259 hours

The countdown timer on the wall of the drop bay started flashing red, and a softly spoken female voice started counting down the numbers in Marriott's ear. Her hypnotic voice jarred with the sudden tempest of nerves growing in his stomach. *Yea, you're scared.* He shook his head.

Five, four...

Above the door was the grab rail. Marriott gripped it, hard, and tried to focus.

Three, two, one...

Marriott took a deep breath and launched himself into space.

352

Chapter 33
Mumbai airspace
December 18th, 0300 hours

Marriott plunged through warm sticky air at terminal velocity. He could make out individual streetlights now, cars moving in slow motion. Enough detail that his hindbrain had started screaming at him to *open the fucking chute!* He shoved the voice out of his head and twisted to deployment position. The HUD timer on his goggles flashed down through *four, three, two, one...*

His chute *snapped* into the onrushing air, and suddenly the roar was replaced with serene peacefulness he didn't notice. He was already sweating like a madman; the thermals they'd needed at thirty-five thousand feet were now a liability in the subtropical air.

The least of his problems. They were still over open ocean, dropping fast. He tugged the toggle and swung out wide in a broad silent arc over Lala Lajpatrai Road. The Royal Indian Turf Club was a giant black hole ahead, and he was sinking into it right on cue.

He didn't look around to check where the rest of his squad was, nothing he could do for them now. He tugged the lines again, and the chute shot forward across the outside barrier of the racetrack. The ground rushed up to meet him, and he yanked up hard on the lines, flaring the chute. His feet crunched into the ground, and he let his knees buckle, ass slamming into the ground and equipment pack crunching painfully into his groin. He groaned and rolled over in a ball, then did a quick inventory of his body; apart from his mildly sore testicles, his ankles, knees, and hips were all fine. That was all the mattered.

A giant bat-like swooping swept overhead as Khawaja hit the ground barely fifteen metres away.

'Nice flying Khawaja!' he hissed with a mad cackle. 'Stick with me, and I'll take you places.'

'Nowhere I want to go, Marriott,' Khawaja muttered back.

A black shadow wafted over them. 'Looks like Edelstein is gonna land nearby as well. Should I ping for an RV?'

Marriott checked the screen strapped to his arm. Everyone was on the ground, and all eight had landed within the confines of the racecourse. Ok, that's a good start. Success was relative though - they were spread over a tract of land more than a kilometre wide.

'Yea, but bring everyone together at Willis' location. He's furthest west and closest to where we need to be.' he stripped his drop gear off and changed into innocuous civilian clothes - loose fitting shirt and sports jacket that could hide the Chinese assault rifles they were toting. 'Let's move,' he said to Khawaja, then checked the time. 'Willis and Johal, go directly to the boat, no need to RV with the rest of the squad. Make sure the thing is there and that it runs, and there's a clear run to sea. Report back. You know what to do.'

'Aye, sir,' said Willis. He swore, after this mission, he was never going near a damned boat again.

Marriott and Carey jogged towards the eastern side of the course, the spot the rest of the team was converging on. He checked his mission timer again. They had four minutes.

Canberra

'They're on the ground - Mahalaxmi Turf Club,' updated Hammersmith. 'Looks like the jump was successful. Willis and Johal are heading south-east to secure the launch, and the rest of the squad are moving west towards the jail.' He was worrying at the stubble on his chin again and forced himself to stop.

'Is everything going to plan?' enquired Laffite. She was giving a good impression of calm, but fidgeting fingers on the tabletop gave the game away.

'So far, yes,' nodded Hammersmith. His eyes darted at the mission update log scrolling down the right side of the screen. They'd just received an update from the diplomatic mission in Mumbai. 'The lawyer is about to leave for the hospital.'

Mumbai

'What in blazes have you signed me up for this time, Kaleb?' The high-pitched whine emanated, confusingly, from the greedy cherub-like mouth of a man whose cavernous chest was couched in a body flowing freely with molten slabs of fat. 'Should we really be blowing up a hospital? I mean, that's pretty fucked up right?' he squeaked. 'And not to mention, it's so late! Nobody else is working at four in the morning.'

Kaleb sighed.

'We're not blowing anything up, you chubby imbecile. We're just creating a scene.'

'Yea, but why? What's the point?'

'As in, why are we here? What is the meaning of life? We're doing it because some rich bastard paid someone in the know who paid someone else and some tiny portion of whatever money was initially paid has found its way into your low-rent pocket, and that's the only reason either of us is doing this. For money.'

What a pointless conversation. Peering at the approaching street sign, Kaleb continued. 'This is Sant Savata Mali Marg. Take this left; the entrance to the hospital should be just around the corner on the right-hand side. Pull into the ambulance bay when you can.'

Kaleb was glad they weren't blowing the building up. It was a beautiful cream coloured art deco block and looked more like a country estate than a hospital. He would've like to stay there if he got sick. Large arched windows afforded patients a view of the small but well-sculpted front gardens, and simple, but elegant ornamental stonework adorned the façade. Only rusty humming boxes that were the ancient air-con units stuck in the

355

windows ruined an image that could have come from the early nineteen hundreds.

The ambulance bay, a small covered section of the drive in front of the main steps, was blocked by an ambulance, so Kaleb told Wandeep to park down the right side of the cream block.

'What do we do know?' asked Wandeep, switching the engine off. The roar of multiple air-conditioners filled the space where the engine noise had been.

'We walk away, and in exactly seventy-five seconds I'll blow the roof off this thing.' He got out of the car and began striding back down the drive. Nobody seemed to have noticed their illegal park; one reason they'd chosen the hospital was because of its lax security.

He heard a wheezing Wandeep hurrying to catch up. 'I thought you said we weren't blowing anything up...?' he hissed.

'The roof of the van, you idiot.' He shook his head in frustration. 'Not the hospital.'

'Oh,' said his partner, audibly relieved. 'Cos when you said that I thought I might have to set you straight on what this mission is actually-'

The little mission timer in Kaleb's watch counted down to zero. He looked around. They were a hundred and fifty metres up the street. He stuck his hand in his pocket and armed the little toggle switch attached to a radio transmitter in there.

He pushed the button.

Pandheer Tendulkar was sitting at the counter of Byculla Police station, barely a stones' throw from Masina Hospital. He was night duty officer and had painstakingly crafted a small dart-shaped paper plane out of sheets of paper he'd liberated from a booklet full of traffic tickets. He'd spied, on the other side of the station waiting room, a large cockroach, and was about to spear that cockroach with his paper kamikaze. He'd set up his phone to record the moment. He lined up the shiny brown bug and exhaled slowly, and was on the verge of release when a loud explosion startled both the cockroach and himself.

The roach scuttled out of sight, and Tendulkar swore. He dropped the plane and got on his radio, calling all available units to investigate.

Barely a minute later, he was fielding frantic reports of a car bomb detonating in the Masina Hospital grounds, the roof of a commercial van had been ripped upwards like a giant fish escaping from an outsized can of tuna. It appeared some sort of poison gas attack from the white vapours surrounding the area: he got on the line to Mumbai Police Central Command and demanded a full terrorist response to his precinct. The dispatch officer transferred Tendulkar to his superior, and before long, the duty officer was speaking directly to the Police Commissioner of Mumbai. The Commissioner immediately ordered Mumbai's counter-terrorism commandos, Force One, to deploy to the suburb around the hospital. They were headquartered in the leafy northern suburb of Goregaon, thirty kilometres north; the commando force would take fifteen minutes to deploy and half an hour to race down the Western Express Highway to scour the area for the bombers and eliminate them.

Canberra

'Local agents have detonated the tear gas bombs,' muttered Hammermith to a silent operations room. 'With luck, this will occupy their response teams so our boys can get in and out without being hassled.'

Nobody replied.

Years ago, when he'd been young lieutenant leading a squad of soldiers in Syria, they'd been on a routine patrol in the outskirts of Homs. The area was supposedly fully pacified, and the patrol had descended into boring routine.

Their infantry vehicle was rumbling slowly down Al Kharab, a road linking the centre of the capital with dormitory suburbs, between which, were, strangely enough, dozens of fields which had been protected from development since biblical times by decree.

It was perfect for an ambush, and when three RPGs had lanced into their APC, there was nothing to do but abandon ship. Henson and Gale got trapped in the wreckage. They'd burned alive.

Incoming fire from insurgents had pinned down the remnants of his squad, and they cowered under a hedge off the side of the road. They could hear the insurgents coming closer, their voices call and catch, hemming them in. Surrender definitely wasn't an option, since the insurgents had a habit of decapitating soldiers for propaganda purposes. Instead, they'd worked their way *towards* the insurgents because it was also where the support they'd called in would arrive.

They'd slid, burnt and bleeding, on their stomachs towards what they all knew was almost certainly death by fire.

That was how he felt right now. Everything he did seemed to take them one step closer to disaster.

Mumbai

'What do we do now, Kaleb?' wheedled the gasping lump of human behind him.

'We're picking up that commercial van you pinched from your uncle's depot, and we're going to drop it off at some posh private school,' answered Kaleb. 'Where did you park it again?'

'It's just around the corner here,' Wandeep replied. 'Why would anyone pay us to park a car in a school?'

'Who gives a shit, Wandeep,' snapped Kaleb. 'it's easy, and it pays the bills. Let me give you some advice. You're the most ignorant moron I know, so this may not apply to you, but generally in life, the less you know, the better. Especially in our business.'

'So what's your point, Kaleb?'

'My point is, stop asking so many stupid fucking questions.'

Thankfully, they'd arrived at the nondescript commercial van. In minutes they'd be done, and he could go home.

Marriott's team huddled behind the inside barrier on the easternmost edge of the Royal Western India Turf Club. Orange light leaked through trees and across the track from streetlamps, and thin, high cloud was racing across the moon, reducing its illumination to a soft glow in the sky; it was good weather to be sneaking around.

He checked the mission timer.

'Time to go, boys. Follow me at fifteen-second intervals and we'll RV corner of,' he checked the map strapped to his arm, 'Babu Sakpal and Ramji Boricha roads.'

With that, he scrambled under the white barrier and trotted across the furrowed dirt of the second last bend of the track. His leather boots sunk into the soft rows of reddish soil and before long he was climbing under the outside rail. Some spindly trees were insulating the course from the main road-gnarled branches spreading sideways as much as up. They looked like giant weeds. He crouched and moved purposefully through them towards Dr E Moses Marg, a disintegrating six-lane road snaking north-south. He dropped his bag at the base of the waist-high cement wall and took a knee, grinding into crumbled concrete. It was three in the morning, and there wasn't much traffic. A small commercial van trundled past, then a petrol tanker. He felt Khawaja drop onto the ground behind him, and then the only incoming headlights were far in the distance; hopefully, the driver wouldn't notice him. He vaulted the concrete barrier and trotted across the road. He picked his way across the rubbish-carpeted pavement, careful not to trip on broken stones jutting through the trash. A couple of rusty scaffold towers mounting peeling Bollywood movie posters loomed over another short fence.

The dirty corrugated iron sheds of Mahalakshmi train station were fifty metres down the road, and tied to a bollard on the station steps was a mangy looking mule, head hung low in sleep. If it started braying, he'd have to shoot it, so he studiously ignored it, and leaned against the fence. Peering south down the railway tracks, he saw they broadened into Mahalaxmi Railway station, from which a soft yellow glow spilled. A couple of silver and purple trains were laid up in the siding, grimy windows staring blackly.

He glanced back and saw two shapes moving towards him from the racecourse, then tapped the fence. Intel had told him this fence would be chain link, and he'd need wire-cutters to get through it. He frowned. Being able to virtually step over it was great, but he wondered what else the intel people had got wrong. Before he'd finished the thought, Khawaja and Edelstein had dropped in silently beside him.

'Let's go,' he said, and they jumped the fence and stole across the tracks.

Locals had built up the other side of the tracks with crooked, double story tin shacks, jammed next to each other as though a giant lateral vice had compressed them together. A makeshift blue tarpaulin leaned out over the tracks from one. From the second story of another hung a colourful tapestry, traditional Maharashtrian reds and blues woven into a golden starburst, with the bald, moustachioed face of a local politician beaming from the corner.

'Can anyone see a way through there?' he subvocalized on their comms net.

Khawaja padded past Marriott south towards the station. 'No gaps in this direction,' he said.

'What if we broke into one of these shops and went through that way?' asked Edelstein.

Marriott shook his head. 'They might be shops, but I bet there are people asleep in there.'

'Well there's no getting through here,' Edelstein subbed. 'I'll take a look further up,' he said, padding away from the station.

Marriott nodded his assent as Marron and Carey picked their way across the tracks and joined them.

'Follow Edelstein - don't want to bunch up too much,' he whispered, and they moved silently away.

'There's a break in the building up here,' Edelstein called quietly. 'The shacks finish, and it's some kind of junkyard or depot. We can loop back to the jail through here.'

'Nice one. Gather in the junkyard and we'll move out together.'

Moments later they gathered in what looked like a depot for a small earthmoving operation; the owners had strewn bits of rusted shovels and digging machinery all over the ground.

They skirted a truck in single file, careful not to knock any of the scraps of metal all over the ground, and the space widened into a small courtyard. A dim orange bulb sputtered weakly in the far corner, casting long shadows.

'What is this place?' muttered Carey. To their right were the shacks they'd just skirted, and opposite, an eight-foot cinder block wall surrounded the space, topped by a row of sleeping birds. Blackened rags and greasy plastic containers were jammed in behind a thick piece of concrete pipe. A splintered cricket bat sat on top.

They padded through a gap in the wall and down the alley. Some spindly trees growing out of garbage piles gave way to makeshift shanties. Cinder block and plywood walls supported corrugated iron rooves; on some of the less sturdy buildings, the occupants had spread thick tarpaulins across wooden poles for shelter. Black pits in the walls for windows, objects glinting on the inside from the flickering light of a buzzing streetlamp.

They snaked around tuk-tuks and barrows, sometimes clambering over mounds of rubble piled randomly between it all, feet crunching. Marriott peered into a concrete box jammed between two plywood homes. Blue and white tiles, chipped but scrubbed spotless, lined each surface. From a second-floor window, the eyes of a child, white and disembodied in the gloom, blinked at him with open curiosity.

Further up, a group of old men were sitting under an umbrella, murmuring to each other, a brazier fire crackling in their midst.

The men fell silent and swivelled to watch as they walked past.

'Act natural,' he murmured.

'But don't *look* like you're acting natural,' chirped Carey.

'Mind on the job, Carey,' he snapped. But he had a point. There was absolutely no reason for eight western businessmen to be walking through this junkyard suburb, now or any other time.

He picked up the pace, and they jogged past a row of parked scooters. Shopfronts crowded further into the street, and a row of apartments loomed to their left.

Up ahead, the north-west watchtower of Arthur Road jail loomed out of the darkness. An orange glow emitted from the guardroom at the top of the tower. The light carved the silhouette of a stocky paramilitary against the window, rifle slung on his back.

Silence solidified between them like glue as the walls loomed over them. In 1926, when the facility had opened, there were no cameras, electric fences or sensors. No sophisticated technology to help keep prisoners on the right side of the walls. Just massive, impervious layers of stone and concrete.

'What a beast,' subbed Edelstein breathlessly as they turned right onto Jivraj Ramji Boricha Road. The immense walls, massive as a mountain, brooded darkly over their left shoulders.

The group sauntered past a long dugout nestled in the crook of the wall. Sleepy paramilitaries slouched on tin stools against the stone. One shuffled along, hunched under the canvas awning, coffee steaming from the tin mug cupped in dirty hands. The soldiers peered at them with a mix of apathy and suspicion. Apathy won, and they continued unmolested. Soon they reached Arthur Road and crossed the street.

On the other side of the road from the dugout were a row of shops; concrete pillboxes with roller doors and layers of corrugated iron for rooves.

'Time to switch on, gentlemen,' growled Marriott. They'd reached the south-eastern corner of the jail, and the intersection of Arthur Road and Jivraj Ramji Boricha Road. The ponderous bulk of the Jacob Circle flyover obscured the sky. Across the road, gleaming under the grimy artificial light was the entrance to Kasturba Hospital. On the right-hand side, a low-roofed bungalow crowded into a clutch of broad-branched trees. A storm had ripped off the roof, and someone had patched it up with an army surplus canvas. On the other side ran an unkempt garden bed thick with tropical weeds and bent trees.

A trio of heavily armed soldiers stood at the entrance.

In the distance, a concussion shook the night. The van parked at Masina Hospital had exploded, right on time.

'That's our cue. Take your positions,' Marriott subbed over the net. The men made a show of shaking hands, as though parting for the evening, and the group split up, with Carey, Marron, and Khawaja heading north up Arthur Road. Marriott, Harley and Edelstein headed south.

At the hospital entrance, the three soldiers cocked their heads. Their CO had come online, barking something about a bomb going off a few blocks away. Marriott watched out the corner of his eye as the soldiers were joined by three more from the bungalow. One of them pointed down Arthur Road and started jogging. The others followed.

Chapter 34
Kasturba Hospital, Mumbai
December 18ᵗʰ, 0130 hours

Robertson staggered weakly into consciousness and moaned softly. The swelling in his groin was now a thudding ache that extended up into his abdomen. Whatever ailed him had twisted his stomach into a dry cramp, a convulsion so hard his breath only came in shallow gasps. The axe was still buried in his head.

'Alice,' he muttered. 'I'm so sorry. It was like an old enemy had come riding around the mountain in a new uniform. The acute pain had just spread into a void that until now, had been filled with a dull ache. He squirmed in a vain attempt to get comfortable. A bright light shone through a crack in his eye, and he noticed distantly that instead of lying on a grimy concrete floor, the surface was soft and crisp. Voices chimed softly in his ear in a language he didn't understand.

One of the voices was attached to a hand; it picked up his listless arm and slid a needle into it. The old enemy suddenly melted back behind the mountain. He frowned on the inside - why did he feel good all of a sudden? The bright light became a small point in his vision. Then the pinprick winked out, and so did he.

A few hours later, Clinton Harvey strode casually under the trees overhanging Kasturba Hospital's driveway. He pretended to look bored. Only the dark patch of sweat on his shirt front betrayed the fact that he was borderline terrified. He chewed gum to disguise the tension in his jaw. He strode confidently up the short flight of steps, and the double-glazed entrance doors slid open, and then he was bathed in septic-scented air-conditioned air. It plucked pleasantly at his sticky clothes.

Harvey pulled out his diplomatic identification and placed it on the reception counter.

'My name is Clinton Harvey, part of the Australian Ambassador's mission representing the interests of Glen Robertson. I believe the embassy has notified you of my visit.'

The young nurse behind the desk shuffled some paper and pretended she had something better to do than admit the lawyer of the most hated man in India.

Finally, she looked up and gave him a questioning look, liberally layered with contempt.

He flashed her a smile. 'I'm here to see my client. Can you tell me where he is, please?'

Marriott's group had worked their way to the south of the Kasturba Hospital block. More low slung shops, more canvas, and metal coverings. Some merchants had attached their shops to the flyover support, like boxy creeper vines made of building scraps.

They had time to kill, and he spotted an old lady turning chicken skewers over a brazier glowing red in the darkness. Marriott ambled across and squatted next to her, fishing some notes out of his pocket.

He pointed at the chicken, and she handed him four skewers which he distributed to the others. They each took a seat and began nibbling. Just a bunch of tourists having a late-night snack.

'Delicious,' opined Khawaja.

'Indeed,' lied Marriott. He scanned around for some chilli sauce. Nothing.

Sirens echoed behind them. Marriott didn't have to check the map to know they were vectored at Masina Hospital, several blocks away. Another group of soldiers appeared from the direction of the gaol. The man in front stared at them suspiciously as they jogged past. Marriott met his stare openly, trying his best to look innocent.

Hiding in plain sight sounded good in theory, but this was bordering on ridiculous. Waiting was always the worst part, and Marriott could sense the nerves in his men. He clamped down on his own jitters and forced himself to relax. He ate some more chicken.

At the hospital, the orderly led Harvey through white corridors. His shoes clicked on the polished vinyl floors, reminding him of Barack Eight in the jail over the road. Gurneys were lined up on the wall; wire baskets attached the foot of each bed. The hospital at night-time was an oddly eerie place. A sinewy old man mopped the floor listlessly, and they skirted around the Caution! Wet Floor sign. Kasturba Hospital was relatively small-only four-hundred and fifty beds and two stories high. So when Harvey asked, he was relieved, but not overly surprised to hear that the isolation ward was on the ground floor.

'If you want to see him, you'll have to put this on,' said the receptionist, pulling a facemask off the wall and handing it to him. She helped him fit it.

'How do I look?'

She ignored him. 'Put these on too,' she said, handing him some surgical gloves. 'We recommend no contact even with the preventative measures.'

'Sounds reasonable to me,' muttered Harvey. He wasn't going anywhere near Robertson.

They opened the door to the ward, and the door sealed shut behind them. The air cycled, and when the room had fully vented, the light flashing red above the inner door turned green. It opened automatically, and they entered.

Robertson was in blue hospital robes, flat on his back. Staff had raised the top half of the gurney slightly, and his head was propped up on pillows. The gowns were sleeveless, and Harvey could see black, pussy boils crusted around his armpits. They looked like a shower of impact craters on the surface of the moon.

He didn't stir when Harvey entered the room. Nurses had strapped an oxygen mask to his face, and a couple of bags full of clear liquid were attached to stands next to the bed.

366

Transparent hoses ran to catheters inserted in the top of Robertson's hand, which looked decidedly gaunt. The ends of his fingers had turned black, like burnt sausages. Harvey looked away, chilled. Seven hundred years ago, half the population of Europe had died like this.

'What's he plugged into?' Harvey asked.

The nurse pointed to the largest bag. 'Saline solution-keep him hydrated. This one is hydromorphone. It's a painkiller.'

'It doesn't look like it's working.' Robertson had set his jaw like concrete, neck sinews straining. Waxy dark bags under his eyes glistened. It looked like he was waging war behind his closed eyelids.

'It's the strongest painkiller on the planet. He's on the highest safe dose. An overdose of this,' the nurse said patting the transparent bag, 'is far more lethal than the infection he's got.'

'I guess that's the antibiotic?' he pointed to the third bag.

'Combination of streptomycin and doxycycline. We're used to treating the plague in Mumbai,' she said, eyeballing him. 'This is our standard response for a high-profile case.'

'What if he wasn't a high-profile case?'

'Well, untreated, the mortality is forty to sixty per cent. Standard treatment protocol with antibiotics can bring this down to twenty per cent. Mr. Robertson has at least an eighty-five per cent chance of recovering,' she said soberly.

Harvey barely repressed a fatalistic laugh. Trading a significant chance of death and a potential international incident for a long shot at avoiding a guaranteed public lynching. He'd heard rumours that the PM had some sort of 'special interest' in getting Robertson home safe, and cynical as he was of conspiracy theories, he was starting to give it more credence, because this was lunacy.

'What do you need to say to him?' asked the nurse. 'I can wake him up if you wish.'

'It's fine,' Harvey said, staring down at the pestilent form of his countryman. He prided himself on being a clear-headed, rational thinker. Emotion made fools of the smartest men (which is why he'd done the rational thing and become a lawyer), but suddenly a strange sentimentality washed through him. Here was a man who had nothing left to lose, apart from his life. Sad.

He looked at the nurse. 'Thank you for showing me him. I've got nothing to tell him that can't wait until he's better.'

She nodded. 'I'll show you out then.'

Ten minutes later, Harvey had decontaminated and was striding back out the hospital entrance into the sweaty Mumbai evening. His car was waiting next to the low, storm damaged entrance bungalow.

'Did you drop off the package?' he asked as he bent himself into the back seat.

'Yea,' the man deadpanned. Had to pretend to hang a piss in the bushes over there,' he nodded at the tangle of growth opposite the bungalow, 'and dropped it out of the front of my pants.'

'OK. Let's get out of here.'

'What about our mark? He gonna be OK?' asked the government driver as he moved to the middle seat.

Harvey read the message he'd prepared on his phone for the third time. Taking a deep breath, he pressed send. *Message sent.*

He exhaled through pursed lips.

'Yea mate,' he said quietly. 'Everything's going to be fine.'

The car eased down an empty Arthur Road. Harvey stared out the window, lost in thought. The car picked up speed, and they drove past a group of drunk tourists eating some chicken from a street vendor. He locked eyes with one, a tall, grizzled man in a rumpled suit. The man was finishing off a skewer. His gaze radiated from lifeless eyes and seemed to penetrate to the back of Harvey's skull. He shivered. The car turned a corner, and the group dropped from view.

368

Canberra

Hammersmith licked his lips. So far, everything had gone to plan. Like clockwork. Too much like clockwork. It was turning his guts to noodles - he wished something would go wrong, and the dread of expectation could finally come crashing down.

'The lawyer - his name's Harvey - has transmitted the exact location of Robertson's ward.'

Laffite merely nodded. She'd barely moved for the last six hours, and she'd kept her hands palms down on the desk in front of her. Hammersmith studied them. Every now and then, she drummed a short pattern on the tabletop.

Stalactite-through-your-heart cold. Suddenly he felt a rush of veneration for the PM. She'd made a call that would probably end her career, and more, and she owned it, front and center. Jacqueline Laffite was a woman he could follow into battle.

He cleared his throat. His apprehension was gone. 'Our squad is in position.' He caught Laffite's eye, and she arched an eyebrow.

'They're the best we've got, Ma'am. The best in the world.'

She smiled.

'I know.'

Mumbai

Marriott wiped his fingers on his leg and spat gristle onto the ground. The meat was somehow running with grease and dissolving like dry ash in their mouths at the same time. By the time they got food-poisoning, he reflected, everything would be over, one way or another.

He'd just traded looks with a slick yet scared-looking middle-office type in the back of an Australian government vehicle. Quite possibly their informer; moments before, headquarters had delivered the precise location of Robertson's whereabouts

369

in the hospital to his mission map. Two minutes had passed - ample time for the lawyer to clear the area.

The chicken lady ignored them as they threw their blackened skewers onto the rubbish pile next to her.

'No tip for you,' said Khawaja mock-seriously as they stood up.

'Gentlemen, your attention please,' subbed Marriott over the comms net. 'We are go, I say again, this is a mission go. Sync your mission clock with mine and execute as planned.'

Marron, Carey, and Khawaja had circled around the hospital to the north, heading up Arthur Road before slinking between two ramshackle shops and vaulting the low concrete wall they were pressed up against. Carey had pulled himself up and kicked off with his boot, dislodging a chunk of concrete from the top which had crunched into the ground. Marron had quickly cleared the edifice, and the men slunk off into the low trees before anybody investigated. Fast and silent, they dodged through a messy garden behind the northern carpark of the hospital. They were going to circle around the top of the hospital and meet Marriott's team on the outside of Robertson's room.

'Weapons free,' subbed Khawaja, and the men unhooked the pieces of their silenced automatics which they'd distributed under their clothing, and assembled them. The weapons contained rubber bullets. Non-lethal, except in case of head-shot; the men were under strict instructions to aim only for the torso of any targets. Marron slung his assembled weapon and put his hand in his jacket pocket, checking, for the fiftieth time, the contents were still there.

'Marron, you ready with our party aids?'

They needed a self-propelled Glen Robertson tonight because carrying a man out of a hospital under fire was not feasible. Problem being, he was on death's door and had been sedated with some of the most powerful opiates on earth. What they had planned for Robertson was like strapping a giant bottle of nitrous oxide to granddad's old station wagon and hoping it all stayed together when they lit the fuse.

In his left jacket pocket were two ampules: One contained naloxone which would block the opiate receptors the hydromorphone bound to in Robertson's body and bring him painfully awake. Beside it was an ampule of pure adrenaline. To give him the energy to run out of the hospital unassisted. The problem with adrenaline was that it was very short-lived and the come-down was quick and nasty.

Robertson only had to stay awake for an hour, but he had to *stay awake*. So, in his right jacket pocket, attached to a dermal patch was a one-hundred and fifty-milligram solution of pure methamphetamine. In the upper range for a hardened crack addict. The medicos who'd come up with this cocktail had joked it was more lethal than his infection. Robertson's chance of survival had gone up in the last twenty-four hours. But not by much.

'Good to go,' he subbed back. 'He's gonna have the time of his life right up to the point his heart explodes.'

The Nirmal Park Railway Quarters were adjacent to Kasturba Hospital to the south, and conveniently dark and empty at this time in the morning. Marriott slipped surreptitiously over the grimy wall fronting Arthur Road. Harley crept behind a canvas shopfront. Edelstein kept walking.

A block down the road was St Ignatius High School. Parked in the student drop-off was a drab grey commercial van. He quickly surveilled the area. A car rolled past, noisy in the night quiet and he kept strolling down the road until it was well past; then turned on his heel and walked back to the van. Got in the driver's side and felt under the seat. The key fob was there, precisely as planned. He leaned the seat back out of view and pretended to sleep.

Chapter 35
Parliament House, Canberra

December 18th, 0500 hours

Hammersmith opened his mouth for an update, but Laffite spoke first.

'They're about to break him out, aren't they?' she said calmly.

Futcher nodded, and Hammersmith answered. 'Yes, ma'am. They've circled around to the back of the hospital. We're hoping the bombs we've set off in other parts of the city will pre-occupy Mumbai security until they're well away.' He shrugged. 'It's barely two clicks from the hospital to the boat that'll take them to the sub.' He cracked his jaw. 'To be honest though, Jacqui, there's so much can go wrong between extraction and egress.'

She nodded, waiting.

'But what has to go right, only has to go right for about ten minutes. This mission is pure Hollywood.' He kneaded his hands. 'And sometimes reality is stranger than fiction. So...'

Laffite repressed a sudden urge to place a comforting hand on the old soldier's wrist.

'So buckle up, Hammersmith. These are your men. And yours,' she said to Futcher, who could barely meet her eye. She nodded firmly. 'I've got faith.'

Mumbai

The five men assembled at the back of the hospital. The red brick building backed onto more unkempt gardens which provided them with a little cover - but not much.

Harley unslung his rucksack and took a knee. He pulled out lengths of three-sided, thirty-millimetre hollow metal rods and lay them on the ground. Then he pulled out a plastic bag full of plastique explosive. Slicing open the bag with his bowie knife, Harley squashed the putty-like substance into the U-shape formed by the open side. When the rods were full, he attached a fuse into one end and wired it up to a detonator. Then he placed the rods onto the red brick wall in a rectangular pattern. When they blew, the men would be able to step straight into Robertson's ward.

Reeling out the detonator, the men crouched against the wall, four metres from the charges.

'Ready to go, Marriott,' subbed Edelstein.

'Acknowledged. Fire in the hole,' said Marriott and triggered a detonator of his own.

The small bomb Harvey's driver had dropped into the bushes through his fly was a combination pyrotechnic and incendiary device. A mix of magnesium, chlorine trifluoride and gunpowder erupted in a loud bang. The magnesium blasted onto the surrounding shrubs and erupted in white-hot flames. The bushes, thick from a wet summer and brown from a recent dry-spell, quickly caught on fire.

Within seconds the garden bed opposite the security bungalow was in flames. Hospital security scrambled to put it out.

Marriott waited fifteen seconds.

'Let's do it, Edelstein,' he subbed, clapping Edelstein hard on the shoulder.

Edelstein clacked the detonator together. An ear-splitting roar and an eruption of red dust and flying brick fragments blew outwards from the wall. From inside the hospital, fluorescent light cast a ghostly glow in the sooty air like a little slice of heaven pouring into the night. Khawaja and Harley stood guard while the rest of the team ran single file into Kasturba Hospital Isolation Ward 1A.

Through the dust and flickering lights, Marriott spied a medical orderly cowering against the wall. When he saw the Australians, he covered his head in hands and shrunk further against the wall keening loudly.

'Cover him!' Marriott shouted at Carey, who levelled his MP5 at the nurse and leaned close.

'Shush, now,' he said. The man stopped keening and squatted, quivering.

'Get to work, Marron!' ordered Marriott.

Marron already had the naloxone ampule in hand. He ripped the cap off the needle, slid it into Robertson's carotid artery and squeezed the little tube empty.

Seconds passed. Robertson shifted. Then he moaned, and then his eyes fluttered open. He squinted at the figures looming over him.

'What the, who the hell are you?' he croaked.

'I'm here with the Australian embassy,' Marron flicked the needle of the adrenaline shot. 'I'm here to rescue you,' he said casually as he slid the needle into Robertson's neck, adjacent to the first shot.

'Nap time's over, Captain Robertson,' said Marriott. He leaned in close. Robertson glared back at him. If this was some elaborate plot to assassinate him, the Indians were even crazier than he thought.

'We're SAS, based outta Perth, here to bring you home. We need you to switch on so we can get you to the egress point.' Greasy chicken smell wafted over Robertson as the block-headed man spoke. 'We've just given you a shot of adrenalin,' which had just reached his CNS judging from the intense sparkle that had suddenly appeared in his eyes, 'now get on your fucking feet, or we're all going to die here.' Robertson's eyes darted furiously.

'We're going to disconnect you from your life support.' Marron hid his distaste as he held up the blackened hand and ripped off the tape holding the catheters in. He expertly slid the needles out. Robertson didn't feel a thing. The machine monitoring his dosing schedule beeped in alarm.

Robertson's mind raced. These guys were obviously Australian; they sounded it, and they all had that slightly weathered look that came with long summers in the sun, especially pronounced on army types. What's more, they were acting with the cool, detached professionalism that was the calling card of all the special-forces guys he'd known over the years. Like they were less highly trained humans and more intricately programmed machines. So maybe they were telling the truth. And, he reflected, he wasn't in the best position to negotiate - he was toast anyway - so if this rescue attempt failed it wasn't like they could execute him twice. He wondered just how in hell they were going to get him out of Mumbai?

'You're all crazy.' He squinted up at Marriott. 'Good crazy. Let's get out of here.' Robertson sat up, wobbled, and grabbed a steadying arm from Marron. He retched weakly and keeled over, shaking.

'Chew on this, Robertson,' said Marron as he slapped the meth patch onto his neck. He drew a ragged breath and his eyed widened in a mix of confusion and slowly building euphoria.

'Move, Commodore!' ordered Marriott, and Robertson slid off the bed. His blackened feet hit the floor, and he straightened his legs with an energy he hadn't felt...ever. The pain in his forearm was consumed by the velvet bliss spreading through his body. He knew with utter certainty he was going to pay in blood for this later, and he didn't care.

He felt...absolutely...incredible.

Marriott crabbed back through the wall. Marron guided Robertson, one hand cradling his MP5, the other on Robertson's shoulder, leading him from behind, and they crashed through the scrub behind the hospital like a brick through a window.

Around the corner, Khawaja was doing his best impression of a passed-out lorry driver, lying across the row of seats, eyes closed and flat on his back. But he was listening to everything through his earpiece and snapped upright when Marriott boomed over the net.

'We're on our way, Khawaja. Get her ready!'

Khawaja pressed the start button next to the steering wheel, and the console lit up glowing softly. He turned the light setting down to zero. The only sound was the quiet rustle of the air con.

Canberra

'They've infiltrated the hospital. The bomb planted in the front garden has gone off, and they've blown a hole into Robertson's isolation ward. It looks like he's responded well to the field stimulus we worked up for him.'

Hammersmith glanced at Laffite. She was chewing her nails.

Mumbai

Marriott's squad jogged through the scrub next to the rear carpark of the hospital. Fire alarms shrieked, and garbled Hindi filled the air.

Vines and skinny trees melded with the ten-foot wire mesh fence separating the southern edge of the hospital carpark and Nirmal Railway Quarters.

Marriott unsheathed the foot-long vibrating blade he had strapped to his leg. He was about to start hacking into the wall of bark and wire when he felt a hand on his shoulder. He turned.

Robertson was there, eyes glittering like a spinning poker machine in the moonlight.

'We going over there?' he grated, pointing towards the railway quarters.

'Yea, now get outta the way so I can make a hole.'

Robertson pushed past him and began scaling the fence. One-armed. His broken arm, splinted and cast, hung uselessly by his side. Regardless, within moments, he was straddling the top and then was gone, dropping through space and landing with a crunch on the other side.

Marron shot Marriott a look then Robertson pressed up against the fence. 'Hurry up, fuckers. I'm guessing we don't have all night.'

'Yea - well I guess that's one way of doing it,' said Marriott, re-sheathing the blade and picking his way up the fence.

'Might've overdone the meth,' he subbed to Marron. 'He's actually having fun.'

'Aren't you?' the medic subbed back breathlessly.

In moments the group was assembled on the other side of the wall.

'Are your feet ok?' Marron asked Robertson as they scuttled through the railway quarters grounds. He'd forgotten to give him footwear and was wondering how the man's blackened bare feet were holding up on the rough ground.

'What if they're not?' the navy man grunted without looking at him.

'Good question.'

Yet another decaying concrete wall. Harley boosted Marriott, then sent Robertson over the top. Marriott softened his landing. When only Harley remained, Marriott and Marron hung on the top of the wall and grabbed Edelstein's wrists as he launched himself upwards. Marriott had only been in Mumbai for half an hour, and it felt like he hadn't stopped hurdling these British-era barriers.

'We're in the school. Khawaja is on the other side of this building. Let's go,' Marriott's team jogged through a schoolyard, skirting to the west. To their left were the class-rooms, to their right yet another concrete wall, separating them from Arthur Road. Sirens howled up the road like a pack of angry wolves. All of a sudden, these old fences were working for them.

They rounded the edge of the block and were suddenly in the school drop-off point. A lone vehicle parked there, looking rather suspicious to Marriott.

377

Without pausing, he rushed to the back of the vehicle, cranked open the door, and the men piled inside.

'Lie flat and cover yourselves with this matting,' Marriott ordered. 'Khawaja, get us out of here!'

The men lay on their backs, positioning their MP5s on their stomachs and pulled the soiled blankets over themselves. In the cramped space, they were pushed tight against each other.

'Could you have got a smaller van?' grumbled Robertson.

'Shut up Robertson, or we'll put you back to sleep,' said Marriott. He checked his locater. They were halfway to the boat where Willis and Johal were waiting to take them to sea.

'We've got company,' Khawaja subbed over the net. 'Lie low. I'll try to bluff my way through this.'

Marriott felt a fidgeting Robertson stiffen next to him. He placed a hand on the man's hip.

'I know you're on another planet, Commodore, but it's time to play dead. Understood?'

A moment's hesitation. 'Yea,' he grunted back. The fidgeting...ceased.

A wailing siren had pulled in behind them, and the van slowed, pulled into the curb.

A few moments passed, and the sound of Khawaja winding down the window emanated into the back of the van.

A local cop flung an angry demand through the window at Khawaja.

'What the hell is going on tonight?' demanded Khawaja in Hindi. 'I've been stopped three times already, and I'm going to be late with my consignment!'

The voice outside shouted something in reply.

'Insurgents this, insurgents that!' Khawaja shot back. 'Do I look like a bloody insurgent? Can't you bastards let an honest man go about in peace?'

The man outside shot a clear instruction back.

'Wow Khawaja,' subbed Marriott. 'You should be in the diplomatic corp.'

378

'You're gonna have company,' Khawaja subbed back. 'Two paras only, automatic weapons. Open fire on my mark. Guidance two seconds after you hear the doors open.'

'Acknowledged,' subbed Marriott. 'On your mark - we can't see shit through these blankets.' At least there were only two of them.

A few seconds passed during which Marriott's heart-rate soared. The door handle clacked and Marriott fingered the trigger of his rifle. He heard one of the other boys two-click his weapon to full auto.

The sound of the doors creaking open...still no word from Khawaja. Indian accented voices soaked over them.

'What the fuck, Khawaja?' panicked Edelstein over the net.

'Fire, fire, fire!' shouted Khawaja and the whipping sound of multiple silenced automatic weapons unloading at once filled the back of the van. The blankets were flung backwards by the bullets, revealing the exploding chests of two Indian military police. The shredded remains of the blankets followed them to the ground like paint-stained shrouds.

'Let's go, Khawaja,' subbed Marriott, changing out his magazine. 'Was that all of them?'

'Yea,' Khawaja replied as the van eased away. 'Only two of them.'

'It appears those rubber rounds are more lethal than the manufacturer's claims,' deadpanned Marron.

'Write a letter,' shot back Marriott.

'Maybe I will,' Marron muttered. Their CO had a heart of dry ice.

The van weaved forward, through potholes and around parked cars, but always closer to the coast.

Lala Lajpatraiu Marg

Willis looked across at Johal, snoring softly against the oil-slicked engine block in the guts of the nondescript launch jammed loosely on the mud-flat off Lala Lajpatraiu Marg. How anybody could fall asleep at a time like this simultaneously baffled, scared and impressed him. Not for the first time, he thought that Johal was a Marriott-level nut case.

He kicked his drooling squad-mate awake. Johal licked his chin and shuffled upright; they were getting comms from the rest of the party.

'Willis, Johal, we're on our way,' Marriott subbed. 'ETA five minutes. We're coming in quiet, but that could change very fucking fast if we get stung by local forces.'

'Acknowledged,' said Willis. 'We'll be ready.'

Johal got up and primed the choke then fired up a turbine heater that had been supplied by whichever gang had sold them the boat. He pointed it at the ancient diesel engine.

'We're gonna warm you up,' muttered Willis, giving the engine an encouraging pat. 'So you better start first time.'

They settled in to wait. Willis was gratified to see Johal fidgeting nervously as he held the turbine heater steady.

In the van, Khawaja turned left onto E Moses Marg. The racecourse was on their right, the ocean dead ahead. All they had to do was get to the end of this road unmolested. While sirens flailed in the distance, the streets here were empty. Willis knew that could change in an instant, and tamped down on the glimmer of hope that was starting to burn in his guts.

In the rear of the van, Robertson shifted restlessly. He was trying so hard to stay still but caught himself going through weird ticks without even realising he'd started.

'So what's the plan, where we going?' he asked.

'There's a Barracuda parked half a mile off the coast,' replied Marriott. 'We've got a launch waiting for us. We're gonna take it and RV with the sub.'

'Who's driving the sub?' asked Robertson.

'Jack Phillips is in charge.'

'I know Jack. We pinged him on the way up to Kolkata - gave him the new acoustic signature data he needed to mitigate that DDS he had strapped on.' He nodded sharply. 'That DDS was for you guys, wasn't it?'

Marriott nodded. 'Yea, we used it to get up the Hoolie. He wasn't happy you found him. Didn't stop bitching about it the whole trip.' A slight exaggeration - he'd mentioned it explicitly once to Marriott - but the man had seemed positively offended at what the DDS had done to his precious acoustic signature.

He thought for a moment. 'So; you found him. I thought those Barracudas were supposed to be invisible.'

'They are, more or less,' said Robertson. 'But yea, we found him.'

'Should we be worried?' asked Marriott. There's a lot of enemy water to navigate before we're home and hosed.'

Robertson didn't hesitate. 'No, you shouldn't. Phillips is brilliant. He's a very, very good sub-driver. As good as any, in a world-class platform.'

'So how did you find him?' asked Marriott sceptically.

Robertson gave him a condescending look.

'I'm the best.' He shrugged, as best as you can shrug crammed between two bodies on a van floor.

'Is this guy kidding?' Edelstein muttered.

Marriott grinned. 'I dunno, but I'm starting to like him.'

Canberra

'How long till they reach the *Kati-Thanda*?' said Laffite to the air in front of her.

Futcher glanced at Hammersmith. 'They're less than a kilometre from the motorboat they've commandeered. *Katie* is ready to surface a click off the coast.' He bit his lip. 'If they make the launch unmolested, all they have to do is putter to the RV. Phillips will bring her to the surface, and they can literally climb on board.'

He bit his lip harder. It sounded so easy.

Mumbai

381

The van slowed, then stopped. 'We're here,' called Willis from the front. 'And clear - we're on our own. We're go for the boat,' he said as he raced around the back of the van and opened the doors from the outside.

The men unfurled themselves from the cramped space and Willis, who had already spotted the boat, took the lead. Willis had parked next to some sort of café, with tables and chairs stacked up next to a shopfront, chained to the wall.

Dr. E Moses Marg intersected with three other streets, forming a large piazza adjacent to the water. Several cars were parked in the space, and Marriott figured it was a giant carpark in the day time.

Their van didn't look so out of place given the other random vehicles dotting the space.

What did look out of place was six heavy-set men in business suits toting automatic weapons piling out the back of it.

A couple of kids were leaning against the low wall beyond which was a rubbish-strewn mudflat and a small white boat bobbing innocuously.

The kids had been launching their skateboards off the wall all night. Now they held their boards close and peered at the Australians like urban meerkats.

'Marriott, we should neutralise them,' subbed Marron. 'They can record everything on their phones and send to authorities.'

'Concur.' Marriott brought his MP5 to bear and fired one, two, three times. The boys cascaded to the ground like dominoes.

'What the hell?' cried Robertson in horror.

'Relax,' said Marriott, leading the group over the wall and vaulting into the mud beyond with a loud squelch. 'They're rubber bullets. Non-lethal.'

Marron shared a look with Edelstein.

Robertson's face contorted in anguish, but he followed Marriott into the tidal swamp.

Perched on the bow of the launch, Johal peered across the swamp, night-vision on his goggles maxed out. The picture was crystal clear, grey-scale; his five squadmates, carrying weapons and gear in wrinkled business suits, and one stocky guy in hospital robes moving in energetic jerky motions like a scarecrow come to life.

He scanned beyond them - the plaza was clear and stayed that way. He'd sworn to himself when Marriott dropped those kids with not a moment's thought. Body shots, apparently, so they should be OK. But still.

'This Robertson guy must have the second-highest body count of all time,' he'd muttered.

'Number one being?' Johal enquired.

'Genghis Khan,' he'd murmured back. 'The area behind them is clear, though. Always count on Marriott to tie up any loose ends.'

An interminable minute passed, and the group had slopped the fifty metres to the boat, wading waist-deep in the waxy water, Robertson was ushered to the front and boosted over the gun-whale by Marriott and Edelstein. He flopped onto the deck like a sodden rug and crawled out of the way - Johal, and Willis were already dragging Edelstein over.

Soon they were all aboard, and Willis moved to the console and keyed the starter. The engine ticked over a couple of times then fired into life, a plume of soot wafting out of the back of the boat.

He moved the throttle out of idle and eased the boat away from the mudflat, keeping the revs low.

Marriott moved to the bow and activated the directional data-link that would ping the *Katie-Tanda*.

They peered over the side anxiously as they navigated around Haji Ali Dargah the giant park in the middle of the bay. A land bridge connected it to the mainland and if they were spotted, a fire team could close to a hundred meters and shoot from the shore.

HMAS *Kathi-Thanda*

'Signal received, bearing ninety-degrees east,' cried the comms officer excitedly. 'Vectored to within fifty metres of our current location, bearing two-seven-four.'

'How long?' demanded Captain Jack Phillips.

'One hundred and five seconds,' replied the sonar officer, updating the console as he answered. A flashing blue dot less than a kilometre to their east appeared on the screen.

'Helmsman, take her to the surface. Nice and easy, and don't use any more air.' The *Kati-Tanda* had been hovering twenty metres below, barely a click off the coast of Mumbai, waiting for word from the SAS boys to surface and pick them up. Now they'd been signalled, they had to surface silently, and that meant not blowing the tanks.

So - they'd pre-blown the tanks and had been using the five-knots forward momentum of the sub coupled with a steep downward push on the planes to stay submerged twenty-five metres. Now, the navigator pinged a location to Marriott that would coincide with one of their loops and ordered the helmsman to go horizontal on the planes.

Like the moon emerging through thunderclouds, the *Kati-Thanda* slowly surfaced.

'There she is,' cried Robertson softly from his vantage point on the bow, awe in his voice.

Marriott was already looking where he was pointing, having the benefit of his mission computer displaying the exact location of the sub, but he too was struck by the sinister majesty of the Barracuda class boat piercing the surface.

'Hang on, boys,' said Willis. 'We're gonna pull up next to her and try to leap across onto the deck.' He eased the launch over to the looming shape and pulled alongside.

The sail jutted out over the ocean, and he pulled up next to the foredeck, the launch bobbing gently against the hull.

Marriott launched himself off the bow of the launch and landed short of the sub. Scrabbling for a handhold, he dragged himself up onto the deck and was composed in time to drag Edelstein, who'd followed him, out of the water

One by one, the rest of the group splashed into the water. Willis was last, shutting down the engines of the launch before he flung himself over the side.

The sodden men quickly moved to the ladder leading up the sail. Marriott shoved up Robertson up the rungs.

'Hurry up, Navy,' he said, as a twitching Robertson clambered up the handholds.

He pulled himself over the last rung. Jack Phillips was at the top, and he grabbed Robertson by the arms and heaved him over the gun-whale. He glared at the gaunt face of his erstwhile brother in arms.

'Robertson, you are one ugly bastard,' said Phillips. 'Welcome aboard the *Kati-Thanda*.'

Thirty seconds later, the Barracuda class sub vanished silently into the sea, and melted, wraith-like, away.

Canberra

'What does that mean,' Laffite asked, her agitation evident. The mission log, scrolling on the right of the screen, had stopped transmitting.

'It means that the rescue team has RV'd with the submarine,' answered Futcher.

Extraction team successful RV with Barracuda SF, comms blackout...blinked silently. It was the last entry. *Katie* wouldn't emit any signals whatsoever until she was within the EEZ of Perth.

'What are the Indians doing?' asked Laffite.

Hammersmith unbuttoned his shirt and regarded Laffite with something approaching reverence.

'From what we can see, they're still scrambling around after all those bombs we set off. We've already stretched their internal response to the limit.'

'Futcher?' the PM asked.

'I don't want to be rash,' he said carefully. 'But with what we know about their anti-sub net and with Jack Phillips at the wheel...' he sat upright.

'My gut says...in ten days Robertson will be back on home soil, Prime Minister.'

The beginnings of hopeful smiles broke on the faces of all the aides in the room.

Laffite nodded. 'Excellent.' She pushed her chair back and stood up. Re-arranged the tumbler and bottled water in front of her.

'Thank you, gentlemen. Today was... an important day in the history of Australia,' she said, pulling her suit-jacket down with a white-knuckle grip, ostensibly to straighten out the creases from a long night, but really to hide the sudden violent tremors in her hands. Jacqui Laffite took a deep breath and nodded again to each of her colleagues, turned, and walked out.

Printed in Poland
by Amazon Fulfillment
Poland Sp. z o.o., Wrocław

53941806R00228